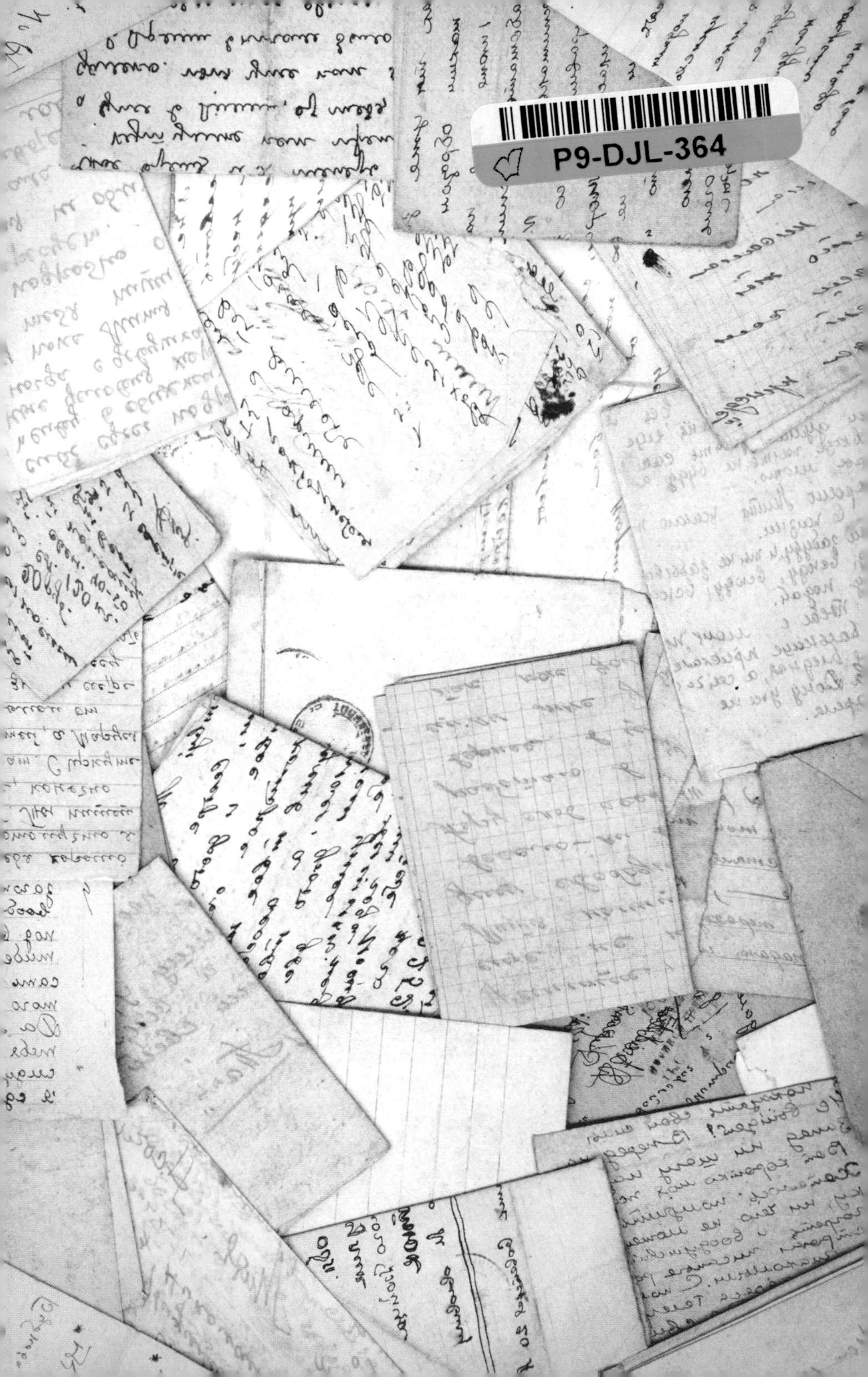

CAT CLARKE

sourcebooks
fire

Published by Sourcebooks Fire, an imprint of Sourcebooks, Inc.

P.O. Box 4410, Naperville, Illinois 60567-4410

(630) 961-3900

Fax: (630) 961-2168

www.sourcebooks.com

Originally published in 2013 in Great Britain by Quercus.

Library of Congress Cataloging-in-Publication Data is on file with the publisher.

Printed and bound in the United States of America.

BG 10 9 8 7 6 5 4 3 2 1

For Lauren

prologue

The boy next door.

It's a terrible cliché, isn't it? The one you eventually realize is The One after having your heart pulverized by an assortment of bad boys. We've all been there. Things were a little different for her though. She realized he was The One before she'd even met any bad boys, let alone had her heart pulverized by one. And in her case The One happened to be very much gay. That pretty much blows the cliché out of the water, don't you think?

From the day his family moved into the house that was slightly nicer and slightly bigger than hers, he was the center of all that she did. They were seven years old.

She was the one to make the first move—surprisingly forward for such a shy little creature. She'd been watching him for half an hour through a hole in the bottom of the fence, studying him to make sure he wasn't the type of boy who pulled the wings off flies or anything like that. He wasn't. He was the type of boy who would lie flat on his back in the middle of the lawn to make sure the sky above was still the same sky he'd left behind in Manchester. She didn't know what he was doing at first, of course. In fact, she thought he might be dead. Just my luck, *she thought.* Emily's moved to the other side of the world and a stupid boy moves into her house and goes and dies.

She briefly considered throwing a stone at his head to check his aliveness, but decided it was probably more sensible just to ask.

"Excuse me?" She was a very polite little girl because she'd been brought up by two very polite parents.

There was no response from the possibly dead boy, so she raised her voice. "EXCUSE ME! Are you dead?"

The boy slowly turned his head so he was looking straight at her face peering through the hole in the fence. His eyes were the same color as the sky and his hair was golden like…gold.

The boy narrowed his eyes. "No, I'm Kai. Are you dead?"

The girl laughed. "Of course not!"

"Good. We can be friends then." The girl liked the sound of that.

It was a good start. And the middle was good too. But the ending? Well, the ending left a lot to be desired. She would have written it differently if she'd had a say in the matter.

Every good story deserves a happy ending—it's a basic rule of storytelling.

The boy next door certainly shouldn't die.

part one

chapter one

I miss Kai more than I can say. It's not something that can be put into words; it's too big. There is a gaping black hole in my life and it's all that I can do not to get sucked into it and disappear forever. He meant everything to me. It sounds like an exaggeration, but it's really not. We took "inseparable" to whole new levels. It wasn't even a week before Kai's dad took a couple of slats out of the fence so that we could wander between the yards as we pleased.

Mom thought it was sweet at first—two peas in a pod, that's what she called us. For the first few years we were actually *three* peas: Kai, me, and his little sister, Louise. She was a gap-toothed, blonde-bunched little ray of sunshine, following us around everywhere whether we liked it or not.

There's a really cute picture that must have been taken when Kai and I were about eight or nine. It was Halloween and Kai was *supposed* to have been dressing up as a wizard but he wanted to look the same as me. He made a better witch than I did. He had green face paint, warts made out of Rice Krispies, and a robe that wasn't made from a black garbage can liner. His dad had even made him a real, proper broomstick. And Louise was dressed as the pinkest, sparkliest fairy you could ever imagine, brandishing a wand at Kai like she was trying to ward off his witchy evilness. That photo used to occupy the red frame on my bedside table, before I replaced it with one of just the two of us—Kai and me—a few years ago.

I wasn't jealous that Kai managed to outshine me every single Halloween. I wasn't jealous that people were drawn to him in a way they were never, ever drawn to me (or to Louise for that matter).

I didn't even know *how* to be jealous of Kai. I think I was a little bit in awe of everything he did.

Kai was clever and funny and kind. I was ten years old when I realized I wanted to marry him. My idea of married life might not have been entirely realistic, since it involved us living in adjacent houses. I didn't get as far as picturing us having children, because where would they have lived?

I was devastated when Kai and his family moved the day after my tenth birthday, even though the new house was only a four-minute walk away (four minutes and twenty-three seconds at normal walking pace, Kai proudly informed me the day after the move).

It wasn't till I was eleven or so that Mom started to worry about me spending every second of every minute of every day with him. It was around then that she stopped us sleeping in the same bed (eliciting total outrage from me and mild indignation from Kai. He never really got outraged about anything). She wouldn't tell me why it wasn't OK for us to share a bed anymore, and I was so cross I didn't speak to her for three and a half hours (until she coaxed me downstairs with the promise of Nutella on toast).

"Aren't there any girls at school you'd like to invite over for a sleepover?" Mom asked one day in the car on the way to the super-market. She glanced at me quickly before returning her attention to the traffic.

"Nope."

"What about that Jasmine girl you used to talk about?"

"What *about* her? She's so boring. All she talks about is horses

4

and hair, and it's not like her hair's even that nice. It's so long it makes me feel a bit sick."

Mom reached over and tugged at a stray lock of *my* hair. It was way too short—not a good look for me, but I didn't care back then. It was practical. "There's nothing wrong with long hair. Louise's hair is lovely, don't you think? You know…I think you'd look really pretty if you let yours grow out a bit."

I stuck out my bottom lip and crossed my arms over my chest. "You mean I don't look pretty *now?*"

Mom managed to raise an eyebrow at me without taking her eyes off the road. "You, my dear, are the prettiest girl in the world. You just don't know it yet." The day after my thirteenth birthday (two days before *his* thirteenth birthday), I asked Kai if he thought I was pretty. I'd wanted to ask him for the longest time, but I'd always chickened out at the last minute. I was worried he'd make fun of me.

We were lying on his bed watching a DVD. He sat up and made me do the same. Then he held his hands up as if to frame my face. He told me to look straight at him and not smile, so obviously I couldn't help but laugh.

"Stop that! This is a serious question and it needs a serious answer!" He narrowed his eyes and nodded slowly.

"Just answer the question, you idiot!" I pulled a face that was anything but pretty and I waited…and waited.

"OK, I have deduced the following…you have unnaturally symmetrical features. Your skin is clear and looks healthy even though you hardly ever go outside. Your eyes are pretty. Your nose is a very fine example of the genre. Your hair is…well, the less said about that the better. Your lips are a perfect medium, and your teeth are reasonably straight. In conclusion I'd say that, yes, you *are* pretty. Congratulations."

I grabbed a pillow and walloped Kai across the face with it.

"Thanks for that, Einstein! I wasn't expecting you to be so... scientific about it!"

Kai laughed and said, "I thought you'd appreciate a bit of objectivity." (Kai was always using long words.)

I wouldn't meet his eye and I was suddenly burning up with embarrassment. "Jem? What's up? I said you're pretty! You should be pleased...shouldn't you? Is it the hair thing? Look, I'm sorry I said anything. You hair's fine. Really. Honestly. Have I ever lied to you?"

"I don't know...*have* you?"

"No! Never!"

I should have stopped there to spare us both any further embarrassment. But I didn't.

"OK then, tell me truthfully—do *you* think I'm pretty?" I still couldn't bear to look at him.

"I said so, didn't I?" His voice was soft.

"Not exactly."

"I think you're beautiful, Jemima Halliday."

I had to look to check he wasn't making fun of me. His face was serious and I took this as a positive sign.

"Would you like to kiss me?" I must have been feeling particularly brave that day.

I'm not sure what kind of reaction I was expecting, but it wasn't hysterical laughter. He stopped laughing when he saw the look on my face. "What's so funny?"

"Sorry. It's just...I thought you *knew*." He was sort of wincing now.

"Knew what?" I had no idea what he was talking about.

"That I'm gay."

⌒

I'd had no clue whatsoever. The thought had never ever crossed my mind. Very-nearly-thirteen-year-old boys were not gay. Of course there were gay men on the TV and stuff, but they were *grown-up* men. The only gay man I knew in real life was a random cousin of Dad's, and I'd only met him once. He danced with me at a family wedding, twirling me around the dance floor until I nearly puked. Then he danced with his ridiculously good-looking boyfriend, which was the first time I'd ever seen two men dance together.

I tried to act cool, like people telling me they're gay was an everyday occurrence for me. I shrugged and said, "Oh yeah, I totally knew. I was just messing around." I could tell Kai wasn't buying it, but he let me off because that's the kind of person he was.

So my crazy dreams of marrying Kai went straight out the window, of course. But I never lost the certainty that he was the perfect boy. The perfect boy for me anyway. I just tried not to think about it because it made me ache inside.

Only four people knew about Kai being gay. His parents knew and were totally cool with it. I knew and was totally mixed up about it. Then Louise found out and was very definitely totally not cool with it.

I was never quite sure *how* Louise found out; Kai refused to tell me. But things changed between the three of us almost instantly. She didn't follow us round like a little lost puppy anymore. And although I'd always acted like her constant attention annoyed me, I actually missed it. I could tell Kai did too, but he didn't like to talk about it. I only realized Louise wasn't OK with the whole gay thing when she caught me and Kai ogling some shirtless guy on the Internet one day (Kai was doing most of the ogling; I was merely agreeing with everything he said). She rolled her eyes and made a sound in her throat that could only be interpreted as one thing: disgust.

Kai quickly closed the browser window, blushing like he'd

been caught doing something seedy and shameful. I was baffled. "What?" I asked her.

She flicked her hair (an annoying habit she'd acquired since starting middle school) and said a sullen "Nothing."

"It didn't sound like nothing." Kai put his hand on my wrist and told me to leave it. I shook him off.

"Louise? Is there something you'd like to share with the group?" This was my new favorite catchphrase; I'd picked it up from my English teacher, who I hated with a fiery passion.

Louise sighed and twirled some hair between her fingers, acting as if checking for split ends was more interesting than talking to me and Kai. "It's, like, gross." This was something else Louise had picked up in the last few months—a completely new way of speaking that drove her parents crazy.

I asked her what was gross, because I genuinely had no idea what she was talking about.

She sighed again, even louder this time. "Boys liking boys. Becky's dad says it's sinful."

I'd never heard Louise mention Becky before, let alone Becky's dad. I laughed. "Are you for real?" The looks between Kai and Louise answered my question. This ground had clearly been covered before. "What does Becky's dad know about anything anyway?"

Louise narrowed her eyes at me. "He's, like, a really important businessman. He drives a BMW."

"Good for him."

The sarcasm was lost on her. "I know, right? Anyway, he said it's probably just a phase." Louise looked shifty all of a sudden.

I felt Kai's grip tighten around my wrist but he still said nothing. So it was down to me. "*What's* probably just a phase?"

"Kai. Being…you know…bent."

My temper flared. I couldn't believe what I was hearing. "You take that back. Right now."

Louise stuck out her bottom lip. "Will not, and you can't make me."

I pushed my chair back fast and Louise backed away, but Kai's hand was still clamped to my wrist.

"Jem, leave it. Please. She doesn't understand. It's OK. Really."

She was smirking, knowing full well that her brother would protect her even though she was the one who was attacking *him*. For the very first time, I hated her. The gap-toothed, cute-as-a-button, only-slightly-annoying little sister had turned into someone else—almost overnight, it seemed. And I wasn't sure I liked this someone else. At all.

Kai said it didn't bother him, that Louise was young and would come around to the idea eventually. My argument that she was only a year younger than we were and that she shouldn't give two hoots if he was gay because HE WAS HER BROTHER fell on deaf ears.

She *did* come around to the idea eventually. She certainly stopped saying stupid things in front of me, at least. But that might have had something to do with the fact that Louise and I started studiously ignoring each other—as if by some unspoken arrangement. I couldn't forgive her for being horrible to Kai, and she… well, I was never quite sure why she started ignoring me. Maybe because I started dying my hair and wearing black and listening to decent music and she turned into a plastic, popular person. It was as if some kind of mystical divergence had occurred, leaving Kai in the middle, loving us both, wishing everybody could just get along. He never did get his wish. And now he won't ever get his driver's license. Or buy alcohol in a pub. Or vote. Or fall in love.

Kai will do none of these things. All because of what they did to him.

chapter two

The idea of life without Kai was unthinkable. My brain couldn't accept it. The thought of going to school every day. Alone. Evenings and weekends. Alone. My whole life stretching out in front of me—without him. It was unacceptable.

For the first couple of weeks I couldn't even get out of bed. Mom was frantic, begging me to talk about it. Pleading with me to get up and get on with my life. I couldn't even hear her. I became a master at tuning everything and everyone out of my mind. Everyone except him. Kai was all I wanted to think about. Thinking about anything else felt like a betrayal, and I felt like he'd *know*.

Mom and Dad were on suicide watch. They'd spoken to a counselor about it and apparently there was a "significant risk" that I would off myself. I can't really blame them for thinking like that. After all, I *was* spending a considerable amount of time working out the best way to do it.

After much deliberation, I settled on pills—a quiet, peaceful way to die. Not too traumatic for my parents either. I mean, obviously I knew it would be traumatic, but this would be significantly less traumatic than if I hung myself in the garage or slit my wrists in the bath. Or jumped off the suspension bridge.

I'd talked about suicide since I was fourteen or so. Some people were sporty or musical or collected model animals…I was into death. It was kind of my thing. People didn't necessarily *know* that about me, but the black hair and the black clothes identified me as emo or goth or whatever other inaccurate label they wanted to pin on me. I hated them for it. No one knew me. No one except Kai. He was the only one who bothered to look beyond the facade. Kai was the one who would listen to me moan about the world and how unfair everything was and how I was never going to be happy and how I hated my parents and how no one understood. He never acted bored or tried to change the subject. He *listened*. I didn't know how lucky I was to have someone who really listened. Someone who understood me on every level. Who seemed to love me despite me being a whining, miserable bitch.

I mean, I wasn't like that *all* the time or anything. We had fun together too. We made each other laugh. Best friends for life, that's what we said. And despite the fact that I liked to talk about death and suicide, I think we both believed we'd end up growing old together (if not *together* together). But Kai will never grow old.

I was sure I wanted to die. There didn't seem to be any other option. I was going to polish off Mom's Valium. There were thirty-one pills left in the bottle. I figured that was more than enough.

Every day I woke up thinking that today would be the day, and every day I found some excuse not to do it. Every day Mom nagged me about going back to school, and every day I told her to leave me alone. Since I refused point blank to leave the house she even got the doctor to make a house call and she somehow persuaded him to sign me off school for longer than he wanted to. The school was fine with it as long as I kept up with my work, because (as everyone and their dog kept mentioning) this was a big exam year. Like I cared about stupid exams.

A month to the day after Kai's death, I was finally ready. I told myself there was something poetic about the timing. I tried not to think about Mom or Dad or Noah, telling myself they'd get over it in time. They'd understand. It's amazing, the lies you can tell yourself. Even more amazing, the lies you can believe if you're desperate enough.

I wrote a pretty standard sort of note: I said I was sorry, how much I loved them, told them they shouldn't feel bad. It was painfully inadequate, but it was the best I could do. And it was better than nothing. Marginally.

For the past few weeks, they'd been taking turns staying home, using up their vacation days in a vain attempt to make sure I didn't kill myself. But their bosses were only sympathetic for so long, so they'd eventually resigned themselves to leaving me on my own for a few hours a day.

Mom and Dad were at work and Noah was at school and I was going to be dead by the time they got home. I would get a glass of water, or maybe a bottle, because there were a lot of pills to be swallowed. I didn't want to be ten pills down and suddenly realize I couldn't swallow them because I was out of water. It would be disastrous if I passed out without finishing the job. That would mean being rushed to the hospital, having my stomach pumped, having to face my parents, having to face Noah.

Thinking about Noah hurt the most. He wouldn't understand. He was only ten, and for some reason he still thought his big sister was awesome. He had yet to discover what the rest of the world thought of her. Emo. Loser. Goth. Freak.

Noah would be better off without me though. Mom and Dad would pay him loads of attention to compensate for the trauma of having a dead sister. He'd get spoiled rotten. He might even be allowed that mountain bike he's been after forever. Those were the kind of lies I told myself.

After a long, hot shower, I raided the fridge to make a sandwich.

My last meal. I would have preferred something like Mom's lasagna or Chinese takeout, but Mom hadn't made lasagna since Kai died and it seemed crazy weird (even for me) to order up a Chinese banquet before I offed myself.

The sandwich was dry and tasted terrible, even though it had all my favorite things and plenty of mayonnaise. I didn't even manage to eat half of it, probably because I couldn't shake the image of what it would look like in my stomach—all chewed up and partially digested. There was a good chance that I would choke on my own vomit. That's how you die, sometimes. The drugs knock you out, your stomach revolts against what's in it, you spew, but you're still knocked out, so you choke and drown in your own vomit. Pretty disgusting, really.

I was regretting not considering this sooner and carefully washing the chopping board, knife, and plate when the doorbell rang. It was probably the postman; our stupidly small mailbox means that only the slimmest of envelopes make it through.

The doorbell rang again and again. *Go away! Go the fuck away!* I covered my ears with my hands to try to block out the sound. *Why won't they leave me alone? Why won't everybody just leave me alone?* I felt like stabbing myself with the knife then and there.

Then whoever it was started banging on the front door with their fist. The banging interspersed with the ringing made me reconsider stabbing myself and think about stabbing the mystery caller instead. Then there was a voice. A voice I recognized, shouting, "Jem! I know you're in there so just answer the fucking door, OK? I've got better things to do than hang around here all day. Jem!"

I froze. It was Louise. *Shit.*

I couldn't ignore her. No matter how I felt about her, she was still his sister. Kai wouldn't want me to ignore her. Kai would probably want us to reforge a friendship based on our mutual grief.

I trudged toward the front door to find her peering through the letter box like some kind of crazy stalker. As I was opening the door I heard her mutter "About bloody time."

I was slightly lost for words at the sight of her. It was like looking in a mirror. A strange sort of mirror. We still looked worlds apart—she hadn't gone and dyed her hair black or anything. Her hair was still way blonder than the natural, beautiful golden color she'd shared with Kai. But she wasn't wearing a scrap of makeup, which was pretty much unthinkable to her lot—the popular, slutty girls she was friends with. There was something in her face that I recognized—something I'd seen whenever I'd looked in the mirror since Kai's death. There was something hopeless about us both. Like we'd disappeared into a place that no one else could reach. I almost wanted to hug her (and wanted her to hug me). But that would probably have freaked her out. I'd steered well clear of her at the funeral to avoid potential hugging scenarios. And because I'd started having some kind of weird panic attack, which meant Mom had to escort me out of the church halfway through the service.

"Aren't you going to invite me in?" This was more like the Louise I knew.

"Sorry, of course, yes." I stepped aside to let her pass. She was carrying a big brown envelope.

She rushed into the living room and sat down on the sofa. I couldn't get over how different she looked with no makeup on.

"Um…do you want a cup of tea or something?"

I hovered in the doorway to the kitchen.

Louise shook her head and didn't even bother to say, *No, thanks*.

I perched on Dad's chair in the corner. As far away from Louise as it was possible to get without actually leaving the room. Trying not to show how antsy I was about her eating into my valuable suicide time. "So…how are you doing?" It was a stupid question, but that's what people do—ask each other stupid things they don't even want to know the answer to.

She gave me a scathing look. The same look I gave Mom or Dad whenever they asked me that very question. "I can't stay long. There's something I have to give you." She waved the envelope. "I don't want you freaking out about it or anything, OK?"

I nodded. Anything to get rid of her so I could get on with the business of getting dead.

Louise hauled herself up from the sofa, which seemed to take considerable effort. She came over and handed the envelope to me. I turned it over to see the front. *Oh God.*

She saw the look on my face and said, "You promised not to freak out, remember?" A vague nod is hardly the same as promising, but I said nothing. I had lost the ability to speak. "It's from him."

I knew that, of course. The handwriting was almost as familiar to me as my own (and a hell of a lot neater).

Louise's words spilled out, answering all the questions swimming around my head. "He left me a note with strict instructions to give this to you today—exactly a month after…He said if I didn't do it he'd come back and haunt me…I think that was supposed to be funny. Anyway, I don't know what's in it, so don't even ask. And he didn't want me to tell Mom and Dad about it. Or the police. So you probably shouldn't either. Um…so…I've done what he wanted and that's it." Her face crumpled like a scrunched-up piece of paper. "I have to…" She practically ran from the room. I heard the front door slam.

I should maybe have followed her to check she was OK, but all I could think about was the envelope, which I was holding like it was the most precious, fragile thing in the world.

JEM (in big purple letters, underlined three times; purple was his favorite color).

In much smaller letters underneath was: *If Lol hasn't delivered this on November 23rd, you have my permission to tell everyone at school that she genuinely believes that one day her and Mr. Franklin will get married and have babies. And that she's started working on a top-secret scrapbook of wedding ideas for the occasion.* (Mr. Franklin's one of the youngest teachers at Allander. He wears his shirtsleeves rolled up and his tie is always loose. That's how you know he's supposed to be cool. I could easily believe that Louise might fancy him or something, but the wedding stuff was clearly bollocks. Kai was always making up silly stories to make me smile.)

Then: *If there's any sign that Lol's opened this envelope and read the contents, you have my permission to tell everyone at school that she once let Barney Jennings kiss her for five seconds as payment for copying his math homework.* (Barney Jennings has horrible teeth, a greasy-plate face, and a definite problem with personal hygiene. There was no way Louise would let him anywhere near her.) And then: *Laters, Kiddo. xxx*

I traced the three kisses with my finger. My throat tightened.

Laters, Kiddo.

chapter three

I sat cross-legged on my bed with the envelope in front of me. I fought against the instinct to ignore it and get on with taking the pills.

I *had* to see what was inside. I opened it up and tipped the contents onto the bed. There were lots of smaller white envelopes. Twelve in all. Each was marked with a month—the same fat purple pen he'd used on the bigger envelope. The one marked "November" also said: "Open this one first…obviously!"

I checked inside the big envelope just in case there was anything else, and sure enough there was something lodged in the crease at the bottom. It was a perfect origami bird made from lined notepaper. Written on it in tiny capital letters were the words

"I AM THE TINY ORIGAMI BIRD OF JOY. I AM NOT, I REPEAT NOT, A TOY! I'M HERE TO CHEER YOU UP WHEN YOU ARE BLUE. SO CHEER THE FUCK UP, YOU SILLY MOO." I couldn't help but laugh. It was so typically Kai.

I brought the bird up to my nose and sniffed it. A silly thing to do, but I was hoping for a tiny reminder of Kai. He always wore this stupidly expensive citrusy aftershave that I adored, and I was suddenly desperate to smell it again. The thought that it had faded from my memory forever made me panic. Unsurprisingly, the origami bird smelled of paper.

I lay the bird on my pillow and picked up the November envelope. There was more writing on the back: "*Sealed with a big fat slobbery snog—with tongues and EVERYTHING.*" I winced when I broke the envelope's seal, ripping his words apart.

Inside were two sheets of creamy paper filled with Kai's impossibly neat handwriting.

I closed my eyes to steady myself and then started to read.

My Dearest Jemima,

Hey! Don't look at me like that! It's your real name and it's about time you got used to it, missy. First things first: you'd better be reading this...because if you're not, there's a chance you might have done something stupid. If that's the case, I'll be so cross with you. I mean really, bloody cross. I'm pretty sure you WON'T have done that, but you never know, do you? And it's not like you never talked about it before, Little Miss Morbid. Anyway...I'm here (well, not <u>here</u> exactly) to tell you that you CAN and WILL be perfectly fine without me. So you'd better not be dead, Ok? I'll feel pretty stupid for wasting my time with this little endeavor, and you wouldn't want me to feel stupid AND cross, would you?

Second things second: I'm sorry. I'm so sorry I can't begin to explain it. People say sorry all the time for the silliest things. But you have to know this: I'm sorry in the biggest, hugest way it's possible to be sorry. I hope you can find a way to forgive me one day. I know you'll be angry and I can't blame you for that. If things were the other way around, I would be SO furious with you for leaving me behind. So I guess what I'm saying is, I think I understand what you feel right now, but I don't think you'll always feel this way. You're just going to have to trust me on that. And if my words aren't enough to convince you, might I suggest conjuring up an image of my rakishly charming smile? I think that might help. Or just look at that photo on your phone. You know the one—don't pretend you don't. "Devilishly handsome" were your exact words, I believe. (If this was a text message and I was not so vehemently opposed to such nonsense, I would probably be going for a winky-face right now...)

Don't worry, this isn't a suicide note. I'm not going to be all "woe is me!" or anything. You know why I'm doing this. There's nothing to be gained from going on about it. What's done is done. At least, it will be by the time you're reading this. Unless I chickened out and couldn't go through with it. In which case, you won't be reading this, because I'll probably have put it through the shredder in Dad's office. But I really don't think I'm going to chicken out. I'm sorry. I'll stop apologizing in a minute, but God, Jem, I'm going to miss you so much.

You are my favorite person in the world. You KNOW that, don't you? I love you more than I love the History Channel. I love you more than I love my sunglasses (and you know how much I love those aviators). I love you more than I love Tim Riggins. I love you more than all of these things combined. That's a whole lot of love. Infinite in fact. Please forgive me for being a tad sentimental, but I think the circumstances warrant it, don't you?

Jem. (That's a serious Jem-listen-to-me-very-carefully sort of Jem, in case you were wondering.) You have to get over this. Move forward with your life and go kick the world in the balls, just like we always planned.

Right, let's cut to the chase. I hadn't intended
to be quite so long-winded, but you know me—
I'm not exactly known for succinctness. You'll
notice that there are eleven more envelopes—one
a month. Today's the 23rd, so I think it makes
sense if you open the next one on the 23rd
of December (just in time for Christmas!)
and the following one on the 23rd of January,
etc. etc. You get the picture. Please, please,
PLEASE don't open them early. That's cheating,
and nobody likes a cheat. (Confession time:
I cheated at Monopoly every single time we
played. You really shouldn't have let me be the
banker...all that power went to my head. So you
only have yourself to blame, really.)

That's about all I have for November...except
for a couple of favors. Please could you look
out for Lol for me? I know she's not exactly
your favorite person, but she's my sister.
She needs someone to keep an eye on her. That
should be my job, but I've failed. I've well and
truly failed at being a brother, Jem, and it
breaks my heart. I'm not quite sure what I'm
asking you to do exactly. I suppose maybe you
could just BE there. Just in case.

The other thing I need you to do is not obsess about what happened. It's done. It was unfortunate and I wish to God it hadn't happened, but it did. You need to forget about it, Ok? I don't want you playing girl detective or anything. It doesn't matter now. None of it matters. The only thing that matters now is you. You need to look after YOU. You're going to do good things in this world, I just know it. Speak to you next month, my little pickle.

Kai
xxx

P.S. I think you'd look ravishing with blonde hair. Always have. Why don't you give it a go... for me? I believe the technical term for this is "emotional blackmail," but that doesn't sound very nice. Maybe a dare would be better? I DARE you to dye your hair blonde—just for a little while. (Yes, I'm fully aware that this is an incredibly immature thing to do. Oh well.)

chapter four

Every word was a needle pricking at my heart. I read the letter five times, crying harder and harder so that it got really difficult to see the words.

Then I lay curled up in a little ball, my thoughts tumbling round my head. Monopoly. Kai's face in *that* photo. Kai didn't know (obviously), but I used to look at it every night before I went to sleep. There was something about it that made me think that even though life seemed bleak, maybe it could all turn out OK. With Kai in the world, it was a brighter, friendlier place. I hadn't looked at the photo since he died.

I couldn't believe Kai had gone to all this trouble, but at the same time it was such a Kai thing to do. Even at his lowest, his life in tatters, he was thinking of me. He didn't have a selfish gene in his body. I know people think suicide is selfish, and maybe sometimes it really is. But what happened to Kai was beyond what anyone should have to cope with. I didn't blame him, not really. It just broke my heart that I wasn't enough to keep him here. That he couldn't hold on a couple more years until we could get out of this godforsaken place and go seek our fortunes in London. That was the plan. That had *always* been the plan.

Kai was right. I *had* been angry with him. Not right away. The first week or so was pure grief—raw and ugly and dark. But then that morphed into something else. The sadness was still there and still huge, but then I felt abandoned. I kept on having this ridiculous thought that Kai was the only person who could possibly comfort me. I needed him to hug me and hold me and tell me that everything was going to be OK without him; how dare he not be here for me? He'd always been that person for me. That one person I could go to and *know* that he would make me feel better. And now I needed him more than ever and he was gone. For good. I wanted to punch him and shake him and shout, "HOW COULD YOU DO THIS TO ME?"

I was angry, and confused about the fact that I was angry with someone who was dead. But that stage didn't last long either. That was when I knew I was going to kill myself, and I felt better as soon as I'd made up my mind. It gave me something to focus on and, weirdly, something to look forward to. But the letters changed everything.

I took my note—my *suicide* note—out of my bedside drawer. What had seemed so reasonable an hour before now looked pathetic. I tore it into tiny, unreadable pieces just in case Mom decided to go rummaging through my garbage can.

I couldn't do it now, could I? I wanted to. So badly. The thought of going to sleep forever was delicious. I was so very tired.

But I couldn't do it to him. Not now. I couldn't ignore what Kai had done for me. I wouldn't let him down like that; I let him down enough when he was alive.

I couldn't get over the timing of it all. As if he knew me so well—every single thing, to the very core of me—that he'd somehow *known* that today was supposed to be the day. He'd known, even though I'd had no idea. Of course, the rational part of my brain knew that this was stupid, just one of those crazy coincidences that life is filled with. This one just happened to be a lot spookier than most, that's all.

I was going to have to wait. Somehow I would have to find a way to get through each day without him. I would be patient and read his letters when he wanted me to, even though the waiting would be complete torture. Maybe the letters would help (and maybe they wouldn't).

Twelve months. One year. I could survive one measly year for him. But once that year was up…The Valium might be gone, but there would always be another way.

First things first: I had to get my hands on some hair dye.

⌒

I blinked against the overly bright sunshine. I was like a hedgehog coming out of hibernation. It was a bit of a shock to see that everything looked the same as it always had. The world had been going about its business while I'd been cooped up in my bedroom. I was on my way to the drugstore to get the blonde version of my usual black dye when a girl stopped me on the street. She was about my age and rather orange.

"Excuse me? Can I just ask, do you dye your hair?" I'd been stopped by them before—the trainee hairdressers prowling the streets for new clients. I'd always ignored them—why spend thirty quid when you don't have to? But this girl's hair was awesome. It looked natural but you could tell it wasn't, if that makes sense. I imagined that only people in California had hair like that.

She pointed me in the direction of the salon. They were doing half-price cut and highlights for students, and when I checked my wallet, I had just enough cash. It seemed like fate. It seemed like Kai had arranged for this girl (Kayleigh…her name even began with a K, for Christ's sake!) to cross my path.

The hairdresser barely suppressed a grimace when he looked at the state of my hair. "Don't you worry, we'll have you looking spick-and-span in no time, little one. Fernando will work his magic, I can promise you that." I wanted to run screaming from the salon. People who talk about themselves in the third person are near the top of my shit list, but I gritted my teeth and thought of Kai (and tried to ignore Fernando's terrifyingly overtweaked eyebrows). I looked through a book of sample colors, but in the end told him I wanted something like Kayleigh's. He smiled knowingly. "Ooh, our Kayleigh's the best advertising we've got!" He looked over his shoulder furtively and then leaned in close to me. "Shame about the 'tan' though, yes?" He did that fingers thing for the quote marks.

I laughed along with him and thought maybe this wouldn't be complete torture after all. It felt strange to laugh again after so long, but the muscles in my face seemed to remember how to do it. And it felt good.

I'd only asked for a half head of highlights, since that was all I could afford, but Fernando winked at me and said, "Don't you worry, my love, I'll do whatever it takes to get rid of this, how you say, *funeral* black, and then"—he paused to ruffle my lank locks—"then I will work my magic!" I kept on smiling despite the funeral reference. It was out of the question for me to cry in a place called Kool Cutz.

Two hours later I slumped down in front of the mirror, exhausted from Fernando's incessant chatter. My hair was still wet, but that didn't lessen the shock. I had been dying it black (much to Mom's horror) since I was thirteen. My natural hair color is a nothingy sort of shade—like baked mud. There was nothing remotely mud-like about this—I was *properly* blonde. Fernando had been as good as his word.

My eyes looked blue. They've always been bluish, I suppose, but now they were BLUE. Seriously, piercingly blue. My whole face looked different somehow—less pale, less like someone who'd only left the house once in the last four weeks.

The shock was even greater by the time Fernando had finished snipping away and done his stuff with the hairdryer and the straighteners. He stepped back to admire his handiwork, a look of supreme smugness on his face. "*Madre de Dios*, I am *gooooooood*."

He wasn't wrong; he had worked a small miracle.

I didn't look like me. To be perfectly honest, it scared me a little. You get so used to seeing the same thing in the mirror every day you stop thinking about what you look like—or at least *I* did anyway. To suddenly see someone else—someone blonde, for Christ's sake—is disconcerting to say the least.

"Ah, Fernando thinks the boys will be knocking at your door before you know it," he said as he brushed the hairs from my neck.

"What makes you think they weren't already?"

"Ha! You're funny. I like you. You can come back anytime!"

How rude.

⌒

Everyone was back by the time I got home. Mom was unpacking the shopping, Dad was chopping onions, and Noah was stretched out on the sofa. The scene was so perfectly normal that it stopped me in my tracks. I'd been so wrapped up in my own world that I hadn't given them a second thought. Even when I'd been thinking about them—thinking about them finding my body, reading the note—I hadn't really been thinking about *them*. I'd been thinking about me.

Noah didn't even look up when I passed right in front of him; he was in full-on slack-jawed TV zombie mode. Dad had his back to me. His shirt was looking especially rumpled that day. Mom froze in the middle of whatever she was saying. She had a pack of bacon in one hand and a head of broccoli in the other.

"Oh!" Her eyes were wide and the corners or her mouth twitched, as if they couldn't quite make up their mind what to do next.

29

Dad whirled around with a huge knife in his hand.

"Oh my!"

I said nothing. Just tugged nervously at the ends of my hair.

Mom put down the shopping, rushed over, and cupped my face in her hands. "Oh, Jem! We were so worried when you weren't here when we got home. Didn't you get my messages?" She didn't pause to let me answer. "But now I see why! My beautiful, beautiful girl. What brought this on, eh? Feeling a bit brighter, are you?" She smoothed down my hair (not that it needed any smoothing…Fernando really *was* some kind of crazy hair-tweaking genius).

The truth is, Mom's comments deserved some kind of snarky response, but I couldn't even think of one. And I didn't want to. I settled for blushing instead.

Dad nudged Mom and said, "Eh, Cath, doesn't she look like you when you were that age?!" Which was just massively creepy.

Mom giggled and bumped him with her hip. "I wish I'd looked half as good! No, she gets that bone structure from you."

I wanted to escape before they started snogging (or worse). "I'm going to…yeah…tidy my room or something."

Mom tried to hide her delight at this little announcement. "Would you like a hand, sweetie?"

I shook my head. "No. Thank you. And…er…I might go back to school tomorrow." I hadn't planned to say those words. I hadn't even thought about going back to school until the words spilled out.

Mom and Dad shared a look, then Mom squeezed my arm. There were tears in her eyes, but we both pretended not to notice. "Good girl." I nodded and left the kitchen before I started bawling too.

Noah *did* look up on the return journey. His reaction? "YEEEEEEEEEUUURGH! What have you done?! You look all fake and…weird." That made me smile. I wouldn't have expected anything less from the little smart-ass.

The sight of my bedroom was almost as big a shock as my new hair, but not in a good way. It was disgusting. I couldn't remember the last time my sheets had been changed. There were clothes all over the carpet, four mugs, three plates, and seven chip bags. And the smell was something else.

Every time Mom had come in to try and sort it out, I'd shouted at her to leave me alone. And every time, instead of telling me what a snotty little bitch I was, she nodded and left without a word. Thinking about it made me cringe with shame. Things were going to change. I had a year left. I could be a better daughter for that long, at least.

I'd take one day at a time. There were thirty days to get through before Kai's next letter.

chapter five

My life had started to come undone at the start of the school year, and I didn't even know it. There was no big flashing neon sign saying: THIS IS THE YEAR THAT WILL CHANGE EVERYTHING. Nothing seemed different after the summer; the popular kids were still popular (and somehow more tanned and healthy-looking than the rest of us), the unpopular kids were still unpopular. The Ignored were still well and truly ignored. This was my category. I wasn't geeky enough to be a target. Sure, I was the target of the occasional "goth" or "emo loser," but it was nothing I couldn't handle.

There was only one new boy. Max. Whenever anyone new arrives you check them out and you try to figure out where they're going to fit in. Are they someone you might want to talk to? Do you fancy them? Are they one of Them? I had Max pegged from the start. Artfully messy black hair, lazy smile, tall, and lean. Good-looking in a generic sort of way. He was one of Them, for sure. As predicted, Max was sucked into the popular crowd with Dyson-like speed.

Team Popular was the name I'd (unimaginatively) given to our year's so-called in-crowd. There were six of them, seven including Max. I was always watching them, talking about them, analyzing them. Kai joined in for the most part, but he drew the line at me talking about Louise; hard as it was to believe, she was well and truly part of the in-crowd.

At the end of tenth grade, I'd come up with a new theory: Allander Park was a zoo and everyone in it corresponded to a member of the animal kingdom. I'd taken great care in categorizing each member of Team Popular. (Kai said I had way too much time on my hands, but he still chipped in with his own opinions on the matter.)

Lucas Mahoney was the easiest to categorize. He was a lion, obviously. He even had the mane to prove it—possibly with slightly more hair product than the average lion would go for. Blond and chiseled, strutting about the place like the king of the fucking jungle. It was a well-known fact that every girl *had* to have a crush on Lucas at one time or another. Except me. And any secret lesbians among the student body.

Kai reckoned that Sasha Evans had to be a lioness—she was Lucas's girlfriend, after all. But it was my game, so I had the deciding vote. To me, she was more like a leopard—all slinky and sexy. Chestnut-colored hair, perfect body. I hated her.

Stu Hicks was Allander Park's officially designated joker. He liked to play with his food. Yes, he was *that* boy—the one who puts chips up his nose to make the girls laugh. And they *did* laugh like they found him genuinely hilarious. He was shorter than the other boys, but wiry and strong with it—majorly into martial arts apparently. I went for a chimpanzee in the end—harmless enough on the outside, but just wait till he bares his teeth. I've never quite trusted chimpanzees…there's something sinister about them.

Bugs was the odd man out in Team Popular. Huge and ginger, he was a big slab of meat with orange mold on top. Apparently he was some kind of big deal on the rugby team, but that wasn't usually enough to make you popular. Perhaps he was the exception that proved the rule? You'd often see the girls cuddling up to him, and the other lads never seemed to mind. They knew he was no competition—not really. I had Bugs pegged as some kind of bear. A pretty useless bear who was long overdue for extinction.

Amber Sheldon—dyed red hair, massive boobs, and an idiotic high-pitched laugh that made me think violent thoughts. A brightly plumed, noisy parrot. One that would start pulling out its own feathers if it didn't get enough attention.

I'd secretly decided that Louise was a snake, but I didn't say anything to Kai. I had no good reason for my choice, other than the fact that I really, really don't like snakes. And it would at least go some way to explain how she'd managed to slither her way into the in-crowd despite being in the year below.

So that was Team Popular. As far as I was concerned, they were an alien race with an evil plan to take over the world with their shiny hair and in-jokes.

Within a couple of weeks Max and Louise were going out. This was something new; Louise had never had a proper boyfriend before, unless you counted that brief dalliance with Stu last year. Why bother having a boyfriend when you could have someone new every day of the week? Why choose one flavor of ice cream when you can alternate between vanilla, coffee, and chocolate (or even go for a couple of different flavors in the same bowl… Gross, I know, but if the rumors about Louise were true, then she'd been there, done that). Kai hated the fact that everyone thought his sister was a slut, but there was nothing he could do about it because it happened to be true.

Max and Louise specialized in public displays of affection that even put Lucas and Sasha to shame. It was vomit inducing. I accidentally saw them in an empty classroom one day, and all I'm going to say about that little scene is it would definitely *not* have made it into a PG movie. And I probably watched for a few seconds longer than was strictly necessary. Not because I'm a perv or anything. It was like when you're driving down the highway and there's been an accident and there's police and ambulances everywhere. You know you shouldn't look at the person on the stretcher. Nothing good is going to come of it, but you're curious. What kind of person wouldn't be curious?

Anyway, I didn't tell Kai about the little performance I'd witnessed. There are some things a brother doesn't need to know about his baby sister, and this was definitely one of them. Besides, he heard that kind of talk from everyone else. According to Kai, Louise was really falling for Max. She talked about him nonstop at home. Kai seemed happy about it; he thought Max was good for Louise. I translated this as meaning, "Thank God she's not shagging everything that moves anymore."

So that was how things were looking. The ranks of the chosen ones had swollen by one, Kai's sister was no longer the school bike, and the rest of us were just going about our lives as normal. And yes, I'm well aware that it sounds like I was more than a little bit obsessed with the lives of people I never even talked to. I *was* kind of obsessed. But what else was there to do? School was boring; Kai was my only friend. It was like my hobby or something. A very weird, very sad sort of hobby that was made SO much easier by the new addition of an upperclassmen common room to Allander Park. The common room's a crucial part of the principal's strategy to try to make us act like grown-ups. I mean, he didn't use those exact words at the grand opening ceremony at the start of the year, but that was pretty much the gist of it.

There was one tiny change I haven't mentioned, but in the interests of full disclosure I probably should. There had been a subtle shift in my friendship with Kai. We still talked on the phone almost every night after school, just in case we might have missed something crucial in each other's lives in the few hours we *hadn't* spent together that day, but for the first time in our friendship, there were times when I couldn't get hold of him. Sometimes he didn't answer his phone, and sometimes it took him an hour or more to reply to my texts. This might sound normal (healthy, even), but it wasn't the way things worked between me and Kai.

I didn't say anything at first because I didn't want to look needy. I *was* needy, but I liked to pretend otherwise. And it wasn't that big a deal. He always called or texted *eventually*, but it bothered me because it was different, and I have never, ever been good with change. Change makes me anxious, which is kind of funny when you think of it now, all things considered.

I was never able to hide my feelings from Kai—he could wheedle his way through my defenses with consummate ease. All it took was him to say something like, *What's up, pickle?* and I would be spilling my guts in no time. (If anyone else on this planet ever called me pickle, I would break their face. Kai had special dispensation to use bizarre terms of endearment.)

We were hanging out in my room one day when he asked what was wrong. And I told him (mumbling and blushing) and he was great about it, of course. He reassured me that there was nothing to worry about—that I was still his very bestest friend in the whole wide world—and then he distracted me so perfectly I didn't even realize it was happening. "Oh, I have news! Very interesting news too. Except you might not find it all that appealing. Hear me out though, OK?"

Kai always prefaced announcements like that—building things up to be bigger than they were. He couldn't help himself. I nodded. We were lying on his bed, side by side, staring at the ceiling. We used to do that a lot.

"So…there's this party. At Max's place. And we're invited."

"*What?*" I understood all the words Kai was saying, but there was a crucial one missing, surely. A "not" between "we're" and "invited."

"I know! So anyway, it's this Saturday and everyone's going and his parents are away and his house is massive…according to Lol anyway." He was speaking super fast, which was something he only ever did when he was excited.

I hauled myself up into a sitting position and prodded his stomach with my finger, harder than was strictly necessary. "Define 'everyone.'"

"Ow! Look, I know my washboard stomach is pretty hard to resist, but please be gentle!" He sat up rubbing his stomach. He lifted up his shirt and inspected his belly as if I'd poked him hard enough to leave a mark. The sight of his stomach made *my* stomach flip and I was relieved when he covered it up again.

"Everyone…is everyone. You know, the usual."

I didn't know, and clearly neither did he. "You mean *them*? Team Popular?"

"Yeah, I guess. Not just them though—that would be a pretty lame party, wouldn't it? I think Max's brother is home from college with a bunch of his friends or something. Anyway, haven't you heard people talking about it at school?"

I hadn't. In order for that to happen, I'd have had to talk to someone who was not Kai. And I tried to avoid doing that because it was mostly unrewarding. Kai *did* talk to other people though, because Kai was a friendly sort of person. He was my link to the real world. I didn't feel the need to participate in it as long as he was there to do it for me.

"I'm not being funny, Kai, but are you sure we're invited? I mean, have you ever spoken to Max?"

"He is going out with my sister, *remember*? But it was Lol who invited us. She's practically cohosting it."

"And she told you to invite *me*? Who are you trying to kid?"

"OK, maybe she didn't say that in so many words. But she knows we come as a package, so inviting me is practically the same thing as inviting you—like we're married or something. Imagine us two married! It doesn't bear thinking about! But I digress... anyway, Lol doesn't *mind* you; she just doesn't get you like I do. No one gets you like I do. That's the problem." He got up to change the music.

"Sorry, I suppose I've never really thought of myself as a *problem* before." I suddenly thought I might cry. I didn't like crying in front of him. Crying was something to be done at home, alone.

He smiled over at me. "Don't go twisting my words, you little minx. All I'm saying is that I think we should go. You never know, it might actually be...gasp...fun! A little drinking, a little dancing...maybe we could hook up with a couple of tall, dark, handsome strangers."

The idea filled me with horror. The kind of party he was talking about was pretty much my exact worst nightmare. And he knew it. He knew how anxious I got and he was normally really good about it. But he obviously really, really wanted to go to this particular party. *Why?*

"Why would your sister suddenly invite you to something like this? It's like cross-pollination or something. It's messing with the natural order of the universe! It's not right!"

Kai sighed. "I thought we'd agreed that *I'm* the drama queen in this relationship. Besides, how do you know Lol doesn't invite me to parties ALL the time?"

"Because you tell me *everything*, idiot."

He jumped onto the bed, clasped my hands between his, and gave me his very best puppy-dog eyes.

"Pleasecomewithmepleasecomewithmepleasepleaseplease?" Kai's puppy-dog eyes were a very effective weapon. They never failed on me. But this was different; he was asking too much.

I decided that whining was my best defense. "But whyyyyyyy? Why would you want to hang out with those people? They're all shiny and fake and—"

"And nothing, Little Miss Judgmental! It's about time we did something different, don't you think? Something WILD…not that this is a massively wild thing to do, but it's a start, right? Say you'll come! If you come, I'll love you forever."

"You'll love me forever *anyway*, doofus." I was on the verge of giving in, mostly just to shut him up.

He could tell victory was near but was equally aware that anything he might say could mess it up. So he just looked at me, waiting.

"OK, OK, I'll go. But there are conditions. One: there will be no dancing. I do not dance. Two: don't expect me to have a good time. Three: don't expect me to be nice to people. Four: I'm allowed to leave whenever I want and you're banned from using your pouty face to get me to stay. Five: you have to buy the booze. There is no way I can face this thing sober. Six: um…there is no six. Just stop grinning like the bloody Cheshire Cat, OK?"

Kai did a terrible job of stifling his grin. "I solemnly accept the aforementioned conditions in relation to the forthcoming gathering at Maxwell Miller's abode. Miss Halliday, you've got yourself a deal." He held out his hand for me to shake.

chapter six

"This is a terrible idea." A wave of nausea crashed over me. I wondered what kind of impression a slick of vomit down Max's front door would make.

Kai hooked his arm into mine and leaned into me.

"It's going to be great, I promise. Don't forget…I'm wearing my lucky shirt. When has the Shirt of Good Fortune ever let us down?" He smelled *so* good. I breathed in the scent of him and it calmed me a little. That "lucky shirt" thing was utter bollocks, but everything would be OK as long as I was with Kai. This would be over soon. I could go home at any point. I'd been reminding myself of these things all day, but it hadn't done anything to ease my anxiety.

Max opened the door and smiled broadly. His teeth were incredibly straight and regimented—like little soldiers. "Hey! Come on in! Quick, Stu's threatening to chuck Bugs in the bonfire." Unsurprisingly, Max's greeting was aimed at Kai, with barely a first glance (let alone a second) at me.

Kai led the way through the house toward the sound of some terrible bass-heavy music. We stopped by the fridge (one of those huge fancy ones) to drop off our beer. I grabbed a bottle and looked around for a bottle opener. Max was there, quick as a flash, brandishing one like he'd just pulled a rabbit from a hat.

"Um…thanks."

"You're Jem, right? Sorry, we haven't officially met. I'm Max."
He held out his hand.

"Yeah, nice to…um…meet you." His handshake was firm but
not overly macho. And not at all sweaty, thank goodness.

Kai nudged me as we followed Max into the yard. "See? Told
you it'd be fine!" he whispered. Slightly prematurely, I couldn't
help thinking.

There were flaming torches dotted around the yard and a
massive bonfire smack bang in the middle. I wondered if Max's
parents would be pissed off when they came back to find a big
scorch mark in the center of their pristine lawn.

It helped to focus on the yard, the torches, and the bonfire.
It stopped me focusing on the people; the people really freaked
me out. It wasn't the number of them that bothered me so much,
even though there were *a lot* of them. It was seeing people from
school away from their normal environment. Everyone looked
different…dangerous somehow.

I kept my thoughts to myself; Kai wouldn't have got it. He
would have nodded and been all understanding and stuff, but he
wouldn't have *really* understood. No one did.

Louise came rushing up and coiled her arms around Max. She
wasn't wearing a coat. In fact, most of the girls weren't wearing
coats, despite the fact that the temperature wasn't exactly tropical.
She kissed Max as if he'd just returned from a six-month voyage
at sea. It was so desperate I was almost embarrassed for her. Why
would you do something like that in front of your *brother*?

Max pulled away and said, "Easy, tiger!"

Louise pouted, and it was almost exactly like Kai's pout but
somehow a lot less attractive. For the first time, she turned and
looked at us. "Hey, brother dear. And hey, brother dear's special
sidekick." Her eyes looked weird—the pupils were massive. She
must have been on something.

"Be nice, sister dear. You *promised*," said Kai. Louise shrugged, made a "W" with her hands, and said, "What*ever*," in a stupid Valley girl accent. She grabbed Max's hand and dragged him toward the bonfire. I imagined her stumbling and falling face first into it.

One hour later and I was ready to bail. I'd necked two beers already, which was a lot for someone who didn't really drink. Kai and I had managed to find a couple of nonawful people to talk to. Well, he was doing most of the talking. I was mostly nodding and sipping my drink and smiling at what I thought were appropriate points in the conversation. He kept giving me these looks whenever the talk strayed into a topic I would normally be interested in. I kept ignoring the looks.

My attention strayed toward the bonfire every few seconds. The strict social hierarchy from school was firmly in place. It would almost have been funny if it wasn't so tragic. The most popular people were closest to the fire, bathed in its orangey glow, which made them look extra beautiful (except for Bugs…no one but a mother could ever describe Bugs as beautiful). Some of them were dancing. Sasha was grinding against Lucas in a way that gave me far too much insight into their relationship.

Bugs had Stu in a headlock, rubbing his knuckles across Stu's shaved head. They didn't have girlfriends as far as I knew. Stu was a bit like Louise in that respect, except he was considered to be a stud rather than a slut. It made perfect sense that those two had done the nasty last year. At school I couldn't help noticing the way Stu looked at girls as they walked past, like he was grading them in his head. Calculating if it was worth his time to try to make them laugh. Everyone (including Kai) seemed to think he was harmless, but I saw something in him…something predatory and not remotely funny. Not that I'd ever talked to him, of course.

I saw Max and Louise standing a little bit away from the others. From the look of things, Louise was *not* a happy bunny (snake). Her arms were flailing around and her chin jutted out aggressively. Max's hands were raised in a gesture of surrender. I wished the music wasn't so loud—this was better than watching TV. Kai had been right—I was having fun, in a weird sort of way.

I was about to tune back into the conversation Kai was having with Bland Boy A and Bland Girl B, but Louise chose that very moment to storm off into the house. Max didn't go after her, and you could tell she'd expected him to, because she looked over her shoulder when she reached the kitchen door. He wasn't even watching her; he'd stormed off to the other end of the yard. Interesting.

The next thing I knew, Kai grabbed my arm and said, "Excuse us for a second, would you? I need to get another drink." But he wasn't talking to me—he was talking to the Blands.

"Would you mind letting go of my arm?" I said when we were nearly at the house.

"Could you be any more rude? I mean, God! The least you could do is *pretend* to engage with people!" He was serious. He was *actually* being serious.

"Come off it, Kai. They're so boring my eyes have now got double glazing…no wait, *triple* glazing." I giggled.

"Are you drunk? Oh God, please don't tell me you're drunk. You've only had two beers! How is that even possible?"

"I'm not drunk! Get me another beer this instant, my good man!"

Kai rolled his eyes and opened the door to the kitchen. The room was now packed with people and we had to squeeze our way through toward the fridge, which was almost empty of anything a normal person would choose to drink. Our beers were gone so Kai grabbed us a couple of dubious-looking alcopops.

We clinked our bottles together and Kai said, "That's your limit, OK? You're on the soft drinks after that one."

I saluted and nearly elbowed someone in the face.

"Aye aye, cap'n."

Kai sighed. "I definitely prefer you sober. Now…what do you say we split up for a while…I've always fancied myself a bit of a lone wolf."

That made me laugh. Kai was SO not a wolf, but if he wanted to tell himself that…

"OK, whatever. Go do your wolfy thing. I'll be fine. Me and my alarmingly blue drink will be just fine."

"Promise me you'll talk to someone new. How about that guy over there? He looks normal. And he definitely doesn't go to our school, which has got to be a bonus."

I looked to where Kai was not so subtly pointing. The boy in question did indeed look normal, friendly even. "If it'll make you happy, I'll talk to him. Now fly away, you little social butterfly!"

Kai kissed me on the cheek and threaded his way through the crowd. I took another look at the boy Kai had picked out and he turned and saw me looking. *Awkward.* I concentrated on taking a swig of my drink. When I looked back he was still looking. *Mega-awkward.* He smiled a little bit and I turned away. There was no way I could talk to him. What would I say? "Do you come here often?" or "Great party, shame about the people," or "I like your shirt. It fits really well." His shirt did fit really well, but somehow it didn't look try-hard on him, like Lucas did showing off every muscle in his tight, white T-shirts.

I felt trapped and vulnerable. I needed Kai by my side to remind me how normal people interacted with each other. Suddenly I was finding it hard to catch my breath and I felt too hot. Fresh air. I needed fresh air. And space. There were too many people in the kitchen, all laughing and joking and crowding in on me. I bolted for the door, spilling someone's drink and tripping over someone else's foot on the way. I didn't *think* the foot had been placed in my path on purpose, but you never can tell for sure.

I closed the door behind me, but not before I heard someone shout, "Who invited *that* freak?" I couldn't be sure if the voice belonged to someone I knew or a complete stranger, but it was nothing I hadn't heard before.

I felt loads better as soon as I was outside. The air was crisp and cool and I breathed it in as deeply as I could. I tried not to think about the boy in the kitchen. He probably hadn't been smiling at me anyway. He was probably looking at someone standing next to me. Yeah, that would be it.

I took another long gulp of my disgusting drink, because there was nothing else to do. I didn't want to talk to anyone. If I was interested in talking to people, I would do it at school, where at least you had a decent excuse to start a conversation—like borrowing their notes for a class you missed or something. I looked at my watch and groaned to see that it wasn't even ten o'clock yet. Kai and I had agreed to leave at eleven. I could have stayed out later—Mom and Dad have never been that big on curfews—but Kai had agreed to an early departure since I was doing him such a huge favor by being here. Thinking about it, it was kind of strange that he'd wanted me here. He clearly wasn't interested in hanging out with me (I ignored the little voice in my head that said maybe he didn't want to hang out with me because I was being so obnoxious).

I couldn't see him near the bonfire. I could see a lot of torsos though—Kai was missing out big time. Some of the boys were doing some kind of tribal dance round the fire, beating their chests and whooping. Lucas the Lion was leading them, of course. His chest had red markings on it—it looked like paint but was probably lipstick. He must have been sweating, because his chest was sort of glistening in the firelight. His jeans were slung low and you could see the black band of his underwear.

Lots of the girls were blatantly ogling Lucas. *Idiots.* I turned away and wandered down a little path toward the end of the yard, which was a lot bigger than it looked. I swore as I nearly fell over a couple grappling on the grass behind a bush. They didn't even notice me—all that grunting and moaning must have masked my voice. I recognized the girl straightaway—Amber Sheldon (aka Parrot Girl)—but I couldn't tell who the boy was. His face was buried in her neck and his bare ass didn't provide any clues.

I shuddered and hurried on. I couldn't believe people really did things like that in real life. Shagging in the yard at some random party? Degrading doesn't even come close to covering it. Didn't these people have any self-respect? Mind you, if I was Amber Sheldon, I wouldn't particularly respect myself either.

At the end of the yard I found a vegetable patch and a greenhouse. I'd never been in a greenhouse before and now seemed like the right time to explore one. I peered through the glass to check there were no more bare asses or bare anythings. It was empty so I went on in. It was weirdly warm inside. I couldn't work out how that was possible (*that's* how drunk I was), and when I remembered the Greenhouse Effect, I laughed out loud and then swiftly covered my mouth because laughing when you're alone is just plain weird.

There was a long wooden bench with lots of little pots on it and lots of green things growing in the little pots. You could hardly hear the music from the house. It was peaceful and warm and made me feel sleepy. And there just happened to be a comfy chair in the back corner which looked like it was begging me to sit in it. I swear it was like a scene from Goldilocks or something.

I collapsed into the chair and closed my eyes, relieved to have escaped the madness of the party. I'd curl up here for an hour or so, then go and find Kai and drag his ass home. I wouldn't mind going to more parties if they all had a safe haven like this.

Then my safe haven was destroyed. By a chimpanzee. A horny, sinister chimpanzee.

chapter seven

"Hello? Drunk girl? Are you in here? Helloooo?"

I didn't recognize the voice, but I didn't *have to* recognize it to know it was someone I did not want to deal with. I stayed quiet, cowering down into the seat, trying to make myself as small as possible. There was a crash and a "Shit!" as he banged into the bench.

"Ah, there you are. Why are you hiding back there?" It was Stu Hicks. And he wasn't wearing a top. Someone had scrawled "COCK" in black marker across his chest. I hoped it was permanent.

"I'm not…hiding."

He started wagging his finger at me, smiling and nodding. "You! I know you. You're that girl, aren't you?"

I wanted to get up, but now he was standing right over me. He stank of beer and sweat and something else that I put down to miscellaneous monkey scent. I sighed and gulped down the last of my drink, trying my best to look nonchalant. "What girl? Yes, I am *a* girl. Gold star for noticing. Now could you please fuck off and leave me alone?"

"Heeeeey, no need to be like that! I was just being friendly! Sorry, let's start again. Hi, I'm Stuart. Nice to meet you." Then he bowed so low his face was practically in my lap. I think that was probably the idea.

"Um. I'm Jem."

"Jem! That's it! I *knew* I knew you. Never forget a face—one of my many talents." He had an OK sort of smile actually—when he wasn't smirking. He didn't look so sinister after all. "Mind if I take a pew?" I said nothing, so he perched on the corner of the workbench. His legs dangled so that one of them was touching mine. "I'm knackered—I had to do laps round the yard. Which wouldn't be so bad if I didn't have Bugs on my back riding me like a fucking supersize jockey." I stifled a laugh and Stu grinned. "So you can smile after all! I was beginning to wonder."

"Aren't you cold?"

He looked down as if he'd forgotten he wasn't wearing a top. "Nah, I'm hard as nails, me. Anyway, it's pretty toasty in here, isn't it? Kind of cozy."

I shrugged. I'd run out of things to say. He was watching me carefully, head tilted to one side, eyes slightly narrowed. Analyzing me. "Can I kiss you?"

I definitely wasn't expecting that. "Why would you want to do that?"

He shrugged. "I dunno. Bored I guess." He saw the look on my face and held up his hands. "Kidding!" He shrugged again. "I like kissing...and you seem nice. Those seem like two pretty good reasons to me."

My head was spinning. Stu Hicks aka Mr. Studly wanted to kiss *me*. It had to be a joke. It *had* to be. My mouth was dry and I coughed nervously. "This is a joke, right? Your mates are watching outside or something..."

Stu hopped from his perch and knelt in front of me. I had an absurd drunken thought that maybe he was going to whip out a diamond ring from the pocket of his jeans and ask for my hand in marriage. He put his hands on my thighs and I didn't stop him. His voice was low and serious when he said, "This is not a joke. Trust me."

Trust me. People who say things like that are usually *deeply* untrustworthy or trying to get you to do something you don't want to do. But I was slightly drunk and a boy wanted to kiss me. That's a poor excuse for an excuse, I know, but it's all I've got. A part of my brain was whispering that this was a terrible idea and something I would never ever do when sober. But a bigger, bossier part of my brain was saying, *Go on, do it. Live a little. So what if he's a total slimeball? It could be fun…*"OK."

Stu grinned. "Good girl." He leaned in close and I did the same, a bit more tentatively. The smell of sweat and beer was almost overwhelming, but I tried to ignore it. Our lips met and I nearly laughed again. *This is utterly insane.* But then I kind of got into it. The kissing was soft and gentle and not at all like I would have imagined it. I put one of my hands on his chest and could feel his heartbeat. After a couple of minutes Stu pulled away. "Man, my knees are killing me…Why don't you get down here with me?"

The look I gave him must have been dripping in skepticism, because he smiled a really sweet smile and said, "Seriously, I'm still trying to get over a tae kwon do injury…help me out here."

So I slid off the chair and settled myself with my back against it. His hand was back on my thigh in no time, stroking. "There… that's better, isn't it?"

I shrugged. Something about this boy had turned me into a malleable, brainless idiot. This time I made the move to kiss him. Drunk Me had decided that kissing Stu was a Fun Thing To Do.

Before I knew what was happening, Drunk Me was lying on the dusty floor of a greenhouse with a boy on top of her. The kissing was considerably less gentle. Stu's tongue was scouring my mouth, and it felt more like being at the dentist than anything else. His hands were everywhere—on my breasts and between my legs, and they kept on squeezing and stroking and probing as if they couldn't make up their mind where to settle.

The part of my brain that thought this wasn't such a good idea was now working harder to make itself heard. It was practically screaming now. But sometimes he'd do something right and my breath would catch in my throat.

It was only when he unbuttoned my jeans and tried to jam his hand into my underwear that I came to my senses. I grabbed his hand and held it. "Come on," he murmured into my ear. His hot breath made me think of a dog. "I just want to make you feel good."

I burst out laughing. "That is the cheesiest thing I have ever heard! Don't tell me girls actually fall for that."

He stopped kissing my neck and looked at me strangely. I was suddenly aware of the weight of him crushing down on me. "Don't you trust me?" Now his hand was meandering up and down my stomach. It tickled.

"Honestly? I don't even know you."

"We can soon change that, can't we?" He dived in for another kiss and his hand snaked down and tried to sneak into my underwear again. When he touched me there it felt so good (seriously good) that I knew it had to stop. Now.

I pushed at his chest. "I…I have to go."

He kissed me again. "You're kidding, right?"

"I've got a curfew. My parents will kill me if I'm late." I tried to squirm out from under him but he didn't move. "Can you…um… get off me, please?"

"C'mon, let's just…it won't take long, I promise."

"No, I really have to go."

Stu wasn't smiling anymore. That look was back. The one that warned any girl with half a brain to stay away. For the very first time, I realized the predicament I was in and I wanted to kick myself.

He grabbed both my wrists and pinned them down on either side of my head. "You're not going anywhere till I say so." His voice was so menacing that I felt a stab of genuine ice-cold fear. *I am about to get raped. This cannot be happening to me. I cannot get raped by this boy.*

I couldn't move—at all. He was crazily strong. The muscles in his arms stood out like ropes underneath his skin. The only part of my body that I could move was my head. Which was exactly what I did. I head-butted him as hard as I could and caught him on the nose.

"Ah, fuck! FUCK!" His hands flew up to his nose and he rolled off me.

I scrabbled to my feet and stood over him. There was blood trickling between his fingers. "What the fuck did you do that for, you stupid bitch?" He looked up at me and his eyes were brimming with tears.

I was breathing hard and shaking. I knew I should probably run and get help, but Stu looked so pathetic. There was nothing remotely menacing about him anymore. "You were going to…"

"Going to *what?*" His voice had gone nasal, thick with blood.

"You know…"

He snorted and a fine spray of blood showered his chest. "What…like, rape you or something?! You're fucking certifiable, you know that? I was joking, for fuck's sake! You didn't need to break my bloody nose, you mad cow."

That stopped me. "No, you…" I didn't believe him. I didn't. But what if he was telling the truth?

"You were *joking?*"

He staggered to his feet, using one bloody hand to steady himself against the workbench. "Of course I was joking! You honestly think I need to go around raping girls to get some action?" He shook his head and looked at me like I was insane. "They're right about you, aren't they? You *are* a freak."

I was shaking my head, trying to clear the fuzziness and confusion that had replaced the fear. "I was…I was scared."

Stu shook his head in disgust. "Haven't you ever had it rough before? Girls usually love it. Then again, you're not exactly my usual type." How someone who was bleeding so profusely could manage a look of such disdain was beyond me.

Girls actually *liked* being treated like that? I found that very hard to believe. It was just so…twisted. And I hadn't imagined the look on his face, had I? Total power, total dominance. But maybe this is what people did. Maybe I *was* a freak? I didn't know what to think anymore. I wanted to be at home in my own bed so I could pretend nothing had happened. So I could pretend that I hadn't very nearly had sex with someone I despised who may or may not have wanted to rape me.

He looked around for something to mop up the blood and I handed him some tissues from my pocket. "Hadn't you better get home? That curfew, remember? I think it's way past your bedtime, little girl."

"I…I'm sorry. I didn't mean to…"

He moved toward me and I backed up against the wall. His eyes were hard, unforgiving. "You, darlin', are what's known as a cock tease. You want to watch yourself in the future…You never know what could happen to a girl like you." His voice was a raw whisper and the rusty smell of blood nearly made me gag.

"Are you threatening me?" I pushed him hard on the chest and he stumbled backward.

He laughed, but there was no humor in it whatsoever. "I wouldn't dream of it, darlin'. I'm a gentleman. Think of it more like a friendly warning. Now get the fuck out of here. And if you breathe a word of this to anyone…" He didn't bother to finish the sentence.

chapter eight

I grabbed my jacket and ran out of the greenhouse before he could say anything else. Nothing had changed back in the real world. The bonfire was still blazing; people were still drunk. And no one had any idea what had just happened. Maybe if I pretended hard enough, I could convince myself that it had been a bad dream. But I could still feel his hands all over me, his tongue in my mouth. I could still taste the panic.

I hurried to another quiet corner of the yard and took out my mobile with shaking hands. I texted Kai: Home. Now. Please. x

I waited for a few minutes—no reply. I kept looking over my shoulder, half expecting Stu to jump out at me like some horror movie psychopath.

Right. Pull yourself together. Kai's probably left his phone some-where. Find him and go home. Pretend that nothing happened. Easy. I'd already decided not to tell Kai, without even making a conscious decision about it. It wasn't even an option. He wouldn't understand. There was no way he would be able to comprehend why I would do something like that. Why I'd put myself in that situation. He probably wouldn't have even been able to get past the idea of me kissing Stuart Hicks. He'd think less of me, that was a given.

How could I ever begin to explain it to him? What could I possibly say that would make him understand, even a little bit?

Because I was drunk. Because I was curious. Because I was horny. Because he was there. And you weren't.

⌒

I ran my hands through my hair and dusted down the back of my jeans, took a deep breath and headed back into the melee. *Just put on a brave face for a few more minutes, then you'll be on your way home.*

I couldn't see Kai outside anywhere. I asked a couple people (only those with friendly-ish faces), but no one had seen him. A quick scan of the ground floor of the house revealed the following: Bugs pretending to hump Lucas as he bent over to get something out of the fridge; a couple getting busy on the sofa while some other people watched, jeering and laughing; some boys looking at porn on the computer in the study; Stu sitting in a corner smirking at his phone, probably trying to distract himself from the bits of tissue stuffed up his nose. I backed away fast before he noticed me.

I stood in the (thankfully empty) hallway trying to figure out what to do. I phoned Kai but he didn't answer. If he'd bailed on me, I was going to be so pissed off. And if he was off having fun without me somewhere, I was going to be equally pissed off. I wondered briefly if I should check out upstairs, but there was a baby-gate across the bottom of the stairs with a handwritten sign taped to it: "ACCESS DENIED. If you ignore this sign, I will kill you. (Bugs and Stu: I will kill you twice as hard, so don't even think about it.)"

Considering what was going on in the living room, I didn't want to think about what might be going on upstairs. And the last thing I wanted to do was make an enemy of Max as well as Stu. If Kai was up there, he was going to have to fend for himself. I texted him to say I was heading home and that I hoped he was enjoying his lone-wolf adventure. The relief when I closed the front door behind me was so immense that I just stood there savoring it for a few seconds.

I breathed in the night air and got a lungful of smoke instead. Louise was sitting leaning against the wall. She had a bottle of wine in one hand and a cigarette in the other. *Classy lady.*

"Louise, hi! Have you seen Kai anywhere? I've been looking for him for ages and no one seems to have seen him."

She turned to look at me and I saw her eyes were red. "How about you just fuck off home, OK?"

And there I'd been just about to ask if she was all right. Charming. "Right. Delightful talking to you—as per usual. Look, if you see Kai, can you tell him I had to go home? I'm not feeling too well."

She looked at me like I'd just asked her to solve a particularly complex equation and eventually answered with a not-very-helpful "Whatever."

"Thanks, I really appreciate it." I kept any trace of sarcasm out of my voice, because somehow I thought she'd find it more irritating this way. I hoped so, anyway.

⌒

The walk home was cold and lonely. Except I'm not all that sure it *was* cold—I just couldn't stop shivering. I was angry at Kai for making me go to the stupid party in the first place and then deserting me. Angry at Stu for doing whatever it was that he'd done. Angry at Louise for living down to expectations and being a total mega-bitch at every opportunity. And angry at myself most of all for so many reasons I couldn't hold them all in my head at the same time.

Somehow I managed to negotiate the notoriously tricky parental greeting. Dad had gone to bed, but Mom was still up, curled up on the sofa with a cup of tea. No matter how many times I told her she didn't have to wait up for me, she always did. She asked lots of questions about the party and each answer took us further and further away from the truth. She was so interested and so lovely I wanted to cry. But then she went and ruined it all by saying, "I'm so pleased you're making some new friends. You know what they say—it's never a good idea to put all your eggs in one basket."

I rolled my eyes. "Kai is not a basket, *Mother*. He's my best friend."

"I know he is, sweetie. And I love Kai to bits—you know that! But a girl needs to be around other girls from time to time."

I picked myself up from the sofa and kissed Mom on the forehead. I wasn't in the mood for an argument.

"Whatever you say, Mother."

She tutted and said, "Enough with the *Mother* thing! You only call me that when you want me to shut up."

I raised my eyebrows and said nothing. She laughed and said, "Off to bed with you. We're going to IKEA first thing in the morning and you're not getting out of it just because you're tired…or hung over." Now it was her chance to raise her eyebrows and smile knowingly. I took off while the going was good. Mom doesn't mind me having the occasional drink; she's pretty cool that way.

The tears appeared as soon as I shut my bedroom door. I shouldn't have been surprised but somehow I was. I lay on my bed and sobbed and sobbed until my tear ducts were dry and my pillow was sodden.

I couldn't stop thinking about Stu. It didn't seem real. It didn't seem like something that could happen to me. The world must have tilted on its axis or something, and somehow *I'd* ended up in that greenhouse instead of Amber Sheldon or Louise or any of those girls who thought that wearing as few clothes as possible was a good look for them. Why had Stu followed me in there? He must have followed me, surely? Because he didn't exactly strike me as the horticultural type. And what was I thinking, letting someone like him kiss me? It pretty much went against everything I stood for. Had I really been flattered by the attention? Perhaps I wasn't so different from those girls after all.

The biggest question of all was one I would never know the answer to. What would have happened if I hadn't stopped him?

chapter nine

There was a knock at the front door while we were still unpacking the IKEA purchases. I was quizzing Mom about why she'd felt the need to buy two hundred tea lights, and she was going on and on about "mood lighting."

Kai stood on the doorstep looking sheepish and tired. His hair was all over the place—a look that I was hardly ever allowed to see. He was wearing an old T-shirt that was at least two sizes too small for him and I could see a narrow strip of skin between it and his jeans. "Before you say anything…I'm sorry I didn't get your messages. And you shouldn't have walked home on your own— that was a really stupid thing to do."

I dragged him inside and upstairs before he could say anything else. "Mom doesn't know I came home alone and I'd like it to stay that way, thank you very much. Where *were* you?"

He dived onto the bed and landed face first. "I'm sooooo tired." His voice was muffled by the duvet.

"Kai! I looked everywhere for you!"

"I looked everywhere for *you*! And I lost my phone and spent half the night looking for that." I couldn't see his face, which made it very hard to tell if he was telling the truth.

"But I asked around and no one had seen you."

"Probably because only about four people there knew my name!

Anyway, missy, I've got a bone to pick with you…" He turned over so he was lying on his back. His T-shirt had ridden up his belly. It was smooth and flat and made me think about Stu. "Get your ass over here." He patted the bed beside him and I lay on my side so that I was facing him. Kai's face was great in profile.

"Go ahead…pick your…*bone*."

"I usually prefer to do that in the privacy of my own bedroom, now that you mention it."

"You are disgusting."

"Awwww, that's the nicest thing you've ever said to me… Anyway…a little birdie told me that you got down and dirty with Stuart Hicks in the potting shed last night." He turned onto his side so we were face to face, almost close enough to kiss. "And I told the little birdie that it couldn't possibly be true because Stuart Hicks is revolting and probably has more STDs than a whole clinic. But the birdie was pretty adamant that you'd been spotted heading off into a quiet corner of the yard with Mr. Hicks hot on your heels. So…what do you say, Halliday? True or false?"

I tried to keep my face neutral even though my heart was racing and I could feel a blush creeping up my neck. "False! And quite frankly I'm offended you even felt the need to ask. Who was this little birdie anyway?" I tried to go for a slightly less neutral facial expression, because neutral can be extra-suspicious sometimes. Still, my tone was maybe not as indignant as it would have been if the accusation had actually been false. If Kai had accused me of getting off with Stu Hicks a couple of days ago, I would have probably decked him.

Kai just looked at me, saying nothing. I matched his silence, knowing full well that I could wait him out. Sure enough, after ten seconds or so he said, "I couldn't possibly divulge my sources. And I'm sorry for even mentioning such scurrilous rumors. I mean, I knew it couldn't *possibly* be true, and I said as much last night. But you never know, do you? The crackling of the bonfire, the twin-kling stars in the sky…it could make a girl crave a little romance, couldn't it?" He wiggled his eyebrows with such fake lasciviousness that I had to laugh.

"Are we talking about me or you now, hmmm? Are you trying to tell me you got a bit of hot boy-on-boy action last night? Don't tell me…Bugs, right? I've always wondered about him. How was it? Rather sweaty and gross, I'd imagine."

He put his hand up to his forehead and swooned back onto the bed. "I do declare that you have uncovered my deepest, darkest secret!" His Southern Belle accent was one of his favorites, but I hadn't heard it for a long time. "That Bugs is just so *manly*. He was like an animal, I tell you!"

"That reminds me…we haven't decided on Max yet! Which animal do you reckon he is? Think carefully now—this is VERY important."

Kai laughed and shook his head. "You know what, Jem? You think about things waaaaay too much. I love you for it, but you are batshit crazy."

Fair point, well made.

⌒

The rumor mill went into overdrive at school on Monday. Most people were talking about the party, especially the ones who hadn't been invited. Kai relayed his personal favorites: there had been an orgy in Max's parents' bedroom; someone had given hash cakes to the dog; and Stu Hicks had tried to prove how hard he was by running face first into a tree, breaking his nose in the process.

Kai was especially thrilled about the last one, given his feelings about Stu. When we caught sight of him at break time, Kai clapped his hands. "Oh my God, it's true! Look at his face!" I thought he might choke, he was laughing so hard. I tried not to wince at the sight. Stu had a white strip of bandage across the bridge of his nose and there was ugly yellowish/purple bruising under his eyes.

He seemed to be OK though—laughing and joking around as usual. People kept on coming up to him and asking about his nose and you could tell he was loving the attention. At one point he looked over from the bench where he was holding court and his eyes passed right over me like I wasn't even there. I should have been grateful, but a part of me wanted him to acknowledge what had happened between us. I wanted him to acknowledge *me*. Kai was right: I was batshit crazy.

～

It wasn't until Wednesday night that everything turned insane. I was in my bedroom doing my homework and trying not to think about Stu. My phone rang. It was Kai. At least the caller ID told me it was Kai; it certainly didn't sound like Kai. "Have you checked your email?"

"Not recently—why? Have you sent me another one of those cat videos?" I clicked on my laptop to bring up the Internet.

"I don't know what to do. I just…Check your emails, OK?"

He disconnected the call. I had no idea what he was talking about. But it was Kai…how bad could it be?

Really very bad.

chapter ten

I opened up my email account to find three new messages. One was from Kai, sent that morning. It *was* a link to a cat video. The second was spam. The third was from a sender I didn't recognize: Captain Outrage. The email appeared to have been sent to Kai, but I must have been copied in and hidden.

A video file was attached. I opened it even though I'd never normally open files from someone I don't know. It wasn't very good quality—kind of grainy, and whoever had been holding the camera (or phone...yes, it was probably a phone) had a very shaky hand. There were two guys in the frame. One of them was sitting on the edge of a bed. The other one was kneeling in front of him, head buried in his crotch. It was pretty bloody obvious what was going on. The face and torso of the guy on the bed had been obscured somehow—like some kind of special effect or something. He hadn't been blacked out completely, but his face and body were a mass of pixels. Like they do on TV when they're trying to hide someone's identity.

The other guy (or rather *boy*) hadn't been afforded the same pixelation treatment. I'd have known him anywhere. Even if I hadn't recognized the so-called "lucky" shirt, the sight of the back of his head was enough, despite the fact that I hadn't seen him doing *that* before. But I didn't think many people would have known it was him…not until they finished and he turned toward the camera, wiping his mouth. He didn't seem to realize he was being filmed.

Just in case there was any doubt left in anyone's mind, the frame froze on his face and the image stayed up there for a few good seconds. His hair was messed up where the other guy had been clutching his head, and he was smiling. The smile was so typically *him* that it caused an actual, physical pain in my heart.

Kai.

∽

I slammed the lid of my laptop down, legged it down the stairs and out the front door. Made it to Kai's in far less than four minutes and twenty-three seconds. Louise answered the door, looking a lot better than the last time I'd seen her. She didn't even bother saying hi, which was fine with me. I rushed past her and up the stairs into Kai's room.

The room was dark and at first I thought he wasn't there. But then I saw his bare feet poking out from under the desk. He was tucked up under there like a hibernating animal. "Kai? It's only me. Are you going to come out?" I said gently, as if he *was* a small animal that I was trying to coax out of its hiding place.

No response.

I sat down on the floor in front of him. "Kai? Talk to me. Please?"

Still nothing.

"You're kind of scaring me. Please say something." He cleared his throat. His voice sounded rusty.

"You watched it then?"

"Yeah, I watched it. But it's OK, Kai. It's nothing to be… ashamed of."

"You think? Why don't you take a look at my inbox?"

His laptop was on the bed. I opened the lid and listened to it whirr to life. The screen was filled with unopened emails. I clicked on one at random and immediately wished I hadn't. Words jumped out at me from the screen: i hope you die of AIDS you fuckin homo.

I didn't recognize any of the email addresses—they were clearly fakes. People had gone out of their way to set up new accounts so they could do this without risking getting caught. *God, how many people has that link been sent to?* I clicked on another message: Always thought you loookd queer as fuck. Looked lik you was enjoying that, u little bitch.

"How many are there now? There were seventeen the last time I looked."

Twenty-nine. There were twenty-nine more messages. "Oh, Kai, I'm sorry! Who would do something like this? I mean, *why* would anyone do something like this?"

Kai laughed. "You don't need an excuse to out a fag, do you? They probably thought they were doing a public service or something."

"When…when did you get the email?"

"The video was in my inbox by the time I got home from school. Whoever this Captain Outrage is, he sent it to me first."

I scrolled back and found the original email. The subject line read: READY FOR SOME FUN AND GAMES?

"OK, let's think about this rationally. Kai, are you going to come out from there?"

"I…I can't."

"What do you mean, you can't?"

"I don't want you to see me."

"Don't be stupid, Kai. This is *me*…Can I at least put the light on?"

"I'd rather you didn't." His voice sounded so hopeless, so small and pathetic, so not Kai.

I felt helpless. "Do you want to talk about this? I really think we should talk about this."

"There's nothing to say, is there? Everyone knows. *Everyone* knows."

"Who cares? You're gay. So what? Lots of people are gay. It's normal."

"Yeah? Tell that to all the people who've emailed me, calling me shirtlifter or fudge packer or pedophile. That's my favorite. *Pedophile.* Like I'm some kind of deviant just because I want to have sex with men…"

"No one thinks that. I mean, no one who matters anyway. Your parents are cool with it, aren't they? There are always going to be idiots in the world, but they don't matter. Come on, you *know* this. They're ignorant, that's all." I knew the words were woefully inadequate, but I said them anyway.

"I wasn't *ready*, Jem. I wasn't ready to come out. I wanted to do it on my own terms, you know? And that's not even the point… That video is…"

"Yes, it's embarrassing…"

"Embarrassing? Are you serious? It's fucking mortifying! Are you trying to tell me you'd be completely OK with a video of you doing something like…that plastered all over the Internet? God, Jem, I'm asking for some support here!" He started to sob.

I crawled under the desk to sit next to Kai. There wasn't really enough room for two people. I leaned my head against him. "I'm here for you. Whatever you need. We'll get you through this, OK? Tomorrow you'll walk into school with your head held high. You've done nothing wrong. Fuck the lot of them, yeah? They can only make you feel ashamed if you *let* them…And anyway, in two years' time, we'll be out of this place and they'll still be here, working in McDonalds or something. Try to remember the plan—Kai and Jem take on London and WIN! Two measly years, that's all."

He reached out and squeezed my hand, then let out a long shuddery breath. "OK."

"Really? Is that a real OK? Or a please-stop-talking-before-I-punch-you-in-the-face OK?"

He laughed softly. That was progress, I thought.

"It's a real OK—honest."

"That's more like it. Now…I'm going to delete all those emails, OK? You're banned from looking at your inbox until all the fuss has died down. And it *will* die down, I promise you."

"You're a good friend, you know that, don't you?"

I patted his knee. "The *best*. And you're not so bad yourself."

I'm not sure why I didn't ask Kai who the mystery boy was. I guess I thought he'd tell me if he wanted to. His privacy had already been invaded in the worst way imaginable and I wasn't about to add to that. That's not to say I wasn't curious. Actually, curious wasn't even the right word. I was *dying* to know the identity of Mr. Pixel. And I couldn't help wondering why Kai hadn't mentioned him when he came over on Sunday. At least now I knew the reason for his little disappearing act. But why the hell hadn't he told me? He was always going on and on about boys, so I'd have expected him to tell me as soon as he'd snagged himself a real live one.

Then again, I hadn't told him about Stu. But that was different. At least, I *told* myself it was different. Still, if someone had secretly filmed what had happened in the greenhouse and emailed it around, I wouldn't have wanted to show my face at school. Or anywhere for that matter. Kai was stronger than me, though. He'd get through this and be OK, I was sure of it.

I eventually managed to coax him out from under the desk and he even let me turn the light on. He looked terrible—wrecked. I hugged him and told him over and over again that it would be all right, that people have short memories and no doubt the next scandal would be right around the corner, that whoever had done this to him was a sad little person with nothing better to do with their life. And it seemed like I was getting through to him. It really did. He nodded and even smiled a couple of times.

I cleared out his email without reading any more of the vile messages. I gave him one last pep talk before I left. He practically shooed me out the door, saying, "I'll be fine," over and over again until I actually believed it.

Kai could always make me believe whatever he wanted me to believe.

chapter eleven

The next morning I knocked on Kai's front door just like I'd done every single school day for years and years. I was ready to go into battle. I was worried about what people might say, but I was ready. Kai and I would get through this—together.

Mrs. McBride answered the door, looking even more tired than usual. She was a nurse and worked night shifts at the emergency department at the hospital. She was usually drinking coffee or yawning or rushing off somewhere. Just looking at her made me feel exhausted. "Jem, sweetheart, I'm afraid he's not coming in today. He's not well."

I wasn't surprised. If it were me, I'd have cut off my arm with a rusty knife if it meant I'd get out of going to school for a while. "Can I see him?"

"Why don't you come round after school? He's sleeping at the mo, the poor love."

"OK, just tell him…tell him I hope he feels better soon."

She smiled a watery smile. "I will do. I'm not used to him being ill—I can't even *remember* the last time! Strong as an ox, that boy. Right, I've got to pop the washing on and then it's bedtime for me. Have a good day at school, Jem."

Mrs. McBride shut the door and I was left standing on the doorstep, wondering if there was any way I could stay home too. I had to go in though; I had to face them. For him.

It was bad. People *looked* at me, which was a new experience. An entirely new experience that I didn't like one little bit. It seemed like everyone had their phones out and little groups were huddled together watching the screen, laughing. Maybe they were watching videos of skateboarding dogs or something. Maybe I was just paranoid…but I didn't think so.

People I'd never talked to in my life asked me about Kai. Most of them were smirking idiots, but one or two people were worried. Bland Boy A and Bland Girl B seemed genuinely concerned, which made me feel a bit bad for being a bitch about them. But even their concern was measured, in a bland sort of way.

I texted Kai a few times but didn't get any reply. Fair enough. I'd give him the day to get over it, but then he really would have to deal with it. Being there by myself was hideous. I'd never felt so lonely. It felt a little bit like my first day all over again—everything and everyone seemed sinister and unfriendly. I must have looked at my watch a thousand times, willing time to move faster so I could run home and see him.

I avoided the cafeteria at lunchtime. There were limits to the torture I was willing and able to endure. I found an empty classroom and sat on the floor under the window so that anyone who walked past wouldn't see me. I sat there nibbling at an apple, feeling sorry for myself. I mean, obviously I was feeling sorry for Kai most of all, but since he wasn't there I felt like a little bit of self-pity was allowed.

Kai would bounce back soon enough. I was almost sure of it. He had to. There was no other option.

Toward the end of lunchtime, Louise came into the classroom. For once in my life I was actually glad to see her. I scrambled up from my hiding place, making her jump. "Fuck! What were you…? Actually, I don't want to know."

"How's he doing?"

"He'll be OK." Her face gave nothing away.

"God, I hope so. He was a total mess last night. I swear, if I find out who did this to him, I'll…"

"You'll what?"

I shrugged. "I…I don't know. I just feel so…helpless."

"That's because you *are*. There's nothing you or me or Kai can do. We just have to pretend it never happened and wait for all the fuss to die down." She seemed resigned, weary, just like her mother.

"Don't you want to find out who did it?"

Louise shook her head and went back to staring out the window. There was a game of soccer going on. Stu Hicks was in the middle of some complicated goal celebration. Max and Lucas were high-fiving each other like something genuinely amazing had just happened rather than some easy goal against the boys from the year below. Boys were pathetic sometimes. She eventually turned to face me. "What does it matter? What's done is done."

"How can you say that? We could go to the police or something. There are laws against this sort of thing…" I wasn't quite sure this was true, but it sounded like it could be.

"You really think Kai wants the police seeing that video? Yeah, that would make everything *so* much better. Kai would be even more humiliated and you'd be even less popular than you are already…if that's even possible."

"I don't give a fuck about being popular! I just want to find out who did this to him. And if you don't give a crap, I'll just have to do it myself."

"Do you have any idea how ridiculous you sound?" Strangely enough, I was completely aware of how ridiculous I sounded.

I wanted to hurt her. "Is everything OK with you and Max?" I asked in my sweetest, most innocent voice.

She blinked quickly a few times. "Not that it's any of your business, but things are going great."

"Really? Because it sort of looked like you were fighting at the party the other night."

She shrugged her shoulders and grabbed her bag from the windowsill. "That was nothing. It's half the fun of being in a relationship…having little *disagreements*. It's totally worth it for the make-up sex." She smirked. "You know how it is, don't you? Oh wait. You *don't*…I forget you've never had a boyfriend. Silly me."

She patted me on the shoulder and left me standing there thinking of all the things I could have said. The best I could come up with was, *Well, at least I'm not a slut.* And that would have been lame by anyone's standards.

I hated that girl almost as much as I loved her brother. It was as if she'd become the price I had to pay to have someone as amazing as Kai in my life. On balance, it was definitely a price worth paying. But at that moment, standing alone in that classroom, my cheeks burning with shame…it was a close-run thing.

⁓

The school day had one more unpleasant thing to throw at me before it spat me out at three thirty. I bumped into Stu in the corridor between classes. And when I say "bumped into," I mean it literally. I'd swear in a court of law that he did it on purpose, but I'd never be able to prove it.

"Oops! Sorry!" Because that's what you say when you bump into someone, before you realize it's someone you'd gladly headbutt (again).

He grabbed my shoulders as if he was trying to steady me—except I'd never been in any danger of falling over. I was very aware of his thumbs pressing into my collarbones. "Oh, it's you!"

"Er…can I just…? I'm going to be late for math."

Instead of letting go, he leaned toward me and whispered in my ear. "Always late for something, aren't you? Curfew…math…I wonder what's next…Late for your period, perhaps? No, of course not. How could you *possibly* get laid when you spend all your time following that little gay boy around?" His face was so close to mine that people must have thought something was going on between us. He laughed and kissed me on the cheek before I had a chance to dodge him.

I rubbed my cheek with my sleeve.

"Don't ever touch me again."

"Don't you worry about that. I wouldn't touch you if someone paid me." He did this fake shuddery thing as if he found me physically repulsive.

"Ditto. Shame you didn't feel that way on Saturday." I don't know why I was talking back to him. I don't know where the courage came from. Normally I would just scurry away without saying anything.

"Yeah…about Saturday…that was a *dare*, you stupid little fuck. What's *your* excuse, eh?"

"You're lying."

"Whatever you say, darling. Whatever you say. Anyway, it's been nice talking to you, but I'd better be off. Things to see, people to do."

He swaggered off down the hallway, leaving me standing there feeling…feeling *what* exactly? It was hard to separate all the different things I was feeling at that moment. Angry, definitely. Annoyed. Embarrassed. I could handle those three. They were what I'd have expected. But there was something else lurking at the edges. Something like disappointment. Something like sadness. And that made no sense whatsoever.

chapter twelve

I went straight to Kai's after school and was surprised that he was the one to answer the door. And doubly surprised to find him smiling. He ushered me in and we went straight upstairs. He bounded up there like an overenthusiastic puppy. I trudged up there like I'd had the worst day ever. Which I pretty much had.

Kai sat at his desk, where it looked like he'd been working all day. There were four empty cups sitting there, which was unusual for Kai who was usually so fastidious.

"Um…you seem…better?"

"I *am* better, thanks."

"Really?" I wasn't buying it. Considering the state he'd been in the night before.

"Really." He was fidgeting. His hands drummed a beat on his thighs.

"Kai, this is me here. Be honest."

He laughed and it was a genuine Kai belly laugh.

"I *am* being honest. OK, here's the deal. This video thing has happened and I wish it hadn't happened, but it has and there's nothing I can do about it. There's no point crying about it like a little girl, is there? I've got to man up. Nut up or shut up, don't you think?" I said nothing, which was OK because he carried on talking without giving me a chance to answer. "So the plan is, I'm going to stay home tomorrow. No point going back on a Friday, is there? Then I've got Saturday and Sunday, and by the time Monday comes around, people will have something new to talk about. Hopefully there will be another party this weekend and someone will do something even more embarrassing and they'll forget all about me…" His voice trailed off into nothingness and he stopped fidgeting.

The onslaught of words was like hailstones battering my head. But even though he'd been speaking at the speed of light, I'd still caught it. "So it *was* at the party?" It was the first time I'd broached the subject; I'd been waiting for him to say something first.

"I didn't say that." His words were measured now.

"Kai, I recognized your stupid shirt as soon as I saw it."

He shook his head and slapped his cheeks, and completely ignored what I'd just said. Under normal circumstances he'd *never* let me get away with dissing his sartorial choices. "God, I'm so tired. Not enough coffee. Not *nearly* enough coffee. Right, anyway, you'd better get going before Mom wakes up. Faking an illness is so much trickier when your mom's a nurse." He jumped up from his chair and held out his hand to me. "Off you go now. I bet you've got homework you should be doing, haven't you?"

I nodded and allowed myself to be led downstairs.

"Kai, are you sure you're OK? You're acting a little weird."

He kissed me on the forehead. "Ah, Jemima! Weirdness is one of my many charms, don't you think?" Then he grabbed me in a bear hug and squeezed so hard I thought I might pass out.

I went to pull away after a couple of seconds, but he squeezed even harder and whispered in my ear.

"Nope. I'm not quite ready for this hug to end. It's a particularly good one, I think."

So we stood there in the doorway for a good couple of minutes and it was nice. Kai's hugs never failed to make the world seem a better, safer place. He didn't smell *quite* as good as usual. The aroma of stale coffee was added into the mix, but at least that explained some of the weirdness. Kai and caffeine never did get on well.

⌒

When he finally let me go, he put his hands on my shoulders and it couldn't have felt more different from that little scene with Stu in the corridor. "I love you, Jem. If I was one of those horrible heteros, I would ravish you this instant!" He buried his face in my neck and pretended to ravish, whatever that meant.

I squirmed and jumped away. "Get off me, you big idiot! And don't lie—if you were straight you would *totally* end up with someone like Sasha Evans."

He tilted his head to the side and considered this for a moment. "Yeah, you're probably right. I'm, like, waaaaay out of your league." I tried to hit him but he danced out of the way. "If you sorted out that hair though…I totally *would*."

I shook my head and turned to walk down the garden path. "You know I'm kidding, right? You're beautiful." His voice was different then, more serious. I turned back and looked at him. His face was serious too.

"You are a big fat liar, Kai McBride." I stuck my tongue out at him.

Then I walked away. Without a backward glance. I never saw him again.

chapter thirteen

I called him a liar. That was the last thing I ever said to him. Sure, we texted loads the next day, but that's not the same, is it? *You are a big fat liar, Kai McBride.* I was joking, and he *knew* I was joking. But that doesn't make me feel any better.

I knew something wasn't quite right. I knew I shouldn't have let him shoo me out of the house. My excuse? I was so bloody relieved he wasn't in the state he'd been in the night before. I wanted to believe that he really *was* feeling better about everything. I think I thought he was trying to talk himself into it, and if he needed me to play along, then that's what I'd do.

It was only later that night that I realized he hadn't asked me about school. Which was the first thing I'd have done as soon as he'd walked through the door if the situation had been reversed. I might not have *wanted* to know how bad it was, but I would have *needed* to know. I'd have needed to know what I was up against, how I was going to get through the next few days and weeks and months.

That's what should have set the alarm bells ringing—if I had half a brain. But I shrugged it off, blaming his overly caffeinated state. And when he still didn't ask during the flurry of text messages the next day? I was glad. Relieved I didn't have to explain that everyone was still talking about him. People were still coming up to me and asking questions or saying horrible, ugly things or smirking from a distance like Stu.

Friday night was a family night out—something I usually enjoyed, despite moaning and whining about it every time. Without even planning to, I seemed to have made it my mission to never ever show any enthusiasm about anything arranged by my parents. Still, despite my best efforts, I think they secretly knew that I sort of liked spending time with them. I liked it when we were all sitting at a table together. There was something appealing about the ritual of it. Dad would pour Mom a glass of wine, Noah would crunch his ice cubes before drinking his Coke. Mom would tell him he'd break his teeth if he wasn't careful. I would sit and observe. It was nice. The venue for this particular family night out was Mr. Chow's. Dad and I loved Chinese food, while Mom and Noah weren't all that keen about it. But it was OK, because they'd get their choice (Mexican) next week. We had the best table in the whole place—the one in the bay window.

I was sitting with my back to the restaurant, so I didn't see them come in. Mom did though. "Oh look, there's Louise! And who's that she's with? He's rather good-looking, isn't he?" My grip tightened on my glass of water. I half turned in what was hopefully a subtle way, but Mom had to go and ruin it by waving and calling out, "Hi! Louise!" Louise had always been perfectly polite to my parents, so they had no idea what a poisonous bitch she'd turned into over the past couple of years.

"Mom!" I hissed through gritted teeth. "Everyone's looking!"

Mom laughed. "Don't be silly! No one's looking…no one even cares!"

Louise was looking though. And so was Max. And so were his parents. His mom was tiny and round shouldered, with a string of pearls that looked tight enough to choke her. His dad was older, with furry gray caterpillar eyebrows that were knit together in a formidable frown. Louise smiled and waved, but carried on walking to her table, thank goodness. Max nodded to acknowledge me, which was more than I would have expected, and his parents smiled politely before sitting down.

I wondered if this was the first time Louise had met Max's parents. I glanced over every so often, but it was hard to tell. Louise seemed completely at ease as if she did this kind of thing every day. I would have been crazy nervous in her position—minding my table manners, struggling to eat spare ribs in a ladylike fashion, making sure I laughed in all the right places and didn't laugh in the wrong ones. At least Max looked awkward—more than awkward enough for both of them, in fact. Whenever I looked over he seemed to be concentrating on his food. Louise was getting on so well with his folks it almost seemed like he was surplus to requirements.

Mom quizzed me about Max and Louise. *How long have they been together? What's he like? Is he a friend of yours?* That last one made me laugh and roll my eyes. Mom was disappointed that the answer was an emphatic NO.

My phone buzzed in the pocket of my jeans. It was Kai: How's family night working out for you? xxx

I replied while Mom and Dad were distracted by the waiter explaining the dessert specials: Good, thanks. Except for the unexpected bonus of your sister and her boyf.

I kept my phone on my lap, waiting for a response that never came.

chapter fourteen

There were witnesses. People saw him do it and didn't do a thing to stop him. I don't blame them—not really. I can't imagine I would have had the guts to intervene either. Not if it was a complete stranger.

The only reason they thought to look twice at him was that he wasn't exactly dressed for the weather. There was torrential rain—like nothing I'd ever seen before. Except I was indoors, watching a DVD with Noah (James Bond was his latest obsession). And Kai was out there, wearing nothing but a tank top and jeans and flip-flops.

They said he looked like he was out for a stroll. Like he hadn't a care in the world. He wasn't ranting or raving or looking mental.

Reports differ about what happened next. One witness said he hopped on the barrier and stood there for a few moments. One said he crossed himself. One said he didn't hesitate—that there was no time at all between climbing the barrier and jumping. All the witnesses agreed on one thing though. He went head first.

The last person to jump from the bridge was a man named Gordon Powter a few months before. He'd been laid off and was thousands of pounds in debt. He left behind a wife and three young sons. I knew the details because I'd read every article I could find about it. I made Kai go with me to the bridge, even though he thought it was morbid. He was always humoring me like that.

We'd leaned over the railings and watched the white water gush over the jagged rocks. I'd wondered out loud if the rocks had killed Gordon Powter or whether he'd drowned. Maybe that's what gave Kai the idea. Maybe if I hadn't made him go with me it never would have crossed his mind to kill himself in that way. I couldn't allow myself to feel guilty though—not for that. Kai probably chose the bridge because he loved the stupid river so much. He liked nothing more than to sit on a bench and watch the water flow by.

In the local paper they put a picture of Gordon Powter next to a picture of Kai, under the headline "BRIDGE OF DESPAIR." Mom or Dad had clearly tried to hide it from me, but I found it in the recycling bin on one of my midnight forays for food. I put it in my desk drawer. I didn't like the thought of Kai being recycled.

I was so relieved to see there wasn't anything about why Kai had jumped, but I thought it was only a matter of time before some nosy journalist found out. Everyone at school was obviously keeping quiet about it—for now. Probably because they didn't want to get in trouble.

The focus of the article seemed to be firmly on the bridge itself. I didn't get that at all. The bridge was just a bridge. It could have been anything—a tall building, a razor blade, a bottle of pills. If people are going to kill themselves, they'll find a way. The bridge just happened to be an efficient way to get the job done. There was hardly any chance you'd survive a fall like that, and even if you did, you'd be knocked unconscious and drowned in no time. Kai died straightaway, or so they said. He hit his head on the rocks jutting from the middle of the river. I bet he was aiming for them.

Three days after it happened the police came to interview me. I refused to get out of bed (Mom was furious) so the two officers had to come up to my room. The female officer stood, while the male officer sat on my desk chair. I couldn't stop looking at their shoes; they were so shiny and sturdy. Mom hovered in the doorway, looking awkward.

The woman did most of the talking. She was very brisk and businesslike, as if talking to me was just a formality. Which it was. They clearly hadn't checked his emails, because they had no idea about the video. I was relieved; the thought of Kai's private life being raked over by the police (and leaked to the papers, no doubt) was unbearable. And if the papers did manage to get hold of the story, it'd surely only be a matter of time before the video found its way onto the Internet. That's all anyone would think about when they remembered Kai, and God knows what it would do to his parents. Louise can't have said anything, and I followed her lead. It helped that the police seemed to be going through the motions, as if they'd done this a thousand times before and it wasn't getting any more interesting. They mentioned that Kai had left a suicide note, saying he was sorry and not a lot else. I guessed the McBrides must have given them permission to tell me that. Maybe they thought it would be a comfort to me.

I answered most of the questions with one-word answers, and they didn't exactly try to grill me. The McBrides must have told them he was gay, because they asked me about his sexuality. I just shrugged and told them we never talked about stuff like that. The female officer raised an eyebrow at that but she didn't accuse me of lying or anything. Mom didn't bat an eyelid, which made me wonder if Mrs. McBride had told *her* too. The whole ordeal lasted no more than twenty minutes, but it was exhausting. Part of me *wanted* to tell them, because then they'd be forced to do a proper investigation and find out who was responsible. But I knew that Kai would have wanted me to keep quiet, and what Kai wanted was the most important thing of all.

The police left, saying that they'd be in touch if they had any more questions. Mom showed them out, then came back up to my room and perched on the edge of my bed, in the exact same place she'd sat three days ago. I relived it over and over again—the moment when she shattered my whole world.

⌒

She wasn't crying when she came into my room, but I could tell that tears were lurking just below the surface. She was wringing her hands together and fiddling with the cuffs of her sweater—a gesture I recognized as one of my own. I don't remember ever seeing her do that before. I wonder if I picked it up from her or she picked it up from me.

She perched on the edge of my bed and I pulled out my headphones, only realizing how loud the music was when I could still decipher every word. "What's up? Mom…are you OK?"

She tucked a few strands of hair behind her ear and nodded. She didn't say anything though, which is when I really started to worry. "Mom? You look…is it…is there something wrong with Granddad?" He'd been battling colon cancer for the past few years and no one had expected him to survive this long.

Mom shook her head and put her hand on my knee. The gesture did nothing to comfort me. It only ramped up the panic. "No, darling, your granddad's doing fine. The latest round of chemo was pretty rough, but he sounded cheerful enough when I spoke to him yesterday. Well, as cheerful as you can expect, anyway."

Then she started talking about how we'd go up to visit him in a few weeks and how much he enjoyed seeing me and Noah. "He says you two are better than anything the doctors could ever give him."

"Mom?" I was wondering why the hell she was going on and on about Granddad when she'd just said he was fine.

She looked at me and her eyes were filled with something that scared me. She'd never looked at me like that before. I'd seen it before though—albeit in a smaller, more measured way. When she watched some tragedy unfolding on the news. When my aunt came to stay after her husband left her. When Noah's guinea pig died.

It was pity.

"Oh sweetie, I'm so sorry. It's Kai."

And I *knew*. She didn't even have to tell me. I knew. But she told me anyway.

I screamed. A raw, animal sound that I would never have imagined could come out of my body.

Then I blacked out.

When I woke up, he was still dead.

chapter fifteen

I nearly chickened out of going back to school the day after Fernando worked his magic on me. Mom was extra nice to me at breakfast; she made me a cup of tea and poured cornflakes into my favorite bowl. I sipped the tea and watched the cornflakes turn into a soggy milky mush.

By some unspoken agreement Mom gave me a lift to school. She chattered the whole way, trying to keep my mind off the ordeal ahead. I couldn't stop staring at my reflection in the side mirror. I was looking at a complete stranger—a blonde stranger who went to school with her mom. What had happened to the black-haired girl with her satchel slung over her shoulder, meandering down the street arm in arm with her favorite boy?

We arrived just as the bell was ringing, so there was hardly anyone milling around outside. I think Mom must have planned it that way.

She hugged me and told me everything was going to be OK. I didn't believe her.

⌒

It was brutal. If I thought it was bad showing my face the day after people saw the video, it was a hundred times worse now. Everyone looked at me when I walked into my classroom. Mr. Donovan's sad eyes looked extra sad and his droopy mustache looked extra droopy. He squeezed my shoulder so hard it actually hurt.

I kept fidgeting with my hair, running my fingers through it, tucking it behind my ears. I wanted to know if people were staring because of Kai or staring because of the stupid new look. Probably a bit of both. I kept my head down, not wanting to catch anyone's eye. Not wanting to see the sympathy or curiosity or disdain plastered across their faces.

Time crawled by. I went to the cafeteria at lunchtime because it seemed sensible to get the hard stuff out of the way first. My hands were shaking as I paid for a packet of prawn-cocktail chips. No one was sitting at the table—*our* table. I sat in my usual chair and focused every last bit of my attention on the chips. I forced myself to eat slowly, determined to brave it for as long as possible. I kept my gaze away from his empty chair. Then I folded the packet into a tiny little square and stood up to leave.

I could feel them watching the whole time. All of them watching, judging. But I refused to give them the satisfaction of knowing they were getting to me.

The route to the bin took me past Team Popular's table. They were quieter than normal too, or maybe that was just my imagination. Max and Louise were nowhere to be seen, so the ranks were depleted.

Classes were just about bearable because I didn't have an empty chair next to me, reminding me of what was missing. Kai had been in the top set for everything, so we hadn't shared any of the same classes. Somehow I managed to focus on equations and past participles and neutrons, taking notes and trying to keep my handwriting as neat as possible. Two teachers kept me back after class to tell me that they were "here for me," like I was supposed to find that comforting. A couple girls came up to me throughout the day to say they were sorry, which was nice of them, I guess.

Undone

History was the last class of the day. I've sat next to Jasmine James in history for two years and I've known her ever since elementary school. She's a nice girl, but we've never really been what you'd call friends, not exactly. More "people who talk to each other in a friendly manner but would never dream of seeing each other outside of school." Mom had long since given up on nagging me about being friends with her.

When I sat down next to Jasmine she said a timid hi, followed by, "It's good to see you," then finished off with, "I'm really, really sorry about Kai." It was the first time I'd heard his name all day and it very nearly broke me. I thanked her and stared straight ahead, hoping she'd get the hint without thinking I was a hideous bitch.

At the end of the class, she rummaged in her bag (the type of rucksack you might take on a huge expedition) and handed me an envelope. For a bizarre, heart-stopping moment I thought it might be from Kai, but then she said, "I…er…wrote this a couple weeks ago. I've been carrying it around because I wasn't sure when you'd be back. Um. OK, see you tomorrow, bye." Then she took off.

The envelope was dog-eared and the blue ink that my name was written in was a little smudged. Inside was a card with white flowers on the front. The words "With sympathy" were written in gold flouncy lettering. Inside Jasmine had written, "Jem, I know we're not exactly best friends or anything, but I just wanted you to know that if you ever need to talk to someone, or just sit beside someone and not say anything, or copy someone's homework, I'm available for any of these things. And if you don't want any of those things, that's OK too. I'm sorry about Kai. He was a good person." She'd written her mobile number at the bottom of the card.

The classroom was empty by the time I scrunched up the card and envelope and put them in the trash can.

⌒

It's not that I didn't appreciate the sentiment and the effort she'd gone to; it was that I couldn't deal with it. I couldn't deal with this girl who I'd never really made an effort with, other than to talk vaguely about the TV we'd watched on the weekend. I couldn't bear the thought of her being nice to me.

The first day back was the hardest, but every day after that was awful in its own way. Being at Allander Park without Kai was suffocating. I sank into some kind of altered, robotic state where I didn't let myself *feel*. I went from class to class to lunchtime to class with one thought in my mind: the letters. I just had to get through each day until I could open his next letter. That was all that mattered.

I saw Louise a few times, but she was only with Max—never with the rest of Team Popular. If I'd been a better person I would have stopped her and asked how she was doing. But I didn't. And it would have been pointless because anyone with eyes could see how she wasn't doing well. She didn't look good. She'd lost weight, her roots were really bad, and she just looked washed-out and exhausted. She didn't swan down the corridor like she used to; she just walked like a regular person. I felt bad for her, but there was nothing I could do to help her, just like there was nothing she could do to help me. We had to bear our grief alone. At least she had Max. All I had was Kai's letters, but I clung to the thought of them so tightly there was no room to think of anything or anyone else.

Mom and Dad gradually stopped treating me like I was going to break and by mid-December they'd even started nagging me about chores and homework. Noah stopped watching me carefully and being so quiet and polite. And he never missed an opportunity to tell me he hated my new hair (*"You don't look real!*"), but it was oddly reassuring that he'd resumed his role as annoying little brother.

Everyone thought that things were getting back to normal. They had no idea that normal didn't exist for me anymore. *Normal* had been smashed on the rocks beneath the bridge.

chapter sixteen

I opened the second letter two days before Christmas. Kai had drawn holly leaves and berries on the corners of the page.

Jem,
    Are you decking the halls with boughs
    of holly? Are you jingling those bells?
Are you feeling goodwill to all men?

Hmm. Maybe not. Nevertheless, I would like
to wish you and your family a very happy
Christmas. I hope Noah gets lots of presents,
I hope your mom isn't too stressed, I hope
your dad doesn't get drunk like last year,
and, most of all, I hope you get ~~everything you
wish for~~ left in peace, I guess.

I can't help wondering who sang the solo at
the Christmas concert and whether it was as

brilliant as the time Melanie Donkin sang the whole of "Away in a Manger" (ever so slightly flat, remember?) before she realized her skirt was tucked into her knickers. Last year was good though, wasn't it? I know you said you hated every minute, but I could tell you liked it a little bit because I saw you smiling whenever you thought I wasn't looking. I hope Melanie gets a chance to redeem herself before we you leave school. It's not fair that all anyone can think about when they look at her is her underwear...but honestly, who would have had her pegged as a red-lace sort of girl?!

How's the whole "getting on with your life" thing working out for you? Better, I hope. And did you blondly go where no Jem has ever gone before? I'm going to go out on a limb here and guess you DID...in which case: YAY! Thank you. I bet you look fantastic and I bet you love it even though you tell yourself that you don't care and you only did it because it was practically my dying wish (no pun intended).

The whole emo look was perfectly lovely, but I never quite thought of it as YOU, you know?

(I'm <u>so</u> glad I'm not there for you to hit me right now.) And all that kohl around your eyes really doesn't do them justice. So here's your next mission: try going easy on the eyeliner for a while. Let's be clear...I'm not forbidding you to use the stuff—I'm not a total monster! You are fully within your rights to ignore everything I say and I promise I won't come back and haunt you. I won't even send one of my new poltergeist chums to freak you out by moving stuff around your room.

This is your life and you can do whatever the hell you like with it. But I am BEGGING you to live that life and try to enjoy that life and try to see the good in people when you're making an effort to be nice to you in that life. This is most definitely a case of DO AS I SAY, NOT AS I DO.

But if you <u>are</u> up for a challenge, why don't you try going the next month without emo makeup? Just until my next letter. And if it hasn't worked out for you, by all means go back to plastering on the kohl. But let me tell you this: it makes it really very hard to tell how pretty your eyes are. And you do have very pretty eyes, my dear. Forgive the amateur psychology here, but you know what I think? I think that's the whole point. You don't want people noticing how pretty your eyes are. You don't want people to notice you at all. But maybe now you _need_ people to notice you, you just don't know it yet. Jem, _I_ want people to notice you, and I want them to see you for who you really are, not for who you pretend want them to believe you are. I was lucky enough to see you and know you and my life was so much better for it.

Anyway, I'd better get on. Ten more letters to write and my wrist is starting to hurt already. Email would have been so much quicker, right? But there's something so lovely about a good old-fashioned handwritten letter in an envelope. An unopened envelope holds a certain promise. Anything could be in there...anything at all. Well, anything as long as it's a letter. But the letter could be a declaration of love or an apology or a get well soon card. I suppose these letters count as all three.

I hope Father Christmas is good to you, but don't let him anywhere near your chimney—he's such an old perv.

I love you, kiddo.

Kai
x x x

This one was easier to deal with than the first. It still hurt, but there was something comforting about it too. It was like hearing his voice. And I missed hearing his voice so much I found it hard to breathe sometimes.

I had no idea who'd sung the solo at the Christmas concert, because I hadn't gone. He should have known that I wouldn't have gone without him.

As for the "mission," it was all getting to be a bit too much like one of those TV makeover programs I never watched. I was sort of pissed off that it seemed like he was trying to change me, but he was right about one thing. I did like the new hair; it suited me. I'd even booked another appointment with Fernando to sort out my roots before I went back to school in January.

The truth is, I'd already realized that the heavy-on-the-kohl panda eyes didn't exactly look good with my new hair. They didn't match somehow. So either the hair had to go back to black or the makeup had to change. Neither was a particularly appealing prospect.

The first time Mom ever saw me with the black eye makeup

she burst out laughing and asked if I'd been in a fight. It didn't amuse her quite so much the second time or the third time or all the times after that. It's not like we argued about it—not exactly. But I knew she hated it, and that was enough to make me want to keep it. The hair was more of an issue with her—probably because hair is the one thing she's vain about. She goes to the most expensive salon in town every four weeks. If she's a week late because of a holiday or something, she gets really antsy. It's pretty funny.

Christmas wasn't as awful as I'd expected. I mean, it was awful, but I'd steeled myself for it to be excruciating. The hardest bit was Christmas Eve, when Kai and I always used to exchange presents. I had a tiny fake Christmas tree on my desk and we'd put each other's presents under it about a week before Christmas. Kai had made this super-cheesy Christmas playlist that we had to listen to every year without fail.

I didn't play it this year. And when Mom brought my little Christmas tree down from the attic I told her to put it in Noah's room. For a second there I thought she was going to protest, but she didn't and I was relieved.

Some of Kai's wishes came true at least. Noah did get a lot of presents and I did get left alone—for the most part. Mom didn't get stressed, even though the turkey turned out to be even more overcooked than usual. But Dad *did* get drunk. Still, three out of four wasn't bad.

It was a sort of tradition in our family that you opened your best present last. Of course the problem was, you didn't *know* which was the best present, so you had to rely on parental advice. Mom kept aside this big box for me to open after everything else. Big boxes were usually a good bet. Soft parcels were rarely good because soft parcels meant clothes. Mom's idea of the sort of clothes I should wear and my idea of the sort of clothes I should wear had been mutually exclusive since I was ten years old.

When she handed over the parcel, she was smiling. She was proud of herself, which both annoyed and worried me. I hated having to pretend I liked things—summoning up that fake enthusiasm never came easily.

It was a fancy gift box from some crazy-expensive cosmetics company. Nestled among red tissue paper were little pots and pencils, brushes and bottles, and things I couldn't even identify. It was more makeup than I'd ever seen outside of Boots. It must have cost an absolute fortune.

"Mom, this is…"

"Do you like it? Oh, I do hope you like it! I had such fun choosing it all. I must have been in the shop for hours!"

I couldn't get over the timing of it. For a mad second there, I thought she must have read Kai's letter, but of course she hadn't. I didn't know how to feel. I was sort of annoyed that she was trying to change me too. And horrified that she'd spent so much money. And, more worryingly, I was a little bit excited. But I'd never have admitted that to anyone in a million years.

When I took my presents up to my room after lunch, I took each item out of the box and lined them up on my desk. Then I took out the ancient pencil case that had served as makeup bag for the past couple of years (covered in pen, holes punched through with a compass, complete with bits of pencil shavings). There was some cheap foundation that was two years out of date and completely the wrong color, my trusty kohl, some waterproof mascara (unopened), and some blusher I'd never used. That was it. My makeup collection in all its glory. It was truly a pathetic sight.

Without even thinking I chucked the whole thing in the garbage can, kohl and all. Then I came to my senses and retrieved the pencil case (sentimental value) and the kohl (just in case). When

Mom emptied my bin the next day she didn't say anything, but she definitely noticed the new makeup lined up on the desk. It was there again—that almost-smile that made me want to punch something. I wanted to shout, JUST 'CAUSE I'VE THROWN OUT SOME CRUSTY OLD MAKEUP, IT DOESN'T MEAN ANYTHING'S CHANGED! IT DOESN'T MEAN *I'VE* CHANGED.

Kai had it all wrong with his amateur psychology. If I hadn't wanted people to notice me, I would have probably gone for no makeup at all and my natural baked-mud hair. That would have been the best way to blend in with all the others. They wouldn't have called me freak or goth or emo then, would they? No. There's no deep, dark reason for the way I looked. It seemed like a good idea at the time, that's all. And once you do something like that, it's pretty much making a statement: this is who I am. And once the statement's been made, it can be hard to take it back.

I spent a fair chunk of the Christmas holidays messing around with the new makeup. It was all subtle and muted and under-stated, but that's not to say it looked good straightaway. Far from it. I looked like some strange version of myself whose skin didn't exactly look like skin anymore. But the more I experimented, the better I got. I'd always liked art at school and this was sort of similar. But I couldn't shake the feeling of embarrassment. It felt shameful to be wasting all that time on something so meaningless. And I couldn't escape the feeling that I was using the makeup to plaster on a shiny, happy face so no one would know I was drowning. I don't think that was quite what Kai had in mind.

chapter seventeen

On New Year's Eve, we watched the usual crap TV. Noah was hyper because he was allowed to stay up till midnight for the first time. Mom let me have a couple of glasses of champagne, and we all hugged each other as the fireworks erupted over London on the TV.

As she was hugging me, Mom whispered in my ear, "This year will be easier, sweetheart. I promise." She had no idea that this time next year I wouldn't be here. I'd be dead. Just like him.

There was only one thing on my mind as the minutes after midnight ticked by, stretching the bond between me and Kai even further. Suddenly, he was *last* year. The way I saw it, I had a choice: I could sleepwalk my way through the days and weeks and months between Kai's letters, or I could *do* something.

I'd wasted so much time already—two whole months of self-indulgent grief had got me precisely nowhere. It was time to put all that aside (or at least bury it deep enough inside so that no one else could see it). Somehow I'd allowed myself to forget that I'd wanted revenge even *before* he died. Kai's humiliation was enough to make me want to hurt someone. But his death had forced me into some kind of suspended animation.

It was time to wake up. I was going to do exactly what Kai had told me not to do in his first letter. I was going to do whatever it took to find out who filmed him. Then I was going to punish them.

Against my better judgment, my first port of call was Louise. There were two reasons for this: she was the only other person (other than his parents) who cared about him as much as I did; and she was bound to know most of the people who'd been at Max's party. That was enough to outweigh the fact that I was practically allergic to her.

I texted her on New Year's Day, not even bothering with the usual pleasantries: Louise, I need to find out who filmed him. You in or not?

No reply. Four hours later I texted: Well? (This wasn't just me being impatient—I knew for a fact that she was practically surgically attached to her phone, so there was really no excuse for the radio silence.) Still no reply. One last try the next day: You going to bother replying?

She didn't bother replying—of course she didn't. But you can't say I didn't try.

My next idea was to talk to Bland Boy A and Bland Girl B. They might have seen something at the party, and at least *they* would be sympathetic.

I went kohl-less the first day back at school after Christmas; I even trialed some of my new makeup. Nothing much, just a bit of foundation and powder, a dab of lip gloss, a tiny bit of eye pencil. No one said anything, but I was uber-sensitive to any looks I got. I felt exposed. Judged. At least no one could tell I was blushing, I guess.

As it happened, nowhere near as many people noticed as I would have expected. I suppose I just assumed everyone was like me—noticing and commenting on every little thing, whether it be

Lucas's obvious affection for hair products or the length of Amber Sheldon's skirts. But they *deserved* to be looked at, analyzed, and criticized. That was the price they paid for being popular.

I thought Mom was going to burst into tears when she came downstairs at breakfast time to find me looking the way I did. She knew better than to mention it, thank Christ. If she'd said anything, I'd have run upstairs and scrubbed off all the new makeup just to spite her. She must have been feeling *so* proud of herself. Thinking if only she'd known that all it was going to take to turn me into a normal daughter was shelling out at the makeup counter, she'd have done it years ago. I wasn't about to tell her what was actually going on…mostly because the new look seemed to keep her off my back a bit. I was given more leeway, just because of a bit of hair dye and some chemicals slapped on my face. I'm not exactly sure what this says about my mother, but it can't be anything good.

I found Jon (Bland Boy A) and Vicky (Bland Girl B) in the cafeteria at lunchtime. They were now a couple (or maybe they'd been a couple since forever and I just hadn't noticed) and they held hands the entire time I talked to them. The hand-holding irritated me out of all proportion; my eyes kept drifting away from their nondescript faces toward their nondescript hands clutching one another. She seemed to be doing most of the clutching, like she couldn't *bear* to let go even if it meant trying to cut through the tough cafeteria meat (also nondescript) with the side of her fork instead of her knife.

They were useless—utterly useless. They'd barely set foot in the house all night; they hadn't seen or heard anything suspicious (and had the cheek to look at me weirdly when I asked if they *had*). I wasn't even back to square one—I'd never left square one in the first place. When I got up to leave the table, Jon looked like he was about to say something, but he half shook his head and turned his attention back to the girl. Like I said—useless.

I spent the afternoon classes kicking myself. As if it was going to be that easy: "Well, now that you mention it, Jem, we did happen to see a suspicious character sneaking away from the scene of the crime, rubbing his hands in glee and laughing maniacally." I was a fucking idiot, plain and simple.

It wasn't until I spotted Max in the chaos after the bell at three thirty that it occurred to me to ask him. Even if he hadn't known everyone at the party, his brother would be able to help for sure. Unfortunately Max had Louise in tow. She was like one of those suckerfish that attach themselves to a shark to hitch a ride—Max couldn't shake her off even if he wanted to. I couldn't help noticing that Louise wasn't looking any better after the Christmas break. It must have been hideous at the McBride house; they'd always been into Christmas in a big way. Especially Kai.

"Max! Hey, how's it going?" As if I talked to him all the time and it was completely normal for me to inquire after his well-being at any given moment.

"Hey..." There was this strange missed beat where I thought he was going to say my name but then didn't. As if he suddenly remembered that I was one of the little people.

I tried to ignore the fact that Louise was hovering behind him, standing way too close, so that if you squinted a little it sort of looked like he had two heads. "Um, I was wondering if I could talk to you about something. About your party...the night when...?"

His face was perfectly blank; it was clear he had no idea what I was talking about. I was going to have to say the words out loud. Louise faked a yawn, probably not realizing how very ugly it made her look. I tried again.

"Look, can we go somewhere a bit quieter? I'll…buy you a coffee or something." It sounded like I was asking him out on a date.

Louise rolled her eyes but (surprisingly) kept her mouth shut. Max ran his hand through his hair and shrugged. "Er…yeah. Maybe tomorrow? I've got practice at four." He held up his hand so I could see the goggles dangling from his wrist. Swimming. Hence the massive shoulders.

"Cool. OK. Fine." How many words could I use to say exactly the same thing? "I'll…see you then. Then." I gave an awkward little wave and turned away, walking smack bang into Mr. Franklin, who grabbed my arms to steady me and said, "Where's the fire?" I apologized and scurried away, blushing furiously no doubt.

That night I was feeling pretty good about things. I'd made progress; I congratulated myself on my bravery. I was finally doing something instead of just thinking about doing something. I wasn't one hundred percent convinced that Max would be able to help, but I had to give it a try.

I hardly slept that night, playing out possible conversations with Max in my head, unable to imagine what it would *actually* be like to sit down and talk with him.

Mom knocked on my door when I was doing my makeup. "Morning, love. Looks like you've got a secret admirer…bit early for Valentine's Day though, eh?" She held out an envelope. My name was written on it in blue pen: *Jem Halliday*.

Mom hovered over me, swigging black coffee from her "Number One Mom" mug that Noah (well, Dad really) got her for Christmas. "Aren't you going to open it?"

I gave her The Look, which was all it took for her to retreat. "Yes, yes, you need your 'space'…Promise you'll tell me later though? I do love a bit of intrigue." She kissed me on the forehead and left me in peace.

The envelope was one of those long, business ones. More a

reminder-for-a-dentist-appointment sort of envelope than a secret admirer sort of envelope. There was no stamp or address, which was obviously what had made Mom jump to conclusions.

Inside was a piece of lined notepaper torn out of an exercise book. The same blue pen had been used to write the words on it in unremarkable neat capital letters.

There were six words, evenly spaced in pairs:

STUART HICKS

LUCAS MAHONEY

DEREK BUNNEY

It took me a few seconds to realize who Derek Bunney was. It took me a few seconds more to realize what the names meant.

chapter eighteen

I didn't need to bother talking to Max; I knew who was to blame. Finally. It didn't take a genius to work out who the note was from. Jon must have seen something at the party after all—he just didn't want to say anything in front of his new girlfriend.

There was no shock, no surprise. Which was shocking and surprising in itself, really. As soon as I'd processed what the names meant, I realized I already knew. Stuart Hicks. It made perfect sense. It was as if my brain had hidden the answer from me until I was ready to deal with it…slipped it down the back of the sofa or something, until this piece of torn paper jolted it free.

Stuart Hicks. It didn't take a genius to work out why he'd done it, and that was what made it hard to accept—the knowledge that if I'd had sex with Stu none of this would have happened. Because it was obvious he'd done it to get back at me. I'd wounded his pride or ego or whatever, and he'd filmed Kai to punish me.

My first instinct was to blame myself for everything. But after a couple of hours of sobbing and self-loathing, that started to lessen somehow. It was like Kai was there, talking me through it, soothing my conscience. Yes, Kai might still be alive if I'd had sex with Stu. But that didn't mean that having sex with Stu would have been the right thing to do. Maybe I shouldn't have head-butted him, but what happened afterward was down to him. *He* decided to humiliate Kai. *He* made it happen. It was his fault. Not mine.

I repeated this mantra over and over until I started to believe it. His fault. Not mine.

⌒

I couldn't help thinking the whole thing had been a setup. Maybe he'd got one of his stupid mates to try it on with Kai and Kai had been too drunk to say no. Or maybe Stu had paid some wasted guy to take one for the team. That would explain why the mystery boy's identity had been hidden. It didn't really matter. I wasn't even interested in the mystery boy anymore; there was nothing to be gained from tracking him down. I didn't doubt for one minute that Stu had been the ringleader. But every ringleader needs his loyal sidekicks. Ruining someone's life was no fun unless you had someone to laugh with about it. Maybe Bugs and Lucas hadn't done the filming or uploaded the video or sent the emails—but that didn't make them any less guilty in my eyes. Or maybe they had. Maybe one of them had held the door open while Stu filmed or kept a lookout in case anyone caught them in the act. But it was almost irrelevant. Either one of them could have stopped him. My Kai would still be alive if one of them had stopped him.

When I thought back to that night, things that had seemed meaningless now seemed to be colored with red flashing lights and maybe a neon sign saying: PAY ATTENTION. Bugs pretending to fuck Lucas as he bent down. Stu smirking at his phone. How could I have been so fucking stupid?

⌒

I told Mom I'd make my own way to school and she tried to hide the relief on her face. She didn't think I knew that the lifts she'd been giving me had made her late for work more than once. It didn't occur to her for a minute that I would walk halfway to school, turn around, and walk right back home again, letting myself into the now empty house.

Stuart Hicks. Lucas Mahoney. Derek Bunney. How on earth was I supposed to punish them?

They ruled the fucking school, for fuck's sake. They were as close to royalty as you got at Allander Park.

It was so tempting to just go to the police and let them handle it. But I couldn't do it to Kai. I couldn't humiliate him even more, even if he wasn't around to see it.

It dawned on me that I couldn't tell *anyone*, because they might not be as worried about Kai's dignity as I was. Louise was the only other person I knew for sure would never tell the police in a million years. But those three were her *friends*. Even if I could convince her they were the ones who'd done this to Kai, she wouldn't risk everything to punish them. There was no way.

So it was left to me. A complete nobody. Somehow this complete nobody was going to have to find a way to take down the three most popular boys in school. And I would do it. No matter what I had to do or how long it took, I *would* do it.

From the outside it looked like they were impossible to get to. It would be so much easier if I knew more about them—knew their weaknesses rather than their strengths. There was only so much information you could glean from staring at people in the cafeteria every lunchtime.

And I was just one person—a friendless person at that. I came up with a few lame ideas to humiliate them but dismissed them straightaway. I didn't want to rush in and do the wrong thing. I was willing to bide my time if that was what it took.

As it happened, I didn't have to wait long at all.

chapter nineteen

It was basic science; all it took was a catalyst to start the reaction. It was kind of fitting that the catalyst appeared in the science block a few days after the note had been delivered.

Since the start of the term I'd got into the habit of going to the bathroom at break time to check that my face was looking OK. This isn't as vain as it sounds. Well, it sort of *is* as vain as it sounds, actually, but it was also an opportunity to escape from people. I always went to the bathroom in the science block because they were the quietest. The other ones were usually invaded by gangs of girls fighting for mirror space. I could just imagine the looks they'd give me if I sidled up to them and got out my makeup bag. (Yes, I had a bag now. The pencil case had returned to its original purpose in life and I'd borrowed a little zip-up purse thing from Mom. She had a whole drawer full of stuff like that, so I figured she wouldn't miss it.)

That morning I headed to the science block, struggling through the hordes, swimming against the tide, making for the cafeteria. When I got to the bathroom I bent down to check the stalls were all empty. Since the start of term I had never once come across anyone else in there. Those toilets were a haven of peace and quiet in the madhouse. Shame they smelled so bad really. There was a notice on the door saying something about a problem with the drains. Thinking about it, that's probably why they were always deserted. I put my makeup bag next to the sink farthest from the door and inspected myself in the mirror. My reflection still shocked me. There was still that fraction of a second where I thought I was looking at someone else. But then I saw me. I was there, lurking under the surface. Trying not to drown down there.

The door slammed open, making me drop my powder in the sink. An explosion of beige. It was Sasha Evans, and she looked as surprised to see me as I was to see her.

She was breathing hard. Tears streaked her face. Her hair still looked perfect though, and her crying wasn't ugly in the way mine is. She cried like someone in a glossy soap opera set in Los Angeles. When I cry I look more like someone from *EastEnders*.

Sasha stayed by the door and I stayed by the sink, and at first we said nothing. Then it got weird that no one was saying anything, so I broke the silence. "Are you OK?" I could have kicked myself. I didn't care if she was OK. She was Sasha Evans—of course she was OK. The tears were probably over some chipped nail polish or a broken clasp on her very expensive bag.

She wiped at her tears with her dainty little fingers.

"I'm fine. Thank you." Her voice wasn't cold, exactly. It was tepid. Neutral.

"OK." I turned on the tap and swooshed water around the sink to clear up the powder. I watched it swirling down the drain. *There goes at least twenty quid's worth.* I'd have to go to the shop after school and replace it. Just as well I still had some Christmas money left over—otherwise I'd be asking Sasha to pay up. (Who was I kidding? I would never, ever have asked her such a thing.)

Sasha went into a stall and came out with some toilet paper. She dabbed it around her eyes, careful not to smudge her mascara. It seemed like the tears had stopped for now.

"What are you looking at?"

I did my best to adopt her neutral tone instead of responding to this slightly more aggressive one.

"Nothing."

Sasha sighed in a deeply dramatic way. "I'm sorry. And I'm sorry about that." She waved a hand at the sink. *Nice of her to notice.* "I'm just…I wasn't expecting anyone to be in here. No one's ever in here and I wanted to be alone."

"You and me both." I turned away so I was looking in the mirror. It was easier to talk to her when I didn't have to look at her. I ran my fingers through my hair just for something to do.

"Sorry. Let me just get my shit together and I'll leave you to it." There was something different in her voice. Something slightly warmer, maybe.

I shrugged. "You don't have to. It's a free country." Sasha snorted and I wasn't sure what to make of that, so I had to look at her after all. The snort was a laugh. A stifled, snotty sort of laugh. "What's so funny?"

"My little sister says that all the time: *It's a free country*. She's only eight and I'm pretty sure she has no idea what it even means." Great. I was being compared to an eight-year-old.

I said nothing. Zipped up my makeup bag and shoved it into my school bag.

As I walked past her, she reached out and put her hand on my arm. I stopped. Sasha Evans was touching me. "Sorry, I didn't mean anything by it…You're Jemima, aren't you?"

Sasha Evans knew my name. This was getting weirder and weirder by the minute. "I…Jem, yeah."

"I was really sorry about your friend. I wanted to say something sooner, but I…well, I didn't know you and I didn't want to intrude."

I looked at her then. Searching for any hint of sarcasm or fakeness. I didn't see any, but that wasn't to say it wasn't there. She seemed genuine though. I couldn't very well say what I was thinking—that I was almost certain one of her so-called friends had been responsible for Kai's death. "Thanks."

She was still touching my arm and I think we both realized it at the same time. She pulled her hand away.

"You look really different now."

I shrugged again. What was I supposed to say to that?

"Can I say something? Promise you won't be offended?"

Another shrug. Shrugging was so much easier than talking.

"You should go easy on the powder. And that one's at least two shades too dark for your skin tone. I'm not trying to be mean or anything. God, you should have seen me a few years ago. All cakey orange foundation and no clue whatsoever."

"What, like Amber Sheldon?" I winced as soon as I said it, but Sasha just laughed.

"Worse than Amber, even! And don't get me wrong—you look *nothing* like that. You look…good."

"Um…thanks." My insides were crawling with embarrassment.

"Now why don't you get out of here and let me cry in peace, eh?" She smiled and it was warm. Definitely warm. She certainly didn't look like she was about to cry again.

"Are you going to be OK? What are you…what's the matter?" One compliment from Sasha and I was suddenly all concerned about her.

Sasha shook her head and went back to staring in the mirror. "I'll be fine. I'll be just fine." It looked like she was trying to convince her reflection as much as me.

I left her there, looking at herself. No good-bye. No "well, this has been lovely." Not even a "please stay away in the future, this is MY space, not yours."

I replayed the conversation in my head for the rest of the day and I kept on coming back to one, unbelievable thing: Sasha Evans had been nice to *me*.

Sort of.

⁓

A tiny kernel of an idea popped into my head that night, but I dismissed it immediately. It would be impossible, surely? But I kept on going back to the fact that Sasha Evans, the most popular girl in school, had talked to *me*. This never would have happened a few months ago. I had Kai and Mom to thank for that. For one thing, I'd never have been in the science block bathroom if it wasn't for my newfound vanity.

It would be so much easier to get back at Stu and the others if I wasn't such a loner, such an outsider. I kept thinking, WHAT IF…?

What if it was possible for me to somehow become friends with Sasha Evans?

What if she introduced me to the rest of her hideously popular friends?

What if I was able to get my revenge on Stu, Lucas, and Bugs *from the inside* and hurt them all the more because of it?

What if…?

chapter twenty

Jem,

January. The worst month of the year.
Nobody likes January, do they? It's all post-
Christmas doom and gloom and it's always
cold and dark and depressing. Still, there's
only a few days left, so let's look on the
bright side.

I bet you've been dreading what I was going
to ask you to do this month. Well, fear
not, I thought I'd give you the month off...
mostly because I don't want you to hate
me! Just one thing though...you haven't
talked to Lol yet, have you? If you have,
please accept my humble apologies. But if
you haven't, please just check on her. For
me. She's not as bad as you think. ~~She's
not as bad as SHE thinks.~~

Ooh, I've just realized that Valentine's Day is coming up! And you know how much I ADORE Valentine's Day. The avalanche of cards and flowers, the chocolates, the candlelit dinners! Be still, my beating heart. I wouldn't be surprised if you got a card or two this year, what with your fancy new hair and all. If you do, please don't rip them up. And go easy on the poor boy (or girl!). It takes guts to put yourself out there like that. Unless of course the card is anonymous, in which case whoever sent it is lame and not worthy of your affections.

Anyway, if you <u>don't</u> happen to get any cards, might I suggest an all-night horror movie marathon to cheer yourself up? I do hope you're continuing our fine tradition in my absence? I'd tell you to watch Halloween on Valentine's Day, but I'm nothing if not true to my word—no silly missions this month. This is merely a <u>suggestion</u>, you understand. (But you really SHOULD watch it...you know full well nothing cheers you up quite like some empty-headed girls

getting chased through a dark house by a
psychopath with a big knife.)

Same time next month, yes?

Kai
x x x

This time I threw down the letter in annoyance. How did he
know? How could he *possibly* know that I wouldn't have talked to
Louise. At least, not like he wanted me to.

I couldn't do it. I *wouldn't* do it. I even had a semidecent excuse:
I hardly saw her anymore. Max and Louise never seemed to be
with the others in the cafeteria. At first I'd assumed it was a blip,
that Team Popular would be back to full strength ASAP. But then
I began to wonder if there was more to it. Mom was the one who
ended up supplying the solution to this little mystery.

She broached the subject at the dinner table one day, which I
thought was spectacularly poor timing. Noah didn't need to hear
that kind of stuff; it was hard enough for him to understand that
Kai was gone. Mom dabbed at her mouth with her napkin and
cleared her throat. That's how I knew she was going to say something annoying.

"So…Jem, have you seen much of Louise at school?"

I shrugged and speared another piece of slightly overcooked
rigatoni. Noah was taking the opportunity to hide his veg under
a small mound of pasta. He tried this almost every night; it
never worked.

"Janice said she's in a pretty bad way, you know."

"Yeah?" I couldn't have sounded any less interested.

"Yes. Janice says she barely leaves her room these days. She's cut herself off from all her friends, Janice said—apart from that boyfriend of hers. You know she's been in counseling? Twice a week, apparently. It doesn't seem to be helping yet, but you can't expect these things to work overnight. There's no miracle cure, is there?" She fell into silence and then shook herself like she remembered that she had actually had a point that she wanted to raise after all. "You know, it might be nice if you invited her over sometime. You've been coping so well…really getting on with things. I thought it might help if you talked to her."

I looked at Dad for help, but he was busy adding yet more salt to his pasta. I wanted to remind Mom that Louise and I were not friends—and hadn't been for years. But she knew that and clearly thought it was irrelevant. I was angry that she thought I was coping so well. I was angry that every time she asked how I was, I said, "fine," and she actually believed me. I was so fucking angry. But for once I wasn't interested in causing a scene. She meant well. I just had to keep telling myself that. Over and over again until I believed it.

"Yeah, I'll do that."

Dad stopped with the salt-shaking and Noah stopped with the broccoli-burying and Mom stopped breathing. Me not being an awkward, snarky bitch was a massive deal, obviously. They'd better get used to it, because I fully intended on being a semireasonable, mostly nice daughter and sister for the next nine months. It was the least I could do.

The news about Louise was interesting. It made me wonder if the counseling made things even a tiny bit better for her. It made me wonder why Mom hadn't suggested counseling for me. It did *not* make me want to reach out to Louise. Not even a little bit.

Soon after the Louise news, it was clear that Team Popular had drafted in a replacement from the subs bench. Nina was blonde and pretty and pointless. A former conquest of Stu's, if the rumors were to be believed (and I always believed the rumors). There was no Max replacement though. Suitable boys were obviously harder to come by.

I was *glad* I didn't have to see Louise every day. I could just about cope with passing her in the corridor once or twice a week. But her retreat into depression or whatever meant I was spared that punch-in-the-gut daily reminder of Kai. I didn't need reminding.

Seeing Mr. and Mrs. McBride was even worse than seeing Louise. My parents had them over a few times and I hid in my room, plugged into my iPod so I wouldn't even have to hear them. I wouldn't budge, even when Mom begged me to come down and say hello, even when she hissed that I was being selfish and I should think about someone other than myself for a change.

The one time I *did* see them (because they arrived early and I was still in the kitchen gathering supplies for the evening) I couldn't believe the change. They looked terrible: shadowy and beaten. Mr. McBride had lost weight. Kai always said his dad could do with losing a few pounds, but he would never have wanted it to happen like this. Mrs. McBride hugged me and I thought she was never going to let go.

The McBrides were going through the motions of their lives. Even smiling and joking occasionally, but you could tell that something inside them had died. The heart had been ripped out of them in the cruelest way imaginable.

I tried my very best to ignore the thought that I would be doing the exact same thing to my parents. Except this would be worse, because I'd *seen* the pain and anguish firsthand. I'd lived it.

chapter twenty-one

I nearly choked on my apple the day Sasha sat down next to me in the cafeteria. At least she didn't sit in his chair. I'm not sure what I'd have done if she'd sat in his chair.

It was a good couple of weeks since we'd talked in the bathroom and I was beginning to think we'd never get any further than random hellos and half smiles in the corridors. But as soon as she sat with me—looking like it was the most normal thing in the world—that was when I knew. For some inexplicable reason, this girl wanted to be friends with me. She was playing right into my hands and she had no clue.

"Hey, Jem, how's it going?" Every movement Sasha made was graceful, and I wondered if that was something I could work on or whether it was something you were born with. She smoothed down her already very smooth hair and started nibbling on a slice of cucumber. All she had on her plate was salad and a Diet Coke, of course. Suddenly I wished that my ketchup-splattered plate would disappear. At least you couldn't tell it had been home to a mountain of fries only a few minutes ago. The evidence had disappeared.

"Hey. It's going…fine, I guess." I discarded my apple, knowing better than to try to eat and talk at the same time. I looked over at her usual table, but none of them were looking this way. They all seemed absorbed in watching Stu do something disgusting with his food.

"Good, good. You don't mind me sitting here, do you? It's just Stu kind of puts me off my lunch sometimes."

I shrugged. "I don't mind. I was just finishing up anyway."

"Oh? Stay a while, will you? Keep me company so I'm not sitting here like a billy-no-mates." She grimaced and looked truly ugly if only for a fraction of a second. "Sorry! I wasn't implying that you don't have any friends...you know that, don't you? You've got that whole mysterious who-needs-friends-anyway vibe going on, whereas I've got that desperate needs-to-be-around-people-all-the-time thing happening. I know which I'd prefer."

This was bizarre. She seemed really worried that she'd offended me. Surely people like her were put on earth to offend people like me. I didn't know what to say, so I shrugged.

She laughed. "You're just too cool for school, aren't you?"

I shrugged again, but this time I couldn't help but laugh. "Yeah, too cool for school, that's me."

The ice was broken, and while I didn't exactly feel at ease, my guard came down a little and I was able to talk to her without thinking I sounded like a complete idiot. We didn't talk about anything in particular. Sasha's conversational technique was to flit from subject to subject like a butterfly. Sometimes the changes of direction were so random it was hard for my brain to keep track. We talked about teachers we had in common (a safe topic), the food in the cafeteria (still safe), Stu (not so safe), and even (now this is the really weird one) the fact that she was thinking about breaking up with Lucas. I had no idea why she would want to talk to me about something so personal, but I was going to run with it. Sasha confiding in me was exactly what I wanted, but that didn't stop it from freaking me out.

"Why would you break up with Lucas?" The incredulity in my voice was obvious.

Sasha leaned forward in her chair and I did the same. "It's not that I don't like him. I mean, *of course* I like him." *Like* him? I thought they were like Romeo and bloody Juliet or something. "It's just…I don't exactly enjoy just being known as Lucas Mahoney's girlfriend, you know? I swear that's all people know about me. I'm sick of it."

"But…he's *Lucas Mahoney*. Most girls would kill to be his girlfriend."

A sly smile from Sasha. "You included?"

"No! I…no."

The sly smile spread into a full-on grin. "Yeah, yeah, whatever you say, Jem! You're right though—I've seen the way the girls here look at me. They *hate* me."

"They don't…"

"Yeah, they do. And don't think I never noticed the evil glares you've been giving me for the past year or so."

How could she…? I'd never even seen her look my way—not once. People like Sasha Evans did not notice people like me. They just *didn't*. I felt embarrassed. Exposed.

"It's OK, Jem. Really. So anyway, I thought I might try *not* being Lucas Mahoney's girlfriend for a while. See if that makes a difference. I want to stay friends with him…I really do. It's not like I think he's going to be devastated or anything. Lately it's been feeling more like friends with benefits than anything else, so maybe we can just move on to being friends *without* benefits?"

There was a question mark there and Sasha seemed to want something from me. The thing she wanted—the thing we all want, really—was validation. "Yeah, maybe."

Sasha nodded slightly, then followed it up with a more convincing nod. It looked as if she'd made up her mind.

"You're really good to talk to, you know that?"

I didn't laugh, even though I really wanted to. If I was Sasha's definition of someone who was good to talk to, then God help her. I would have almost felt sorry for her if she wasn't one of the founding members of Team Popular.

⌒

That was the day the Plan crystallized; for the first time I thought there was a chance I could really do it. I knew it wouldn't happen overnight, and it wouldn't be easy (or fun), but it seemed *possible* at least.

I guess the Plan had been floating around in my brain, just out of reach, since that incident in the bathroom. But that was the day I managed to grab hold of it with both hands. The Plan started with befriending Sasha. Do whatever it took to make her like me. Do whatever it took to make me think I was like her. Somehow become a part of Team Popular—even a very peripheral part. I just had to get closer to them. To Lucas and Bugs and Stu. Then I'd find a way to take them down for what they did to Kai. By the time I was finished with them, they'd know exactly how it felt to be humiliated.

It was easy enough to ignore the little voice telling me this was precisely what Kai *didn't* want me to do. I just had to remember that Kai was (very occasionally) wrong about things and this happened to be one of those times.

Admittedly there were a few things I hadn't exactly thought through. Like the fact that just because Sasha seemed to not hate me, it didn't mean the others would feel the same way. And the fact that these people made me really, really nervous, and how was I ever going to pretend to be one of them? And the Stu problem. And I had no idea what I was actually going to do to them. Yeah, there were a fair few details that had to be ironed out.

I was sure that Amber wouldn't be a problem—as long as Sasha was cool with me, she would be too. Same deal for Bugs, probably.

Nina should be OK, being such a newbie herself. King Lucas would be tricky though. And there was no point even thinking about Stu right now. That particularly nasty bridge would be crossed when I came to it. I was in this for the long haul. *As long as it takes.*

People's reactions to the hair and the makeup had at least proved that they saw me differently now. That was the first step. The new look needed time to sink in—enough time for people to start forgetting the old me. Since most of them had never even noticed the old me I didn't think it would take long. It really was that simple—a new look and people thought you were a different person. They thought you were one of them. People really are that shallow. It made me sick.

Next stop was the clothes. It shouldn't have surprised me that Kai mentioned that particular subject in his next letter. Somehow he was managing to facilitate a plan he'd had no idea about—a plan to do the very thing he'd expressly begged me not to do. It's funny (not really) how things work out.

I opened the letter on February 23. Needless to say, Valentine's had come and gone with zero admirers, secret or otherwise. I had watched *Halloween* though. And it *had* made me feel a little better, especially when I thought about Kai pretending to hide behind a cushion every time Michael Myers popped out from behind a hedge.

Jem,
Ah, February! Like January but mercifully shorter. You're getting there though, inching toward spring. Everything seems better in springtime, don't you think? The air is full of promise and the lambs are frolicking now and again.

~~I can't help thinking about Mom's birthday.~~
~~I hope~~ So I let you off last month, because
that's the kind of guy I am. But you didn't
honestly think I was going to go easy on you
this month too, did you? (Cue evil laugh.)
This month is all about SHOPPING! Your very
favorite thing, right?! S H O P P I N G! Are
the capital letters sufficient to ignite a tiny
spark of excitement somewhere deep within you?
No? Ah well, you can't blame a chap for trying.

It's simple. All you have to do is go into
town on Saturday and go into That Shop. You
know the one, so don't even pretend you don't.
Remember that time you said you'd rather
stick toothpicks in your eyeballs than go
inside? Well, I'm here to tell you that I've been
in there and it's really not as bad as you
think. Lol loves it, and so does pretty much
every girl in the known universe. But you have
to be different, don't you? And that's why I
love you so much. This is just a bit of fun, Ok?
No need to freak out about me trying to change
you or whatever it is you're thinking right
now. I'm merely attempting to open your mind.
Not that I think you're narrow-minded...but you

can be just a teensy bit judgmental sometimes.
And I like judgmental. Judgmental can be fun.
But so is trying new things once in a while.
Trust me.

Your mission is to go into That Shop and buy
something. Don't think you can get away with
a bracelet or some underwear or something,
because that doesn't count. You have to buy
something you would absolutely not wear in
the course of your everyday life. It has to be
colorful (and no, gray is not going to cut it
this time). Ideally it would be a dress but
that's probably pushing my luck somewhat,
so I'm thinking a top maybe. No sleeves. And
if it could show a hint of cleavage, all the
better. Nothing too expensive though—I don't
want to bankrupt you.

There. Simple. Buy one top/dress. You don't
have to wear it though...not yet anyway. Baby
steps, yes?

Don't hate me. I'm doing this for your own
good. And maybe a little bit for my own
amusement. It almost makes me wish

133

It's nice picturing you doing all these things. I like thinking about all the wonderful things Future Jem has in store for her.

I love you, pickle. Never, ever forget that.

Kai
xxx

← FROLICKING LAMB

Kai's missions (demands) were getting a little bit old. I was tired of playing puppet to his puppet master. I promised myself I wouldn't do anything else unless I wanted to—unless it fit in with the Plan. It just so happened that most of what he'd asked me to do so far had worked out that way. But it wasn't cute or funny anymore. It was a major pain in the ass.

To fortify myself on Saturday, I started off in a shop I didn't *completely* despise. I bought a few T-shirts, one skirt, and a pair of jeans (nothing black or gray). I wouldn't go so far as to say it was fun, but it certainly wasn't as bad as I'd been expecting. The things I bought were still *me*—as in, they weren't bright or garish or particularly revealing—they were just things I wouldn't necessarily have thought to wear *before*. I had a brief look at the shoes, but that was one step too far. It would take more than a crazy revenge plan to make me forgo my trusty old biker boots (Converse in summer, obviously).

While I was on a roll, I rushed next door into The Shop That Shall Not Be Named, grabbed a top in my size off the rail closest to the door, and headed straight to the counter. I was in and out in five minutes. It would have been four if the hung-over girl with the talon-like nails hadn't taken her sweet time folding the top oh-so-carefully, like it was made of the finest silk instead of fifty percent acrylic.

The stupid thing went straight to the back of my wardrobe as soon as I got home.

chapter twenty-two

The news about Sasha and Lucas spread through the school faster than you would believe. The unthinkable had happened. The Golden Couple was officially no more. I imagined a stampede of girls heading to the bathroom, checking themselves out, fixing their hair and makeup just in case he was ready to audition for a replacement.

Lucas Mahoney had dumped Sasha Evans. Opinions varied from *I told you she wasn't good enough for him* to *I thought they'd be together forever and have the most beautiful babies the world has ever seen.*

At lunchtime all eyes were on their table, everyone gleefully expecting a Sasha-shaped hole in the ranks. I'll admit that I was semigleefully expecting the exact same thing.

But there she was, sandwiched between Bugs and Stu. She looked completely at ease, as if she hadn't even noticed that the eyes of the whole school were on her. Lucas looked as calm and relaxed and Lucas-like as usual, leaning back in his chair, legs spread wide as if his bollocks were so huge they really needed that much room. Amber Sheldon was sitting on his right side and I could smell the desperation from where I was sitting. *Not a chance, love. Not a chance.*

I was leaving the school premises with my customary

speed—something akin to a death row inmate given a last-minute reprieve—when I felt a hand on my shoulder. Sasha.

"Wow, you're pretty speedy, aren't you? Didn't you hear me calling you?" I'd been thinking about Kai. Wishing he'd been here today for the Lucas/Sasha speculation; he would have loved it. "Don't suppose you fancy grabbing a coffee or something? It's been a bit of a crazy day and I could really do with the company… if you've got nothing better to do, that is."

It was like Sasha Evans was asking me out on a date. Of course, I knew she *wasn't* asking me out on a date, but that's exactly what it felt like. Not that I was particularly accustomed to being asked out or anything. I'd been asked out twice in my whole life. (Twice if you're being generous, once if you're not.)

I felt cornered. I wanted to say no but I couldn't think up a decent excuse quick enough. Potential ways out would flood my brain minutes later—dentist, doctor, babysitting for Noah. So many plausible excuses, but none of them available when I needed them most. I should be happy, I reminded myself. This was exactly what I wanted; Sasha was my way in. She was my golden ticket to the realm of the in-crowd. And for some bizarre reason she was playing right into my hands. I wasn't even having to work for it. It was almost as if she *actually* wanted to be friends with me or something. Incomprehensible.

So I said yes and we had coffee. Well, Sasha had coffee (double soy something latte) and I had a pot of tea. Without even asking, I got the low-down on the whole Lucas situation: she broke up with him after sex because she figured he'd be more chilled out; he *was* pretty chilled out about it and they agreed to stay friends; Lucas wanted to keep the *benefits* but Sasha was having none of it; she sweetened the pill by saying he could tell people *he* was the one to break up with *her*. I couldn't believe she was OK with everyone thinking she was the one who'd been dumped, but Sasha just shrugged and said, "What does it matter? People can believe what they like—I know the truth and that's what counts, isn't it? Besides…boys' egos are so very fragile." She laughed and I laughed right along with her.

It was starting to dawn on me that Sasha was a decent person. This made me deeply uncomfortable for a couple of reasons: it meant that I was a truly terrible judge of character, and it made me feel a little bit guilty.

I was using her.

I'd never really thought of myself as the kind of person who would use someone.

That was the day I read Kai's fifth letter.

Dear Jem,
I hope you're not bored of me yet? Wishing I'd
shut the hell up and get on with being dead?
Let me cut to the chase…

You are the best friend a boy could ever wish
for. I never needed anyone else, you know? You
were always more than enough. Why bother
making new friends when I already had the
best one in the galaxy? But I think maybe it
was unfair of me to keep you to myself. It was
selfish of me. I can't help thinking that if
we'd both had other friends—real, proper ones
rather than people we merely talked to now
and then (and said horribly mean things about

later)—things would be easier for you now. With that in mind, this month's mission is this: talk to someone new. Bonus points (and who wouldn't want bonus points?!) for going completely out of your comfort zone. For the record, "comfort zone" may be defined thusly: anyone you sit next to in class. You never know, that girl sitting next to you in the cafeteria line could well be ~~your new best~~ someone who shares your questionable taste in music.

What I'm trying to say is that you never really know a person until you know a person. Pretty deep, right? They'll probably print that on a dish cloth one day.

Oh God, Jem. I'm scared. I know it's hideously unfair of me to be telling you this, because there's really nothing you can do about it, is there? I'm sorry. I wish I could talk to you right now, but you're at Mr. Chow's for family night. I wish my family could have done that once in a while. I can't even remember the last time the four of us had dinner together. They always blame it on Mom's shift work, but I know it's not that. There's nothing to stop her sitting down with a bowl of cornflakes while we eat our dinner, is there?

You're lucky. I know you've never believed that, but it's true.

If I could talk to you right this second, I'd ask if I was doing the right thing. And I know you'd say no.

Of course you'd say no. But if you were in my shoes I honestly think you'd understand. It's too hard. It's all too hard. It's not just the video. Jem, I don't think I could ever be happy in this world—a world where people are ashamed to admit who they really are.

I know what you're thinking, but I'm <u>not</u> ashamed of who I am. I happen to think I'm a fairly decent human being, all things considered—one with exemplary manners and style, for that matter. But that's not enough to keep me going. ~~And you're not enough.~~

Let's be brutally honest here, because what's the point in kidding ourselves now? The London plan was never going to work out, was it? It was always my dream, not yours. You hate big cities—they make you nervous. But I know you'd have done it for me. You'd have applied to any university I chose, just to keep your promise. But you'd have been miserable, and I would have been miserable knowing you were miserable. And what would have happened if either of us got a boyfriend? I know I'd have been insanely jealous and watching like a hawk to make sure he treated you like you deserve to be treated—and you'd probably have been the same way.

What it comes down to is the fact that I'm not strong enough to be here anymore. But you <u>are.</u> You don't know how strong you are, but maybe Future Jem (five months older, five months wiser) is starting to have some idea. I hope more than anything in the world that you're beginning to realize how truly amazing you are.

~~Fuck.~~ Wow. Sorry about that, my dear. I was trying to keep these letters light and fluffy, dagnammit.

Must. Try. Harder.
Until next month,

Love,

Kai
x x x

I wanted to forget I'd ever read this letter. I *hated* this letter.

Still, there was a certain grim satisfaction, knowing that I'd already achieved this month's annoying mission. With bonus points. Even in Kai's craziest dreams he would never have imagined that I would be hanging out in a coffee shop with Sasha Evans. It felt like I'd beaten him at his own game.

❦

Two weeks later, coffee with Sasha paled into insignificance when I somehow found myself sitting next to Lucas Mahoney in the common room. If he'd wanted to, he could have reached out and pushed my hair behind my ear. If I'd wanted to, I could have reached out and touched the stray eyelash that was perched on his cheek. Of course there was no hair-pushing or eyelash-touching or any touching at all for that matter.

Bugs and Sasha were dominating the conversation—for very different reasons. Bugs because he was Bugs—talking was his default state. Sasha because she was clearly trying to make an effort to make this seem normal for everyone, despite the fact that there was an interloper in their midst.

I wanted to disappear into the graffiti-strewn bench we were sitting on. I willed myself to melt and trickle through the cracks, but it didn't seem to be working. Sasha was trying her best to include me in the conversation, but I wasn't exactly helping, with my one-word answers and blatant awkwardness. Things weren't quite going to plan.

I was full of grand ideas about how I was going to take these people down, like some kind of (slightly tame) movie vigilante… yet here I was, nodding along and smiling shyly. Yes, I despised these people and everything they represented. And I knew full well that one or more of them was ultimately responsible for my best friend's death. I was full of righteous indignation and anger and a whole lot of scheming. But I had to admit an uncomfortable truth: these people intimidated the hell out of me.

I hadn't meant to do anything so soon, but the opportunity seemed too good to miss. I'd been sitting in the common room, pretending to read a book for English. Team Popular was occupying their usual spot by the pool table, being obnoxiously loud. Normally Sasha was right in the thick of it, messing around with Bugs or giggling with the girls, but today she was sitting a few feet away, reading the same book as me. I gathered my stuff before I had a chance to chicken out, then I walked over to where she was sitting. The direct approach seemed like the best option.

I coughed to announce my arrival, and Sasha looked up and smiled. I held up my book. "Snap!"

She grimaced. "You too, huh? Talk about the most boring book in the entire history of the universe."

I sighed. "Tell me about it. I'm not even halfway through yet and I already want to slit…" Slit my wrists. That's what I'd been about to say—on purpose, of course. It did the job, because Sasha winced and jumped in with, "Hey, why don't you sit with us? I can't take any more misery on the moors right now."

I paused before nodding shyly, as if this hadn't been what I wanted all along. Sasha shoved the book in her bag and jumped up, steering me toward the others with a hand on my arm.

They were all looking at me and I was wondering if my hair looked OK. I couldn't check though—I wouldn't even allow myself to run my fingers through just to make sure. Because then they'd know how uneasy I was.

Lucas was smiling up at me. "What have we here?" Just what I'd have expected. I was a *what* rather than a *who*.

Sasha answered before I had a chance to embarrass myself. "Everyone, this is Jem. Jem, this is everyone." She might as well have said, *This is anyone who's anyone.*

I said an awkward "Hi, everyone," and Lucas said, "Hello, Jem. Sit." He patted the space next to him and I sat like an obedient dog. If anyone else had said something like that to me, I would have told them where to go, but this was Lucas and it was all part of the Plan and there was something commanding about him that made it impossible to refuse.

The reactions of the others ranged from entirely uninterested (Amber and Nina, aka New Blonde Girl, who probably hadn't been granted the right to speak yet), the friendly (Bugs), and the hostile (Stu). He was careful not to let the others see him glare at me, because then he might have had some explaining to do. After a minute or two he jumped up and challenged some random boy to a game of pool.

Then Bugs and Sasha started talking and Amber asked for Nina's opinion about whether her boobs were looking saggy or not and all I could do was try to remember to breathe. I was determined to keep my mouth shut and listen, because that was the only way I was going to come up with some decent ideas of how to hurt them. *Know your enemy—isn't that what they say?*

A couple of minutes later and I'd stopped listening to Bugs

and Sasha's conversation. I couldn't help thinking about how different it was to sit here. The whole common room looked different from this angle. Was it the most desirable place to sit purely because they sat there? Or did they choose that spot because it was the most desirable place to sit? Maybe it was the best seat in the house because it was next to the pool table, or because it was farthest away from the door so you weren't subjected to that blast of cold air every time someone came in or out? No. I was pretty sure it was *them*. They made it desirable. In truth, it was as uncomfortable and shabby here as it was anywhere else.

I was vaguely aware of Lucas turning to face me. He didn't say anything at first, so I didn't turn toward him. But I could see his face in the corner of my vision and he was definitely looking right at me. Heat crawled all over me, but I tried to ignore the sensation and concentrate on what Sasha was saying.

"Hey," he said softly.

I had to turn to look at him then, didn't I? I couldn't very well sit there and ignore him. "Hey." I had never seen his face so close up before. It was as ridiculously perfect as it was at a distance—maybe even more so. Lots of people look good from a distance, but not many hold up to close scrutiny. This was Lucas Mahoney in High Definition. His eyes were such an impossible blue that I wondered if they might be contact lenses. Looking at his stupidly perfect face made my skin itch. If a baseball bat had magically appeared in my hands, I wouldn't have hesitated to smash his face with it. Of course, that would have got me arrested, but it would almost have been worth it, just to rearrange those perfect features.

"So, Jem, what do you have to say for yourself?"

"I...nothing much, really."

He smiled, but not unkindly. "I find that very hard to believe.

OK, tell me something about you that no one else knows. Here, I'll go first. Um…right, I've got one. Up until last year, I still had a night-light in my bedroom. It was shaped like an alien and glowed green in the dark."

"You're scared of the dark?" I didn't want to smile but I couldn't help myself.

"Past tense, thanks very much! I've managed to face my fears and now I don't even have to leave my bedroom door open to see that crack of light from the hallway. Pretty impressive, right?"

I know what you're doing. This is supposed to be charming and endearing. But why are you doing it? Either he was just trying to put me at ease, make me feel comfortable, because he recognized this must be weird for me, or this was what he did with everyone. This was what made him King Lucas. Insincere self-deprecation and a sweet smile. I had to admit it was a pretty effective combination, but I could see through this boy like a pane of newly polished glass.

"Yeah, that *is* pretty impressive. Your parents must be so proud." My sarcasm was carefully judged—enough so he knew it was there, not enough for him to think I was a bitch.

His smile faltered a little. "Parent. Singular." He fiddled with a thin strip of leather tied around his wrist.

That stumped me. "Oh. Right…" I trailed off, not wanting to ask what he meant but not wanting to gloss over it either.

"It's all right, it's no big drama or anything. I never knew my dad—he took off before I was even born. Bastard."

"I'm sorry." This seemed like the right thing to say. I couldn't help wondering why Lucas had brought it up. There was no need for it really. He could have just ignored my proud parents remark, couldn't he? That's what I'd have done. Did he want me to feel sorry for him? Was that it?

Lucas shook his head. "No need to be sorry. My mom's

pretty amazing…and she's clearly done an awesome job raising me, right?"

"I…yeah."

He laughed. "Jeez, I was kidding! How arrogant do you think I am?" I chose not to answer that. "So come on then, fair's fair. Tell me a secret." He leaned a little closer and I had to force myself not to lean back.

"I don't have any secrets."

"Everyone's got secrets, Jem. It's what makes people interesting." The way he was looking at me made me feel naked. His gaze was magnetic. Maybe that's why he was so popular—he hypnotized people into liking him.

I hate you and your friends and the only reason I'm sitting here right now is because I want to destroy you. I'll do whatever it takes.

"I used to go line dancing with my mom." I have never been line dancing in my life.

Lucas burst out laughing and slapped his knee in a totally disproportionate way. "Now that's a good one! That's almost worse than being scared of the dark. So when did you hang up your cowboy boots?"

"A couple years ago. You know, line dancing is a lot harder than it looks. There's a lot of skill involved."

"Is that so? Maybe you could teach me some tricks some time?"

The invitation hung in the air, inhabiting the space between us. There was that strange exposed feeling again—like he had the measure of me. I knew he didn't. I knew he couldn't possibly know what I was thinking, but that didn't stop me from looking away, embarrassed.

I was saved by Bugs shouting over, "Hey, Lucas, stop flirting with the poor girl! You're so bloody *obvious*, mate. You want to take a few lessons from the Bugsmeister, my friend." He raised one ginger eyebrow with faux suaveness, then yawned and stretched his arm around Sasha. Before she knew what was happening, she was pulled into his embrace. She squealed as Bugs pretended to maul her like the big bear he was.

I'd never been so glad to hear the bell ring for classes. I grabbed my bag and jumped up; the others carried on like they hadn't even heard it. Lucas was watching me, amused. "Blimey, you're keen."

"I've got geography with Mr. Lynch. He makes you stand outside if you're late. It's embarrassing." *Why do I feel the need to explain myself to him?*

"Well, we wouldn't want you being embarrassed now, would we? On you go." I couldn't tell if he was mocking me. That smile was really quite distracting.

"Actually, I'll let you go on one condition." His legs were blocking my escape route, so I had no choice but to stand and wait. "Sit with us at lunch? It's kind of a downer seeing you sitting in the corner all by yourself." Once again I found it hard to believe that a member of Team Popular had deigned to acknowledge the existence of an outsider. The thought of them watching me made my skin creep and crawl.

"OK."

Lucas smiled.

I smiled back. I was in.

It was that simple.

chapter twenty-three

Of course, it wasn't actually *that* simple. After lunch, I was silently congratulating myself on getting through a whole hour in their company, marveling at the fact that I hadn't spilled any food on myself or choked on my water or sprayed food in anyone's face. *Maybe this won't be so tricky after all.* Then there was a voice in my ear as I lined up to hand over my empty tray. "What are you doing here? Nobody wants you here." I could smell onions on his breath.

I didn't turn to face him as I spoke. "I don't know what you're talking about."

He waited until the others had walked out of the cafeteria ahead of us. "What are you playing at? With all this?" He flicked my hair, his finger grazing my ear in the process.

I'd seen the way he'd looked at me all through lunch, emitting all kinds of bad vibes from the other end of the table. At one point, I'd heard Nina asking him what was up—his response was a grunted "nothing." I knew I was going to have to deal with him sooner or later. I'd just expected it to be later, that's all. But I'd already worked out how I was going to handle him.

I looked over my shoulder in a really obvious way, then pulled him away from the crowds pouring out of the cafeteria. My touch on his arm was enough to confuse him. I leaned in close, steeling myself against the onion breath. "Look, I'm really sorry about what happened. I'm sorry about your nose."

"Yeah? You didn't seem sorry after it happened, *remember*?"

"I know. I was just…messed up, I suppose." I averted my gaze from his.

"What do you mean by that?" His eyes were suspicious, but I knew they wouldn't be for much longer if I played this exactly right.

"I can't talk about it. I'm sorry. Please, you have to understand." I touched his arm again and left it there for a second or two.

"I haven't got a bloody clue what you're talking about. All I know is we were having a good time and then you went and freaked out like a lunatic."

I took a shaky breath and looked him square in the eye. "If I tell you something, will you promise not to tell anyone?" This performance was turning out to be truly Oscar worthy.

"Yeah, I won't tell anyone." He was looking uncomfortable now. Clearly he wasn't accustomed to girls telling him secrets.

"You have to promise, Stu. This is serious. You can't tell Lucas or Bugs or *anyone*. No one knows. I've never told anyone before."

"I promise." His voice softened. "You can tell me." He sounded almost sincere.

I leaned even closer and whispered the words into his ear. The words I knew would get me off the hook with him. Three little words.

"I was raped."

⁓

A stab of guilt as I said the words. A stab of guilt that had to be ignored.

Stu's eyes widened and he flinched as if I'd hit him.

"What?"

"It happened a long time ago and I guess…I guess I thought I was over it. But I haven't…y'know…*been* with anyone since then. I thought I was ready. But I wasn't and I freaked out and I'm sorry. It wasn't your fault." Those last words almost stuck in my throat. Part of my brain was truly appalled at what I was doing, that I'd even come up with this idea in the first place. The other part was pragmatic, reassuring me that I had to do this. It was the only way.

Stu leaned against the wall and breathed out.

"*God.* That's…I had no idea. That's pretty hardcore." Only an idiot like Stu would think hardcore was an appropriate word to use when talking about rape. "I'm sorry. That's terrible. If I'd known, I never would have…I mean, *obviously*."

"I know you wouldn't."

"Who…? Did you go to the police?"

I shook my head. "No point. My word against his. Look, Stu, I shouldn't have told you…but I wanted you to understand why I freaked out like I did. You do understand, don't you?" I was all but fluttering my eyelashes at the boy.

"Of course! God, I'm so sorry." He went to touch my arm and then stopped when he realized that maybe being touched by him was not something I would want.

"So we're OK? You won't mind me hanging out with you guys sometimes? It helps, you know? I feel like I'm finally fitting in, after all this time." I nearly winced, sure that I'd gone too far. That he wouldn't buy it.

"I don't mind at all. I'm sorry I was a dick." Again with the poor choice of words. This boy seriously needed to work on his vocabulary. He rubbed his hand over his head in a nervous gesture.

"You've nothing to apologize for. I'm just glad I was able to explain. And you promise you won't tell anyone? I couldn't bear it if people knew. I want to get on with my life and forget it ever happened."

"I understand." I'd never seen him look so serious before. It didn't suit him.

"Thank you. Well, I'd better get to English. I'll see you later, OK?" Stu nodded but didn't make a move to leave.

"Jem, there's something I…I want you to know that it wasn't a dare. Me and you. Nobody dared me to pull you. I made that up." He shrugged and smiled sheepishly. "Wounded pride or something. Sorry," he mumbled, looking at his feet.

I smiled and it was genuine. "That's OK. Thanks for telling me. I really appreciate it. See you later, Stu." I left him leaning against the wall. As soon as I was out of the cafeteria I had to stop myself from doing a lame little victory dance or punching the air. I walked calmly down the corridor, but I couldn't keep the smile off my face.

I'd done it. I'd really done it. Stu wasn't going to be a problem. He'd been officially neutralized. And it had been so much easier than I could have imagined.

It was almost scary how easy it was to get away with a story like that. I'd half expected him to call me a liar, but it would be a very brave person to say that to someone who'd just admitted to being raped. You'd have to be absolutely sure you were in the right. And Stu didn't know me well enough to know anything of the sort. Stu didn't know me at all.

The admission about the dare was what pleased me the most. Either he was now telling the truth and there'd been no dare— he'd followed me into the greenhouse for his own reasons. Or he was lying, in which case he felt bad enough to want to protect my feelings. It was win-win.

When I lay in bed that night, I tried to ignore the question my conscience kept coming back to: had I *enjoyed* telling that lie? Even just a little bit?

No. *No.*

Maybe.

chapter twenty-four

I've done it. Somehow I've achieved the impossible. I am officially one of Them. I thought it would take a lot longer to infiltrate Team Popular, but I suppose once they decide you're in, you're *really* in. There are no half measures where this bunch is concerned.

I wonder if everyone would do this if they knew how effortless it is. I wonder if people look at me and wonder how I did it. I bet they put it down to the hair and the makeup and the stuff they can see on the outside. And that was the start of it, no doubt. This would not have happened if I hadn't changed all that, if I hadn't molded myself into an approximation of a face that fits. But there's more to it than that: it's about watching and listening and saying the things they want to hear. It's about knowing when to speak and when to shut up. It's about learning the dynamics of the group. Looking in from the outside, I thought I knew exactly how they operated. Luke was King and everyone bowed down to him. The others were his loyal subjects, who existed solely to make him look good. I was wrong.

Lucas and the boys are louder than the girls—they *seem* dominant. The girls laugh and roll their eyes at the boys' antics. You'd be forgiven for thinking they're simpering idiots, clinging on to the boys with their manicured fingernails, knowing that if they put a foot wrong they risk losing their place in Team Popular. But the more I watch, the more I realize it's the girls who hold the real power. Pretty much everything the boys do is to impress the girls. Even the things that are gross or violent or incredibly stupid—it's all about the girls. Especially Sasha. She's the center of the group, which explains why she wasn't ousted for dumping Lucas. It also helps explain why it was so easy for her to bring me in from the wastelands of the general school population. It's Sasha who's made the Plan possible really. I must remember to thank her one day.

Anyone can see that Bugs is in love with Sasha. Any opportunity to touch her or hug her and he's there. Lucas doesn't seem to mind or even notice—probably because it's Bugs. Bugs can get away with stuff purely by virtue of being Bugs. The other boys don't see him as a threat—at all. I'm willing to bet that if it was Stu who was all over his ex-girlfriend like a rash, Lucas wouldn't be so cool about it. Sasha doesn't seem to mind either; I think she likes the attention. And because she doesn't see Bugs in *that* way, she can cuddle him or sit on his lap or ruffle his hair without even thinking about it.

It must drive Bugs crazy. He knows nothing's ever going to happen there—never in a million years—but he takes what he can get, like a dog waiting for scraps from the table. It's kind of sad actually. Or utterly pathetic, depending on how charitable I'm feeling.

Even Nina the Pointless Blonde has her own subtle sort of power over Stu. He's clearly keen for this particular former conquest to become an ongoing one. Nina seems to be resisting his charms at the moment, but it's only a matter of time. She said as much to me and Sasha the other day. Her exact words were, "I reckon I'll let him have sex with me soon." Sasha laughed and said, "I knew it!" A smile was the best I could do, mostly because the thought of anyone having sex with Stuart Hicks was repugnant. And there was something about the way she said it—that she'd *let* him. She would allow him to do it to her. Like she wouldn't even be a willing participant. Like sex is something that a boy does to a girl, not something they do together. It was disturbing.

⤙

I've been watching them, analyzing them, and they have no idea. They think I'm just another harmless girl, filling up the ranks. Maybe they let me in because they realized that Nina doesn't really add up to one whole useful person.

I've decided to go for Bugs first. It didn't take long to come up with the idea. Captain of the rugby team, with the biggest crush in the world on his mate's ex? Anyone can see where his weakness lies. And considering what they did to Kai, it really couldn't be more perfect. I just need to wait for the right moment. I've been dropping hints whenever I've spoken to Bugs, feigning interest when he goes on and on about his car. Bugs is a year older than the rest of us. I listened to the whole long, boring story about some childhood illness that meant he was in and out of hospital. Any kid with half a brain would have been able to catch up on all that missed schoolwork, but Bugs isn't the brightest crayon in the box so he was kept back a year. He's reaping the benefits now though—the only kid in our year who's turned seventeen well before junior year. And since he somehow learned to drive before he turned seventeen (I'm sure he mentioned something about an older brother and an airfield but it's really hard to stay conscious during car-related chat), he's on course to pass his test in a couple weeks. I've made it clear that I'm very keen to go for a drive some-time, and Bugs seems more than keen to play chauffeur.

He has no idea he's playing right into my hands.

chapter twenty-five

I've been dreading Kai's next letter. And not just because the last one was so brutal. I know what he's going to talk about, and it's something I've been trying my best to ignore.

Jem,
It's April. Our month. I'm sorry I'm not there to bake you a bizarre-tasting, slightly-crispy-round-the-edges birthday cake like I did last year. Maybe your mom will get you a cake from Marks & Spencer—one that people can actually eat. I'm sorry I'm not there to get you a birthday present too. Something amazing that you've secretly always wanted.

I'm sorry I wasn't around for _my_ birthday, mostly because you always enjoyed mine more than yours for some reason. (You never did like being the center of attention, did you? Even when it meant cards and presents and cake.)

Anyway, I hope it wasn't too awful. It's just a day like any other, after all. It will get easier, I'm sure. I hope that one day in the not too distant future you'll be able to raise a glass of champagne on April 19th and maybe remember me and smile a little bit? I would really like that. And I do hope you've got something special planned for your birthday. Something that involves leaving the house, at least. But if you don't feel up to doing much, that's Ok too, you know? Not that you need my permission or anything.

Shit. I'm sorry, Jem. I hate to think of you being alone on your birthday. ~~It almost~~ I'm sorry for being a selfish bastard.

Ok, I need to move on to May now because this is too hard to think about. I was all ready with a challenge and everything (socializing at the weekend, maybe wearing your new top/dress/whatever, in case you're curious), but all I really want is for you to get through these few days. That's all I <u>really</u> care about. I'm sorry I had to go and make things so hard for you, pickle, I really am.

162

Your loving best friend,

Kai
x x x

DON'T FORGET TO
BLOW OUT ALL THE
CANDLES

He's right. His birthday was bad. I stayed in my room all day. Mom didn't even try to coax me out. Just brought me food on a tray, no questions asked. She said she was here for me if I wanted to talk but understood if I didn't. I tried not to think about how much worse it would be in the McBride house. I tried not to wonder what they would be doing to mark the day. I tried not to think of Kai never getting any older. The boy who never grew up.

My birthday isn't much better. Mom and Dad and Noah make a real effort to make it special and they try not to look disappointed when I barely manage to crack a smile. Mom and Noah even baked a cake together; Noah's proud little face almost breaks me. I try to forget that this will be *my* last birthday. The girl who never grew up.

I didn't tell anyone my birthday was coming up, and I've always had it hidden on Facebook (mostly to avoid the shame of having *nobody* write on my wall, since Kai prided himself on his complete ignorance of any and all social networks). I receive a single card from someone who's not a member of my family: Jasmine. The last card I got from her must have been when I was about twelve, so it's a little odd that she remembered the date.

I especially didn't want Sasha to know it's my birthday, so it's definitely more than a little weird that I'm a little disappointed not to receive a birthday text from her. She does text though, to ask me if I want to hang out at her place tomorrow. She reckons I need a break from studying, which is a joke because I've barely started. Anyway, tomorrow happens to be Sunday. So I guess I've completed Kai's little challenge after all, even if he didn't actually set it. It's almost enough to make me smile.

My new top is a little tight; I'm only wearing it because Kai *didn't* ask me to. Sasha said it's just going to be the two of us, watching a few DVDs and eating pizza. So it's a bit of a surprise when Lucas Mahoney answers the door. I manage to hide my feelings and plaster an easy smile on my face when I say hi. He's not wearing any shoes. There's something about him not wearing shoes that makes him look more normal, less Lucas. And I'm not sure how I feel about that.

"Hey, come on in." I wrestle my way out of my jacket in a most unladylike fashion and he says, "I like your top. It's…nice."

I mumble thanks and follow him into the living room. They're all there, sprawled on sofas or on the floor. None of them look surprised to see *me*, which is irritating. I perch next to Nina on the edge of the sofa nearest the door and listen as the banter ramps up. After the obligatory moaning about studying, today's topic of choice is Lucas and how he hasn't had any action since his breakup with Sasha. Lucas and Sasha don't seem bothered by this discussion in the slightest. Sasha just rolls her eyes and goes to sort out the pizzas in the kitchen. Stu and Bugs are shouting out the names of girls at school and listing their various attributes. Amber and Nina add their (nearly always unfavorable) verdict on the girls in question. And Lucas mostly laughs and shakes his head, with the odd grimace thrown in if he particularly disapproves.

It's surprisingly easy—and very enlightening—to sit here and just listen. The thing that does my head in is that so much of what's said are things I've thought to myself or things I said to Kai hundreds of times. I can't bear the idea that I've ever had the same thoughts as these people. Like the fact that Bella Colgan has an unusually large head. Or that Caroline Forbes's eyes are so close together it makes her look like a giant spider. Or that Marnie Dent's breasts are so big they don't look like they belong on her body. Amber nods away as if this isn't the biggest pot/kettle/black situation the world has ever seen.

And then Stu throws a new name into the mix.

Jasmine James. I feel guilty every time I see Jasmine—throwing away that card she gave me was a crappy thing to do, pure and simple.

Everyone's quiet for a minute, weighing up Jasmine's attributes or lack thereof. They're all taking this very seriously, really getting into it.

Amber's just about to open her mouth when I speak without even thinking. "Hermaphrodite Girl?" They all turn to face me and I can feel my cheeks start to burn. Stu barks out a laugh and Bugs reaches over to high five me. Nina gives an ugly snort and immediately puts her hand to her face as if she can stuff the snort back up there if she's quick enough. Amber smiles and takes a sip of her drink. They approve, clearly. Lucas is the only one who doesn't show any visible reaction.

I don't even know why I said it. I've no idea which ugly dark place in my brain the words came from. *Obviously* it's not true. Sure, Jasmine maybe looks a little masculine if you ignore the long shiny hair—broad shoulders, no boobs to speak of. And her voice is maybe a bit deeper than most. But not so much that anyone would ever notice…until someone drew their attention to it, that is.

I feel sick, but everyone's laughing and joking and taking the hermaphrodite idea way too far, so no one notices that I retreat into myself. Lucas is the only one who doesn't seem to find it particularly funny. He picks up the *Sky* magazine on the coffee table and starts flicking through the pages.

I have to get out of here. I can't listen to Stu speculating about what genitalia Jasmine might or might not possess. *Please forgive me, Jasmine. It's part of the Plan. They* have *to believe that I belong.*

I mumble something about helping Sasha and escape into the kitchen. She's standing in front of the open fridge, staring into it like she's trying to memorize the contents.

"Hey, need a hand with anything?"

Sasha doesn't seem to hear so I repeat the question. She turns and blinks exaggeratedly. "Oh, hi. No, I think I've got everything covered, thanks." She peers into the oven, then turns to face me. "By the way…sorry about the ambush."

I wasn't going to mention it; I didn't want to sound ungrateful or pathetic. And I should be glad that I've been thrown into this situation unawares so I didn't have time to get all worked up about it. Playing dumb seems like the best tactic. The person Sasha thinks I am wouldn't bat an eyelid at the change of plans. The more, the merrier—that's what Sasha's version of me would think. "Ambush?"

Sasha does that extreme blinking thing again. It reminds me of a robot, even though as far as I know, robots don't need to blink. She waves an arm in the direction of the living room. "I should have told you the others were coming too."

I shrug and run my fingers along the worktop. No crumbs or tea stains or stray milk bottle tops here, just shiny perfection. "No worries."

"I'm just sorry it's not a girls' night in like we planned." This is surprising.

I smile. "I don't mind at all—the more, the merrier, I reckon."

Sasha hops up onto the worktop next to me and folds a pair of oven gloves on her lap. "He likes you."

My heart performs an anxious somersault. "Who?"

"You know who." A sly smile.

I swallow. "Stu?"

"Ha! No! You're not exactly his type—and trust me, that's a good thing. Am I going to have to spell this out for you? Name starts with 'L,' ends in 'ucas'? Ringing any bells?"

I can't help but laugh. "What are you talking about?"

"He *likes* you. I can tell." She looks awfully pleased with herself. The cat that got the cream, with a side order of dead mouse.

"You're out of your mind. Why would he…? You're kidding, right?"

"Nope. That boy is so easy to read it's not even funny."

I don't know where to look or what to think. She's watching me, waiting to see how I react. But how the fuck am I *meant* to react in this situation? What are you supposed to say when a boy's ex-girlfriend (very recently *ex*) tells you he likes you? And how are you supposed to *feel*?

"I…You're wrong."

Sasha shakes her head and smiles. "Ah, Jem, you have so much to learn. I'm never wrong about things like this. Never. It's a gift. So what do you think? Reckon you might go for it?"

"He…I mean, you and him were…"

She rolls her eyes. "Ancient history! Well, not exactly ancient, but you know what I mean. I'm so over that—and clearly Lucas is too. No need to be awkward and weird about it." She places her hand on my head and puts on this deep, solemn sort of voice.

"By the power vested in me as The Ex-Girlfriend, I hereby give you permission to do whatever the hell you like with Lucas Mahoney. I give you my blessing."

I giggle and scoot out from under her hand. "You're crazy. People at school have no idea how crazy you truly are, do they?"

She pulls a face. "Nope, and I'd like to keep it that way, thank you very much! Now, seriously—Lucas…yay or nay? On the pro side, I can tell you that the sex is exceptionally good. I've trained him well—you can thank me later."

"Ewww! I don't want to hear it!"

"On the con side, he spends far too much time in front of the mirror. And his obsession with soccer might get on your nerves a bit. Any questions?"

I'm blushing; I can feel it. The redness *must* be powerful enough to break through the layers of makeup. "Why are you telling me all this? It's…kind of weird, isn't it?"

"Here's the way I see it. I like Lucas and I want him to be happy. I like you and I want *you* to be happy. Lucas fancies you but it remains to be seen whether you fancy him. So…? Do you?"

"I—"

An insistent beeping sound comes from the oven timer and Sasha leaps off the counter, brandishing the oven gloves. "Saved by the bell!" She goes to open the oven, then changes her mind and turns to face me.

"Actually…I'm not going to let you squirm out of this that easily. I'm not getting those pizzas out until you tell me. If everyone has to eat burnt pepperoni I'm going to blame you, so you'd better spill…What do you think of him?" She flicks the oven gloves over her shoulder, then crosses her arms looking as smug as you like.

Something tells me that Bugs wouldn't be too happy if I ruined his dinner, and Sasha's clearly not budging, so I have to say *something*. My mind flits between all the possible things I could say before eventually settling on the truth.

"I have no idea how I feel about him."

It feels good to tell the truth for a change.

Sasha narrows her eyes and she's about to say something when Bugs comes barreling into the kitchen shouting, "I WANT MY PIZZA, WOMAN!" He picks Sasha up, hoists her over his shoulder, and proceeds to circle the kitchen making an assortment of unappealing grunting noises.

For the rest of the night, I do my best to make sure I'm not left alone with Sasha, and I watch Lucas for any signs that Sasha could be right. But it's so far outside the realms of possibility that my brain has difficulty taking it seriously. Still, Sasha seemed so sure, and why would she say something like that if she didn't think it was true? And Lucas *has* been friendly to me—way friendlier than I would have expected after observing him from a distance for all those years. But this is ME we're talking about. I might look different now, but underneath it all I'm still Jem Halliday. And Jem Halliday is definitely not the sort of girl to catch the eye of someone like Lucas Mahoney. Stand me next to Sasha and it's not even a contest.

But I can't seem to silence the tiny stupid voice in my head whispering, *What if it is true? What would you do then?* There's no doubt that getting in with Lucas would give me more options when it comes to the Plan. Some *very* interesting options. It's got to be easier to humiliate someone you're really close to—especially if they tell you their secrets, their hopes and dreams. Of course, you'd usually *care* about someone you're close to, so humiliating them would be the last thing on your mind. But the beauty here is that I *don't* care—not even a little bit. I keep coming back to Sasha breaking up with Lucas and him not wanting anyone to know that *he* was the one who'd been dumped. This useful little nugget of information is firmly lodged in my brain.

But could I actually do it? Could I pretend to like Lucas for Kai's sake?

Finally a question I know the answer to without even thinking. Of course I could.

chapter twenty-six

I didn't have much time for plotting before exams crept up on me. Tests are pretty much all I can think about right now, which is strange, because I've never really cared about this stuff before. But now I'm actually studying and it's sort of nice to have something else to focus on. Of course I've been complaining to Mom and Dad every chance I get. They'd think there's something seriously wrong with me if they knew I was enjoying studying.

I'm pretty sure I'll do better than my teachers are expecting, but not as well as Dad thinks I will. He seems to think that hard work should mean top marks, but he should know better. Life's not like that. Some people don't need to lift a finger, and they'll get more A's than any one person could possibly need. And some people will sweat and toil away for weeks on end and come away with mediocre grades at best. Life *isn't* fair. It's the same with popularity if you think about it. You can't make it happen by being nice and friendly and kind—otherwise, Jasmine James would rule the school instead of having to deal with the repercussions of rumors started by yours truly.

I've been trying to tell myself it's not my fault, but it's *clearly* my fault and I feel horrible about it. I really do. I don't know for sure which one of Team Popular decided it was perfectly OK to start spouting off about it at school, but it doesn't matter. The fact is, I should have known this would happen.

I've overheard at least three people talking about it already this week, and I'm ninety-nine percent sure Jasmine knows. Yesterday in history I had this awful feeling that she wanted to talk to me about it. I could sense her glancing over at me way more than she normally does. I've never stared so hard at a textbook before. It must have done the trick; she didn't say a word.

Hopefully everyone will forget all about it soon, what with the exams and everything. If not, all I can do is hope that Jasmine's strong enough to weather the storm. Unlike Kai.

I devour the May letter far too quickly. I've got a math exam today; I hate math more than anything. My head is swimming with equations and right-angled triangles. I stuff the letter under my pillow and promise myself I'll read it again as soon as I get home.

Jemster,
Sorry about the last letter. And I'm sorry about all the apologizing I seem to be doing. It must be rather irritating, but I can't seem to help myself. ~~Sorry.~~

I'll keep this brief, because you must be in the middle of your exams and I'd hate to be the reason for you failing. (Not that I think there's the remotest chance of you failing. Failure is NOT an option, my dear.)

Undone

I hope you're not missing your study buddy too much. Not that I was ever much use—more of a hindrance than a help really. Too easily distracted—that's always been my problem.

My three tips for getting through these trying times are as follows:

1. Steer clear of caffeine late at night. Caffeine will drive you crazy. Trust me. (I'm surprised I'm still able to form coherent sentences right now…or maybe I'm just babbling incoherently and I can't even tell.)
2. Rest your brain every so often. It's a little-known fact that watching horror films is almost as good for the brain as eating oily fish. (I'd recommend something on the sillier end of the spectrum. *Friday the 13th Part VIII: Jason Takes Manhattan*, perhaps?)
3. Try not to get too nervous—they're only exams for God's sake. ~~Life's too short to worry about.~~
I'm going to leave you in peace. Go do some studying…NOW. Step to it, soldier! And get your mom to test you—you know how much she loves playing the quizmaster.

Good luck, pickle. Break a leg and all that.

Love,

Kai
x x x

Today's the day. Bugs passed his test without even a single minor fault. I even hugged him when he told us the news.

Mom's been nagging me about studying, but she eventually came around to the idea that a day out might be just what I need. Plus I told her I'd work extra hard as soon as I get home this afternoon—I said she can even test me if she likes (Kai was right— it's one of her favorite mother–daughter activities). Besides, she's over the bloody moon about my "new friends" as she keeps calling them. She's always asking questions about Sasha.

I went to the shop first thing this morning. Right on the other side of town, of course. There was an old lady behind the counter and she gave me the longest, hardest look. The old Jem would have crumbled and mumbled and reddened under the gaze of her watery eyes. I just stared right back at her, daring her to say something. She was the first to look away. When it comes down to it, most people are weak. Too afraid to say what they're really thinking—especially to a stranger.

I shoved my purchases into my bag, looking over my shoulder to check no one was watching. Which is exactly the kind of shifty behavior that makes people notice you.

I breathed a shaky sigh of relief as soon as I escaped from the shop, swiftly followed by a giggle that bubbled up from nowhere. Also the kind of shifty (or deranged) behavior that makes people notice you. Sure enough, a kid leaning against the shop window looked at me strangely. Normally I'd ignore this and scurry away like a particularly pathetic mouse. Not this time though; this time I told him to fuck off. His eyes widened and he looked embarrassed. I felt bad. I wanted to apologize. But I didn't. I walked away feeling ashamed of myself. He was just some poor kid who happened to look at some mad girl who was laughing to herself. What was wrong with that? What was wrong with me?

∽

I couldn't resist taking a peek at what I'd bought as soon as I got home, especially since I didn't exactly take time to study them in the shop. It was more a case of grab whatever I could off the shelves as quickly as possible. There was no more giggling. Looking at them made me feel beyond uncomfortable, and of course Noah chose that exact moment to burst into my room without knocking. Lucky for me he's so spectacularly unobservant I was able to cover up the evidence with a pillow. He wasn't even watching. He narrowed his eyes, dived under my bed, and stayed there for a second or two before scrambling out again. "Good. No zombies. You're safe. As you were, soldier." Then he did what I can only assume was some kind of commando roll, saluted me, and ran from the room, ignoring my shout to "CLOSE THE BLOODY DOOR!" My brother might just be even weirder than I am.

∽

They arrive thirteen minutes late. No one bothers to ring the doorbell. Instead, the car horn toots some irritatingly unplaceable tune and I hurriedly shove things into my bag and run down the stairs, nearly spraining my ankle jumping the last four steps all at once. I shout good-bye to Mom and take off before she can ask me where I'm going and what time I'll be back.

The car is as ridiculous as I expected. It's white, for a start. What kind of an idiot chooses a white car? Especially when you're as slobbish as Bugs. It has this weird sort of wing thing on the back, which is supposed to make it look more aerodynamic, I guess. The windows are tinted, and the rims are super shiny. But take all that away and you're left with a car your mom would drive.

This is the first official outing for what Stu has christened "The Pussy Magnet," in typically revolting fashion. Bugs has been dreaming of this car for years. I assumed his parents had bought it for him, but he took great pride in telling me that he'd saved up every penny. Three years it had taken him. I'm more impressed than I'd like to admit.

The pavement is practically vibrating with the thumping bass. I can only hope my ears make it through this experience intact. The tinted windows make it impossible to see who's in the car, so opening the door is a little like dipping your toe into waters you're pretty sure are infested with sharks.

Bugs is in the driver's seat, his big moon face looming between the seats, meaty arm slung over the passenger seat. Sasha's sitting next to him, and you can just tell by the look on his face that this is a dream come true for him. Well, it would be if it weren't for the boys in the back. I squeeze in next to Stu, which I definitely wouldn't have done if the stupid windows hadn't deprived me of the choice. Getting up close and personal with Lucas would have been a far more attractive option. There's only room for five in the car, so that means no Amber, no Nina. I can't help thinking this could be significant—am I higher up the pecking order *already*? Or am I reading too much into things, as per usual?

The backseat is cozy, to say the least. Stu's leg presses up against mine and I can feel the strength there. There's a hole in the knee of his jeans. I remember it from that night in the greenhouse. His knobbly knee sticks through, and if you weren't careful you might find it kind of endearing. You'd think he was a little boy who'd fallen off his bicycle. You would be very, very wrong.

We head out of town, and Bugs's driving is way better than I would have expected. Boy racer he is not. Every time I glance at the speedometer, it's *exactly* the same as the speed limit. Stu keeps taking the piss, saying things like, "My gran drives faster than this…and she's been dead for two years," and, "What's the point in that beast of an engine if you're going to drive like a woman?" The latter is swiftly followed by a "no offense, ladies" and what he thinks is a disarming grin. Stu's ability to be a complete tool never ceases to amaze me.

Bugs tells Stu to shut up on more than one occasion, and every furtive sideways glance at Sasha (of which there are many) makes it abundantly clear that *she's* the reason he's driving so carefully. Either he doesn't want to crash the car and risk damaging her beautiful face or he wants her to think he's mature and sensible and other things he most definitely is not.

The journey takes about an hour, which is a very long time to be trapped in a tiny car with anyone, let alone four people you can't stand. I mostly stay quiet and look out the window. If I try really hard, I can block them out and imagine I'm on my way to somewhere amazing. With someone amazing.

By the time we pull into the car park, it's starting to rain. The prospect of this little outing being ruined cheers me up a little. The others have this big debate about what we should do. Bugs and Sasha want to head to a cafe; Lucas and Stu want to go to the beach ("It's only a bit of rain, for fuck's sake. We're waterproof, aren't we?"). Sasha's worried about her hair, and if I'm being completely honest, I'm worried about mine too. I never used to be the kind of girl who worried about her hair.

Everyone clambers out of the car and that's when I make my move. It doesn't even take two seconds. Not enough time for anyone to wonder about later. It's almost too easy. It doesn't even feel like I'm doing something shifty. My level of guilt is precisely zero.

This is going to be good.

chapter twenty-seven

Lucas buys everyone hot chocolate and doughnuts in this cafe overlooking the beach. Sasha takes ages deciding whether or not to have a doughnut, and it's only when Stu makes a grab for the last one (having eaten his own in two monstrous bites) that she smacks his hand away and nibbles on it in the most dainty way possible. I eat mine like a normal person.

We sit around until the rain becomes drizzle, and sit around some more until the drizzle becomes nothing. Then we walk on the beach and the boys engage in one of their obligatory wrestling matches. Sasha and I ignore them and walk ahead. She's quieter than usual, which is disconcerting, because if she's the quiet one, then I have to think of something to say to fill the silence. And all I can come up with is, "I like the sea," which is too stupid for words.

We sit on the damp sand and Sasha uses her finger to draw a heart with JH and LM inside it. I scuff over it with my boot while she laughs. "You're hilarious. Truly." I can tell she thinks my sarcasm is cute, which makes me never want to be sarcastic ever again.

The boys arrive back at the car a few minutes after us, all ruddy-faced and sandy. Lucas leans over and ruffles his hair for ages, trying to get every last grain of sand out. Everyone agrees that we should head back home. There's some boxing match on

TV that the boys are going to watch at Stu's house. Watching two sweaty guys beating the shit out of each other is exactly the sort of entertainment I would expect them to enjoy.

I'm more talkative on the way back, mostly because I'm trying to disguise the fact that my foot is ever so slowly sliding something out from under the driver's seat. Little by little, it edges out until anyone looking down at my feet would see it. But of course no one is looking down at my feet.

I ask Bugs to drop me off in town, claiming I have to pick something up for Mom. I say my good-byes and slam the door and I swear Bugs winces. I take a few steps away from the car before turning around. Stu's watching me through the open window. I think he likes the way my butt looks in these jeans. For once I'm grateful for his utter sleaziness.

"I forgot my bag! Stu, would you mind…?"

He nods and reaches down to grab my bag. His brow furrows. His eyes widen.

He laughs. No, it's more like a guffaw.

"Well, well, well, what have we got here?! Bugs…something you want to tell us, mate?"

I open the car door. I'm the first one to say, "What's that?" This might not seem important, but it is.

Lucas makes a grab for the magazine in Stu's hand, while Stu reaches down and rummages under Bugs's seat. "Wait! There's more!" He pulls out two more magazines with a look on his face that can only be described as gleeful.

Sasha and Bugs are both leaning over their shoulders, trying to see what all the fuss is about. Stu treats them to a particularly graphic page—he has a lot to choose from. Sasha's hand flies to her mouth in a gesture that I was pretty sure no one actually did in real life. Turns out I was wrong. Bugs's eyes bug out. I laugh, because that's what I should do in this situation.

"What the fuck?! They're not mine!" And it sounds like he's lying, which is just brilliant.

Lucas joins in the fun. "Yeah, yeah, that's what they ALL say. That's exactly what you said when your mom found that weed in your bedroom, remember?" Bugs tries to grab the magazines from Stu, but Stu's ready for him. "Hands off! I'm learning a lot...this picture in particular is very...er...educational." The photo shows bodies in positions I didn't know bodies could get into. And lots and lots of penises.

Sasha's blushing almost as much as Bugs. I didn't have her marked down a prude, but maybe she's just embarrassed *for* him.

Bugs jumps out of the car and nudges me out of the way. His enormous bulk hides Stu and Lucas from view, but from the sounds of things there's a struggle going on. There's laughter, swearing, and a pleasing "ow!" from Stu. I'm transfixed by the sight of Bugs's butt crack peeking over the top of his jeans. A few ginger hairs are sprouting here and there.

Lucas and Stu spill out of the other side of the car and Bugs reverses out of this side, nearly flooring me in the process. A chase ensues, but Bugs has no chance. Lucas has one magazine, Stu has the other two—and they run in opposite directions. Bugs is huffing and puffing like an angry asthmatic bear and the other two are taunting him—waving the magazines in front of him.

Stu shouts, "Mate, you should have told me...It's nothing to be ashamed of." He bends over and looks between his legs. "You want a piece of this sweet, sweet ass? Come and get it, big boy!" Bugs almost gets him this time, but Stu dodges out of the way with expert ease.

"You fucking fuck! You put them there, didn't you? I'm going to kill you, you little bastard." He's focusing the chase on Stu now, the obvious candidate for planting the magazines. That's the price you have to pay for playing pathetic practical jokes all the time, I guess.

Sasha gets out of the car and this is when I have to be careful, because she may be many things, but stupid isn't one of them. "Poor Bugs," she says.

"I know. *So* embarrassing. I had no idea."

"No idea about what?"

"That he's, y'know…"

"Gay?! Bugs isn't gay! No way…no chance. Stu planted those magazines, I bet you anything."

"You think? That'd be kind of a low thing to do. I mean, that stuff looks pretty hardcore…literally." Sasha doesn't laugh at my lame attempt at humor.

"There's no way." She shakes her head and frowns. "No way."

"Are you sure? It'd be pretty tough for the big rugby star to admit…even to himself." I think I might have gone too far. I sound like a character in a "very special episode" of some crappy teen show—the one where the jock comes out of the closet. "You're probably right though. It *is* the kind of thing Stu would do, isn't it?"

Now she's looking thoughtful. That reversal of tactics was a wise move. "Yeah, maybe. You know, I always thought Bugs fancied me…but…"

"But what?" It's like reeling in a fish—a very small fish that's not even struggling.

She shakes her head because Stu is running toward us, with Bugs close on his heels. He dodges the car at the last minute and the two of them carry on up the street. "I don't know. Why would he keep them *there*, though? Pretty weird, don't you think?"

She has a point, but I counter with, "That's teenage boys for you," meaning they like to get their rocks off at any opportunity.

I don't push it any further. There's no need. The seed of doubt is there, planted deep inside her brain. She'll never be able to look at him in the same way, no matter what he does to convince her.

And with a bit of luck, this rumor will spread through the school and into the boys' locker room. Even if the boys on the rugby team don't believe it, they'll still take the piss out of him. Mercilessly. And that's good enough for me. He'll know what it's like to have people staring at you, whispering about you.

Kai would hate this. There's no doubt about that. He'd say something about me sinking down to their level. And he'd ask me if I thought this was *really* the right way to go about things. Knowing full well that if I really, truly thought about it, the answer would be no. But it's the only way I know. I've come too far to backtrack. And they deserve everything that's coming to them— let's not forget that.

⌒

The pointless chase around the town center ends eventually. Sasha's the peacemaker. She takes the magazines from Stu and Lucas and hands them back to Bugs. He puts his hands up as if the very act of touching them might make him a little bit gay. "No! I TOLD you! They're not mine. Chuck 'em in a garbage can or something. Stu, you are so gonna pay for this, man. It's not funny."

Stu's still grinning like this is the best thing that's ever happened. "OK, two things: first of all, it is *fucking* hilarious. And second of all, I had nothing to do with it. I wish I had! So either you're a closet homo with a serious addiction to wanking off—in the car though, dude? Really?—or someone else put them there. My money is totally on you being queer though—all those sweaty bodies in the changing rooms after rugby…how can you resist?" He dodges Bugs's attempt to hit him by hiding behind Sasha and using her as a shield.

Stu and Lucas are making the most of this, really enjoying themselves. But there's no way they believe it. They *know* Bugs isn't gay. I'd like to think that if they suspected there was even the tiniest chance he might be, they'd be slightly more sensitive to the situation. He *is* their mate, after all. Unlike Kai.

Sasha's different though. She's not so sure. And everyone else at school will be in the same boat as her. They don't know Bugs well enough—that's the beauty of it. And people love nothing more than gossip. It doesn't need to be true, just *possible*.

I make a show of looking at my watch and saying I'm going to be late for dinner if I don't hurry up. So I don't see how they leave things. All I know is that when I walk away (triumphant grin kept in check—for now), Bugs is angry as hell, embarrassed like he's never been embarrassed in his life, and trying desperately to convince Sasha that he has no idea how those magazines found their way into his car. Lucas and Stu are leafing through the magazines, pointing and laughing like eight-year-olds. And Sasha's standing there with her arms crossed, not sure what to say or do. Probably weighing up the possibility that the one boy she could rely on to worship the ground she walks on might in fact bat for the other team.

It's bloody brilliant.

⌒

The rumor *has* spread around school. To such an extent that no one seems to be talking about Jasmine James anymore. To such an extent that Stu and Lucas have stopped taking the piss out of Bugs. It's not so funny for them anymore.

Bugs seems to be going out of his way to prove his sexuality. Lewd comments at any opportunity. Most of his lewdness is aimed at Sasha; I don't think she'll be sitting on his knee or snuggling up to him anytime soon. His cluelessness is truly breathtaking.

People will forget about it in a couple of weeks, with the exams and everything. But it's enough just to see Bugs shuffling down the corridors looking unhappy. It doesn't matter that it won't last.

It's enough—for him, anyway. Bugs should count his lucky stars he clearly couldn't be considered the brains behind any kind of operation, let alone one as cruelly calculating as what they did to Kai.

One down, two go.

chapter twenty-eight

Something happened yesterday. Or rather, something didn't happen. I forgot to open Kai's letter. I wouldn't have thought that was possible. With the other letters, I was thinking about them days, even weeks before. Sometimes as soon as I'd opened one I'd be counting down the days to the next one. It took so much willpower not to open them early, just to hear his voice again.

But yesterday was the last day of term and it was madness. Bugs and Stu were determined to make it the best ever—"the stuff of legend" were the exact words Bugs used. I've always thought it's kind of stupid that the eleventh graders go crazy every year, running rampage through the school like they're engaged in some kind of prison riot. I think they forget that they're going to be coming back after the summer. That teacher you throw a water balloon at might well be teaching you in September, and everyone knows that teachers have longer memories than elephants.

But it's *tradition* at Allander Park. And even though we all despise that word when it's used about the tedious assemblies or the lame school song or the horrible brown ties we have to wear, suddenly we don't mind it at all. It's *tradition* for people to scrawl obscene messages on each other's shirts; it's *tradition* to steal the portrait of the headmaster from outside his office and replace it with something funnier than last year's class managed;

it's *tradition* to cause as much trouble as possible in whatever way you can think of. On the last day of term Allander doesn't so much resemble a zoo, as a zoo where someone's unlocked all the cages after pumping the animals full of caffeine and sugar. Hyper doesn't even begin to cover it.

Last year Kai and I hid out in the library at break and lunchtime. It seemed like the safest place to be. The rampaging eleventh graders usually left other students alone, but you could never be sure. At the end of lunchtime a bunch of boys stumbled in—soaking wet even though it wasn't raining outside—and asked loudly if they could borrow *The Joy of Sex*. The librarian was not amused. The leader of the gang leaned right over her desk and said, "Come on, we *know* you've got a copy stashed under there. Knowledge should be shared, you know? That's what Mr. Slater always says…"

Kai rolled his eyes at me and I shook my head. We thought we were terribly mature, looking down on these idiots even though we were a year younger. I never would have expected that this year I'd be in the thick of things. And I certainly never would have expected to enjoy it so much, but there was something infectious about the excitement. I even threw a water balloon. Kai would not be pleased.

I couldn't help wondering if the only reason I'd disapproved of the end-of-term shenanigans before was because I knew I wouldn't be allowed to get involved. The real fun was reserved for the popular or semipopular kids or even the kids who were just *there*. People like me (the *old* me) didn't get a look in—apart from the odd bit of shirt-signing. But somehow I found myself being given a piggyback by Bugs, acting like I ruled the school. Acting like one of them—and loving it.

Bugs was just glad to have a girl's legs wrapped around him, I think. He made a point of running round the entire building, making sure as many people as possible saw us. Hoping to lay those gay rumors to rest once and for all. We nearly floored Louise when we slammed through a set of doors. She told him to watch where he was fucking going and gave me the kind of look that would shrivel flowers in a Disney movie. I read a lot into that look of hers—more than the simple hatred that was probably intended. To me it seemed like she was saying, *Enjoy it while it lasts. It's only a matter of time before they realize you're not one of them.*

After school we headed to the park and lounged around talking about our summer plans. Nina's the only one who's doing anything remotely interesting—two months in New York with her dad. I wish *my* dad lived in New York…but I suppose that would mean my parents would have to be divorced and that would mostly be a bad thing. Still, I wouldn't say no to an apartment overlooking Central Park. It beats a couple weeks in Spain, which is the sum total of our summer holiday plans.

There was also the obligatory reminiscing about the day. You could tell the boys enjoyed talking about the things they'd gotten up to almost as much as they'd enjoyed doing them. Exaggerations were already starting to creep into the story of the day—especially from Stu: "Did you hear about me pelting Mr. Watt with eggs? Man, you should have seen his face!" (I was pretty sure no eggs had been involved.)

Lucas sat close to me, and when I said I wanted to go on the swings, he volunteered to push me. I ignored the meaningful look from Sasha as we left the others. It was fine hanging out with Lucas without the others. We didn't talk about anything much—I was too busy giggling like an idiot and he was too busy pushing me as high as he could, trying to show off how strong he was.

I came home to raised eyebrows from Mom and Dad when they saw the state of my shirt (and my tie, which I was wearing like a headband for some reason). They didn't say anything though—just asked if I'd had a nice time and seemed pleased when I said yes. I fell into bed after a late dinner, completely exhausted. My mind was buzzing from the day's activities but somehow I fell asleep quicker than I'd done in months.

I realized as soon as I woke up. I'd forgotten. How could I have forgotten?

⌒

I sit staring at the envelope for a few minutes. The date is wrong. I mean, the date is right. But it's yesterday's date. I feel like I've betrayed Kai. I know it doesn't matter when I open the letter—as long as I read it. And I know that Kai's not going to *know*. But *I* know, and that's enough to make me want to crawl back under the covers and cry.

I open the envelope, being extra careful not to tear the letter inside.

Jem,

If my calculations are correct (and you know how good I am at math), it should be the start of summer vacation right about now. I hope the exams weren't too traumatic. I bet you've done better than you expected. That's always the way with you.

If everything's gone to plan, you should be set up for a pretty good summer. If everything hasn't gone to plan (and I know how stubborn you can be), then you're in for a pretty standard sort of summer—only you won't have me around to stave off the boredom. ~~Sorry.~~

I keep wondering whether you're playing along with my silly challenges. I wouldn't like to bet on it, but I do hope you are. And I really, really hope you're having <u>FUN.</u> Even just a little bit? I wouldn't be surprised if you'd snagged yourself a boyfriend by now (can't quite imagine you going for someone at school though...unless you've been keeping secrets from me and you're secretly in love with Marc Fishman. Please don't be in love with Marc Fishman. That name is just too hideous to even contemplate. But if you DO happen to be in love with him, you're not allowed to get married until you're at least twenty-eight...and you absolutely MUST keep your name. Agreed? Good.)

And if it turns out that you don't have a boyfriend—<u>WHO CARES?!</u> It's not like you need some random boy to tell you how amazing you are, because hopefully you're starting to believe what this nonrandom boy has been telling you for years. <u>YOU ARE AMAZING.</u> So there. ~~Anyway, boys are more trouble than~~

191

I'll keep this brief.
It's summer.
Go outside. (It's nice out there, honest.
Fresh air is good for the soul.)

Enjoy the sunshine.
Have fun.
Simple.

Love you always, pickle,

Kai
x x x

P.S. I was going to suggest you get a bikini
and do a bit of sunbathing in the park
but I think I'll quit while I'm ahead. Count
yourself lucky.
P.P.S. Remember that summer we put the
paddling pool in your yard and pretended to be
marine biologists? That was brilliant.

THIS IS THE SUN.
← IT IS NOT YOUR
ENEMY.

chapter twenty-nine

A week into the summer holidays and I haven't done a bloody thing. Mom's been on my back to "get out and do something." As soon as she gets home from work she seems to have the uncanny ability to deduce that I've been on the sofa all day. Maybe it's the imprint my butt makes on the faux leather.

I miss him so much. It doesn't get any easier. No matter what they say, time doesn't heal the wound. Time just unravels and shows you new and more painful ways to miss someone. The longer they've been gone, the worse it is. You start to forget their smile or the way they tilted their head when they were confused or the way they looked at you and knew exactly what you were thinking. You can look at them in photos, but it's not even close to the real thing, and pretty soon you feel like your real memories are being replaced by the photo memories—like the only way you can picture them anymore is in one of those photographs. They become two-dimensional, and it rips your heart out whenever you think about it so you really try not to.

At least I've got the letters. That's more than most people get. But it won't be long before I run out. The stack is dwindling way too fast. Four more, then I'll be left with nothing—apart from the satisfaction of knowing I at least did *something* to get back at the people responsible for his death. It's not enough though. It's not nearly enough.

I've decided to focus my attentions on Lucas for the moment. If all goes to plan, I'll be having the sort of summer romance that would put Sandra Dee to shame.

He's making things easy for me. It's getting more and more obvious that he maybe kind of sort of *does* like me a little bit. He's been texting me (not that I'd ever admit that to Sasha). Nothing serious—just stuff like "Are you coming to Sasha's tonight?" and "Would it be wrong to kill my sister? :)" It's not exactly flirting, but Stu and Bugs have never texted me, so it's got to mean something.

After yet another exchange of innocuous messages, I decide it's time. I compose a message and amend it several times before the wording is just right: Want to hang out today? Just us two? ;)

The reply is almost instant: Finally. ;)

I smile to myself, not because I'm happy or excited, but because he's playing right into my hands. The thought of spending time with Lucas without the others around makes me nauseous, but it has to be done. It will be worth it in the end.

I meet Lucas in the park. He's slouching on a bench with his legs far apart, casually twirling a Frisbee on his finger like one of those plate-spinning idiots you see on TV. He's wearing jeans and a black-and-red checked shirt with the sleeves rolled halfway up his biceps. Ray-Bans and a pair of flip-flops (Havaianas, of course) complete the look.

He sits up straighter when he sees me coming. He smiles that ultraconfident smile that has every girl hooked and he calls, "Catch!" as he launches the Frisbee. I have a moment of panic when I'm certain it's headed straight for my face, but somehow I manage to catch it cleanly—which I've done maybe one other time in my whole life. I try to disguise how surprised I am at making the catch while Lucas claps and whoops like I'm a particularly skilled performing seal.

I sit down next to him and hand over the Frisbee.

"Impressive! I didn't have you down as a world champion Frisbee player."

I shrug. "What can I say? I've got some mad skills."

"Clearly! I hesitate to ask if you fancy a game…I fear my fragile ego might be in for a battering…"

"Don't worry, I'll go easy on you." I nudge his arm with my elbow and he looks delighted. Meanwhile I'm thinking, *I bet Sasha was some kind of Frisbee fiend. You, on the other hand, are about to make a complete fool of yourself, Jemima.*

But I don't. Somehow I don't. I have to concentrate really, really hard, but somehow I manage. I think God must have temporarily granted me an ability to catch and throw that has been lacking my whole life—much to the disappointment of Noah, who's always trying to get me to throw a rugby ball with him in the backyard. If Noah could see me now, he'd be the proudest brother in the world.

Lucas throws and catches the Frisbee the same way he seems to do everything else in life—with ease. As if he was born knowing how to do everything. It makes me want to hit him, so I do the next best thing, which is aim for his perfect face. But he ducks out of the way and manages to catch the disk with an easy swoop of his left hand (even though he's right-handed). "Whoa there! Are you trying to kill me?"

I grimace. "Sorry!"

"Maybe we'd better quit while we're ahead—or before I get maimed for life!" He jogs toward me.

"Good idea. I wouldn't want to break your sunglasses…they look pretty expensive."

He pulls them up, rests them on top of his head, and then looks over his shoulder. "Don't tell anyone, but these are fakes. My sister got them for me on her gap year."

I like it better now that I can see his eyes. Talking to someone with sunglasses makes me nervous—you can never tell where they're looking. "Nothing wrong with that. I'd be more worried if you'd spent a hundred quid on a pair, to be honest."

Lucas laughs loudly. "Somehow that doesn't surprise me! You're like the opposite of Sasha or something."

I look away and then back at him, fixing him in my gaze. "Is that a good thing?" My voice is lower and quieter.

"That's *definitely* a good thing." He bites his lip and I don't know what's going to happen next. I'd find the lip-biting thing pretty damn adorable if I actually liked him. But there's a calculated cuteness about it that I can see right through. It's a move he's used before to great effect, probably to get a girl focusing on his mouth, wondering what it would be like to kiss him. I'm wondering too, because I know it's going to happen. It's only a matter of time before it happens.

Lucas takes a step closer to me and he's definitely invading my personal space now. I have to fight the instinct to take a step back. I stand my ground and look up at him. It's getting awkward—neither of us has said a word for a few seconds. I do not know Lucas well enough to be sharing comfortable silences with him. It's a deeply, deeply uncomfortable silence—for me at least. He seems to be enjoying himself.

He leans down and I'm sure this is it. I am going to kiss Lucas Mahoney right here in this park in broad daylight. There are heaps of people around and they're going to see us kissing. Some of them might think it's sweet; some of them might think we should get a room; most of them probably couldn't care less. But whether they realize it or not, they're all about to witness something impossible happening.

I tilt my head back a little, so that he knows I'm OK with the idea of him kissing me. He leans even closer and I'm just about to close my eyes in anticipation when something entirely unexpected happens. I feel something on my head—a flat and plastic something.

Lucas has not kissed me. He's balanced the bloody Frisbee on my head!

I don't move, so the Frisbee stays in place. "Er…what are you doing?"

He smiles. "Frisbees are the height of fashion this summer, don't you know? And this one really suits you. Wait, let me take a picture on my phone." As he fumbles in his pocket, I whip the Frisbee off my head and whack him on the chest with it.

"You're an idiot." He laughs and cowers under the onslaught of Frisbee blows. I can't help laughing, mostly to cover my embarrassment for thinking he was going to kiss me.

And then he grabs me. And kisses me.

I drop the Frisbee on the ground and I am kissing Lucas Mahoney. My lips are touching his and his hand is pressed flat against my back and I don't know whether to gag or push him away or just go with it. It repulses me, the thought of doing this. But the *actual* doing this, the actual kissing, is sort of OK. Conflicted doesn't even begin to describe the way I'm feeling.

The kiss lasts maybe five seconds before he steps back and looks at me like he's just done a very bad thing. "I'm sorry."

I wonder if this is part of his usual routine, pretending to feel bad about kissing you. It would be very endearing if you liked that sort of thing. "Why sorry?"

He shrugs. "I wasn't sure if you wanted to…" He seems embarrassed—he's not used to having to explain himself.

I smile with a confidence I definitely do not possess. "Don't worry about it. If I hadn't been OK with it, you would have known about it. Trust me." Who is this person who looks like me and thinks like me and speaks with my voice but says ridiculous things like this?

The easy smile is back on his face and it's dangerously close to a smirk. He likes this false me. She's feisty. "You're different, you know that?" He steps in close again.

"Different? Is that supposed to be a compliment? You're going to have to try harder than that, especially if you want to…" I lean up and kiss him swiftly. I can't get over how easy this is, this game of make-believe.

"It *is* a compliment. You're more…I dunno…than I thought you'd be."

"Wow. Eloquent." We're standing so very close, our faces inches apart.

"Hey! Are you making fun of me?" He looks like he's very much OK with me making fun of him—as long as there's going to be more kissing.

"Yes, I think I am."

I steel myself and kiss him again to soften the blow.

⌒

Later I'm lying on my bed, thinking about the kissing. I can't stop grinning; it was so easy. So basic and simple and uncomplicated. It's amazing to me that I can say something and know exactly how he's going to react, despite the fact that my previous experience with boys is practically nonexistent.

Has this version of me been lurking there all the time, somewhere deep below the surface, biding its time, waiting for its chance to make an appearance? Or do I just have some random talent for acting that I never knew existed? Should I have been auditioning for school plays all these years instead of taking the piss out of those ultraconfident drama kids?

There's some part of me—a stupid, hippy-dippy spiritual part—that wonders if somehow Kai has something to do with this. Like he might be guiding me from beyond the grave. Stupid, I know, but the idea is sort of comforting.

Lucas and I kissed for a long time, only stopping when a tiny yappy dog skipped over and got itself and its long leash tangled around our legs. Lucas laughed and bent down to disentangle the dog, which then proceeded to try and mount his leg.

"Someone's popular today!"

"What can I say? I'm irresistible to women, dogs, pretty much any species you can think of. I think they call it 'animal magnetism.'" This is exactly the kind of thing I'd expect a boy like Lucas to say, but there's a mocking glint in his eye and I can't quite tell if he's mocking me or himself.

"You're an idiot."

He treated me to another devastating smile. "A cute idiot though, right?"

I shrugged and walked away. Sure enough, he followed like a little puppy.

We got ice creams (which Lucas paid for) from the cafe in the middle of the park. Lucas held out his cone and said, "Fancy a lick?" while wiggling his eyebrows suggestively.

"Maybe later," I said just as suggestively. Normal shy and retiring Jem was screaming, YOU DO REALIZE YOU'RE TALKING ABOUT GIVING HIM A BLOW JOB, DON'T YOU? And this new version of Jem was shrugging, not even a little bit bothered (because that is never ever going to happen). I have to draw the line somewhere, and right now I choose to draw it at exactly the level of Lucas's belt.

chapter thirty

"Lucas told me." Sasha's tone is casual in a very noncasual sort of way.

My hand stops flicking through the hangers. "Lucas told you what?"

Sasha grabs the hanger out of my hand. "Perfect! You found my size." She holds it up against herself and tilts her head. "What do you think? The ultimate outfit?"

I nod. It's definitely the perfect outfit—slinky and sexy and black. "Sasha, what did Lucas tell you?"

"Nice try, Jem, but there's no point playing dumb with me. It's OK, you know. I *told* you it's OK. He really likes you—there's no way he'd have told me unless he really liked you. I guess he was looking for my blessing or something, or at least making sure I wouldn't kill him…or you."

"I…I don't know what to say." There are some things in life that are beyond imagination. Going shopping for clothes with Sasha Evans and talking to her about kissing her ex-boyfriend is pretty high up on my list of whatthefuckery.

Sasha smiles and flounces past me to flick through a rack of even slinkier clothes. "You don't have to say anything. I get that it must be a bit awkward for you, but if I'm not being weird about it, then I refuse to let you be weird about it. So let's make a deal. No weirdness, OK?"

"No weirdness. But—"

She holds her index finger up to her perfectly pouty lips. "Hush! I said NO WEIRDNESS."

So I can't ask her why she's being so ridiculously reasonable about this and why it doesn't seem to bother her one little bit that I had my tongue in her ex-boyfriend's mouth. I thought it was like the first rule of friendship or something—you stay away from friends' boyfriends and ex-boyfriends and even boys they used to have a vague crush on. Clearly I have a lot to learn about friendship. Or perhaps Sasha's the exception that proves the rule.

She throws a hanger at me and I fail to catch it. I must have used up my quota of catches playing Frisbee with Lucas. "You should try that on. He'll like it."

Now this is crossing the line into major oddness.

She wants me to try on a top because *Lucas* will like it. Not because she likes it or because I would like it. Don't get me wrong— I'm *glad* she hasn't flipped her lid about the Lucas situation. If she did have a problem with it, Lucas might want to cool things, and how the fuck would I be able to hurt him then?

I'm really glad *he* was the one to tell her, because I would have had no idea what to say. I'll admit, I was maybe slightly looking forward to seeing her reaction, just for the surrealness of it. I'd even gone so far as to picture it in my head—the drama, the tears, maybe a slap thrown in for good measure.

We head into the changing rooms to try stuff on, and miraculously we're the only ones in there. I try on the top Sasha picked out and inspect myself in the mirror from every possible angle. I don't know whether Lucas will like it, but I definitely do. It fits well but it's not too tight. Green's not a color I would normally wear. There's something fresh and cheerful about it. It's a summery sort of top; I usually go out of my way to avoid anything remotely summery. Summer is my least favorite season by some distance. Give me autumn or winter any day. You'll never find me complaining about a cold rainy day—it gives me the perfect excuse to stay in and watch TV. Kai always loved summer. He was a sunny sort of person. No one would ever accuse me of being summery—even *with* the blonde hair.

I think Kai would approve of this top. I care more about that than I do about what Lucas thinks.

"Are you ready for this?" Sasha knocks on the door. I step out of the cubicle and pretty much the only thing I can focus on is Sasha's cleavage. Her breasts are just *there*, like they've been laid out on a silver platter.

"Wow."

"Too much? What does this top say to *you*?" She sashays toward the huge mirror at the end of the changing rooms.

"It says…'Hello, boys! Come get me.'" As soon as I've said it I wonder if I've gone too far—after all, I don't exactly know Sasha that well, no matter how much she's started to act like my BFF.

"Ha! That's precisely what I want it to say!" She pushes up her breasts and I'm pretty sure they're about to spill out. She turns and looks me up and down, head nodding approvingly. "Nice. It's his favorite color, you know."

Suddenly I feel deeply uncomfortable. "I didn't know that. Um…I'm not going to buy it. I'm broke."

She grabs my upper arms in a vicelike grip. "You *have* to buy it! You have to you have to you have to! Go on, treat yourself."

I wriggle out of her grip. "Sasha! I'm broke!"

Sasha sighs. "Let me buy it for you then."

I didn't think I could feel any more uncomfortable. I was wrong. "I can't let you do that. It's really…nice of you and everything, but…"

"Nonsense. I'm buying it. That's what friends are for, right? You'd do the same for me if you had some extra cash." She couldn't be more wrong. If I had extra cash, it would be going straight into my savings account.

She's clearly not going to give up—if the expression on her face is anything to go by. For some bizarre reason she really, really wants to buy me this top that she's so convinced Lucas will like. I'm not sure if she's doing this for me or for him. "OK, you can buy it. But on one condition: I'm paying you back as soon as I've got the cash."

"Yeah, yeah, whatever," she says with a glint in her eye. She thinks I'm going to forget, but I won't. I always pay my debts. Always. It used to drive Kai crazy that I kept a mental tally of things like that—if he bought me a can of Coke one week I'd make damn sure to buy one for him the week after. I don't know why it makes me so antsy, accepting gifts from people. I've never had a problem accepting things from Mom and Dad, but that's different, isn't it? They're supposed to spend money on you—it's practically their main purpose in life. I just don't like being treated like a charity case, that's all.

~

By lunchtime Sasha has accumulated five bags of clothes and shoes. Three pairs of shoes! That was the arduous bit—trying to maintain enthusiasm as she tried on pair after pair, mulling over the pros and cons as if this was something that actually mattered. Sasha doesn't seem to notice my impatience, because all that's required of me is to agree with her. There's a lot of nodding involved.

We get sandwiches from Marks & Spencer and sit on a bench. Something tells me this isn't Sasha's usual mid-shopping lunch. She strikes me more like the type to get sushi from that posh Japanese place that opened last year. I appreciate what is almost certainly a concession to my poverty (even though I'm not *actually* broke). There's more to this girl than meets the eye. Sometimes (like right now) I find myself wondering whether I actually *like* her. But then I think about Kai and I know it's not possible. She is not, and never will be, my friend.

I'm eating the last bite of my sandwich when she says,

"He's good at the kissing, isn't he?"

I chew my mouthful way more times than is strictly necessary because I have no idea how to respond to this. She laughs and says, "Are you ever going to swallow that?"

I swallow with some difficulty. "It's good for the digestion… um…lots of chewing."

"You're hilarious, you know that? Anyway, feel free to thank me for his kissing skills. He learned everything he knows from me…and I mean *everything*." She nudges me with her elbow and I narrowly avoid spilling water all down myself.

"You mean he was…before you two…?"

"Virgin? Yup. The biggest, greenest, scaredest virgin on the planet, bless him."

This news doesn't just come as a surprise. It's almost enough to knock me off the bench. Lucas Mahoney, the school stud. I was sure he was one of those boys who'd been having sex since he was about thirteen. And I don't think I'm the only person in school who thought/thinks this way. He exudes sexual experience like some kind of pungent aftershave. Mind you, maybe he and Sasha had *a lot* of practice.

Sasha's watching me and I don't know where to look. "It's OK to talk about stuff like this, you know. There's nothing to be embarrassed about." I can't tell if she's being kind or patronizing—or kind of patronizing.

"I know…it's just…I'm not sure Lucas would like it."

"Who cares whether Lucas would like it or not?! It's girl talk and therefore strictly classified. What's said on the bench stays on the bench…or something. So, how long are you going to make him wait?"

I would like nothing more than to teleport myself away from this bench. I wouldn't mind where—pretty much anywhere would be preferable to this. "Um…we're not even going out or anything. I don't…"

The dismissive sound she makes is something like *Pssscccchhh*. "Since when have you needed to be going out with a guy to do the nasty? I don't mean you as in YOU; I mean you as in ONE—like the Queen. Although she probably didn't put out till she was married. Ewwww, now I'm grossing *myself* out. Anyway, where was I? Oh yes, you have to promise you'll tell me when you've had sex with Lucas."

This has gone far enough. "No! And I'm not going to have sex with him! Not in the foreseeable future anyway." I grab the M&S bag and start clearing the remnants of lunch just to give me something to do to hide my extreme awkwardness.

"We'll see about that." Her knowing smile makes me want to ram a straw up her nose.

"Can we talk about something else, please? *Anything* else?"

"Whatever you say. As long as you know that if you need some-one to talk to about that sort of thing, you can talk to me…Look, I know it must be hard for you. Anyone could see how close you and Kai were. I don't know if you two ever talked about this kind of thing, but just in case you did…I'm here. I mean, I'm obviously no substitute for him, but I'll try my best."

I can't believe she said his name. Usually people go out of their way not to say it. No one should be allowed to say his name without my permission. And the idea that she could ever be anything close to a substitute for him is laughable. AND WHY THE HELL IS SHE BEING SO NICE TO ME?! If she keeps on like this, there's a danger I might actually start feeling guilty about using her. "Thank you. I'm…I guess I'm sort of private about that kind of stuff." As if there'd been any of "that kind of stuff" to be private about!

"That's cool. I'll do my best to rein in my curiosity, I promise…I'll say one last thing on the matter and then we can talk about a subject of your choosing: you should definitely have sex with Lucas. Trust me, you won't regret it."

This time I sideswiped her with the bag of garbage.

"Are you finished now? In that case, we're going to talk about something really, really boring. Like the weather. Yes, let's talk about the weather. Hasn't it been lovely this last week? I don't like the look of those clouds though, do you?"

chapter thirty-one

Lucas texts me later: Gd shopping with S? Buy anything nice? Talk about me much? ;)

I reply: Gd, thanks. Got a top and didn't talk about you AT ALL.

He texts back at warp speed: Liar! ;)

Lucas Mahoney is grand master of the winky face. I choose not to reply, since I don't appreciate being accused of lying even when (especially when?) I actually am.

He texts again ten minutes later: Fancy seeing a movie later? I knew he'd text again. It's as if I've had some kind of How Lucas Works manual implanted into my brain.

I wait fifteen minutes before replying this time. I'm starting to enjoy myself: Bit busy but movie sounds good.

Not sure he'll necessarily believe the bit about me being busy, but how's he to know I spend most waking minutes either in front of the TV or listening to music in my room?

We arrange to meet outside the cinema at eight. The movie sounds terrible—something to do with fast cars. Yawn.

I stand in front of my wardrobe trying to decide what to wear. It's a sea of black and gray and very dark purple, apart from a little splash of brightness on the right-hand side where my most recent clothes purchases reside. And then there's the bag I chucked carelessly on the floor as soon as I got in. The bag with the green top in it. The green top that Lucas would "love."

I heave a great big sigh even though there's no one to hear me. I'm going to have to wear it, aren't I?

⌒

Mom can barely disguise her glee when she sees me coming down the stairs. I've finally turned into the daughter she always wanted. A daughter she can be proud of. She can finally compete with those wine-swilling book-club harpies when they brag about their daughters. It's always the daughters they brag about; none of the sons appears to have ever done anything particularly bragworthy. Or perhaps it's just that Mom only tells me about the daughters. Either she doesn't realize that I couldn't care less about the achievements of these girls I've never met, or she knows full well and tells me anyway. Maybe hoping to inspire me to reach such dizzy heights as Getting a Boyfriend and Having a Hollywood-themed Birthday Party.

At least Mom manages to keep her mouth shut though. Dad's the one who says, "And where are you off to, looking all fancy?"

Mom nudges him in the chest with her foot, which is easy enough to do, since she's lying on the sofa with her feet in his lap. She knows me too well. She can sense that the slightest thing will make me run back upstairs to change my clothes.

I try a breezy, nonchalant look on for size, knowing that the next words out of my mouth will floor them.

"I've got a date." I struggle to maintain eye contact with Dad, but it's worth it because I get to witness his eyes widening as far as they can go.

"A date? With a *boy*?"

"Yes, Dad. A date with a boy."

"Well. That's just…um…Cath?" He looks at Mom and she rolls her eyes.

"That's just wonderful, Jem." She's doing a fair job of hiding her excitement at this revelation, I'll give her that. She grabs the remote control and mutes the TV. "Who's the lucky boy…if you don't mind me asking?"

"His name's Lucas. You don't know him."

"Lucas? Nice name, isn't it? Very…manly."

My mother has lost the plot. I have to get out of here pronto, even if it means diving through the double-glazed (closed) window.

"And when will we get to meet this Lucas character?" says Dad. "I'm not sure I like the idea of you going out on the town with some strange boy we've never even met."

"Greg!" Mom gives him another kick, less gentle this time. "We're not living in the Stone Age. I'm sure Jem will introduce us to her boyfriend when she's good and ready."

"Moooooooom! He's not my boyfriend. Can we just…not do this? I'm gonna be late. I'll see you guys later, OK?" I'm backing out of the living room, desperate to escape.

The last thing I hear before I slam the door is Dad shouting, "No funny business, OK?" and Mom admonishing him with an extra-stern "GREG!"

Well, that was almost exactly as awkward as I would have expected. I have no earthly idea why I told them about Lucas. I could have said ANYTHING. Anything in the world and they'd have believed me. But no. I went for the truth.

I kick myself all the way down the street and halfway to the cinema, reliving every cringeworthy moment of the conversation. And then I realize something. I *wanted* them to know. I wanted to see how they'd react. To see what it would be like for them to have a normal daughter who did normal things, instead of a freakish daughter obsessed with her dead best friend.

It was a mistake though. I shouldn't give them false hope. It'll only make it that much harder for them when this version of me ceases to exist. When any version of me ceases to exist.

Only four months to go.

There are loads of people milling around the cinema entrance. Lucas is sitting on the front steps, leaning back on his elbows, catching some rays. His perfect face is bathed in sunlight. He looks like the sun should be worshipping him rather than the other way around. A bunch of twelve-year-old girls sit a few feet away, staring and giggling and nudging each other. I bet he gets that all the time. He probably doesn't even notice anymore—he's so used to people looking at him wherever he goes.

I stand right over him, blocking out the sun. Putting him in the shade. I like the way it feels, standing over him like this.

He sits up and smiles. "Hey, you. You look really nice. Is that new?"

I shrug and look down at my top. "Nah, just something I found lurking in the back of the wardrobe." I sit down next to him on the steps. Not too close.

He smiles again and I can tell he *knows*. I bought it for his benefit and he *knows*. Arrogant bastard. "Don't I get a hello kiss?"

Another shrug from me. "Hmm…unsure. I think you have to work a little harder to earn a kiss." The twelve-year-olds are watching us. I'd usually feel uncomfortable under this kind of scrutiny, but today I don't care. I'm pretty sure they think Lucas is out of my league, but I couldn't be less bothered. There's only one person I need to fool tonight, and from the way he's looking at me, it's not going to be too hard.

Or so I thought. "Oi! Mahoney! Think fast." A scrunched-up Coke can hits Lucas on the chest. Lucas leaps up and launches himself at his assailant, rugby-tackling him round the waist and lifting him off the ground. Stu. And lurking behind him, looking brainless, Nina.

Nina sidles over and sits next to me and we watch the boys

grapple with each other in a way that can only be described as homoerotic.

I have to make an effort to talk to her. She is one of Them after all, even if she is a peripheral bit of fluff. "I thought you'd be in New York by now."

She twirls her hair around her finger and I can't tell if it's a nervous tick or if she just really likes how it feels. "I'm off on Saturday."

"Oh." This is going to be hard work. "So…are you and Stu…?"

"Are me and Stu what?" Either she's playing games or she really is as stupid as she looks.

"Um…y'know…a couple?"

She stops staring at the boys for a second and there's a spark of *something* in her eyes. "Yeah, I suppose we are. I mean, it's not, like, official or anything. We don't need to put, you know, labels on it. We both know where we stand, and yeah, it's good." She nods emphatically, like she's trying to convince herself.

"Cool." I turn my attention back to the boys, who are now chasing each other around the art installation in the middle of the square—the one the local paper ran a big feature on last year. "IS THIS ART?" was the headline. Stu certainly seems to like it—he's currently trying to hump it.

Lucas is laughing this loud, booming laugh, but then he looks over at me and he stops straightaway and jogs over. That was a mistake—letting my true face show, even for a second. I need to be more careful.

"Sorry about that," is accompanied by a bashful little boy face.

I give him what I hope is an indulgent smile and say nothing.

Stu stops humping when he gets a stern look from this tiny old lady in a lilac hat. He meanders over, walking with this strange rolling sort of gait—half gangsta, half I've-just-filled-my-diaper. He slumps down next to Nina and slings an arm over her shoulders. "So, what are you guys doing here?"

I refrain from saying, *What the fuck do you think we could possibly be doing, sitting right outside the cinema?*

To cut a not very long story even shorter, Stu and Nina decide to join us. It turns out Nina really likes action films and car crashes and explosions and that sort of thing. Odd.

Lucas goes off to buy the tickets—his treat. I think this gesture is supposed to impress me, like he deserves a fucking medal for spending Mommy's money. He does get a gentle punch on the shoulder and a "nice one, mate" from Stu, so I guess that'll have to do.

Nina heads off to the bathroom, and somehow me and Stu are left with the crucial task of choosing pick 'n' mix. I head straight for the fizzy cola bottles while he goes for the licorice allsorts, which tells you everything you need to know about what kind of person he is.

He carefully counts ten candies into his bag, while I shovel a whole scoop of cola bottles into mine. I stand back and consider my next choice. It's a serious business, pick 'n' mix. One bad choice can ruin the whole bag. Those big gummy strawberries might be my next victim. Suddenly I'm aware of him. He's just standing there, watching me. It's weird. I pretend to ignore him, but the truth is he's standing way too close to ignore. "I didn't realize you and Lucas were…" His voice is low and somehow conspiratorial.

I don't know what to say to this, so I shrug.

"I mean, you are…this is a date, right?"

"I guess so."

"That's…good. I mean, it's cool. I mean, um…Lucas is a good guy." This is not the Stu I know and hate. This is new, improved Stu—with added mumbles.

I look over my shoulder, praying that Lucas will rescue me from this. I'd even settle for Nina. *That's* how awkward this is.

Neither of them are anywhere to be seen. I'm going to have to say something, dammit.

"Yeah, he seems nice." That's the best I can do? YEAH, HE SEEMS NICE? Nina would be proud of such extreme levels of vapidity.

Stu leans in even closer and I lean away, masking the action by reaching for another scoop of sweets.

"Does he know? About…what you told me?"

I should have known this would come back to bite me on the ass. "No. And I'd like to keep it that way, OK?"

He nods and runs his hand over his fuzzy head.

"Of course. I would never say anything. You can trust me, you know that? I know we got off to a bad start and everything, but I…er…didn't know…about…yeah." The idea that Stu thinks I would ever trust him is almost enough to make me laugh, but laughing would ruin everything. I've got him right where I want him—firmly on my side—and if I have to pretend he's my confidant or whatever, then that's what I'll do. For now.

chapter thirty-two

Kai and I always used to sit three rows from the front. I try not to look at our usual seats as Lucas leads us up the stairs toward the back.

Somehow I end up sitting between Lucas and Stu. It doesn't bother me at first, but as the movie goes on (and on and on) I start to feel as if I'm in one of those films where the hero is trapped in a room and the walls start closing in from both sides. Suddenly I feel out of my depth, trapped between these boys who are bigger and stronger than me. These boys who could do anything to me and I would be powerless to stop them. I don't know where this train of thought comes from, but once it starts, it's impossible to stop. I make myself as small as I possibly can in my seat, pulling my elbows in tight. Luckily Lucas got us tickets in the posh seats, so it's actually possible for me to avoid touching either of them. It's not that I think they are going to *do* anything. Not here.

About halfway through the movie, when yet another car has somersaulted through the air and burst into flames, Lucas leans over to me. I have to lean toward him so that he can whisper in my ear. His breath is warm and tickles my ear as he speaks. "Are you OK?"

I nod and turn my attention back to the movie, like I can't bear to tear my eyes away for one second in case I miss someone getting shot.

"Are you sure?"

I need to do something. I can't sit here on the verge of a panic attack. I have two options: get out of here and never look back. Forget about this stupid plan and go back to being Normal Jem who would never ever find herself sandwiched between two boys in the posh seats of the cinema. Or I need to forget about being scared, forget how intimidating and strong these boys are, and start doing the things they'd expect of New Jem. The things they'd expect of any girl, really.

I nod again, but this time I lean in very close, so our mouths are almost touching. "This movie is terrible." He nods but he's not thinking about the movie anymore. He's not thinking about anything except kissing me. Just as he goes in for the kill, I lean back. He's grinning now; this is some kind of game to him.

I lean in again and he does the same. This time I bite his bottom lip ever so gently before pulling away. I try my best to ignore the fact that Stu is sitting so close. I try not to think about him watching. Hopefully he's too into the film or busy trying to get his hands down Nina's pants to notice what Lucas and I are up to.

I let him kiss me. And somehow I feel much calmer when we're kissing. Like it's OK and not scary because I made it happen. I am in control of this.

After a while Lucas's hands start to wander. I knew they would. I resist the urge to grab his filthy hand and snap every one of his fingers. I have to be OK with this. I have to pretend to want this. My breath catches in my throat and a soft sound escapes from me. It's the sort of noise you'd make if you were enjoying yourself—if you liked how you were being touched.

The sound is a lie.

⁓

The four of us go for milkshakes after the movie. Stu decides to try and down three milkshakes in five minutes if Lucas will pay for them. Nobody dared him to do something this stupid—he came up with the idea all by himself. I wonder if he has a notebook at home to record all his ideas of Stupid Things I Can Do Involving Food and Drink. Or maybe he just comes up with them on the spot. Perhaps it's a gift.

We chant, "Down it, down it" and thump our hands on the Formica table, much to the annoyance of every other customer. None of them asks us to pipe down though—not even the lady with the helmet hair who's glaring at us every time I look over. I give her a little wave accompanied by a sugar-sweet smile and she looks away in disgust, muttering something to her husband/boyfriend, whose hair is equally disastrous. I would never have done something like this a few months ago. Strangers were to be ignored, or feared, or whispered about. They were not to be confronted or taunted or laughed at—at least not openly.

I turn my attention back to Stu—two milkshakes down and going strong. I try not to think about helmet-hair woman. I try not to think about the possibility that maybe she's had a really crap day at work or maybe her dog's just died or maybe she's just really not in the mood to put up with a bunch of noisy, irritating teenagers. I try not to think about the possibility that maybe this is her first night out in ages because she's been so busy looking after the kids. Maybe she was really looking forward to a burger and onion rings and a night of peace and quiet. I try not to think about her. People like me do not think about people like her. We don't even give them a second thought. Why would we?

Stu completes the challenge and Lucas slaps him on the back—hard. I think he's trying to make him spew. Stu's looking massively proud of himself and only a little nauseous. "Come on, mate, cough up!" He holds out his hand and Lucas hands over a tenner. I'm starting to think that Lucas really does have a never-ending supply of cash. I wonder what that must be like.

Nina seems impressed by Stu's antics. Milkshake downing must be high up on her list of desirable qualities in a boy. They start kissing and it looks like she's using her tongue to try and get every last drop of milkshakey goodness from Stu's mouth. It's about as revolting as you'd expect.

I excuse myself to go to the bathroom, ignoring the unimpressed look on Lucas's face. He doesn't want to witness this display of grossness any more than I do. He needn't worry though, because Nina disengages herself from Stu's mouth, grabs her bag, and scoots out of the booth too. Fantastic. Just what I need. Girl talk with Miss Vapid.

Nina heads straight for one of the two stalls in the bathroom, but I hesitate because a) I don't really need the bathroom anyway, and b) there's no way I could pee with her in the next stall. Nina's totally cool with it though. She starts talking, but I find it really hard to concentrate while I can hear her peeing. I study myself in the mirror instead; you can tell I've been kissing.

Nina's still going on and on about Stu as she washes her hands. I'm not sure how much more of this I can take. Maybe it's time to have a little fun—lay some groundwork for getting back at Stu. "I think it's really great that he's making such an effort, you know."

Nina's expression is even more confused than usual.

"Well, it can't be easy for him, can it? He's not exactly a 'one-woman man,' is he?" I even do that annoying air quotes thing with my fingers, which I have never, ever done before.

She shrugs and says, "That was before," with a tiny yet unmistakable pout.

"Oh yeah, I know. He really likes you. I mean, he didn't even flirt with that girl at the cinema."

It's a real struggle not to laugh at Nina's face in the mirror. "Which girl?"

"The one at the pick 'n' mix counter. She was after him for sure. I kind of got the feeling that he'd…that they'd…Sometimes you can just tell, can't you? But it's so great that you can trust him."

Nina looks thoughtful as she applies sticky pink gloss to her lips and smacks them together a couple of times before saying, "I *do* trust him." The emphasis there betrays her true feelings.

I put my hand on her arm and give it a squeeze. "I think that's great." Add a patronizing nod into the mix and that's all it takes for the seeds of doubt to turn into full-blown paranoia.

"Was she pretty?"

I run my fingers through my hair and pretend to think. "I dunno…I *guess* so. She looked a bit like you, now you mention it. Maybe a bit curvier?"

That went down about as well as expected. "I'm going to ask him about her."

"Okaaaaaay. If you really think that's a good idea…"

"Why wouldn't it be?" It's too much for Nina to get her head around, all this thinking. Her poor brain just isn't used to it.

I roll my eyes as if the answer couldn't be more obvious. "He'll think you don't trust him, won't he? And he'll be so hurt and pissed off, he'll probably head straight around to whatsherface's house for a rummage in her pick 'n' mix." I stop to let that sink in.

"You're right. I guess I'll just have to keep an eye on him, won't I? Just in case?" She's looking at me like I'm some kind of relationship guru. It's hilarious.

I nod with all the (fake) sincerity I can muster. "That sounds like a good idea…We'd better get back—the boys will be wondering where we are!"

Now it's Nina's turn to put her hand on my arm.

"Thanks for telling me, Jem. You're a good friend." She hugs me and I watch myself grin in the mirror.

⌒

Lucas offers to walk me home and I say no. I can't stand the idea that I'm a defenseless female in need of a chaperone. We go back and forth for a few minutes—him insisting and me refusing. He's obviously used to getting his own way. It's getting tiresome, so I relent and agree to him walking me halfway. At least that means he's not going too far out of his way. Not that I *care* about him going out of his way—it's the principle of the thing. He thinks I need looking after, protecting. It's patronizing in the extreme. (Of course, there's always the possibility that he's just being nice. But I can't allow myself to think things like that.)

He takes my hand and we meander through the streets. It's a nice evening to be strolling hand in hand with a boy. It's just a shame it has to be this particular boy. I wish with all my heart I could be doing this with *my* boy. Kai.

I let him walk me more than halfway—more like two thirds. It's not that I'm enjoying his company or anything; we've some-how ended up in the middle of a heated debate about movies. I maintain that *Halloween* is the greatest horror movie ever made. Lucas is foolish enough to disagree with me. I stop in the middle of the pavement and reel off ten reasons why he couldn't be more wrong.

He holds up his hands and laughs. "OK, OK, I give up! You win! I can't compete with such in-depth—and frankly scary—knowledge." He gives me a sly look. "And if I'm being one hundred percent honest…I've only seen the remake."

"Whaaaaat? Why the hell were you arguing with me if you haven't even seen it?!"

"That wasn't arguing—that was *discussing*. There's a differ-ence. Arguing is stressful; discussing is fun. Plus it's kind of funny watching you get all wound up about it."

I narrow my eyes and plant my hands on his chest. His T-shirt is so thin that I can feel the heat of him underneath. I push him toward the side of the pavement. He backs up against a low wall and sits on it, his legs planted wide as usual. He looks up at me and grins. "You're stronger than you look."

"Don't patronize me, Lucas Mahoney. Don't you dare." My voice is lower and throatier than normal. I can tell he likes it. He grabs me round the waist and pulls me close. I feel trapped again, but I keep my smile in place. His hands feel huge and strong, even though I know full well they're just normal boy-sized hands. In fact, his hands are rather dainty and refined if you really stop to look at them.

Now Lucas has to look up at me. It makes a nice change from me straining my neck to look up at him. I prefer it this way.

"I wouldn't dream of patronizing you. You are unpatronizable."

"That's not a real word."

"I know. Can I kiss you now?"

Lucas Mahoney is staring at my mouth. He looks hungry. I shrug and say, "I suppose so…" He lunges in and I duck my head out of the way. "On one condition…"

"And what might that be?"

"You have to promise you'll watch *Halloween* with me." And as soon as the words are out of my mouth, it feels like the worst possible betrayal of Kai. *Halloween* was *our* thing. I won't taint that by watching it with Lucas. I won't.

Lucas slips his hand behind my neck and gently pulls my head toward his. "I think I can agree to those terms." After a few seconds of kissing, I forget about *Halloween*. After a couple of minutes, I forget about Kai.

We kiss until an angry bald man knocks on the bay window of his living room and follows it up with a gesture I can only interpret as *Stop shoving your tongues in each other's mouths on my front wall.*

Lucas and I run away laughing, hand in hand, like a couple of naughty kids. Then we stop in an alleyway and do more kissing. I have a feeling there's going to have to be a lot more kissing before this is over. And maybe some other stuff too.

And maybe I don't mind.

chapter thirty-three

Mom and Dad want to meet Lucas. I tried telling them it was not going to happen—under any circumstances—but Dad's coming over all Father-in-a-crap-American-sitcom. You know the ones... the daughter's going to prom or whatever and her date arrives to pick her up. Dad answers the door and interrogates the poor boy while the daughter puts the finishing touches to her makeup upstairs. I have no idea whether this actually happens in real life.

I don't like what I see in my parents' eyes when they ask about Lucas. It's worse with Mom, but I can see Dad feels it too, even though he's making a show of being the gruff, overprotective father. It's hope. I put hope in their eyes and soon I'm going to rip it away from them in the worst possible way.

They want me to invite him over for dinner next week. Mom gets all excited looking at recipe books and asking about his likes and dislikes. I don't tell her that I have no clue what he likes to eat and really could not care less. Instead I make stuff up: he likes meat and pasta and Chinese food but isn't too keen on fish or sweetcorn. Mom looks up from her latest cookbook acquisition—with some voluptuous woman on the front, all pouty and ridiculous. "You two must be a match made in heaven—liking all the same things! Actually, thinking about it, he's probably pretending to like what you like. I remember when your father and I met I said I liked that awful music of his, and he said he enjoyed going to the ballet! Ah, the things we do for love…"

She's staring into space, all misty-eyed. I'm staring at her, wondering how we can possibly be related. Noah barrels into the kitchen, looks from me to Mom and back again, says, "You two look weird," grabs an apple from the fruit bowl, and runs out again.

⌒

I call Lucas and he thinks it's just about the funniest thing in the world that my parents are so keen to meet him.

"Sasha wouldn't let me anywhere near her parents till we'd been going out for three months!"

The implication of this statement is enough to stop me in my tracks.

"Jem? Are you still there?"

I clear my throat. "I…yeah."

"Are you OK? You sound a bit…I dunno."

"I'm fine. I…just…Is that what we're doing? Going out?"

He laughs like he doesn't even know the meaning of awkward. "What exactly did you think we were doing?"

I shrug before I realize how pointless that is. "Um…I didn't…I thought we were just hanging out, I guess."

"*Hanging out, I guess?* Huh. Well, how about we make this more formal? Jemima Halliday, would you like to go out with me?" His voice is slick as olive oil.

I leave him hanging for a second longer than is comfortable. "OK."

"OK?! All I get is an OK after laying my heart on the line like that?!" His mock outrage makes me wince.

"Sorry. Yes, Lucas Mahoney, I would like to go out with you."

"That's more like it."

We talk some more—making arrangements for him to come

over for dinner. I can't get off the phone quick enough. When I do, I throw the phone on the bed like *it's* the one to blame for my current situation.

I am officially going out with Lucas Mahoney. Lucas Mahoney is my boyfriend. I'm disgusted with myself. And more than a little bit impressed.

⌒

I've been counting down the days till the July letter. There's no way I'm opening another one late.

Jem,

I've been sitting here for God knows how many hours, slowly but surely losing the plot. I owe you yet another apology. What was I thinking? All these stupid challenges. You must be so ~~fucking~~ angry with me. I wouldn't blame you if you'd torn up every last one of these ridiculous letters and decided to forget all about me. Who ~~the fuck~~ do I think I am? Trying to change you from beyond the grave, like some kind of ghostly Tim Gunn.

Anyway, what I'm trying to say is: I hope you've ignored everything I asked you to do. I hope you've stayed your glorious, lovely self. And if you haven't, well, I hope you're happy with the changes you've made and you don't

hate me too much. It's too late for me to
start again with the letters, I'm afraid. I'm
so very tired. This isn't quite going the way
I planned it. It was all so clear in my mind.
Everything made sense and I was so sure I was
doing the right thing. For everyone.

You know what I wish? I wish more than
anything that I wasn't gay. It's not as easy
as I made it look, you know. ~~There are things
I never told you~~ Everything's so much easier
for you straight people. The world is set up
to work in your favor and you don't even
appreciate it. Before you get righteously
indignant, I'm not talking about YOU you, I'm
talking about the GENERAL you.

Sometimes I used to imagine us two getting
married, can you believe that? I used to
imagine what life would be like if I didn't like
boys. Because you know what? If I didn't like
boys, I would be truly madly deeply in love
with you. ~~But I DO like fucking boys~~. Oops.

I'm not stupid, Jem. I know full well how you
feel about me. I think I've known for longer

than you've known yourself. You're really not that good at hiding your feelings. You should work on that if you don't want to get your heart trampled all over. There I go again—telling you how to live your life…I just can't help myself, can I?! So anyway, all I can say is that I'm flattered. That you would spend all your time with me when you could have been off chasing boys who would actually want to do rude things with you. God, now I sound really up myself, don't I? I can't seem to say the right words no matter how hard I try. I just want you to know that I wish I could have felt the same way about you. I wish that more than anything. I think we could have been happy together, you and me. ~~If only~~

Sorry if that bit's looking a bit blotchy now. I didn't mean to get all heavy there. That's about the least helpful thing I can do, and it's the exact opposite of what these letters are for. Don't be getting maudlin now, my precious Jem.

Anyway, my love, whatever it is that you're doing, I hope with all my heart that you are happy. You deserve to be happy. Because I say so.

And I'm always right about these things.
So there.

Until next month.

Big, huge, fat bear hugs to you,

Kai
xxx

This kind of thinking really isn't helping. Even though everything I'm doing is for Kai, thinking about him really, really doesn't help. If he could see me now...I can't even...

Yes, I've done all the things he asked me to, but I'm kidding myself if I think he'd be happy about what I'm doing. He wouldn't have wanted *this*. But I can't let myself think about that. All I can do is hope that he would understand—why I have to do this. Why I have to take them down.

He's chipping away at my heart with every letter and he doesn't even know it. Wishing he wasn't gay. That's not Kai. He didn't think that way. He *didn't*. Not until they humiliated him anyway. They will pay for making him think that way.

He *knew*. He knew how I felt about him. I don't feel the hot flush of embarrassment that I would have expected. I'm glad. I'm glad he knew that someone loved him like that. It must be nice to know that. He knew I adored him in every possible way. It doesn't matter that he didn't feel the same. (*Why* couldn't he have felt the same? WHY?) I can't help feeling sad that no one will ever love me the way I loved Kai. I'll never, ever know what that feels like. Still, it didn't exactly do him any good. It wasn't enough to keep him here.

chapter thirty-four

Looks like the Dinner of Awkwardness might have to be post-poned. I'm ill. Like, properly ill in a way that I haven't been for years. Never in my life have I been glad to feel so bloody awful, but it feels like this virus or whatever is a gift from God.

I wonder if the thought of being Lucas Mahoney's girlfriend is so horrific that my immune system has revolted against it. Maybe this illness is my body rejecting Lucas like an organ recipient rejects a donated kidney or something. Whatever it is, it feels like someone's been at my throat with a cheese grater and my brain is suddenly two sizes too big for my skull.

Mom comes in before she goes to work and does that feeling-the-temperature-of-my-forehead thing that mothers always do, complete with a look of serious concentration. "Hmm…I think we should call Janice."

My panicked "No!" is followed by a coughing fit.

Mom purses her lips so tight they disappear from view, then checks her watch. "She'll be coming off shift now and I'm sure she wouldn't mind…just to put my mind at rest, you know."

I sit up in bed and somehow manage to ride the undulating wave of extreme dizziness that crashes over me. "Mom, I'm fine. It's just a cold or something. Please don't bother Mrs. McBride. She's always knackered after her shift." I can tell she's wavering. "Besides, she'll just say it's a virus. They always say it's a virus, don't they? I'll just rest up today and I'm sure I'll be fine by the time you get home."

I say a silent prayer to the god of mother–daughter interaction. The thought of having to talk to Mrs. McBride, having to see her sad, pale face…I briefly consider leaping out of bed and doing pushups to prove I'm fine.

Mom sits on the edge of the bed and takes my clammy hand in hers. "OK…but I worry about you, Jem. If anything happened to you, I can't even…" She shakes her head and takes a deep shaky breath. I reckon she might be about to cry.

"Mom, nothing's going to happen to me! It's just a cold. Now stop fussing and get yourself to work. If it'll make you feel any better, you can text me on an hourly basis or something."

She squeezes my hand but says nothing. This is getting a little weird. "You're right. I'm just being silly because…yes. OK, I'm off, but you'd better reply to those texts—unless you're asleep—but try not to leave it too long…"

And then she's gone. Finally. I pull the duvet over my head, feeling twice as exhausted as when I'd woken up. It wasn't as if she had to spell it out. There's only one reason for her newfound concern/paranoia: Kai.

The crazy thing is that she's right to be concerned. She's right to be paranoid. Just not about me getting ill.

$\backsim$

In the end, Mom had to stay home from work for the next two days to look after me. It wasn't just a cold—it's some hideous killer virus from hell which has basically killed a good chunk of my summer holidays. On the plus side, it means the awkward Lucas dinner hasn't happened yet. On the negative side, I feel like crap and can only eat ice cream and soup and melon. (Maybe the ice cream should shift over to the plus side.)

Lucas wanted to visit me, but there's no way I'm letting him see me like this—unwashed, pale, and clammy. I don't want him to think I'm someone who needs looking after. And I definitely don't want *him* seeing me in my pajamas. I texted and said I'd let him know as soon as I'm back in circulation, fit for public viewing. He made some crap joke about coming over to play doctors and nurses; all I could muster up in reply was a smiley face. He texts me every morning to ask how I'm doing; it's kind of irritating.

By day 15 of my confinement I'm starting to feel a little better. Technically I've been feeling a little better since day 9, but I kept my mouth shut. I was starting to enjoy the extra attention from Mom. The soft, sympathetic voice, the blissful lack of nagging.

On Saturday I'm whiling away the afternoon flicking through the pages of one of the many, many magazines Mom bought me… Fashion! Boys! Makeup! More boys! Once I'm over the initial does-she-know-me-at-all revulsion, I actually manage to find some interesting articles. Shameful.

The doorbell goes and I figure it must be one of Noah's mates. It's not until the timid knock at my bedroom door twenty minutes later that I get suspicious. Mom never bothers to knock (she reckons she *forgets*) and Dad's knock is a machine-gun-like rat-a-tat-tat which always scares the crap out of me.

"Come in?" Definitely a question rather than a statement. I'm really not sure I want this person who is most definitely not a member of my family to come through that door. The only person I ever *really* want to see will never walk through that door again.

A plate laden with cupcakes is the first thing I see. Not quite what I was expecting. The hands holding the plate are dainty and girlish and everything you'd want hands to be. It's Sasha, looking prettier and healthier than ever. Crap sandwich.

"You poor thing! Why didn't you call me?! I could have come around and kept you company!"

I clear my throat. "Um...I wasn't really up for company, I guess."

She perches on the side of my bed, a little too close for my liking. "Silly! What do you think friends are for?! I could have made you chicken soup or something." She sets the cupcakes on my bedside table. The frosting's bright pink—it really doesn't look like something you should put in your stomach. "Never mind, I'm here now. With cupcakes." She looks at me with her big brown eyes, all expectant and caring.

"You made cupcakes?" A stupid thing to say, but I'm struggling here. I look like shit. My tank top has holes in it. There's a zit on my chin the size of a golf ball.

And worst of all, I'm not wearing any makeup.

"I bake when I'm bored. And I have been bored. Here, have one." She puts the plate under my nose and I manage not to puke on it.

"That's...um...really kind of you. OK if I have one later though? I feel a bit rough right now."

"Of course! Your mom said you'd been off your food, and now I look at you, you *are* looking kinda skinny. Maybe that's what I could do with the rest of my summer—get ill, lose a few pounds."

"Yeah, like *you* really need to lose weight."

She smiles sweetly at me because that was exactly what I was supposed to say. "So anyway, your mom is so nice! And your dad too. You're so lucky—my parents are just so blah, you know? And Noah's just the cutest thing I've ever seen. He managed to sweet-talk me into giving him a cupcake—he's super smooth, that one."

"Yeah, *so* smooth. It runs in the family. So...what were you and my mom chatting about?" Trying to sound like I don't really care, like I'm just making conversation. But the thought of Sasha talking to Mom makes me feel uneasy. I'd dodged a bullet by getting ill and avoiding Lucas coming over, but I hadn't anticipated one of Them turning up unannounced. I guess that's just the kind of thing you do when you're popular—assume that people will be glad to see you. Assume there's nothing they'd rather do than see your pretty, perfect face when they're looking like utter shit.

"Oh, this and that. You, obviously. And she was asking me about Lucas." She sees the look on my face and rushes on, "Don't worry, I didn't say anything bad. She just wanted to know more about him—said you'd been all secretive."

"Oh God." I pull the duvet up over my head.

Sasha yanks the duvet right back down again.

"Chill out! All I said was he's a good guy. I didn't tell her he was my ex or anything—didn't want her asking anything too…er… intimate. Anyway, how are you feeling?" She doesn't bother to wait for an answer. "So…I hear you two are, like, official and everything. How does it feel?" She's got so much energy she's practically bouncing on the bed.

"Um…good, I guess?"

"You don't sound so sure." She scrapes some frosting off a cupcake with her index finger. Her nail varnish is the exact same color pink. She licks the icing off her finger with feline delicacy.

"I've been a bit preoccupied with fever, phlegm, vomiting…that kind of thing."

"Soooooo…you haven't done the nasty yet, have you?"

I shrug. "You seem to know everything else about me and Lucas—surely you know that too." I don't quite manage to hide the edge in my voice.

"As if I'm going to ask Lucas if he's had sex with his new girl-friend! Give me *some* credit…But I'm well within my rights to ask *you*. It's, like, the law of girl talk." Sasha tilts her head and narrows her eyes like she's considering how to draw a picture of me.

"You know you can trust me, don't you? You can tell me anything.

I'm really good with secrets...unless they're lame secrets that shouldn't even be secrets in the first place."

I open my mouth to tell her that no, Lucas and I have most definitely not had sex. But she holds up her hand to silence me. "It's OK, you don't need to say anything. You haven't done it yet, I can tell. I swear I have a sixth sense about this kind of stuff. You're going to do it soon though, right? Once you're not so... mucustastic of course. I mean, Lucas is patient, but he's not going to hang around forever..."

She witters on and on and on. I want her to leave; she's more than I can cope with in my weakened state. I congratulate Sasha on her *amazing* intuition and admit that I have not "done it." Then I fake a coughing fit that somehow turns into a real coughing fit and ends up with me nearly choking to death. That does the trick. Sasha leaves with promises to come back with more cupcakes soon. I even get a hug, despite my protests that I'm probably highly infectious. I can't help noticing the overwhelming coconutty aroma of her super-shiny hair. It makes me crave a Bounty bar.

All I can think after she leaves is, *Sasha Evans was in my bedroom.*

chapter thirty-five

The timing of the family holiday to Spain couldn't be better. I'm just about recovered enough to have a decent time. I try not to dwell on the fact that it's my last family holiday (or "Halliday" as Dad insists on calling them). Noah will have a room to himself next time.

Once we get back I become the master of excuses, avoiding everyone as much as possible. Mom and Dad seem to have forgotten about having Lucas over for dinner, which is a massive relief. I need to buy some time; I can't make my next move until we go back to school.

The last few weeks of the summer holiday go pretty quickly. Before I know it, texts are flying around comparing exam results and celebrating or commiserating accordingly. Lucas did better than expected, Sasha did worse, and the rest of them performed very much as predicted. Stu's annoyingly smug about his B in biology, making some crap joke about being very familiar with the female anatomy (yawn). Nina's been texting me from New York, pretending she's not checking up on Stu. I've been replying, doing my best to keep her paranoid while trying to make it look like I'm being a supportive, understanding friend. It helps that she's not exactly over-endowed in the brain department. It's good that I'm still able to do *something* to keep the Plan moving forward—even something small.

I manage to avoid a party at Lucas's house the day we get our results. I tell him Mom and Dad had planned this big family dinner, when in actual fact I begged them to take me and Noah out. Mom wanted to know why I didn't want to "celebrate with my friends." There was no point in telling her that I don't have any friends anymore. My *friend* (singular) is dead. I eventually convince her that I'm not missing out on anything, that everyone else is celebrating with their families too. Dad arrives late at the restaurant, then insists on embarrassing me by making a toast to his "little brainbox." Since when has B's and C's been enough to get you labeled as a brainbox? Still, I'll take it. I suppose I get a little bit of dispensation for Kai being dead. Mom as good as said so the night before my results.

~

On August 23rd I wake up early and go downstairs to make a cup of tea. My favorite mug's in the dishwasher so I use Noah's instead. I take the tea upstairs and get back into bed to read Kai's letter. Only two more after this.

Jem,

So did you nail those pesky exams? Are you pondering your future and wondering if maybe a career as an astrophysicist awaits after all?

Honey, I'm afraid I'm going to have to keep this brief. I'm running out of time. I may have slightly underestimated how long this little endeavor would take. It's 4:23 a.m. already.

Undone

The world is sleeping and everything is far
too quiet for my liking. I want to shout and
scream and throw something at the wall
just to break the silence. But if I do that,
they'll <u>know.</u> They'll know I'm not Ok and I
can't have them knowing that until ~~tomorrow~~
today. It's today.

I wish I could talk to you, pickle, but this
is the next best thing. And I <u>am</u> talking to
Future Jem. ~~Do you have rocket booster~~
~~boots and hoverboards yet?~~ I wish I could hug
you one last time. The last hug we shared
was excellent though. Except it was cheating,
because you didn't know it <u>was</u> the last one,
did you? You had no idea. If you had, maybe
you wouldn't have let me go—ever. ~~And maybe I~~
~~wouldn't have wanted you to.~~

Back to school soon, my dear. Better
sharpen all your pencils and whatnot. I know
how much you hate this time of year, Jem.
I know how much you hate going back to
that place and I'm pretty sure I haven't made
things any easier by not being there for you.
I'm sorry. But hey, look on the bright side:

at least you don't have to wear that maroon monstrosity of a uniform anymore. Small victories, remember?

Hugs,

Kai
xxx

chapter thirty-six

The first day back at school I stand at the gates, steeling myself to step through them and face the mayhem. I've been up since half past five, going through all my clothes, trying to work out what to wear. I bet Sasha laid her clothes out last night. She's probably got the whole week's outfits planned, down to the last accessory. I never thought I'd miss the uniform, but I really do. The uniform reminded me of who I was. The girl who used her compass to pick the white threads out of her tie in math class. The girl with holes in the sleeves of her sweater. It didn't matter that the hair was different, the makeup was different, and the people I talked to were very, very different; there was still something left of her. The girl who loved the boy who stared at the sky.

My wistful thoughts are shunted out of my head when someone barges into me. Serves me right for standing here, I suppose. It's not just anyone though. It's someone I haven't seen the whole summer. Someone I've barely even thought about. Louise. And she's running—no, more like frolicking—through the yard, being chased by Max. He catches up with her because she lets him, and he wraps her up in his arms and kisses her like it's not quarter to nine on a dreary September morning.

Louise looks like Louise Version 2.0. She's been rebooted. She's blonder than ever before, without even a hint of roots (unlike me. Should have known better than to pay Fernando a visit in the middle of the summer holidays instead of the end. Rookie error, I guess). The haunted look is well and truly gone. I'd describe her as glowing if that wouldn't imply she looks pregnant. She most definitely does not look pregnant. Her top is tighter than Saran wrap.

The reappearance of Louise on the social radar could be a real problem for me. I can't have her turning the others against me. I've come too far, worked too hard, to let that happen. Why couldn't she have just stayed skulking in the shadows? This is NOT a good start to my day.

I shoulder my way through the crowds toward the bench. The Hallowed Picnic Bench of Popularity.

They're all there, with an added (and most unwelcome) dash of Louise, extra conspicuous because she's the only one wearing a uniform. Nina jumps up and gives me a hug. She only got back from America yesterday, so I *suppose* a hug is warranted. It makes me feel uncomfortable though. Sasha's waiting for a hug too, which is definitely not warranted—I only saw her a couple of days ago. It's not that I've got anything against the act of hugging or anything. I just have no desire to hug these people; their hugs are all bony and ill-fitting.

Lucas is sitting in his usual spot—smack bang in the middle of things. He pats the space next to him and I resist the urge to remind him that I am not, in fact, a dog. I take my allotted seat like a good little girl and nestle myself into the crook of his arm. I try to act like I belong. Like I'm not an imposter.

I can't help checking Louise's reaction, mostly as I want to know if she's been brought up to speed about me and Lucas. She catches me looking, and to my utter surprise, smiles widely. "How was your summer, Jem? Looks like you had a good one."

I smile back and try to make it as genuine as possible. "My

summer was fine, thanks." I don't say, *WHAT THE FUCK ARE YOU DOING HERE? THIS IS MY TERRITORY NOW, BITCH.* Because people might think that was a little weird.

Everyone's acting like nothing's amiss. Like Louise had never cast herself into the social shadows and I'd always been glued to Lucas's side. I guess that's what it's like for them. Nothing fazes them; they just go with the flow and never even bat an eyelid when things change. I can't get over how quickly things can change. One day everyone seems to have forgotten about you, and somehow (HOW?!) the next day you're back in and you're laughing and joking and smiling and ruining things for normal, decent people like me.

Lucas squeezes my knee and whispers, "You look great." This is flattering and irritating in equal measure. Flattering because it's nice to know that the ungodly early start this morning wasn't for nothing; irritating because I don't want him to think I did it for him. Because I didn't. Not even a little bit.

I sit in the middle of the viper nest that is Team Popular and look out at the real world. The normal kids, doing normal things. No one's paying us even a little bit of attention. Which is strange, because when *I* was on the outside I was always watching. Always.

What's the point of being popular if nobody's watching?

⌒

The first chance I get to talk to Sasha alone is at break time. I practically drag her to the science block bathroom.

"What's the rush? Did you drink too much coffee this morning or something?"

I give her a look that can only be described as exasperated, but she seems completely clueless. I have to spell it out for her. "Er… is there something you forgot to tell me, maybe? About Louise?"

Sasha shakes her head dismissively. "Oh. Yeah. She said she's feeling a lot better about…stuff. The counseling really helped." She pouts at herself in the mirror.

"So now she's back and everything's normal again?"

She stops pouting and turns to face me. "I guess so. She came over on the weekend and we talked. It was…nice. She really wants to get her life back on track, you know. Things haven't been easy for her." I stare at her until she says, "I mean, I know things haven't been easy for you too. Obviously."

I get my makeup out, just for something to do. There's no need; it's looking pretty damn flawless if I do say so myself. "Um… Sasha? You do know that Louise isn't exactly my biggest fan?"

"Actually, she told me she was looking forward to hanging out with you. I think she's really changed. She's, like, softer or something." I'm taking this in, trying to make sense of it. But Sasha's moved on and is staring at her reflection as if it holds the answer to the meaning of life. "Can I ask you something important? And you have to be absolutely totally honest with me?" I nod. "Do you think my cheeks look fat? I swear I look more like a hamster every day. God, that summer diet was such a waste of time. Why did I even bother? Why can't I be one of those bitches who just eats what she wants and never gain a milligram of weight…Sorry… you were going to ask me something?"

Sasha and I have had so many variations of this tedious conversation that I know that nothing I say will reassure her. But I'm supposed to say it anyway.

"No, Sasha, you do *not* look like a hamster. You are ridiculously gorgeous and I hate you for it." That makes her smile.

"Ah, little Jem, you're too kind." She pats my cheek. She actually pats my fucking cheek. I want to pat/slap her big fat hamster cheek in return. I can just picture it. I'd hit her so hard she'd lose her balance, maybe knock her head on the corner of the sink. Then I'd have to explain to the police how I'd accidentally killed the most popular girl in school, just because she invaded my personal space in the most patronizing way possible.

I spend most of the day worrying about Louise.

Sasha's clearly forgotten that I've known Louise a lot longer than she has. I swear she forgets who I actually *am* most of the time. She probably doesn't like to think about the fact that she was responsible for bringing a complete nobody into the group.

After *a lot* of fretting, I realize there's no other option. I'm just going to have to accept Louise's reappearance and get on with things. Maybe counseling does work miracles after all. It kind of makes me wonder if I should have had some.

I just have to hope Louise doesn't get in my way. She'd better not. I don't want to have to take her down too. I really don't.

chapter thirty-seven

Lucas invites me over to his house on the weekend, making it quite clear that it'll be just the two of us. One boy. One girl. One empty house. Doesn't take a genius to work out what's on his mind. And I know it couldn't be more perfect for the Plan, but I can't ignore the wave of anxiety that washes over me. I just have to hope it will pass.

I haven't been to his house before. I know exactly where it is. The street is quiet and leafy and idyllic. Until you look over the road at the sprawling graveyard. The spike-topped black railings would be enough to give me shivers. But that's not what bothers me.

Kai's there. His body is in a box under the ground. Layers and layers of cold, wet worm-ridden earth lie between him and the sunlight. I can't even think about it without feeling sick and dizzy. How can it be possible that my Kai is in that place with all those dead people? It's not right. He should be in the forest or in the ocean or somewhere beautiful. Or with me, *alive*.

No one could ever call the cemetery beautiful. It's not one of those ancient, tumbledown ones with ivy creeping up the sides of elaborate Victorian gravestones. No, this place is purely functional. Rows and rows and rows of gravestones, laid out in regimental fashion. As if the neatness and order can make sense of death. As if the manicured lawn is a comfort to anyone.

I haven't been to his grave. I wouldn't even know where it is if Mom hadn't made a point of telling me. She's been trying to get me to go for months. She thinks I should "pay my respects," which sounds like something out of a Dickens novel. Surely you only need to pay your respects to rich great uncles who live in huge mansions?

I didn't even feel bad about not going. Not even a little bit of guilt. I know full well Kai wouldn't give a toss about this sort of thing. But now that I'm walking up the street toward Lucas's house I can't help thinking that that's not exactly the point. And suddenly I need to see it. I need to see what's written there. See where he is. Check that he's OK.

A quick look at my phone tells me if I take a detour into the cemetery, I'm going to be late. Lucas can wait.

It's not hard to find. It's almost as if my body's on autopilot, pulling me toward him. My legs slow down as I approach the grave. They aren't sure that this is such a great idea after all. But I'm not going to turn back now.

The stone is shiny and black and smooth. Granite, I think. The edges have been left rough, which just makes it look as if someone couldn't make up their mind.

There are some sad-looking tulips in a glass jar in front of the gravestone. The flowers droop down toward the grass, as if they're bowing their heads in grief. The water in the jar is murky and greenish. I feel bad that I haven't brought anything. It seems like such a waste though, cutting the stems of something alive and beautiful to bring them to this awful place to die. It's what people do though, isn't it? I've seen it on TV a thousand times. You take the flowers and place them in front of the grave, then take a couple of solemn steps back. And that's when you start talking to the dead person. Ideally there are some tears. And if you're really lucky, the mourner will fall to their knees.

There are no tears today. I feel nothing. Kai's not here—he never was. Whatever made Kai *Kai* isn't rotting away down there. This place has nothing to do with him.

Kai McBride. Beloved son, brother, and friend. Seeing the word "friend" makes me want to thank Mrs. McBride. I bet she chose the wording; Kai's dad would be useless at that kind of thing. I wonder how long it took her, trying to choose the words. Words that strangers would see as they wandered past, looking at the dates and realizing that Kai McBride was only on this earth for sixteen short years.

There are so few words on the gravestone that it makes me wonder if the engraver charges by the letter. Maybe Mrs. McBride wanted to say more. Maybe she wanted to add a poem or something, but the cost put her off. Whatever the reason, I'm glad. There's a simplicity to this gravestone that makes me not hate it. There's no way Kai would approve of the shiny blackness though; it looks like something cheap masquerading as something expensive.

I stand there for I don't know how long. Thinking about him. Missing him. Wanting him to be alive more than anything in the whole world. Wishing that the words in front of me were lies. That the dates would magically change and Kai would have died at the grand old age of ninety-six after the happiest life anyone could ever imagine—jam-packed with adventure and laughter and love.

I turn and walk away. No big melodramatic scene.

chapter thirty-eight

Lucas opens the door and ushers me into his lair. He doesn't mention the fact that I'm late. Perhaps he didn't even notice. Maybe he wasn't pacing around looking nervously at his watch at all. Dammit.

The house is nice. I half expected it to be like a show home, with cushions you're not supposed to sit on and the dining table all set up for a fancy dinner. It's nothing like that though. It's warm and cozy with lots of knick knacks everywhere. Apparently Lucas's mom has a ferocious garage sale habit.

There are photos everywhere. A few pictures of Lucas's sisters, who look like goddesses. Loads of Lucas way back before he realized how good-looking he was. My favorite is one of him wearing nothing but a pair of navy-blue underpants, standing in the middle of a sandpit, gap-toothed and grinning at the person behind the camera.

I pick up the photo to get a better look. How could the boy in this photo have morphed into the Big I Am, Lucas Mahoney?

He grabs the photo from me and holds it behind his back. "Jem, if you want to see me in my underpants, all you have to do is ask." His eyes are locked on mine and he's smiling. For once that smile doesn't look like a smirk.

I make a grab for the picture frame, but he holds it over his head.

"As long as you're not wearing navy Y-fronts…" I hook a finger on to his belt and pull him closer. He chucks the photo onto the sofa, where it lands face down. Little boy Lucas is forgotten and the present-day version is kissing me.

I have to be honest. I sort of like kissing Lucas. Scratch that—I really like kissing Lucas. It took a bit of getting used to at first, and sometimes it still freaks me out a bit, but mostly it seems like a normal thing for me to be doing. But I think that's because I just like kissing. When I close my eyes and let myself sink into the moment, it's like slipping into a hot bath (with bubbles and everything). Lucas isn't Lucas anymore, and I'm not Jem. Weirdly, it's the one time I'm able to forget about Kai and the Plan and the evilness of Team Popular. Even though those are the only reasons I'm kissing him.

I think maybe Lucas is just really, really good at kissing. He definitely had enough practice with Sasha. I don't like thinking about Sasha and Lucas together. The feeling I get is far too close to jealousy.

Before I know what's happening, Lucas is pulling my top over my head. And I let him. At least I'm not wearing one of my ratty old gray bras. This one's purple.

We kiss some more and then I realize the curtains are open and anyone walking past could see me in my purple bra. "Um… Lucas…maybe close the curtains?"

"No need. This is the quietest street in town…unless you count the ghosts from the graveyard." His hands are fiddling with the clasp of my bra and he starts to kiss me again. But I'm not sure his brain can cope with doing both things at once, so he stops the kissing for a moment. Then he stops the fiddling and steps back, wincing. "Shit. I'm sorry. Your friend's buried there, isn't he?"

I feel cold and exposed all of a sudden. "How do you know that?" Guilt. It has to be guilt. Maybe Lucas made a point of finding out where Kai was buried, so he could visit the grave. Perhaps *he* stood over the grave, talking to Kai. Saying sorry.

Lucas shrugs. "It's the biggest cemetery in town. Pretty much everyone gets buried in there. Sorry, I shouldn't have brought it up. I'm such an idiot. Talk about ruining the mood…" He picks up my top from the floor and hands it to me. "Unless you *do* want to talk about it? Because we can totally do that."

I am standing in Lucas's living room in my bra and jeans. And he wants to talk about my dead best friend. This is beyond surreal. I can't find any words to say, so I settle for silence.

Lucas sits down on the sofa. "You never talk about him, you know? It might help if you did. You must miss him so much."

WHY IS HE DOING THIS? It makes no sense. Unless he really *is* feeling guilty. Either that or he's just going out of the way to prove how sensitive he can be. I've never been the best judge of this sort of thing, but he looks genuine. I look in his face and see compassion there. Empathy. Sympathy.

This is not what I was expecting. I don't know what to do.

I'm not sure who Lucas is. The different versions of him are clashing in my head.

But the version in front of me is looking up at me with those amazing eyes and there's only one thing I can do, really. It's the next step in the Plan, and the Plan is the only thing that matters.

chapter thirty-nine

I'm lying in Lucas Mahoney's bed. Naked. Lucas Mahoney is also lying in Lucas Mahoney's bed. Also naked.

There are a couple of odd things about this situation. No. Make that three.

I've had sex.

I've had sex with Lucas Mahoney.

I liked having sex with Lucas Mahoney.

⌒

If I was really going to analyze what happened, it all comes down to a series of choices. Moments in which I could have made a different decision and the outcome would have been entirely different.

I wanted Lucas to stop talking about Kai; I wanted to stop thinking about Kai. Lucas looked surprised and pleased when I let my top drop back to the floor.

And he looked like all his Christmases and birthdays and any other celebration you can think of had come all at once when I knelt in front of him and started unbuckling his belt.

He even gave me the opportunity to stop. "Are you sure you want to do this? You really don't have to…" This was when I could have said, "No, I am not sure I want to do this. I definitely *don't* want to." But I didn't. I went right ahead and unbuckled his jeans.

I didn't have any idea what I was doing, but he seemed to like it. Low standards, I guess. There was a moment when I nearly burst out laughing at the madness of it all. But laughing would have been difficult, given that Lucas Mahoney's penis was in my mouth.

A little voice in my head niggled at me, telling me to check for a hidden camera. But I knew I was just being ridiculous.

The next decision was whether to go upstairs. Whether to take things even further. Once again, Lucas presented me with a get-out clause. Once again I refused. It was like someone else had colonized my brain; Old Jem was in there somewhere, cowering in a corner saying, *Don't do this. Please don't do this. Not with him.* New Jem told her to shut the fuck up.

Lucas's bedroom was the opposite of the rest of the house. White walls, minimal clutter. I barely had time to take it all in before I was on the bed having the rest of my clothes stripped from my body.

He had a box of condoms in his bedside drawer. A half-empty box, which made me think of Sasha again. She'd been exactly where I was, doing exactly what I was doing. And if she was to be believed, she'd taught him everything he knew. I tried to block this thought from my mind, but it kept pushing its way to the forefront. Whenever Lucas touched me or kissed me in a way I liked, I wondered if Sasha had instructed him to do it that way. Unfortunately (or fortunately) Lucas kept touching me and kissing me in ways that felt so good I could hardly stand it. And he was so gentle. He kept stopping and looking at me questioningly. He clearly realized it was my first time. I should have been insulted, but instead I was glad.

⌒

Afterward he asks me if I'm OK and I can't help the smile from spreading across my face. I didn't quite come but I'm not even that bothered—just relieved I got through it OK.

"I didn't hurt you, did I?"

I shake my head and kiss him. Not strictly true; it had hurt a bit. Nothing like some of the horror stories I'd heard though. Lucas props himself up on his elbow.

"Um. I've been wanting to give you something…"

I elbow him in the ribs. "You've already given me plenty, don't you think?" I inwardly cringe; I really have no idea where this stuff comes from sometimes.

Lucas doesn't laugh, which is fine because it really wasn't funny. He's unwinding the thin piece of leather wrapped around his wrist. I've never seen him without it. "I thought maybe you'd like to wear this?" He looks shifty, worried almost.

"Marking your territory, are you?" I'm only half joking.

"Look, if you don't want it, that's fine. I just thought it would be kind of…cool, that's all."

I hold out my left hand and he winds the leather around my wrist. He ties it carefully, then kisses the back of my hand like he's a fairytale prince and I'm some swooning wench.

"Thank you," I say. I have no idea how I should be feeling about this token of his affection. No idea at all.

"I really, really like you, Jem." The way he says it makes it seem like a declaration of the deepest, most sincere love.

I look into his eyes until he blinks. "I like you too, Lucas Mahoney."

He smiles. "Why do you always do that? Call me by my whole name?"

I nuzzle in closer to him. "I just like the way it sounds." A lie, of course. In my head Lucas Mahoney is not a real person. He is a fictional character. A puppet. Someone who exists for me to mess with. I know exactly how I feel about Lucas Mahoney. I despise him. But Lucas? Lucas is very real. Frighteningly real. I'm not sure how I feel about Lucas. And I'm starting to wonder if…

No.

This is the truth of the matter: having sex with Lucas Mahoney was better than I could have ever imagined.

And that's the problem. I want to do it again.

Jem,

How's senior year treating you? Bet Allander Park looks a little different from the dizzy heights of twelfth grade block, right?

I fell asleep, Jem. I was going to rest my head for a minute, ~~decide if I really~~ but I bloody fell asleep. It was only for a few minutes, but I woke up and forgot—for one blissful, perfect moment I forgot. My foolish, caffeine-addled brain thought I must have fallen asleep doing my homework, and you know that sleepy, hazy feeling you have that's halfway between dream world and this world? Well, I could have lived in it forever. I could have curled up inside it and stayed there for good. But everything came crashing back, like it always does, and I remembered that I'm a laughingstock. That people who never gave me a second glance now have an <u>opinion</u> about me. They think I'm disgusting. I'm not, Jem, am I? I need you to know that I'm not. I just made a mistake. A

silly mistake. I thought I could do things with
a boy I liked and that it would be Ok because
no one would know. ~~And maybe one day he
could even be my boyfr~~

I'm almost too embarrassed to admit that I
was planning on giving you some relationship
advice. Now, if that isn't the most ridiculous
thing you've ever heard, I don't know what
is. All I know is that it's supposed to be
amazing, this "love" thing. It's not supposed
to make you sad or angry or ashamed.
It's meant to make things easier, better,
lighter. (And doing rude things with someone
you actually care about? God, Jem, it's
brilliant.) So I guess what I'm trying to
say is, if you find someone that makes you
happy—really, truly happy—then try to hang
on to them. Because I don't think it comes
around all that often.

The sun's coming up now. I was hoping for a
proper, beautiful sunrise, but I think we both
know you don't always get what you wish for.
It's just starting to rain, and maybe it's
better that way.

Bye for now, pickle.

Love,

Kai
x x x

My tea sits untouched on the bedside table. There are no tears this time. I feel numb.

It had never occurred to me before. Maybe it should have, but it really didn't.

Kai had been in love with that boy in the video. He'd been in love and he hadn't felt able to tell me.

I feel numb.

chapter forty

Sasha's grin couldn't be any wider. "You've had sex!"

"What?! No I haven't."

"YOU HAVE! I can tell! You look…different." Sasha wasn't quite jumping up and down with glee, but she wasn't far from it. It was way too early for such levels of enthusiasm. The bell hadn't even rung yet.

"No, I really…I don't look different, do I? Shit. He told you, didn't he?"

"Ha! I *knew* it. Don't be stupid—of course you don't look different! What were you expecting? A rosy glow of sexual satisfaction or something? 'Fraid not. And no, he didn't tell me."

"Then how…?" Maybe there had been a hidden camera after all.

"It was so obvious that's what he had planned—inviting you over when his mom was out. I wouldn't be surprised if he'd lit some candles too…Please tell me there weren't candles. That boy is such a soppy bastard. I see he's handed over his prize possession too." She flicks at the leather on my wrist. "He must reeeeeally like you. Anyway, I saw him yesterday and asked him straight out. I've never seen him so uncomfortable—it was like he was trying to protect your honor or something! Ridiculous boy."

"So he didn't say anything?" This was a surprise. I'd half expected him to brag about it. Maybe he had though—just not to his ex-girlfriend. Stu and Bugs would be a more appropriate audience for that kind of thing. I'd have to wait till break time to see if they'd been told all the gory details.

"Nope, but he blushed and looked shifty. So I was pretty sure, and then you just confirmed it! I swear I'm some kind of evil genius." She slipped her arm through mine and whispered conspiratorially, "So…what did you think? He's pretty good, isn't he? I have to say, that's the one thing I miss about him."

"Sasha, I really don't want to hear about you missing his *one thing*. Can we talk about something else, please?"

Her sigh was so prolonged it sounded like every last molecule of air was leaving her body. "God, you two are as bad as each other. You're, like, perfect for each other. Just for the record, I think it's very selfish of you to deny me the details. It's been so long since I had sex that I'm practically a born-again virgin."

Just for the record, I know for a fact that Sasha shagged some random guy three weeks ago. In a toilet cubicle in Espionage, the crappiest nightclub in town. I've heard enough about it to know that I never, ever want to go there. Sasha says it's only worth going at Christmas or in the summer holidays—when there are likely to be hot boys home from college. She reckons she is "so over" boys our age.

"Sorry, Sasha. You'll just have to get your vicarious…er…pleasure elsewhere."

I'm pleased that the idea that I might have actually lost my virginity to Lucas doesn't even occur to Sasha.

⌒

It's been five days since I lost my virginity to Lucas Mahoney. It's all I can think about. I haven't been concentrating in any of my classes. I've hardly eaten a thing.

When I saw Lucas in the common room at break time on

Monday, I swear I felt my heart contract. *I've seen you naked,* was my first thought. *I would like to see you naked again—soon,* was my second. These were the wrong thoughts though. These thoughts were most definitely not part of the Plan. I gave myself a stern talking-to. Things along the lines of *You cannot allow this to change anything* and *Just because you got laid, it doesn't mean he's not an evil bastard* and *He deserves everything that's coming to him—and more.*

But then he turned and smiled at me and…that smile. It was shy and genuine and full of *something.* Something real.

The sensible part of my brain was thinking that this is perfect. *It's going to be so much easier to make him a laughingstock. I know you didn't exactly plan it to happen this way, but this is awesome.*

The unsensible part of my brain fired some electricity through some synapses or neurons or whatever which caused the corners of my mouth to tilt up and my eyes to twinkle. Twinkling eyes, for fuck's sake. This boy had really done a number on me. When it came down to it, I was no better than every other simpering female in school. No one is immune from the charms of Lucas Mahoney. Not even someone who really, really hates him.

⌒

Sasha decides it would be a good idea for "us girls" to hang out at her place after school. I think she wants to cement Louise's place back in the group with some serious girl time. The very thought of it makes me feel uncomfortable. Things are easier with the boys around. Simpler somehow. Everyone knows what they're supposed to be doing, and the focus is nearly always on the boys and their antics. Take that away and all you're left with is *talking*—and these people don't even speak my language. At least I'm spared the presence of Amber—she's got netball practice. Netball is the most pointless sport in the entire world. I can see why *she* loves it so much. Someone should really do her a favor and inform her about the invention of the sports bra though.

Sasha's bedroom is so huge it even has a seating area. It looks like something from MTV Cribs. I'm the last one in, so I end up sitting on this massive cushion with a swirly black-and-white pattern. I have to look up at the others so I'm at a disadvantage already. Sasha and Nina are on the sofa (Sasha with her feet casually draped over Nina's lap—I had no idea they were so close). Louise is opposite me on the window seat. I think I'd like to have a window seat one day. It will have a spectacular view of something spectacular, and I will sit there thinking deep thoughts about deep things. Then I remember that dead people don't have window seats. It's not the first time that I've found myself forgetting that my days are numbered.

"Jem?"

"Mmm?"

"You and Lucas? I was just telling the girls." Sasha has that look on her face—the one that says she wants to talk about sex and nothing's going to stop her.

There's no way I'm talking about it—especially not in front of Louise. She's still acting all friendly toward me, and I'm starting to think it might not just be for show. Maybe—just maybe—she's realized that she was wrong about me—that I'm *not* a terrible person after all. Or perhaps she's realized that there's no reason to hate me now that Kai's not here. It's not like I'm taking him away from her anymore.

All eyes are on me. I have to say *something*, and it turns out that *something* is ultralame. "I'm afraid I operate a strict anti-kissing-and-telling policy." I try to look cool and smug.

"Bullshit!" Sasha rolls her eyes. "Besides…you two have been doing *a lot* more than kissing."

I mime zipping my lips and throwing away the key. Sasha

needs to learn that however stubborn she thinks she can be, she will *never* be more stubborn than me.

Weirdly enough, it's Louise who comes to my rescue. "So, Nina…how are things with you and Stu? Hot and heavy?" A look passes between me and Louise, in which I acknowledge this favor and she acknowledges my gratitude. Or perhaps it was just a look.

Nina leans forward—she's clearly been gagging to talk about Stu. "Totally hot and heavy! That boy has a…oh, what's the word again? Like, he likes a lot of sex."

"A *voracious* appetite?" The word "voracious" rolls off Sasha's tongue as if she likes the way it tastes.

"Yeah, that's it. He wants it *all* the time, you know? Not that I mind—he's good at it!"

I refrain from saying that maybe it's because he's had so much bloody practice. A monkey can learn to perform a simple task if he has enough attempts at it.

"And lately he's been really sweet, you know? He's different when it's just the two of us."

Louise laughs. "Yeah, the difference is that he has his cock inside you." I half expect one of the others to call her out on being so crude; I should have known better. I can't help wincing though…it's too vile for words.

Nina laughs along with the other two. "Well, there is *that*. But he's started walking me home, and we text *every* day. He's even stopped complaining about using condoms." The fact that she considers these things to be sweet is wrong on so many levels, but Sasha and Louise don't bat an eyelid. "And I know you're not going to believe it but"—she pauses to give me a meaningful look—"last night he asked me to be his girlfriend. He said he doesn't even look at other girls anymore." Another look in my direction as if to say, *You were wrong. So there.*

Sasha sits bolt upright in an exaggerated fashion.

"What?! You have *got* to be kidding me! Stu Hicks in a *proper* relationship?! What the hell have you done to him? Nina, he must like you a lot. I mean, *really* like you."

This is exactly what Nina wants to hear. She's squirming with glee. "Reeeeally?"

"Totally! I never thought I'd see the day..." Sasha shakes her head, like this is some kind of modern-day fucking miracle.

"I *knew* there was more to him than everyone says." Nina sits back, looking massively pleased with herself.

For the first time, I'm actually glad I came. I couldn't be happier that things are (supposedly) going so well between Stu and Nina. It just makes it all the sweeter, really. I'm willing to bet things won't be going so swimmingly by the time I'm finished with him.

chapter forty-one

I wish I hadn't worn jeans today. But how was I supposed to know that Lucas would come back from soccer practice looking like that? Face flushed, wet hair mostly slicked back, a few strands escaping and falling in front of his eyes. Damp patches on his T-shirt like he hadn't had time to dry himself properly after his shower. And how was I supposed to know that the sight of him would produce a reaction in me that was so powerful I was glad I was sitting down?

He jogged over and stood in front of me. "Hey." His smile really was something else.

"Hey." Good to know I hadn't been rendered speechless, at least.

He bent down and gave me a quick kiss on the lips. It wasn't enough. Not even close. I grabbed the front of his T-shirt and pulled him down to me again. This kiss was more satisfactory. This kiss was definitely the kind of kiss you wouldn't want your parents witnessing.

Lucas settled down next to me and took my hand.

"Now that's the kind of welcome a man could get used to."

I was going to make some snide remark about him calling himself a man, but I was distracted by his mouth. I'd never really noticed how utterly perfect it was before. How his lips looked like they were made for kissing. I must have been too busy hating him to notice.

"Jem? Are you OK? You spaced out for a second there."

The bell rang and I shook my head, tried to remember where I was and who I was and what class I had next. Spanish. Fuck.

I've never skipped a class in my life. Sure, I've pretended to be ill and stayed home once or twice, but I've never missed a class when I've actually been on the premises. The others do it all the time, especially now that we're seniors. No one really cares anymore—including the teachers. But we had a test in Spanish, and I'd studied really hard for it. Studying is pretty much the only time I can clear my mind; the only time I'm able to stop thinking about Lucas every two minutes. I looked at my watch even though I knew full well what time it was. "What have you got now?"

"Free period. Stu's challenged me to a high-stakes game of pool—although he hasn't revealed exactly what those stakes *are* yet. Doesn't matter though—he's physically incapable of beating me at pool. I don't know why he keeps trying. It's like a fly bashing its head against a windowpane. Kind of pitiful really."

I wasn't really listening; I was looking at his mouth again. Was I really going to do this? One more look at Lucas was enough to confirm that, yes, I was definitely going to do this. I leaned in close to him, whispered in his ear: "I think you should postpone that game of pool and think of somewhere we can go right now." My lips touched his ear as I spoke.

He pulled away from me so he could see my face.

"What are you...? Where do you want to go? I suppose we could go get a coffee or something. Stu can come too. Maybe Nina's free and we can make it a foursome."

Clueless. Utterly clueless. Clearly I'd have to be more obvious about my intentions. I leaned in again.

"That's not exactly what I had in mind. I meant...somewhere private...so we can..." I couldn't say it. Surely this was enough for him to catch my drift.

His eyes widened. "Ohhhh, you mean you want to…? *Now?*"

I nodded, suddenly feeling awkward. Suddenly afraid that he'd reject me and I'd have to pretend I wasn't all that bothered.

Lucas licked his lips really slowly, and if I hadn't been feeling so damn horny, the gesture might have made me gag a little bit. "I like the way you think." His smile was devastating. He glanced around. "No sign of Stu, anyway. Let's get out of here." He pulled me to my feet and we hurried out of the common room.

The corridors were empty, which was a relief. I was sure anyone who'd seen us would have known what we were up to straightaway. He led me down to the basement corridor—the one I usually try to avoid, since the smell from the boys' bathroom is ten times worse than the science block toilets. The basement is also home to two geography classrooms and I steer clear of geography whenever possible.

Lucas stopped in front of a red door—a door I'd never noticed before. He ushered me inside and switched on the light. The most unflattering, bright white fluorescent light in the known universe. I glanced around to see rows and rows of shelves filled with exercise books and binders and textbooks. Then I hit the light switch, which made Lucas laugh. There was enough light filtering through the tiny window near the ceiling for us to see what we were doing. I wondered how Lucas knew this room existed, unless he was hiding the fact that he's a secret stationery fiend. (Of course I knew exactly how he knew this room existed, but I didn't want to kill the mood by giving Sasha a moment's thought.)

"I know it's hardly the Ritz, but beggars can't be—" I shut him up by kissing him. I backed him against a table, then he turned us around till I was sitting on the table and he was standing in between my legs.

I silenced the voice in my head that was whispering, *This isn't you. You KNOW this isn't you,* because the voice was wrong. This *was* me. This is who I am now.

⌒

We've only been kissing for a minute or two before I start working on Lucas's belt buckle. A minute or so later I'm struggling out of the jeans I wish I hadn't worn. They seem annoyingly reluctant to let me go.

Another minute and I am shagging Lucas Mahoney in the stationery closet. Thank Christ he had a condom in his wallet, because I'm really not sure what I'd have done if he hadn't. Let's just say I'm relieved the issue didn't come up.

The sex is good. Really good. Better than before, even. Less self-conscious. He knows how to push all the right...um...buttons.

It's my first orgasm with a boy. That's some kind of milestone, I guess. All I know is that I want lots more of them (orgasms, not boys). I'm starting to think this sex thing could become slightly addictive.

This is far from ideal.

⌒

We go back to Lucas's house straight after school and do it again. And again. He hasn't said anything, but I can tell he's surprised. As if boys are the only ones who are allowed to be horny or something. He doesn't mind though, obviously.

We lie in his bed and talk for a while. He asks a lot of questions about me and my family. Every question he asks leads to another question, and another. It's like he's storing up information about me for future use. I have never talked about myself so much in my whole life. He must be bored senseless, but he does a good job of pretending to care.

When I'm getting dressed and hunting under the bed for a

272

rogue sock, he says, "I really like talking to you, Jem." He's still lying on the bed, hands behind his head. The duvet is covering him, but only just. Every (straight) girl's dream.

"Er…thanks." I find the rogue sock and sit down on the bed to put it on. Lucas scoots over and kisses my back, which is bare apart from my bra. Tiny kisses sneaking down my spine, making me shiver. Making me want to jump his bones again. But I can't. Mom will kill me if I'm not back in time for dinner.

He lies back again while I pull on my top. "I'm really glad you're in my life, you know."

I lean over and kiss him on the lips. The kiss lasts slightly longer than I'd intended.

I leave him lying there after making arrangements for me to come over again tomorrow. As I plod down the stairs, I can't help thinking about what he said. It was a nice thing to say. It was a nice thing to hear, even from him. I think he probably expected me to say something back.

◦

I make it home as Mom's putting dinner on the table.

"Just in the nick of time!" she says, smiling. She's in a good mood. I wonder what sort of mood she'd be in if she knew I'd been shagging Lucas Mahoney half an hour ago.

She asks where I've been and I stab a piece of broccoli and stuff it in my mouth to give myself time to think. I really should have thought about this before, but this sneaking-around-with-boys thing is still new to me. I chew the broccoli for longer than broccoli (or anything for that matter) would ever need to be chewed. By the time my mouth is rid of every last trace of food, I have it. "I was at the library with Lucas. Study date."

"Study date? Well, that's nice, isn't it? As long as you actually managed to get some work done and didn't spend all your time fluttering your eyelashes at him!" She laughs and Noah laughs too, the little traitor.

I roll my eyes. "Mother. Have you ever known me to flutter my eyelashes…*ever?*"

Noah attempts to flutter his eyelashes; he looks like he's having an epileptic fit.

Mom tries not to laugh at Noah's antics, but she can't help herself. "Sorry, love, but anyone can see you're smitten! You keep staring off into space, you've lost your appetite—although you seem to be quite keen on that broccoli. It's nothing to be embarrassed about…we've all been there."

"*I* haven't!" Noah says with as much indignation as someone with ketchup smeared around their mouth can muster.

I can feel myself blushing, which is too stupid for words. There's no point in arguing with her though—that would only make her more convinced of my smittenness.

Mom takes pity on me when Noah starts pointing and laughing about the fact that I'm blushing. She tells him to shut up and start eating. It seems like a good time to inform Mom that I have another "study date" scheduled for the next day. "Don't study *too* hard," she says, which makes me wonder if she knows that I'm lying after all. She has that Mom-knows-all look going on. But if she knew I was lying, surely she'd ground me or something? Unless she's secretly happy that I'm getting laid at long last.

Later in the evening we're sitting in front of the TV and she says, "You know, you and Lucas are perfectly welcome to study here whenever you like." I turn to look at her, but she keeps her eyes on the TV. It's not that she's smiling, not exactly. There's just something about the look in her eyes, something about the corner of her mouth that looks like it could twitch into full-on smile mode any minute now. She knows. Shit.

chapter forty-two

Today's task is Stu. I could have done it sooner, I suppose. But it'll be all the sweeter now that I've laid the groundwork with Nina.

I get up an hour earlier than usual, which is doubly hard because of the terrible night's sleep I had. I'm leaning against the kitchen counter eating Weetabix and rubbing the sleep out of my eyes by the time Mom comes in. She raises her eyebrows but says nothing.

I have to make a detour on the way to school. I'd hoped that I'd have what I needed at home—or maybe Dad would have something in his office that I could use. But my requirements are very specific—it has to be *exactly* right to make an impact.

There's a big line in WHSmith—mostly people buying newspapers. The back of the store is pretty empty though, so I take my time choosing my weapon.

I buy some other things too—a protractor and some highlighters. I don't know why I bother, because it's not like the sales assistant pays me the least bit of attention (except to ask me if I want a half-price bar of Dairy Milk with my purchase). And it's not like I'm committing a crime or anything. At least…I don't *think* it's a crime. I don't care either way.

⌒

There are a couple of kids in school early, but no one I know. I steer well clear of the common room just to be on the safe side. I head to the science block bathroom first because they're closest. There's a moment of hesitation just before I do it—only a moment though.

There are three more girls' bathrooms to get through. I go to the main ones next; I want to get them out of the way before the normal people start arriving at school. I check my watch. I reckon I have fifteen minutes tops before school starts filling up.

By the time I've finished I'm sweating from the stress. The only person who sees me anywhere near any of the toilets is a tiny little seventh-grade girl. Her blazer is three sizes too big and her skirt is all uneven at the bottom from being taken up by someone who knows jack shit about sewing. She's delving into her school bag (also three sizes too big) and bumps into me as I'm heading out of the door of the last set of toilets. She's all mumbly and apologetic and doesn't really look me in the face. She looks miserable. The school has clearly done a number on her already. She was probably completely normal and happy and smiley until she came to this shithole. I feel bad for her.

But I'm not too worried about her seeing me. No way would she have the balls to say anything, even if she'd caught me in the act. There was something about her though. For some reason I find myself thinking about her for most of the morning. I hope she has a friend to look after her. I hope she has her very own Kai. And I really hope he doesn't go and die on her.

⌒

I can't concentrate at all for the first couple of classes. It's only a matter of time.

I should have chucked away the evidence. I don't know why I didn't think of it before. And I realize I didn't do a very good job of washing my hands, so I keep rubbing at the marks until there's not a trace left. I must look like some kind of weird version of Lady Macbeth or something. No one sees though. That's the benefit of sitting at the back of the classroom in every single class.

The usual suspects are all in the common room at break time. The only one who's missing is Amber, but no one seems to notice when she's not around.

Her presence is not needed in order for the group to feel like the group. Pretty much all she adds is a pair of humongous breasts and that annoying laugh of hers. I've noticed that Bugs has been paying her a lot more attention recently, as if that will offset the gay rumors. Amber loves the attention. The poor girl has no way of knowing that he only notices her when Sasha's not around.

No one else notices when Amber arrives, aims a worried glance at Stu, who's grabbing a can of Coke from the vending machine near the door, and practically drags Sasha into a corner and starts whispering. Lucas is too busy tracing circles on my thigh with his finger, and the others are engaged in a heated debate about something meaningless that I'm trying my best not to get involved in.

I watch Sasha and Amber leave the common room. I don't feel nervous, exactly. It feels a little bit like nerves but slightly different. It's an anticipation that's only one tiny step away from excitement. I wish I could follow Amber and Sasha and listen to what they're saying. I still *could*, I suppose. But I don't want anyone getting suspicious. Speaking of suspicious, I wish Louise would stop looking at me. It's been going on for the past couple of weeks and I really, really don't like it. She keeps catching my eye. I mean, I suppose it's not *that* weird. We hang out in the same group pretty much all the time. I probably wouldn't even notice if it was Nina or Sasha or even one of the boys, but with *her* I always notice. I don't know why it makes me so uncomfortable. She's been perfectly friendly since she and Max wheedled their way back into Team Popular. Not that we've spent any time together on our own or anything, because that would be properly weird. It would be worse than me and Amber hanging out. (I still shudder to remember the time I spent ten minutes with Amber because Sasha was running late. Scintillating conversation is not her strong point. In fact, I'm pretty sure she couldn't even *spell* "scintillating.")

Lucas's hand has crept further and further up my thigh and I didn't even notice. *Now* I notice. No one else can see though, because of the table. He's talking to Bugs about soccer and touching me *there*. Bastard. I should stop him. I really, really should… stop him. Fuck.

My hand grips the edge of the table and there must be some chewing gum or something equally gross stuck on the underside because I feel something disgustingly sticky and pull my hand away. In doing so, I accidentally swipe at the half-empty can of Coke in front of me. Which ends up on Lucas's lap. Which stops him doing what he was doing. Lucas jumps up and swears. And that's when Sasha and Amber reappear. And I'm left wishing some dirty skank had disposed of their gum in the bin. And wishing everyone apart from Lucas would magically disappear so I could help him out of those jeans (and more importantly, he could help me out of mine).

Sasha looks Lucas up and down and rolls her eyes. Then she turns her attention to Stu, who's sitting with Nina on his lap, looking very pleased with himself.

"Stu? Can I have a word?"

Stu does *not* look pleased. "Can it wait? I've kind of…got my hands full right now." He squeezes Nina's waist and she giggles and squirms. "Oh yeah, that's right, baby…don't stop." He throws back his head and groans in mock ecstasy. The boys all laugh at this little performance, even Lucas, who's busy sponging his crotch with a napkin.

Stu smacks Nina's ass as she dismounts from his lap. "Same

time next week, darlin'?" he says in this crap Cockney accent he likes to adopt whenever he's being filthy (which is often). He gestures for Sasha to take Nina's place and she snaps at him, "Stu! Can you be serious for one fucking second?"

It's like a flick of a switch and he's in Serious Mode. Sasha NEVER loses her temper, so everyone knows it must be something important. I notice that more than a few girls are looking over at our table—at Stu specifically. He notices too. "Sasha, what is it?"

She pulls him aside and whispers in his ear, which is totally pointless because everyone else is going to find out in a matter of minutes. He balls his hands into fists and for a second I'm worried that he might really lose his shit, but he just stomps out of the room. Probably going to see for himself.

Sasha fills in the rest of us, and everyone's all *What?! No way! That's bullshit! Who would do something like that?* The *No way!* was my contribution. I think they bought it.

Lucas is the one who suggests we go and find Stu. He doesn't seem embarrassed about walking round school with a wet crotch.

We head for the nearest girls' bathroom en masse. And sure enough, Stu's there, staring into the first cubicle. A couple of girls are standing nearby, whispering. None of them tell the boys to get the fuck out of the bathroom—they want to see how Stu reacts. So do I.

He punches the cubicle door so hard it almost breaks. Then he goes from cubicle to cubicle, checking each one. One more punch—aimed at the wall this time—and then he storms out. Lucas and Bugs follow him. Everyone else stays behind.

I admire my handiwork. The handwriting doesn't look like mine—I made sure of that. A couple of girls in the year below crowd around us, giggling and gossiping. Sasha tells them to fuck off. Nina looks like she might burst into tears. "I don't understand," she says. "Why would anyone say that?"

One of the girls Sasha told to fuck off—it's impossible to tell which one since their backs are turned—mutters, "Probably because it's true," as she walks away. Nina makes as if to go after them, but I grab her arm. "Don't. They're not worth it." She starts to cry and I put my arm around her. "Hey, it's OK, Nina. Don't worry about it. It'll all blow over before you know it." She snuggles into the crook of my arm and really starts bawling. I'm worried she's going to snot all over my shoulder.

Sasha wets a paper towel and starts scrubbing at the wall. It's going to take a lot more than that to get rid of permanent ink. She gives up after a couple of minutes and mutters something about going to find the custodian.

Louise comes in right then and informs us that it's in all the girls' bathrooms—every single cubicle in the whole school. Sasha shakes her head, "What a fucking twisted thing to do…I mean, I know Stu can be a bit full on and stuff, but this is bollocks…isn't it?" I love the uncertainty in her voice. I love that she's not really sure. I love that Nina is so bloody impressionable that I can tell the doubt will start to infect her too—any minute now, probably.

There's a beat or two of silence, which is more telling than any words anyone could ever say, and then Amber chips in, "Of course it's bollocks. *Of course* it is." She couldn't sound less sure if she tried.

This is where I step in. "If it was true, then whoever wrote it would have gone to the police instead of scrawling it on the wall." I give Nina's shoulder a reassuring squeeze. "Don't worry about it, Nina. Really."

"I…I don't want everyone thinking my boyfriend is a…"

Say it. I want her to say the words out loud. But she doesn't. It's OK though, because the writing's on the wall in big fat black letters:

STUART HICKS RAPED ME

chapter forty-three

By lunchtime it's all anyone's talking about. Stu's been called into the principal's office, and the custodian and his assistant (who knew custodians had assistants?) have been dispatched to scrub the walls like they've never scrubbed before.

Nina's doing a brilliant job of playing the victim, which is pretty fun to watch. Lucas (now in his slightly grubby soccer shorts after the crotch-spillage) tried talking to Stu, but Stu was having none of it. Bugs just looks a bit confused by all the drama. He clearly doesn't know what to do with himself since it's probably a little too early to joke about things.

While Stu's in Mr. Heath's office the others can't help but talk about it. The number one question on everyone's lips is obviously the identity of the mystery scribbler. No one actually comes out and says that the accusation might actually be true, but the names thrown up are those of Stu's conquests (of which there are many).

"He probably broke some girl's heart and this is her way of getting revenge," says Sasha, and the others nod and mutter in agreement.

Bugs finally has something to say. His brain must ache from the effort. "Pretty extreme way of getting your own back though. I mean, accusing someone of that is no joke." More nods of agreement even though he hasn't exactly added anything to the debate.

Louise says, "I just can't think who would *do* something like this." And she looks right at me for a fraction of a second. Then she looks at Sasha, then Nina and the others. But she looked at me first. I grip Lucas's hand a little harder and I sense him turn to look at me. I don't look at him though—I can't.

Weirdly, Nina's the first one to mention the police. She asks Lucas if he thinks the school will call them in. I'm not sure why she asks him, like he's the authority on *everything*. "I doubt it. The police have got better things to do than piss about investigating graffiti."

"It's more than graffiti though, isn't it? It's, like, a campaign or something. I mean, why else would you go to so much trouble?" Louise again. I don't know if she looks at me because I won't allow myself to look at her. I stare at my apple core instead.

Nina's voice cracks as she says, "I can't even…I mean, what if it's…?" Then she properly breaks down in tears. Sasha puts her arm around her on one side and Amber does the same on the other side. No one else knows where to look. The sobbing doesn't abate and even Nina eventually seems to realize it's getting a little embarrassing. She pushes her chair back and hurries out of the cafeteria. Sasha and Amber look at each other to decide who's going to follow, and Sasha shrugs and hurries after her.

As soon as they're gone, the atmosphere changes. Everyone relaxes a bit. Lucas doesn't though—he's abnormally quiet *and* he's let go of my hand. I rest my palm on his bare leg and whisper into his ear, asking if he's OK. He nods and shrugs. "We'll talk later, OK? You still coming around after school?"

I stroke his thigh with my thumb. "Definitely. I want you to finish what you started earlier." I worry for a second that he might not be in the mood for this kind of talk, but then I remember that he's a boy and *always* in the mood for this kind of talk.

I sit back and listen to the others talk about Stu. It feels pretty good, but I can't wait for Stu to come back from the principal's office. He's been gone ages and lunchtime's nearly over. It's OK though—I'll get every little detail from Lucas later.

⌒

The girl I sit next to in Spanish (there's really no excuse for such frizzy hair in this day and age—hasn't she heard of John Frieda?) asks me if I think it's true and if I have any idea who might have written it. I'm half tempted to tell her to fuck off and mind her own business, but then I remember that this is exactly what I wanted to happen. Sometimes I find it hard to keep it all straight in my head. I wonder if this is a little bit what it's like being schizophrenic. Probably not.

"Of course it's not true," I say in a perfectly uncertain tone of voice while avoiding eye contact. "And I've got no idea who wrote it…it could have been anyone." I like how this can be taken two ways. It could have been anyone. Or it could have been any *one* of the multitude of girls he's shagged after getting them drunk or giving them drugs or just wearing them down until they're too exhausted to say no or fight him off.

Frizzy girl (Rachael?) nods and goes back to looking at her notepad. I might as well go for broke before she loses interest. "I…I'd better not talk about it though. You know, in case there are *legal* implications…"

Rachael/Frizzy's ears prick up at that, and she looks at me with narrowed eyes. "Why would there be legal implications? Unless… unless it's *true*?"

A quick shake of my head and a half-assed "Don't be ridiculous" and I can practically see the cogs whirring in her mind, thinking about who she's going to tell, what little extra details of her own she'll add when she tells her random friends that she talked to one of Stu Hicks's friends and there might actually be some truth behind the rumors.

Today is a good day.

~

I am an idiot. I didn't really think this through, did I? But then how was I supposed to know that Lucas would be all moody and weird just because one of his best mates got accused of being a rapist? You'd think I'd be happy that the graffiti's affecting everyone, but I could do without it affecting *him* right now. Nothing to do with the fact that I'm horny as hell, of course.

He's quiet on the walk to his house. I decide it's better to tackle the subject head-on, try to get it out of the way before we get back. Otherwise I might as well just give up and go home now. I link my fingers with his and lean in close. "Hey, are you OK? You seem a little distant."

He looks up and smiles, but it's a poor effort.

"Sorry. I'm just worried about Stu…You should have seen him this afternoon. He was in a right state—like, really scared. Apparently Heath gave him a right grilling."

"He doesn't have anything to be scared about. He hasn't done anything wrong."

Lucas says nothing and walks on. "Lucas? What is it? He *hasn't* done anything wrong…" I look at Lucas out of the corner of my eye and he's staring at the pavement in front of him. "…has he?" This is an unexpected turn of events.

He shakes his head and says, "No," but it's not particularly convincing.

I stop walking so Lucas has to stop too. "Lucas, is there something you're not telling me? Because you know you can tell me anything, don't you? You can trust me." *Lie.*

He looks deep into my eyes and I've never seen him look so troubled. Usually he looks like nothing in the world can touch him, but now he looks like an actual human being. "I know I can trust

284

you," he says, but when he kisses me quickly on the lips it doesn't feel right. "It's probably nothing. I mean, I'm *sure* it's nothing. It's just that Stu's slept with *a lot* of girls, you know? And most of them have been one-night stands and…" He shrugs and looks around as if the shop window we're standing next to will have the words he's looking for instead of garish signs advertising six cans of Stella beer for a fiver.

"And what?"

He shrugs again. "I suppose some of the girls haven't always been too happy about it afterward. I'm not saying…it's just you should see the texts they send him, calling him a user and saying he took advantage of them or whatever." Lucas is still searching the window for answers.

"But that doesn't mean he actually raped anyone. Those girls knew what they were getting into—it's not like people don't know what sort of reputation he's got…Unless…He hasn't said anything to you, has he?"

"No, no, nothing like that. It's just…I suppose what I'm trying to say is I can sort of imagine some girl maybe regretting what they'd done, or maybe he kind of…you know, talked her into it a little bit. Maybe gave her an extra shot or two in her drink. Which is a totally different thing, right?"

I can't believe what I'm hearing. It's clear as anything that Lucas thinks Stu might have *actually* raped someone. Because even though *he* might not think it would count as rape, that's exactly what it is. I remember what Stu was like in that greenhouse at the party. But then I also remember what he was like when I lied to him and told him I'd been raped. Suddenly I don't know what to believe anymore.

I say nothing and you can tell Lucas is regretting his choice of words but isn't quite sure what to say to make things better. "He's a good guy though, deep down. I know he is." He nods as if he's convinced by his own words.

I slip my arms around his waist. "I think we should talk about something else, don't you? I'm sure everything will be fine with Stu. And if you say he's a good guy, then I believe you. I trust *you*, Lucas."

This was clearly the right thing to say because the worry disappears from his face and the smile is back. "You trust me, do you? That's good to know." He brings his face close to mine. "Don't think I haven't noticed you checking out my legs all afternoon."

I slap him on the shoulder. "Checking out your legs? AS IF!"

He whispers in my ear. "You probably spilled that Coke on purpose, just so you could see me in shorts. I mean, really, Jem, I thought you were classier than that."

"Yeah, you're right. You've uncovered my evil plan. Next time I'll make sure a vat of Coke gets spilled on you so that you have to walk around school in nothing but your underpants." He laughs and kisses my ear lobe. It tickles.

He takes a step back and grabs my hand. "I think we should hurry up and get back to my place, don't you?" There's no mistaking the look in his eyes. He's gone from stress and worry and doubt about Stu to complete and utter lust in approximately sixty seconds.

chapter forty-four

We have sex on the sofa because it seems that neither of us can wait the extra thirty seconds it would have taken us to get upstairs to his room. It's pretty intense. He's a bit rougher than before, which is weird considering what we'd just been talking about. Don't get me wrong, I *like* it. And he's not *rough* rough or anything weird like that. It's just that there was a noticeable difference in the way he kissed me, the way he touched me.

Afterward, Lucas makes me a sandwich and we've just finished eating when we hear the sound of a key in the door. Lucas's face is priceless. He looks at his watch, grabs our plates, and legs it into the kitchen. As if the fact that we're having a snack in the living room is the worst thing about this situation rather than the fact that my top seems to have been spirited away by invisible elves or something.

When a harassed-looking woman with car keys between her teeth, five bulging bags of shopping in her hands, and a newspaper tucked under one arm walks in, I'm leaning over the back of the sofa on the off-chance the elves might have deposited my top there. At least I've got my bra on. And my jeans. So it's not as embarrassing as it could have been if she'd have arrived half an hour earlier. It's still pretty much the most embarrassing thing that's ever happened to me though.

She lets the car keys drop from her mouth onto a little dish on the sideboard, takes one look at me, and says, "Are you going to give me hand or what?"

A nervous laugh bubbles up from nowhere and I have to do my best to turn it into a cough because the last thing I want is for Lucas's mother to think I'm laughing at her. Because it's obviously Lucas's mom, unless a multitude of middle-aged women barge into his house on a regular basis. I hurry over to her.

"Sorry, I…" She hands me one of the bags, then holds out another, which means I have to abandon my lame attempt to cover my boobs with my right arm.

"No need for modesty, honey. Really. Boobs are boobs…we've all got them."

I'm tempted to drop the bags and run out of the house into oncoming traffic. Then I remember how bloody quiet this street is and decide to act like I'm totally cool with being half-naked in front of this stranger.

Lucas comes back into the room and laughs. He fucking *laughs*, the bastard. He's not wearing a top either, but it's OK for boys, isn't it? The bastards. He holds out his hands to me and says, "Let me take those. You…er…" He makes a flapping gesture in the vague direction of my chest.

I hand over the bags and look around, and that's when I see the corner of my top peeking out from behind a cushion. Thank Christ for that. I pull it over my head and smile at Lucas's mom. "Hi, I'm…"

"Jem, yes, of course you are. I've heard *all* about you." I'm not mad keen on the emphasis she puts on the word "all" there. "I'm Martha. Nice to meet you and all that. Now, could you please take this bag before my bloody arm drops off…And Lucas? Put your shirt on."

She makes me help her unpack the shopping, and it feels like a very odd thing to be doing with a complete stranger. Especially since I have no idea where anything's supposed to go. She keeps on saying things like, "No, not that shelf…*that* one, there's a good girl."

Lucas washes up the knife and chopping board from the sandwich making and directs me toward the right cupboard for the canned tomatoes. It's all too weird for words. His mom doesn't seem in the slightest bit bothered about what we'd been up to. There is no way on earth *my* mom would be so cool about it. Maybe this is what it's like to be a teenage boy—your mother not batting an eyelid at you shagging some random girl on the sofa. But she knows I'm not some random girl, doesn't she? She's heard ALL about me.

Once the shopping's put away, Mrs. Mahoney (there's no *way* I'm calling her Martha) leans back against the counter and sighs, "Put the kettle on, will you, love?" I do as I'm told while Lucas gets three mugs out of the cupboard above the kettle. He doesn't seem to think there's anything awkward about this situation. He keeps catching my eye and smiling. I can't help thinking that he's pleased his mom came home early. I mean, he'd mentioned her a few times and said he thought the two of us would get on. Whenever he did I'd change the subject, since I had less than zero desire to meet the woman who'd spawned Lucas Mahoney. But here we are, sipping tea at the breakfast bar.

Lucas doesn't look like his mom AT ALL. She's small and sharp looking. I guess Lucas must take after his dad (aka That Bastard). From the pictures I've seen, his sisters don't really look like her either. They're girl versions of Lucas.

I sit there sipping my tea, answering the occasional question, mostly listening to them banter back and forth. Mrs. Mahoney's pretty funny. I think she'd get on really well with my mom. Maybe they should meet…

And this is when it hits me. What the fuck am I doing, thinking about my mom meeting his mom? It's beyond insane. I have to get out of here—now.

I let my eyes wander over to the clock on the wall. "God, I'm so late! It's my turn to cook tonight—Mom'll kill me."

Mrs. Mahoney looks at me indulgently and then raises her eyebrows at Lucas. "She can cook too! You'd better make sure you hang on to this one, Luke! I like her."

Lucas smiles into his mug of tea. "I intend to hang on to her for as long as she'll put up with me." Mother and son laugh, and that's when you *can* see the family resemblance. It's also when I feel like I will have a panic attack if I stay in this house for one more minute.

There's nothing I can do to avoid hugging Mrs. Mahoney when we say good-bye. She holds out her arms to me like I'm some long-lost relative from Australia or something. Something about the hug makes me want to cry and I have to swallow hard and scrunch my eyes closed to try and stop that happening. Mrs. Mahoney says something about me coming over for dinner soon and I don't answer because I'm pretty sure my voice will come out all shaky and weird if I dare to speak.

Lucas walks me to the front door and kisses me.

"Nice job winning over The Mother. She loves you."

"She's really nice." It's an effort, but somehow I manage a smile.

"So are you." He hugs me close and whispers into my hair. "I meant what I said, you know. I don't plan on letting you go anytime soon."

"Well, I'm afraid you're going to have to, because my family might give me funny looks if I attempt to cook dinner with you hanging off me."

Lucas laughs at my exceptionally lame attempt at a joke. "You know what I mean, Halliday. Now shut up and kiss me and maybe, just maybe, I'll let you go…on a strictly temporary basis, you understand."

I kiss him, softly at first, then with a hunger that surprises me. It surprises him too; he pulls away after a few seconds and gestures toward the kitchen. I don't know what he's so worried about—the door's closed. I pull him toward me again, but he thwarts my efforts by wrapping me up in a bear hug.

I don't want to hug him. Hugging is intimate. Hugging is me and Kai.

I have to leave now.

Lucas looks slightly puzzled at my hasty exit, but he shrugs it off. It would never occur to him that it was something to do with him. That *he* might be the problem.

It must be nice to never have to question anything. To be so perfectly comfortable in your own skin. I wonder if I could ever feel like that or whether it's something you're just born with. Maybe I'll ask him one day, after all this is over.

Maybe not.

chapter forty-five

It's not going away, the Stu thing. Every time the words get scrubbed off, it's only a matter of hours before they're back—the handwriting might be slightly different, but the words are the same. I think it's one person though. Someone on a mission to keep this thing going—to keep everyone talking about it. It makes me wonder why someone would do that. It makes me wonder a lot of things.

Stu keeps his head down mostly. He doesn't look well. There are dark circles under his eyes as well as a look on his face that I can only describe as *hunted*. He makes the occasional joke, but you can tell it's an effort. Lucas, Bugs, and Max do their best to act like everything's normal, but the girls are all acting differently toward him. Especially Nina. They haven't officially broken up—not yet—but I know she wants to. Anyone can see it's only a matter of time. Instead of sitting with Stu at lunch or in the common room, Nina seeks out Amber and Sasha, or me (if the other two don't happen to be around). And every time she chooses to sit next to someone else instead of taking the empty seat next to him, I make sure I watch him. I like seeing the look on his face. Hopeful at first, then he doesn't even bother to try hiding the disappointment. It's pitiful.

I was walking behind the two of them on the way home from school one day and Stu put his arm around her. She didn't shrug it off, but you could tell her body was angled away from him. You could see daylight between them. Soon you'll be able to drive a fucking truck through the space between them. Part of me wants her just to get it over with, but I'm kind of enjoying the fact that she's stringing him along. Giving him tiny scraps of hope, making him wonder if maybe things will turn out OK when everyone's forgotten about it. But the new mystery graffiti scrawler is making damn sure that isn't happening. I'd like to find out who she is (at least, I *presume* it's a girl) and shake her hand. Or at least ask what her deal is.

⌒

I'm running out of time. It's time to finish this thing. There's only one letter left—the letter that makes it one whole year. I can't even fathom how I've managed to survive twelve months without him.

The perfect opportunity has presented itself. I couldn't have planned it better: Max and his brother are having another party. But the timing of it makes my heart ache: two days before Kai's final letter. Two days before the anniversary of his death. Two days before I die.

The venue leaves a lot to be desired. Apparently Max's parents were majorly pissed off about the state the house was left in last year—especially the bloody great scorch marks in the pristine lawn from the bonfire. So this year they've decided that Boreham Woods would be a more sensible option. Right next to the bridge.

Everyone's so bored of hanging out in the same old places that the idea of partying in the woods is genuinely exciting to them. They probably reckon it's going to be like some American movie—a post-homecoming party with cheerleaders and soccer players and kegs of beer. When the reality is that it'll be the same old people, doing the same old things—with the added bonus of freezing our asses off in the process.

Every time I allow myself to think about going there, I feel my stomach tighten. I've gone out of my way—literally—to avoid that place. Sometimes it's impossible, like when we're going somewhere in the car. But when that happens, I just close my eyes and picture myself somewhere else. I can still tell exactly when we're going over the bridge though. The tires make a different noise. I used to like that sound; I'd listen out for it because it usually meant we were going somewhere exciting (like IKEA). It marked the beginning of an Adventure. Now it marks nothing of the sort. It marks a boy standing in the rain, looking down at his beloved river. Looking down at the rocks below and wondering if they would smash his skull or whether he'd drown first.

With any luck I won't have to even see the bridge. I can enter the woods around the back of that creepy-looking church. It's not the fastest way to get there, but it's my only option. It'll be awful enough *knowing* it's there, but I can't allow myself to get distracted, not now. I'm so very nearly there.

Sasha thinks the party will be "good for the group" after all the crap stuff that's happened recently. And that was before yesterday's little drama, when Nina finally got around to dumping Stu. I'd been getting antsy, thinking she was going to pull that "stand by your man" crap. I should have known she'd come good in the end.

It wasn't as rewarding as I'd hoped actually. I'd been hoping for screaming and shouting, or at the very least some tears. Nope. Nina was classy enough to break up with him off the school premises. They went out for coffee at lunchtime and she came back by herself, looking amazingly composed. You could tell she was upset though. Whenever anyone asked, she'd say, "I'm fine," in this clipped, tense voice that sounded like it was about to shatter at any moment. I was fairly sure I could make her cry if I really wanted to, but that wasn't really the point of the exercise. Nina hadn't done anything wrong—unless you count her terrible taste in boys. It was Stu I wanted to hurt, and by the sounds of things, I'd done a pretty decent job. No one saw him for the rest of the day, and you could tell everyone was glad not to have to deal with him. He's been putting on a brave face today though, and Nina's had the good sense to steer clear. I don't know what this means in terms of position in the group. I wouldn't be surprised if her time was up. Only time will tell, I suppose.

I doubt Nina will come to the party though. Which is a shame, because I actually don't *mind* her that much. Not really. She's harmless, like a little piece of fluff on your favorite top. If she's clever enough (and I have my doubts), in years to come she might realize I did her a massive favor. She might even want to thank me, but of course it'll be too late for that. Anyway, I'd much rather Amber was the one left out in the cold; I really don't see the point of her. Sometimes I get caught up in this stuff, the ins and outs of the group, and then I remember I have precisely zero reasons to care. It's as if my brain forgets that my days in the inner circle are numbered too.

Three more days as one of Them.

Three more days as Lucas Mahoney's girlfriend.

It doesn't seem enough somehow. I think it's time Lucas and I paid another visit to the stationery closet.

～

I get my wish on Wednesday. We do our thing and then head up to the cafeteria to get some lunch. The only person who seems to realize what we've been up to is Sasha. She gives me a knowing, supercilious sort of look and whispers, "God, you two really can't keep your hands off each other, can you? How was your visit to the Stationery Closet of Luuuuurvve?" I *knew* he'd taken her there, and it pisses me off more than I can say. I hate knowing that everything I do with Lucas is something she's already done—and even worse, maybe even something she *taught* him. I debate stabbing Sasha in the eye with my fork but decide that might get me uninvited from the party. And I really need to be at that party. So Sasha's pretty eyes remain intact.

⌒

Today, Lucas and I arrange to meet in the closet as soon as the bell rings for lunch. I get there in record time and loiter around until the corridor clears. There's a bunch of seventh graders standing outside one of the geography classrooms gibbering about some test they've just had that was, like, sooooooo hard. Just my luck one of the girls is the one who saw me leaving the scene of the crime. She's not doing any gibbering though—she's on the edge of things, listening, looking like she wants to say something if only she could be sure she'd say the *right* thing. And if she can't be absolutely sure, she'd rather keep her mouth shut just to be on the safe side.

She sees me watching and is quick to glance away. Then she looks again. The other girls wander off and she follows them, a couple of steps behind the main group. Always a couple of steps behind.

I'm not worried about her. Not really. She probably looked away because that's what you do when you're a tiny little seventh-grade minnow and a twelfth grader looks at you. She probably doesn't even remember bumping into me. And even if she does remember, and even if she made the connection between me and the graffiti that everyone's *still* talking about, who's she going to tell? Besides, after the weekend, it won't matter either way.

I take one last look around to check the coast is clear and open the red door. My very favorite door in all the world.

The light's on, which probably should have lessened my shock at hearing a distinctly UN-Lucaslike voice coming from the shelves to my left. I freeze in the doorway. A man's voice, gruff with a slight speech impediment. It takes a moment to place it.

Mr. Bodley, the deputy head. Married to Mrs. Bodley, who I had for English in eighth grade. As close to a power couple as you can get at this dump. I've only ever heard his voice at assemblies or shouting at kids to tuck their shirts in or screaming, "NO RUNNING IN THE CORRIDORS!" so it's sort of surprising to hear him saying (with some urgency), "That's right, bad girl. Suck it." My hand flies to my mouth, which does nothing to stifle the laughter that escapes. It's OK though, because Mr. Bodley's revolting groans are so very, very loud. I'm just about to reverse out of the room (and scrub the hideous mental picture from my mind by whatever means possible) when I hear, "Ohhhhhh, Donna…"

Mrs. Bodley's first name is not Donna. It's Betty. Betty Bodley. One of the new teaching assistants, however, *is* called Donna. She has ginger hair and strange teeth. She is not attractive by any stretch of *anyone's* imagination. Still, she's a good thirty years younger than Mrs. Bodley, and Mrs. Bodley somehow doesn't seem the type to go down in the comfort of her own home, let alone in the Stationery Closet of Seediness. I'm tempted to try and get a photo of the action on my phone, even though I really have no desire to see Bodley with his trousers around his ankles.

My phone is in my hand before I realize…

No.

Lucas comes running down the corridor as I'm shutting the door. He's out of breath. "Sorry! I couldn't get away from Stu. Man, I really wish he'd stop moping about. It's such a downer." He goes to open the door and I sidestep to block him.

"Um…there's someone in there."

"Shit. Really? Who?"

"Mrs. Bodley. And she didn't seem too happy to see me either… said something about a phantom book thief? Crazy old bitch. Anyway, I'm kind of hungry. Are you hungry? Let's just go to the cafeteria." I take his hand and pull him away from the red door.

"But I thought you wanted to…?"

"I did. And now I don't. That's OK, isn't it?"

The look on his face says it's *so* not OK. But Lucas thinks he's a gentleman, so there really isn't a lot he can say about the matter. "Of course. I *am* starving. Got to carb-load for the match this afternoon anyway."

I barely say a word at lunch. Just sit and watch as Lucas shovels forkful after forkful of pasta into his mouth. I manage two or three bites, tops. He notices and says, "I thought you were hungry, Jem?" I shrug and he turns his attention back to Bugs, who's talking about some girl (fictional, no doubt) he met on the weekend. Apparently he can't bring her to the party tomorrow because she already has plans. None of the others call him on the fact that he's clearly making up an almost-girlfriend to make sure those nasty rumors about him stay dead and buried. Why is he even bothering? No one's gossiping about him anymore. Possible rapist beats possible gay boy any day.

They're all too caught up in their own stuff to notice that I'm not talking. The girls are involved in some in-depth discussion about what to wear to the party tomorrow. The forecast isn't too bad, but it's still October, which means their usual clothing choices may result in a touch of hypothermia. Amber isn't going to let that stop her wearing exactly what she wants though. "Anyway, there's gonna be a fire, isn't there? Plus, we can always find some hot boys to keep us warm…I'm totally bailing if there aren't any hot boys. It's all right for you, Lou, you've got Max. And Jem's got Lucas. It's *so* unfair. Sash, what do you say we head to Espionage if the party ends up being a bust?"

Louise ruffles Max's hair and I think I'm the only one to notice the annoyance flash across his face. She leans her head on his shoulder and goes on to assure Amber that there *will* in fact be decent boys at the party and that she reckons Max's brother is "totally up for it" if Amber can't find anyone else she fancies. Max doesn't react to this nugget of information about his brother.

I sit there messing around with my phone. I scroll through my contacts until I get to him. Then I scroll back through our messages, back before the video appeared. I haven't done this yet. I've wanted to—so many times. Wanted to remember what it was like, how good things were. What it had been like to have someone who *knew* me. I've been too scared though. I needed to hold things together, to not let myself cry and grieve and *feel*. It was difficult enough opening those damn letters. But weirdly, now feels like the right time, even sitting in the middle of the hornets' nest of Team Popular. Suddenly it seems urgent. I need to remember who I am. Because I realized something in that stupid fucking stationery closet, when I was ready to take a photo of Bodley and the slutty teaching assistant. I realized something that scared me more than you can ever imagine: I have no idea who I am anymore.

Who I've become.

chapter forty-six

Lucas wants to hang out after school. He says he wants to "talk," which is pretty much the last thing I want to do. For a millisecond or so I wonder if he's going to break up with me, but from the way he kisses me I can tell that's the last thing on his mind. It would almost be funny if he *did* dump me though. All that planning and scheming—for nothing. Talk about an anticlimax.

Lucas tries to persuade me to go around to his place after dinner, but it's family night in the Halliday household, and the one rule of family night is that nobody bails. We haven't had a proper one in ages 'cause Dad's been so busy at work. We're going back to Mr. Chow's for the first time since last year. I think Mom must have forgotten that we went there the night before he died. Or maybe she knows full well and just doesn't think it's a big deal. I'm sure I could have persuaded them to take us somewhere else, but it seems right somehow.

It's a struggle to leave Lucas after a good fifteen-minute make-out session behind the science block. I think he's as frustrated as I am after our lunchtime sexfail. "Tomorrow night seems a really long way away."

I kiss him lightly on the lips. "Don't worry. It'll be here before you know it. And we can 'talk' then, yeah?" I raise my eyebrows.

"Hey! I *do* want to talk, actually. Not sure tomorrow's quite the right time, but I'll take what I can get."

"There's a good boy…hmm…I've never had sex in the woods before. Better watch out for pine needles." I pat him on the butt and leave him standing there, staring after me. I mean, I don't bother checking, but he's *probably* staring, right?

I've never had sex in the woods before? I can't help shaking my head at my lameness. How come words like that spill out of my mouth so easily these days? I don't even have to think about it anymore. It's scary.

I was already toying with the idea of heading to Boots on the way home, but this makes up my mind. I should have just enough time before we go for dinner. Mom won't be happy. Lucas probably won't be happy. But I need to do this for me, before I disappear completely.

~

I look at myself in the mirror and see me looking back for the first time in forever. It's good to be back. Poor Fernando would have a fit if he saw me now.

Mom nearly chokes on her customary pre-dinner gin and tonic. "Oh, Jem!"

Noah raises his hand for a high five and I can't help but grin. Dad doesn't say anything. He's too busy watching the news to even notice.

I stand with my hands on my hips. "What? WHAT?! I fancied a change, OK?"

Mom takes a sip of her drink and you can tell she's not sure how to play this. She's wondering what she can possibly say to make me change my mind. In the end, she goes for silence. A sensible move on her part, I feel.

I sit down on the edge of the sofa and pretend to watch the news. Some big oil disaster that must have happened a few days ago. The sort of thing I used to care about. I used to watch the news with Dad all the time. It was kind of our thing. I can't remember when it stopped being our thing. I wonder if Dad even noticed. The look he gives me when I sit down next to him tells me that he did. And the guilt hits so hard it brings tears to my eyes.

Mom's the only one who sees, probably because she's still staring at my hair. "Oh, what's the matter, love? Is it your hair? Don't worry, I'll pay for you to go to the salon tomorrow if you like?"

I bite back the snarky comment that would have no doubt completely ruined family night. I somehow manage to focus on the TV through my tears. Lucky for me, there are some tarry-looking seabirds flapping around helplessly on a beach somewhere. Not lucky for them, obviously. "Those poor birds!"

Dad pats my knee in a vaguely reassuring way, and I can tell Mom's still looking at me—not remotely convinced. Why is it that fathers are so much easier to fool than mothers?

We sit through a plane crash, a civil war in some country I've never even heard of, and a house fire that killed a family of five. By the time Dad switches off the TV and grabs his keys, I've kind of lost my appetite.

We sit at our usual table at Mr. Chow's and everyone orders the same thing they usually do and Noah pretends his veggie spring roll is a cigar and Mom gets annoyed and tells him not to play with his food. Mom flirts a little bit with the waiter, just like she always does. Dad puts up with it and says nothing, just like he always does. Everyone plays their roles perfectly. Everything is unbearably normal.

I'm quieter than usual, watching, listening, taking it all in. Absorbing the little things they do and say, trying to etch them permanently into my brain. Because it's only just occurred to me that this will be the last time we're all together like this. And I've only just realized that maybe I should have been spending time with Mom and Dad and Noah instead of wasting my time on this stupid revenge thing. It all suddenly seems a bit ridiculous. Like my priorities have been horribly, obviously wrong, but there hasn't been anyone to tell me. That's a cop-out, really. *Kai's* been telling me, but I haven't been listening. It's too late now.

Mom and Dad have coffee after dinner, and Noah has a hot chocolate. I have nothing. No one noticed that I barely ate any of my food. Mom's a little bit drunk and is now focusing her flirting energies on Dad. Normally this kind of behavior makes me want to throw up a little bit, but tonight it's OK. Tonight I'm glad to see it, because you can tell they really love each other. And I think this means they're going to be OK when I'm gone. They're strong enough to get through it, so I don't need to worry.

Who am I kidding?

chapter forty-seven

Sasha wanted to get ready at my house. I tried to put her off, but she was having none of it. When I finally agreed, she clapped her hands together and said, "Our very first sleepover!" I said nothing. I was too busy wondering how someone coming over to get ready for a party automatically gave them an invite to *sleep* there. It must be some secret girl code no one bothered to tell me about. Anyway, I'm not going to sweat it, since there's no way she'll end up coming back to my place tonight.

No school today because of a teacher training day (which never fails to make Mom go on about teachers being lazy). I spend most of the day sleeping. I can't help feeling like this is a bit of a waste of my last day as a member of Team Popular, but I don't want to see any of them before tonight. An hour or so before Sasha arrives, I sit cross-legged on my bedroom floor and get to work. It makes me think of Christmas Eve and a giggle bubbles up from nowhere. I think I am losing the plot entirely.

Sasha arrives bang on time and her eyes practically pop out of her head when she sees my hair. She doesn't have a chance to say anything though, because Mom's right there asking her how she's been and blah blah blah. So Sasha spends a good twenty minutes chatting to Mom in the kitchen. She's so bloody *comfortable* with people. Mom loves her—that's obvious as anything. She laughs at everything Sasha says, which is stupid because Sasha is not a particularly hilarious person. Even Dad decides to get in on the action by wandering into the kitchen and chipping in to the conversation every now and then. I get the feeling that if I could disappear through the wall I'm leaning on, my parents would be perfectly satisfied with Sasha as a replacement daughter. The one redeeming thing is that I'm pretty sure Noah would prefer *me* as a sister, because I'm not sure Sasha would be up for beating the crap out of him in the various video games he makes us play. Correction: *made* us play. Thinking about it, I can't remember the last time he asked me to play a game with him. I always used to pretend I had better things to do, but I never did. I loved it if I'm honest. It was the perfect opportunity to teach him some pretty choice swear words to impress his friends with.

I think it's probably for the best that I haven't been spending heaps of time with Noah and Mom and Dad recently. If I tell myself this enough times, I might actually be able to believe it.

Mom and Dad and Sasha are all staring at me. I'm clearly supposed to say something. I suppose I *could* risk a "yes" or "no" or "maybe," but I go for a confused-sounding "hmm?" instead.

Dad shakes his head and laughs in that incredibly irritating *What is she like?* way. At least he doesn't start singing the old David Bowie song he normally warbles when I'm not listening to him. That would be too embarrassing for words. "Sasha was just saying her parents have invited you to their house in Scotland for the weekend…?"

Um. What? House in where? This is news to me. Why is Sasha doing this to me?!

Sasha sees my look of utter bafflement and laughs.

"Yeah, sometimes my folks take pity on me having to hang out with them in the middle of the Highlands, so they let me invite a friend along…and I thought you…might like to? It's not for a month or something, so you don't need to decide now." She seems almost shy all of a sudden, as though she genuinely gives a toss whether I go to bloody Scotland or not. I mean, who even has an extra house in Scotland?! A house in France would be acceptable; Italy would be even better.

I fake my most winning smile, which really isn't all that winning, and say, "Sounds cool, I'd be well up for that…Now, we'd better get ready if we don't want to be late." Then I grab Sasha by the shoulders and maneuver her out of the room like a shop dummy. There's zero chance of us being late. We've planned to get to the party no earlier than eight thirty and it's not even six o'clock yet. But Sasha insisted on coming around crazy early. She is *seriously* high maintenance.

I shoo Sasha up the stairs, and as soon as I close the door she says, "What the fuck have you done to your hair?!" Her facial expression is confused more than anything else.

I tug at the ends of my hair, all self-conscious and lame. "I just fancied a bit of a change, that's all."

She throws her bag and coat on my bed and turns to face me. "A *bit* of a change? Moving your part is a *bit* of a change, wearing your hair in a ponytail is a *bit* of a change…this is an *epic* change!" Now she's the one maneuvering me so that we're both standing in front of the mirror that's on the back of the door. She narrows her eyes and looks at me like I'm a painting and she's an art critic and she's not at all sure she likes what she sees. "Hmm…" She starts running her hands through my hair, fluffing it this way and that, and I really, really want her to stop. But I smile and do my best to act like I'm completely comfortable with this situation.

"It's going to take some getting used to, that's for sure. You know…you look kind of *dangerous*. Like you should ride a motorbike and have loads of piercings and drink tequila."

"It's the exact same color my hair used to be." Suddenly I want her to remember that I was a person before. That I didn't just spring to life the moment she noticed me.

"Is it? Mmmm…" Like she's not really listening. "I think it's going to be fine, you know. We can work with this. Maybe red lipstick? I happen to have the *perfect* color, if you don't have any. Has Lucas seen it yet?"

I must remember that it really wouldn't be OK to punch her in the face. "Not yet."

"Ooooh, I wonder what he'll make of it. He'll probably think it's hot. It'll be like having a whole new girlfriend or something." Maybe a small punch would be OK…a quick jab to the jaw perhaps.

I shrug off Sasha's hands, because the touching is going on way too long for my liking. "I'm not all that fussed about what Lucas thinks, to be honest. What I do with my hair isn't really anyone else's business."

I open my wardrobe and stare at the contents so I don't have to witness whatever irritating look Sasha's giving me right now.

"You're so right, you know. I wish I could be more like you."

I can't help it. I snort with laughter and slam the wardrobe doors closed again. "Sasha, that may well be the funniest thing you have ever said." And for some reason I'm laughing hysterically and I couldn't even stop if I wanted to. Luckily it feels so damn good to laugh—to properly laugh like I haven't done in so very long—that I have no desire to stop. I don't even care that she's looking at me like I've completely lost the plot.

I'm laughing so hard I can't even stand up straight. I collapse face first onto the bed. My stomach feels like I've done a thousand crunches. Just as I start to get a grip, I hear Sasha start to giggle, and then the giggles turn into full-on proper laughter. She flops down onto the bed next to me and we're both just lying there laughing our bloody heads off. And I don't want to admit it to myself, but it feels incredible. It feels like *before*.

"Oh my God, Jem! Has anyone ever told you that you're fucking crazy?"

"It may have been mentioned once or twice. Why do you ask?" I prop myself up on one elbow and look at her. Sasha looks more normal, more *human*, than I've ever seen her. Even when she was crying that day in the bathroom. She's hardly wearing any makeup and she looks something close to beautiful.

"Can I tell you something? You have to promise not to laugh, OK?" She looks almost shy.

"I think it's safe to say I'm pretty much laughed out for the time being."

"OK, this is really lame and everything...and I know it's the kind of thing you say when you're, like, twelve...but what the fuck, I'm going to say it anyway. You're...sort of my best friend. And I just wanted you to know that. I mean, Amber and Louise are fine. I like them, I really do. But you're different from them. I feel like we connect on another level or something." She cringes and laughs. "Told you it was lame!"

I'm focusing on the little flash of her toned stomach that's peeking out above her jeans. And all I can think about is lying here all those times with Kai. My *actual* best friend. No one could ever replace him. Certainly not this girl with her perfect hair and perfect body and perfect everything. I only have to pretend for a little longer. You can do anything, say anything, when you know the end is in sight.

"It's not lame. OK, it's really quite lame...but I feel the same way so it's cool." You can say *anything*.

I do my best to match the grin that's spreading across her face. "Yay! We're, like, totes besties!" I think (hope) she's being ironic, but it's really hard to tell. "Shall we hug it out? I think we probably *should*, don't you?" She hauls herself up into a sitting position and I do the same.

While we're hugging she says, "We should probably get a couple of those BFF necklaces, don't you think?"

"Why stop there? Why don't we get those crappy broken-heart pendants…you know, the ones you put together to make the heart whole again? Or matching tattoos, maybe? That would be *such* a good look." Sasha starts to giggle, which makes me laugh.

The weird thing is, I can almost imagine a future in which we *are* the kind of friends she thinks we are now. I'm not entirely sure how I've ended up in a place where I can imagine such a thing, but I really, truly *can*. We would go and stay at her house in Scotland and steal a bottle of something from her dad's drinks cupboard and stay up late talking about boys and go hiking in the mountains the next day. This almost-possible future shimmers in front of me, vanishing whenever I try to focus on it. It's just as well really, because if I could see it properly, it might actually be a future I would want. A future almost worth living for.

chapter forty-eight

Mom and Dad are watching TV when we eventually come downstairs. We're running late, of course. Sasha couldn't make up her mind about what to wear. She brought three tops with her, tried each one on twice, asked me detailed questions about how awesome her rack looked and then ended up wearing something of mine she found by rummaging through my wardrobe when I was in the shower. It's not even new—some old band T-shirt I haven't worn in years. She decided to go for a "rock chick" look, as she calls it, in honor of my new hair. She looks good. I won't be getting the T-shirt back, of course. Not that it matters.

We're both wearing short skirts and boots. Sasha's wearing tights but I'm not. I have my reasons. I'm going to be fucking freezing, but I don't care. I'll just stand right next to the fire for most of the evening or something.

Mom makes us parade in front of her, much to Dad's embarrassment. There's not much a dad can really do in this situation, is there? Nothing he says will be right. Mom says we look lovely—she's not the least bit bothered that my skirt's even shorter than Sasha's. She even compliments Sasha on the bloody T-shirt, which is strange because she never liked *me* wearing stuff like that. ("Couldn't you wear something a bit less…black?") Then she says something ridiculous about us looking like sisters, which really tickles Sasha for some bizarre reason. She slings her arm around my shoulder and calls me "sis" on the way out of the front door. Sasha's slightly drunk. I'm completely sober, even though she thinks I drank as much as she did of the vodka she brought. Not very observant, that girl. There's no way I can risk being drunk this evening.

Mom and Dad think the party is at Lucas's house. I probably didn't need to lie, but you can never be entirely sure about the things parents will freak out about. And Mom knows that I can't stand being anywhere near the bridge these days, so she'd probably think something was up. Dad's given me money to get a taxi to be home by one at the very latest. Sasha's never allowed to stay out past midnight, so she won't shut up about how "cool" my parents are. "I'm staying at your place every Saturday night from now on… you don't mind, do you?"

I link arms with her and say, "Of *course*, I don't mind."

❧

We meet Louise and Amber at the church, which is looking even creepier than usual. I've only ever seen it in the daytime before. The graveyard is one of those really old ones with headstones sticking out of the undergrowth at odd angles. It's nothing like the one where Kai is buried—all regimented rows and manicured grass. He'd have preferred it here. The two of us used to come up here and wander around, reading the inscriptions. There was never anyone else here and it was nice and peaceful among all the dead people.

Amber's wearing a fake fur coat that actually makes hugging her a pleasant experience for once. Louise is wearing as little as possible—not even a coat. She clearly doesn't want to hide her assets, even if it means a slight case of frostbite. I can't tell if she's smirking or smiling when she says, "Nice hair," to me. Amber says she LOVES it and wishes she could get away with something so *extreme*. Extreme hair? Fuckwit.

Louise leads the way through the graveyard—she's even brought a flashlight. There's a beautiful stone archway you have to go under to get to the path through the woods. I have a picture on my phone of Kai standing there with his arms reaching out to touch both sides of the archway. The photo is one of my all-time favorites—he looks a little bit like an angel.

I wonder if Louise is thinking about him or if she genuinely has no problem being this close to the place he died. She certainly seems fine, yammering on about Max, but maybe she's trying to distract herself. Amber's trying to talk to me about Lucas, but all I can think about is how cold my legs are and how I'm a complete fucking idiot for not wearing jeans or long johns or something. The others don't seem the slightest bit bothered by the cold, which makes me wonder if maybe I'm shivering because I'm nervous— scared, even. I keep telling myself that it will all be over soon. A few more hours and I'll be back at home in my own bed and I'll never have to spend another minute in the company of these people.

We hear the party before we see it. Crappy R & B music blaring out through the woods, and it jars somehow. There should be someone playing an acoustic guitar, maybe accompanied by bongo drums or something.

The bonfire is smaller than the one at Max's house last year. I guess someone doesn't want to risk a full-on forest fire breaking out. There are loads of people here already; I recognize some of the faces from last year. That ramps up the anxiety levels a little. Some older boys sitting around the fire don't even try to hide the fact that they're blatantly ogling us the minute we enter the clearing. One of them looks so much like Max that they could be twins. He jumps up and says, "Welcome, ladies! Grab a blanket and make yourselves comfortable." He wraps Louise in a big bear hug. "Hello, dear almost-sister-in-law…always a pleasure." They hug for slightly too long and Sasha and I exchange A Look.

Once the too-long hugging is over, Louise introduces me to Max the Elder (Sebastian, which is the perfect name for a sleazy wanker if ever I heard one). The other girls must have met him last year. Another reminder that things were very, very different back then.

Max and his brother might look the same, but Sebastian makes Max look like a Jane Austen hero (not that I've read any Jane Austen novels, but I've seen enough TV adaptations to give me a fair idea). He hugs each one of us and spends an unnecessary amount of time stroking Amber's fur coat. Amber loves it, obviously.

I look around while Sebastian introduces his equally sleazy mates to Amber and Sasha, who are in full-on girly giggle mode. I'm embarrassed for them.

The boys—*our* boys—are milling around near the "bar."

This consists of three coolers and a few random bottles sitting on a tree stump.

I wander over and snake my hands around Lucas's waist; he doesn't even flinch. He must be used to girls molesting him in public. He slips his hands over mine and I rest my head on his shoulder. I like having my body pressed up against his like this. He feels solid and strong. He'll be broken soon enough.

Bugs rummages in a cooler, cracks open a can of beer, and hands it to me. He looks me up and down.

"Nice pins, Halliday. Not sure about the hair though…!"

Of course now Lucas has to turn around to check me out. "Whoa. You look so…different! Good different, I mean. Not that I didn't like the way you looked before of course…I should proba-bly stop talking now, right?"

"That would probably be a good idea." I'm grinning like a fool; I can't help it. I like it when Lucas acts like one of us normal people.

His eyes flicker down to look at my legs. "You look awesome, babe. *Cold*, but awesome." His kiss tastes like beer.

314

I smile my most un-Jemlike smile. The one Lucas seems to find irresistible. "Well, you'll just have to think of a way to warm me up, won't you?"

His eyes light up. "I'm sure I can come up with *something*."

Bugs starts making alarmingly realistic vomiting sounds. "Jesus, aren't you two over that annoying honeymoon period yet? You're making the rest of us feel bad…ain't that right, Stu?" He elbows Stu in the ribs and Stu gasps and winces. He tries to smile and laugh to cover it up, but we all noticed. "Dude, I hardly touched you! I appreciate you playing along to make me look all strong and manly in front of Halliday here, but it's really not necessary. Anyone can see she wants a piece of the Bugmeister…as soon as she's got over this ridiculous infatuation with Mr. Perfect here." Lucas pretends to be affronted at the slur on my name, and he and Bugs start a sword fight (with invisible swords, of course). Stu and I stand back and watch. He's uncharacteristically silent.

One of us has to say something, and it looks like it's going to be me. "Are you OK?" He looks confused until I indicate the fact that he's still clutching his ribs with one hand.

His hand drops to his side and he takes a massive swig of beer. "Yeah, I'm fine. Just got the shit kicked out of me at tae kwon do last night."

I nod and take a sip of beer just for something to do.

One measly beer isn't going to hurt. I could probably have two or three and still be totally fine. It might help warm me up a bit. My teeth start chattering and Stu gives me an amused look. "You're not exactly dressed for the weather, are you?"

I shake my head, still shivering.

Stu laughs. "Girls are mental. Do you want, like, a blanket or something? I think Seb must have raided the local homeless shelter. Here." He reaches into a bulging black trash bag and hands me a bundle of tartan. I sniff it dubiously just in case he's not kidding about the homeless shelter. It smells fine so I put it over my shoulders.

The shivering starts to abate just as Bugs dies a protracted mock death and Lucas wipes the mock blood from his mock sword on his real jeans. He does this ridiculous sweeping bow in front of me. "May I claim a kiss, my lady? I have vanquished the evil Count Numbnuts, and your reputation as a lady of impeccable taste and virtue has been restored."

I pretend to swoon into his arms. "My hero!" Then we kiss for a bit until I feel a tap on the shoulder.

"Sorry, Luke, urgent girl talk is required." Sasha drags me away from Lucas and behind a tree.

"Nice blanket you've got there, by the way. Refugee is a really good look for you! Right. Here's the deal. One of Sebastian's friends is super hot and clearly into me. I think his name's Rory... or maybe Corey...it's definitely something with a *y* on the end anyway. So...what do you reckon? Should I shag him?" She talks fast and keeps on peeking around the tree as if her prey might make a run for it any minute.

Why the fuck are you asking me? That's what I want to say. But I guess in Sasha's world this is exactly the sort of conversations best friends are supposed to have. "Sash, we've been here all of ten minutes. You don't need to decide now, do you? Why don't you talk to him a bit more? Find out some more about him...starting with his *actual* name, perhaps."

She laughs. "Honey, I'm not looking for a *husband* for Christ's sake...I just want to get laid."

I cringe and she laughs and calls me a prude.

"Hey! I'm *so* not! I just...I don't know. I think you deserve better than a shag with some random posh boy in the woods, that's all." I'm surprised to find I actually mean it.

She smiles at me indulgently like I'm a toddler who's just

said something totally adorable or used a potty for the first time. "Awwww, you're too cute. Really. Thanks for looking out for me, best friend. But don't try to tell me you and Lucas won't be at it like rabbits before the night is out." Her laugh is filthy.

She knows me too well. Even though she doesn't know me at all. "Fine, go shag Rory-Corey-Balamory. I'll catch up with you later, OK?"

She grins. "You're the bestest best friend ever, you know?"

I roll my eyes. "Yeah, yeah." I grab her arm just as she's about to take off. "Make sure he uses a condom, OK?"

"Yes, *Mom*!"

Then I'm alone. I could slip into the woods and head home. I take a single step away from the firelight and music. Then another step. Before I know what's happening, the trees have thinned and I'm standing on the edge of the ravine. Looking down at the river. The bridge is on my right, but I'm careful not to look at it. The lights twinkle in the corner of my eye, trying their best to attract my attention, but I'm stronger than that.

Everything looks eerie and beautiful in the moonlight. It's a scene you could write poems about if you were the sort of person who did that kind of thing.

The sound of the water is loud in my ears, drowning out the music and laughter and shouting from the woods. I stand so close to the edge that the toes of my boots are resting on nothing but thin air.

It would be so easy to take another step. So tempting.

I think of him. Jumping. Did he change his mind as soon as he jumped? Falling. Hitting the rocks. Did it hurt? What if the last thing he felt was unimaginable pain?

I step back from the edge. I have work to do.

chapter forty-nine

By the time I make it back to the clearing a few more people have arrived. Still, it's not a huge party—maybe twenty people in total. More a gathering really. Sasha's nowhere to be seen, so I assume she's with Posh Boy or some other random guy.

There's a couple dancing near the fire. As I get closer, I see that it's Amber and Sebastian, grinding away like no one's looking. Her coat's nowhere to be seen and her boobs are practically hanging out of her too-tight top. The rest of Sebastian's mates are lounging around the fire, watching. Amber's loving the attention. She'd make an excellent stripper.

"Don't suppose there's room for me under that blanket?" Lucas pulls me close to him and I pull the blanket around his shoulders. "Where did you disappear off to? I've been looking for you everywhere."

I bury my face in his neck and breathe him in. There's a vaguely smoky smell as well as the aftershave he wears because he knows I like it so much. I close my eyes and forget, just for a minute.

"Do you want another drink? Or I could toast a marshmallow for you?" He's always doing this, seeing if I want stuff. Checking I'm OK. Almost like he cares.

"That's the best offer I've had all day." I smile up at him and we look into each other's eyes for a moment or two.

So we sit on a log by the fire, snuggled up under the blanket. And Lucas toasts some marshmallows and I burn the roof of my mouth a little and he licks some sticky oozy marshmallow off my fingers and it's all very cute. Anyone watching us would think we're the perfect couple. Unlike Max and Louise, who are sitting across the fire from us. You wouldn't notice anything was wrong unless you were looking, but I'm *always* looking. Max has his arm around Louise's shoulders, but his attention is focused on Bugs, who seems to be involved in some sort of drinking challenge (against himself, of all people, since his usual drinking buddy seems intent on spending his evening staring moodily into the fire). Louise keeps getting her phone out every couple minutes. When she's not busy texting she's sipping from a bottle of wine and looking like she'd rather be anywhere but here. I catch her eye once or twice, but she pretends not to notice. Maybe it's getting to her after all—being close to the bridge.

All of a sudden, I'm hit by a massive wave of guilt and I wish more than anything that I'd done what Kai asked me to. I should have looked out for her. Made her talk to me even though she made it abundantly clear she didn't want to. We could have helped each other, I think. Once we'd got over the whole "hating each other" thing. But it's too late now. I just have to assume she's going to be fine. I hope she'll be OK, I really do.

~

I'm three beers down when Lucas asks me to dance. I shrug off the blanket and he pulls me to my feet. No one else is dancing, but the music is half-decent for the first time all night, so I don't care. Amber and Sebastian are kissing up against a tree on the other side of the clearing. At least, I hope that's all they're doing.

Lucas holds me close as we dance. It's not so much dancing as shuffling from side to side, but it's the first time we've ever danced together. It's a nice thing to do. I wish I'd had a chance to do it more, maybe in some fancy ballroom with twinkly fairy lights and velvet curtains. I close my eyes and listen to the music and imagine Kai's arms wrapped around me. He was about the same height as Lucas, a little slimmer though. We would have danced together at the prom for sure. Except that wouldn't have been in some fancy ballroom. It's held in the school gym, as if a few pink helium balloons are enough to distract everyone from the smell of boy sweat.

"Mind if I cut in?" Sasha, slurring her words a bit. Lucas looks annoyed, but he says nothing.

I step back. "He's all yours."

Sasha snorts. "I don't want to dance with *him*, doofus. Been there, done that. I want to dance with *you*."

"Oh. Right." Lucas and I exchange a puzzled look, but we both know better than to argue with Sasha.

"Don't mind me," he says in a tone that makes it quite clear that he definitely does mind.

"Off you go now." Sasha shoos him away then puts her arms around me and starts to sway. I think the swaying is down to the amount of alcohol she's consumed, because it's definitely not in time with the music.

"Boys are crap." She sticks out her bottom lip and I think I'm supposed to find it endearing.

"Awww, did Corey or whatever his name is not live up to expectations?"

"You could say that. There was nothing *up* about him, if you know what I'm saying."

"Oh. *Oh.*"

"I was better off with Lucas. He never had any problems in that department—not even once. There's no need to look at me like that! I don't want him back, if that's what you're thinking. Besides,

I don't think I could get him back even if I wanted to. Which I don't. He's totally into you...anyone can see that. The way he looks at you when you're not even looking at him. That boy is one smitten kitten, I'll tell you that for nothing."

"You are completely hammered, aren't you? No more booze for you tonight, OK? We should get you some water."

"You think this is drunk? This isn't drunk! I've been waaaaaay drunkerer. Just ask anyone!" She rests her head on my shoulder. Some of the others are watching us; Bugs gives me a sympathetic wave. "I'm so glad we're friends, Jem. Just think...if I hadn't been bawling my eyes out in the bathroom that day, we might never have even talked. Thank God for PMS, eh?"

I let her ramble on some more, all the while slowly maneuvering us toward the others. I sit her down next to Bugs, ask around until I finally get my hands on a bottle of water (a quick sniff to make sure it's not vodka), and hand it to Sasha with the strict instruction that she drink all of it. Bugs assures me he'll look after her. He slings his arm around her shoulder and she snuggles into the crook of his arm; the delight on his face couldn't be any more obvious. She hasn't been near him since the gay rumors started, so he's definitely going to make the most of this opportunity.

There's no room left on any of the logs so Lucas kindly offers me his lap to sit on. I whisper, "Sorry about that. She's pretty wasted."

He wraps his arms around me. "I hate it when she's like that. And her timing sucks."

"Why? Were you about to go all *Dirty Dancing* on me?"

He laughs and I like the feeling of his breath on my neck. "Yup. Nobody puts Jem in a corner."

I nudge him in the ribs. "Wow. You can quote it and everything. *Impressive.*"

"If you tell anyone, I'll never forgive you...but yeah, I might have seen the movie once or twice. Or thirteen times. That's what

comes of being raised in a household full of women. At least…
that's my excuse and I'm sticking to it."

"Your secret's safe with me. I solemnly swear I won't tell Stu
and Bugs the first chance I get." I lean back into him and stare
into the fire. For a minute or so I forget what I'm going to do. I
honestly forget. Too busy getting caught up in how good it feels
to sit here with him.

I'm about to say something when he whispers in my ear. "Can
we go somewhere…to talk?"

This is perfect. "Can't we talk here?" I'm not going to make it
easy for him.

"Um…this is the kind of talking that's really better done
in private."

"Fine. Let's go somewhere private and *talk*. Let me just grab
a blanket. Blankets are *always* useful whenever talking's involved,
I find."

chapter fifty

We walk hand in hand through the woods like Hansel and Gretel. I lead us toward the river, retracing my earlier steps. I lay the blanket down on the ground and we sit.

The sitting progresses to lying pretty quickly, mostly because I push Lucas down onto his back and straddle him. I'm fully aware that this is the very last time this is going to happen; I intend to make the most of it. I kiss him like there's no tomorrow, which is apt because there are very few tomorrows left. It doesn't seem right that Lucas Mahoney is the first, last, and only boy I've ever had sex with. The only consolation is that he's pretty good at it. And at least I won't die a virgin.

I kiss his neck the way he likes and feel his Adam's apple move under my lips when he swallows hard.

I press my body into his and he groans, but it's a different, frustrated sort of groan and it stops me in my tracks. I remove my hand from his crotch and look up at him. "Er…what's wrong?"

He closes his eyes and squirms like he's in pain.

"Believe it or not, I did actually want to talk to you."

"But I thought you wanted to—"

"Jem, if I wanted to have sex with you, I would have said something like, 'Let's go have sex in the woods.' Not very romantic, I know, but it would have got the point across." Lucas never says shagging or fucking. Sometimes I wish he would.

I clamber off him and make a cursory effort to smooth down my tousled hair. "OK, I'm listening. What do you want to talk about? Philosophy? Current affairs?"

He sits up and shakes his head, smiling. "You're such a smart-ass, you know that?"

"Yup, and you *love* it."

His smile vanishes and he's dead serious all of a sudden. "I do, actually."

"Um…OK." I giggle nervously. And the nerves are actually real.

"I love you, Jem. That's why I wanted to talk. Well, it's not so much talking as saying something really. Because you don't have to say anything back. I just had to say it. So…yeah. I love you. Kind of a lot." He doesn't look away. His eyes are on mine the whole time.

I have no words. Because I think he means it. I mean, he can't possibly actually *love* me, because this thing we're doing isn't real. But I think *he* believes it, which is the important thing. Everything has been leading up to this moment, even though I didn't think it would ever happen. I was working hard toward something I never dared think was possible.

The silence continues, neither of us breaking eye contact. I need to say something soon. Now, in fact.

"I love you too." I don't stutter or mumble as I say the words. They're surprisingly easy words to say when it comes down to it. They trip off the tongue so nicely.

"Really?" I wasn't expecting this. It makes him sound…needy.

"*Yes*, really."

"I…I wasn't sure. Of course I hoped you might feel the same, but I…sometimes you seem kind of distant, like you're thinking other things when we're together, but when you're with me—when you're really *with* me—it's…pretty amazing."

The talking needs to stop. "You'd better kiss me now, Lucas Mahoney."

He smiles—a smile to rival the sweetest smile I've ever known. A smile that I would have given anything to see on Kai's face in this situation—or any situation. I would kill to see that smile again.

Lucas pulls me toward him gently. He kisses me and it's all tender and soft. It's not what I want, but I let him lead the way for a minute or two. Then I push him back down onto the blanket and do things my way.

As I unzip his jeans, I realize that I'm angry. I'm angry with him for saying those ridiculous words, and I'm angry with myself for saying them back. I feel as if I've betrayed myself in some fundamental way.

When we're doing it, I'm trying really, really hard not to think about anything. Not to think about the fact that this is the last time I'll ever have sex. I try to focus all my thoughts on how good it feels. How powerful I feel when I'm on top of him.

Lucas is close to coming when the cold realization hits me: I'm angry because I feel something. And that something was definitely not part of the Plan.

Those words were easy to say for a reason.

Those words were easy to say because I meant them.

Fuck.

<hr />

We lie facing each other on the blanket. He tucks a strand of hair behind my ear and rests his hand on my cheek. There is serious gazing going on here and it's not all one way.

There are tears fighting to escape, but I won't let them. Tears would ruin everything.

Eventually I say, "We should probably get back to the party. People might think we've been eaten by wild bears or something."

Lucas smiles lazily. "I'm sure people have a pretty good idea of what we've been doing."

"You're probably right. Still, I think you should go back first. I'll be right behind you."

He's puzzled, which is understandable. But he doesn't question me. He's floating on that hazy post-sex cloud.

He tells me he loves me again, and this time I can't say it back. I just can't. He doesn't seem to mind, because I kiss him like I love him.

He leaves me sitting on the red blanket. Alone in the woods.

I wait a few minutes—five, maybe ten. Longer than I should. Am I really going to do this? Am I brave enough to do this with all those people watching?

I think of him. My Kai. Curled up under his desk. Broken and lost.

Yes. I can do this. I *must* do this.

chapter fifty-one

The first surprise is that a strange sense of calm descends on me as I make my way back to the clearing. I'm ready for this. They can do their worst; I'm immune to whatever they can throw at me. I've no doubt that it's going to be ugly, but I'm fine with it.

The second surprise is that the clearing's almost empty. There are just five people left. Luckily three of those people happen to be the ones I'm after.

Lucas is standing close to the fire. Stu is sitting, leaning against a tree, swigging from a half-empty bottle of whiskey. Bugs still has his arm around Sasha. Her head rests on his shoulder and her eyes are closed. I hope she's not asleep; she probably won't want to miss this. Max is rummaging through the sole remaining cooler for a drink and Louise is watching him. She's always watching him. I wonder if she thinks the same about me with Lucas.

I wander over toward the fire. The flames are different now—paler than before. The heat seems fiercer than it was when we left. "Where did everybody go?!"

Bugs looks up, careful not to dislodge Sasha's head from his shoulder. "Amber had a sudden desire to strut her stuff on a real dance floor so she led everyone off like the bloody Pied Piper of Espionage. No prizes for guessing what *you* were up to. Lukey boy certainly came back with a spring in his step." Lucas shoots him a filthy look. Maybe he thinks he has to protect my honor or something. Bugs just laughs. "Mate, don't look at me like that. If you're gonna get laid as often as this, you have to at least let me take the piss once in a while. It's all I've got, man." I'm tempted to point out that he now has Sasha's drool on his jacket, but I don't.

I saunter over to the now depleted pile of bags where the stereo was earlier. I hadn't noticed the silence until now. It's a peaceful, sleepy kind of silence. And I'm about to shatter it.

I grab my bag and go sit by the fire.

We sit there chatting quietly for a few minutes. Except I'm not really involved in the chatting. Mostly I'm thinking, *Am I really going to do this? Really? Maybe in a minute or two.* Lucas is on my left-hand side, Max on my right. Stu's the only one not really part of our little fireside circle—for now. He's perfected the art of looking mean and moody over there. He'll be meaner and moodier in a matter of minutes. Sasha stirs from her sleep when Bugs accidentally laughs a little too loudly. She yawns and stretches and asks where everybody went. Bugs calls her Sleeping Beauty and she smiles sweetly.

Lucas keeps glancing my way and smiling, like we share a special secret. I look away each time, almost like I'm trying to warn him about what's coming. Like I want him to know that everything's not OK, so that it's not so much of a shock. It doesn't seem to work though, because he keeps smiling goofily. This isn't going to be pretty.

No more stalling. I start to speak, but my mouth is so dry I have to clear my throat and start again. Maybe I could have another drink and *then* do it. But then Bugs says, "You all right there, Halliday?"

"Um. Yeah. I…I've got something for you. It's just…" I take one of the wrapped packages from my bag and lean over to hand it to Bugs.

He looks thoroughly baffled, and the others do too. Bugs laughs—a little awkwardly, I think. "I knew it! I *knew* you were just biding your time with Mahoney until you could get your hands on a real man. What's this? A scrapbook for us to fill with happy memories of our wonderful future as Mr. and Mrs. Bugs? Really, you *shouldn't* have!"

Lucas pouts. "I'm not sure how I feel about this." Bugs shakes his head and looks at Lucas with faux sympathy. "Dude, you're just going to accept that the better man won. I'm sure you'll get over it, in time."

I clear my throat again. I could seriously do with some water. Or vodka. "Don't worry, I've got something for you too. And Stu." I hold out two more wrapped parcels. Stu looks over and it's clear that he couldn't be less interested in what's going on. Still, he pulls himself upright and sort of staggers over. He doesn't sit down though—just stands over me, swaying ever so slightly. He doesn't say anything, just holds out his hand for the "present." I hand the other parcel to Lucas without looking at him.

Bugs looks even more puzzled than before. "So I have rivals for your affections, huh? Should we open our presents at the same time, or would you like one of us to go first?"

I shrug, unsmiling. "Whatever."

Bugs and Stu start to unwrap their parcels. The only sound is the tearing of paper and the crackling of the fire. Bugs gets into his first; Stu's dexterity has clearly been hindered by the booze. I still don't look at Lucas.

"Is this supposed to be funny?" Bugs doesn't look impressed, but he's not majorly pissed off or anything.

Stu looks over to see the magazine in Bugs's hands and he cracks a smile. "Ah, Jem knows you so well! Maybe we should all leave you to have some alone time with those hot, hung homos?"

Bugs gives Stu a withering look, turns to me, and says, "Forgive me if I seem ungrateful, but there's really only one thing to be done with this." He chucks the magazine onto the fire. The flames lick around the edges for a second or two and everyone watches as the ridiculously buff guy on the front cover blackens and turns to ash.

I can feel everyone looking at me, but my attention is focused on Stu, who's finally managed to get his fingers to work properly.

There's no confusion on his face. He *knows*. I don't know how his alcohol-addled mind worked it out so quickly, but it's plain as anything that he knows. He just stares at me and I stare back. I'm not afraid anymore and I'm not sure why.

Sasha breaks the silence. "What's that, Stu?"

He holds up the pen for all to see. It's an unremarkable pen in every way. A thick black marker pen. Permanent ink.

Bugs says, "No offense, Jem, but you could *really* do with some lessons from Santa when it comes to choosing gifts. Just for the record, you can't go wrong with vouchers."

Now it's Sasha's turn to pipe up. "Am I missing something here?"

Stu's gripping the pen so hard I wouldn't be surprised if he crushed it. "It was her."

"What was her? What the fuck are you talking about, mate?" Lucas sounds worried. Somehow he knows this is serious. Maybe he's seen Stu like this before. Or maybe he senses something different about me.

"The graffiti. It was her." And my eyes are still locked on his, as if no one else matters.

"What do you mean, it was her? Don't be stupid." Lucas sounds so very sure. So very convinced that his girlfriend couldn't possibly have done such a thing. I mean, why would she?

"Why don't you ask her then?" There's something dangerous in Stu's voice.

Sasha and Lucas both say, "Jem?" at exactly the same time, but neither one shouts "Jinx" like they normally would.

"Now we're in for some fun and games," murmurs Louise. I wish she'd just disappear.

I could still get away with saying it was a bad joke. The others would believe me, but Stu wouldn't be so easily convinced. He *sees* me now. This is it.

"It was me." Now I look at Lucas, then Sasha. Their faces are identical pictures of confusion. I don't think they believe me. I have to make them believe me. "It was me. I wrote that stuff on the walls." My voice doesn't sound like my own; it's detached. Toneless.

"And you put those magazines in Bugs's car too." There's no question mark at the end of Stu's sentence. He's worked it all out. Clever boy.

"Is that true, Jem?" Bugs's face is more serious than I've ever seen it. Serious looks wrong on him.

"It's true."

"I don't…I don't get it. Why would you do that to me? The whole fucking school thinks I'm queer! I…I thought we were friends?" He looks like a little boy who's just been informed that the tooth fairy's not real. Or that his parents are getting divorced. "What did I ever do to you?"

The question hangs in the air, and I'm not sure that I'm ready to answer it quite yet. I finally look over at Lucas, who's staring at the small parcel in his hands. He opens it slowly, as if he's worried the contents might explode. Tiny strips of leather fall into his lap, and he shakes his head in disbelief. When I see the look on his face, something inside me cracks, but I have to hold myself together because there's no going back now.

Louise stands up and pulls Max up with her. Max looks massively uncomfortable. He doesn't know where to look. Louise speaks to Sasha. "Look, we're just going to go, OK? I can't be dealing with this drama. I'm supposed to be avoiding stressful situations." That must be due to her counselor, because Louise has always been very fond of drama. She squeezes Sasha's shoulder, mutters, "Call me," and then she's walking away. Max trails after her without a word. I got my wish after all.

Everyone starts to talk at once. Lucas puts his hand on my knee. He's the only one I hear. His touch on my bare skin almost makes me lose the plot. "Jem?"

"Don't touch me." The words are cold and hard and he recoils. He removes his hand from my leg.

Still he comes back for more. "Jem? Talk to me, *please*? We can sort this out…I'm sure there must be some explanation, right? I—" The hand is back, more tentative this time.

"I said: don't…fucking…touch me." I brush his hand off and look anywhere but his face. I can't watch his face as I do this.

Sasha's up next. "Jem, just tell them you didn't do it, OK? This is hilarious and all that, but can we just pretend it never happened and go home? You played a practical joke. It backfired. Let's just forget about it. Please?" She crouches down in front of me and tries to score some eye contact. Eventually she succeeds and it's painful to look at her. Her eyes are wide; she looks scared almost.

"Are you fucking stupid or something, Sasha? Actually, don't answer. We all know the answer to *that*. Do you really need me to spell it out for you? *I* put those magazines in Bugs's car. *I* wrote that stuff on the wall. And while we're confessing things, I might as well tell you that there is no *fucking* way I'm your 'best friend.' I can barely stand to be around you. I've never met anyone quite so shallow and self-obsessed before. And I've met *Amber*, so that's saying something."

Sasha takes a moment to process the information. She shakes her head and frowns. "What…why are you doing this?" I think she might cry. I might too if I'm not careful. Just got to hold it together for a little while longer.

Stu's been pacing up and down. "You bitch. You fucking *bitch*.

Do you have any idea what you've done? This is about that night at the party, isn't it? You thought I was trying to...going to..."

"Rape me?" I don't know where this calm person has come from, but she's speaking for me while I cower somewhere deep inside. This person is starting to scare me.

"I would never do something like that! Jesus!" He stalks up and down some more, swigs some more whiskey from the bottle. The others seem to be waiting to see how this plays out. I'm wondering whether it would be a bad idea to ask for some whiskey. Probably.

Stu takes a deep breath, clearly trying to calm himself. "Look, just because it happened to you...before...I'm sorry about that, I really am. But that doesn't mean any guy that wants to fuck you is a potential rapist, OK?"

Lucas flinches next to me and Sasha's eyes go even wider if that's even possible. "What's he talking about, Jem? I don't understand." His voice is gentle.

Stu laughs bitterly. "I'm talking about the night your girlfriend pounced on me at Max's party and then changed her mind about shagging me."

Lucas jumps to his feet and I swear he's about to deck Stu. Bugs holds him back, his brute strength coming in handy. "You shut the fuck up. Let her speak." Even now, Lucas is willing to defend me. Willing to think the best of me despite mounting evidence to the contrary.

I get to my feet. It's nearly time to go.

Sasha stands too, takes hold of my arm, and says quietly, "Did someone rape you? Is that what this is all about?"

I laugh, and I honestly can't tell if it's a real laugh or one I conjured up to piss Stu off even more. "No! Nobody raped me."

Stu's shaking his head now, utterly disbelieving.

"But you told me...What kind of fucked-up chick would lie about something like that?! Louise was right—you're fucking crazy, aren't you?" He gets right up close to me now, his sneering face centimeters from mine, as if we're about to kiss. "You're not going to get away with this." He spits out the words and a fine spray of saliva hits my lips. Lucas muscles his way in between us and shoves Stu away from me.

Stu doubles over in pain, struggling to breathe. He even drops the whiskey bottle. Bugs puts a hand on his shoulder. "Dude, are you OK? What's the matter?"

After a few seconds of panting, he straightens up slowly, painfully. "You really want to know? Fine. Fuck it." He moves closer to the fire and pulls up his hoodie, revealing his perfect abs. And a huge ugly mark under his pecs. It's reddish purple.

Everyone apart from me winces at the sight. "What happened?"

Stu's smiling now, looking even more menacing than before. "Well, Jem, turns out I *didn't* get hurt at tae kwon do last night. Turns out my bastard stepfather beat the crap out of me because he thinks I'm some kind of sex offender. Told my mom he wanted to 'teach the little fucker a lesson he won't forget.' Said he'd be surprised if I went anywhere near another girl after the beating he was going to give me. And she didn't even try to stop him. She never does. And I didn't fight back. I tried that once before and he started on my little brother. Better he uses me as a punch bag than Danny."

Bugs says, "Shit. Why didn't you say anything, mate?"

Stu shrugs. "It's nothing I can't handle. It's not like he does it every week or anything. And it's usually only when he's hammered. Not this time though—he was sober as a fucking judge. Broke a couple of ribs, I'm pretty sure. All because this little bitch decided to get creative with a fucking marker."

Lucas isn't standing quite so close to me anymore. I didn't notice him moving away, but he's closer to Stu now. The unwavering loyalty has started to waver.

Sasha's still close to me though, and there are tears running down her face. It's all too much for her drunk brain to cope with. She takes a deep breath and rakes her fingers through her hair, trying to massage some thoughts into her brain. "Right...this is all completely fucked up. We should talk about this tomorrow when everyone's calmed down."

"No. I think we should talk about this now actually." I walk toward Stu and now I'm the one getting in his face. His breath is vile. "You deserved everything you got, you fucking low-life prick. So what if you haven't *actually* raped anyone? It was only a matter of time. Why do you think someone kept writing it again every time the janitor cleaned it off? Clearly I'm not the only one who knows what you're like. Knows that you're a sleazy, disgusting sexual predator..." I don't know where these words are coming from, but they're streaming out of me. I know I should stop. I know I'm going too far, but I can't help myself. I'm smiling as I say the next words. "And you know what? Your stepfather had the right idea. I only wish he'd kicked a little harder, maybe punctured a lung."

This is what does it. This is what makes him snap. He shoves me, hard. And I stumble backward, not quite losing my balance. I smile again. "See? Using physical violence against a poor, defenseless girl? You're pathetic..." I'm just about to say something about Kai, about Stu as good as killing my best friend. But I don't get a chance, because he rushes at me with a look in his eye. And I know in that second that he's capable of doing some real damage. That he's so full of rage and hurt that he won't stop. I think he'd like me dead in this exact moment. And that would be fine with me.

He grabs me by the shoulders and screams in my face, "I'm going to fucking kill you!" The fact that I show no fear seems to make him even angrier. And I'm genuinely curious to see what he's going to do next, but Lucas is trying to pull him away, shouting at him to calm down, take it easy.

Too many things are happening at once. Stu is shaking me, screaming obscenities. Lucas is behind Stu, arms wrapped around his torso, trying to get him under control. But Stu's stronger than him, even though he's smaller.

Sasha is crying and crying and shouting at everyone to calm down. Then she makes a mistake and tries to get between me and Stu. What is she thinking? If Lucas can't do anything, there's no way she can. But she *does*. She does *something*—and I'm pretty sure she elbows him in that exact spot on his ribs, because he cries out in pain and he pushes her.

The push was pure instinct. He was under threat and in pain, so he lashed out. That's all it was. But the way he catches her on the shoulder spins her around and away from us.

And she trips over something. A tree root, perhaps. She's falling. And there's nothing anyone can do. She's falling and I open my mouth to say something or scream something, but I don't know what.

She's falling.

Face first into the fire.

chapter fifty-two

I was supposed to make a big speech about what they did to Kai. I was supposed to have my moment with all of them looking at me, aghast at my audacious plan. They were supposed to feel guilty and ashamed. I was supposed to humiliate Lucas in front of his friends, tell him I was only going out with him to get my revenge. Tell him I could never love someone like him. He was supposed to be crushed.

I had it all worked out in my head. I'd thought about it for months. The party in the woods seemed like the perfect opportunity. Even the fact that it was so close to where he died seemed right in a way. Like it was meant to be, almost.

I'd pictured it time and time again. Bugs realizing he'd been given a taste of his own medicine. The look on Stu's face when he found out the truth. Breaking Lucas's heart. I'd never truly believed *that* would be possible—I was just going to go for dumping him in front of everyone, call him a lousy shag. But the way he'd been looking at me had changed recently; it had softened somehow. Still, him saying he loved me was almost too good to be true. And the timing couldn't have been better. Like I said: meant to be.

This was not meant to be.

Burning hair and blistering flesh and screaming. So much scream-ing. Mine and hers, different in tone yet merging together in a hellish chorus. I will never forget the sound of her screams for the rest of my life. It will haunt me forever, just as it should.

When I was nine Gran baked a cake for my birthday. She baked one for me every year, but this is the one I remember best. It was chocolate, with more layers than I'd ever seen on a cake. Shavings of chocolate were heaped on top (Dairy Milk, I was pretty sure, since I'd sneaked a taste before the party). Nine can-dles, evenly spaced.

There were lots of kids at the party, but Kai's the only one who's clear in my memory. The others are blank faces. Except for Louise. She was there somewhere, I think. Mom had made me invite her.

I knelt on a chair, hovering over the cake while everyone sang "Happy Birthday" (Kai sang extra loud, of course). They did the whole hip-hip-hooray thing, and then it was time for me to blow out the candles. I took a deep breath and blew as hard as I could, getting six of them in one go. I leaned over the cake to get the two on the far side, and as I did so, the candle nearest me caught my hair. The air filled with that unmistakable smell, I yelped, and Mom grabbed a napkin to extinguish the flame. It was no big drama, really. A few singed strands of hair. It wasn't even the thing that Kai and I talked about after the party (that honor went to Kai eating so much cake that he was sick in my dad's new car on the way to the bowling alley). But I never forgot that smell.

The smell of Sasha's hair burning is lodged at the back of my throat; I can taste it almost. I'm not sure whether to be relieved that it's strong enough to obliterate the memory of the smell of burning flesh.

She's still in the ICU. Apparently they're busy arranging trans-port to a special burns unit in Liverpool. That's all I know. Lucas told me. He wouldn't look at me, but he came and told me at least.

He's in the family waiting room with Sasha's parents. I saw Mr. and Mrs. Evans arrive. He was in a dinner jacket and bow tie, she was wearing a beautiful midnight-blue dress. I think Sasha had said they were going to some charity benefit. They do that kind of thing a lot apparently. Tears were streaming down Sasha's Mom's face; her makeup was a mess. Her dad looked pale and haggard. They didn't notice me lurking at the end of the corridor. I took one look and went through a set of double doors in search of somewhere to wait far away from the others.

She could die. Sasha could die and it would be my fault. Other people might blame Stu for pushing her, but we know the truth.

If she doesn't die, she might wish she had.

❧

I called home, told Mom what had happened. I wasn't even crying. Mom asked me a lot of questions that I couldn't answer; then *she* started to cry. She said they'd be at the hospital in ten minutes and I had to beg her not to come. She couldn't understand why, but I begged and begged until she agreed to give me a few hours at least. She didn't say anything about the fact that we'd been partying in the woods instead of at Lucas's house like I'd told her. I was grateful for that.

❧

I can't stop thinking about her face. Her perfect face.

None of us knew what to do. Once Lucas had put out the flames with a blanket, none of us knew what to do next. Sasha kept screaming and there was nothing we could do to make her stop. Lucas was the only one who was any use. He told Bugs to find some water, then he poured it on her face. I had no idea if this was the right thing to do, but he seemed so confident, so calm.

There was only one bottle of water; everything else was spirits.

Whenever anyone in our family has even the tiniest burn or scald, Mom makes us hold it under the cold tap for at least ten minutes. I don't know what difference it makes, but she's adamant about it. So what good would one measly bottle of water possibly have done? We'd have been better off chucking Sasha in the river.

When the paramedics eventually arrived, they stabilized Sasha before taking her away on a stretcher. Lucas followed closely behind. My feet just kept moving, pulling me in the direction of the hospital even though I would have given anything to be somewhere else. Bugs didn't say a word to me on the way there. He walked a couple of steps in front of me the whole time. Or maybe I walked a couple of steps behind him. I didn't even notice Stu wasn't with us until the automatic doors at the emergency room closed behind us.

Her perfect face. Red, raw eyelids swelling shut. Eyelashes, eyebrows singed to nothing.

She didn't even have a chance to put her hands out to break her fall.

Her perfect face. Ruined.

chapter fifty-three

I'm sitting with my head in my hands when I hear a voice I haven't heard in months. "Jem? Is that you?"

I say a startled hi, then ask her what she's doing here, which is the stupidest question imaginable because I know exactly what she's doing here. "I work here, love. Remember?" Kai's mom is looking at me like I'm deranged. She sits down next to me on a tatty plastic chair. "Is that girl—Sasha, is it?—a friend of yours?"

I nod. And I realize that it's true: Sasha is a friend of mine. Or was, might have been, could have been.

"It's a terrible thing…were you there when it happened?" Another nod from me and she puts her hand on my arm. "Oh, you poor love! You've been through so much."

I don't deserve her pity, but I stay silent.

"She's getting the best possible care, you know? You mustn't worry. Listen, I clock off in a few minutes. How about I give you a lift home? You look exhausted…and there's nothing you can do here."

I finally meet her eye and it's all I can do not to fall into her arms sobbing. I look away fast before that happens. "Thank you, but I'd like to stay here. Until they move her. I just feel like I should *be* here, you know? In case…"

"Oh, Jem. You have to stay positive, OK? If there's one thing

I've learned in the past year, it's that you *have* to stay positive." Her voice wavers but doesn't crack. "We've missed you, Jem. No, no, you don't need to say anything; I understand how painful it must be for you. But you're always welcome in our house. I want you to know that. I meant what I said at the funeral…you're like a second daughter to me. So if you ever need someone to talk to—about anything—you need to know I'm here…and since my own daughter barely speaks to me anymore, God knows I could do with the company." I smile awkwardly, not a clue what to say. "Thank goodness Louise wasn't with you girls tonight…the thought of losing her too…doesn't bear thinking about. Not that your friend's going to…I'm sorry. I'm exhausted. I'll leave you in peace." She hugs me and her shoulder blades feel all bony. She was always skinny, but now she's skeletal.

I wonder where she thinks Louise was tonight. And I wonder where Louise is now. I should call her, I know that. She needs to know what's happened. I already tried calling Amber, but she must have left her phone in the cloakroom at Espionage. Maybe Lucas has already called Louise; there's no way I can ask him though.

I should go home. There's no reason for me to be here. Sasha wouldn't want me here. But the thought of going over and over things with Mom and Dad is more than I can cope with. And I want to wait in case there's news.

I text Lucas: I'll be in the cafeteria in case you hear anything.

I don't expect a reply and I don't get one.

⌒

Half an hour later I'm in the cafeteria, sitting in the corner furthest from the door. The only other people in there are a man with a mop, who has done precisely no mopping since I arrived, and a forty-something female doctor who looks like she might be trying to chat up the hot young guy she's sitting opposite. He looks interested—knackered, but interested.

I'm drinking a carton of orange juice—the kind I used to have in my packed lunch when I was ten. It feels sour and wrong in my stomach, but I keep sucking juice through the tiny straw just for something to do. The straw is making alarmingly loud gurgling noises, trying to suck up every last drop of juice, when he comes in.

He looks wrecked. Like he's been through the spin cycle in a washing machine a couple times. It's when he's close enough for me to see that his eyes are red that my entire body floods with panic. I feel it through my whole body, right to my fingertips. She's dead. I'm sure of it.

I put my hands flat on the table to steady myself. The nail varnish I put on earlier is chipped already. Sasha told me it would last for days when she was painting my nails. She was wearing the same shade. It's her favorite color. A deep red so dark it's almost black.

"Is she…?"

He slumps into the chair opposite me. "She's gone." He sees my reaction and says, "No! They've taken her in the ambulance. She's not…"

The adrenaline doesn't dissipate, in spite of the epic relief. "What do the doctors say?"

"What do you care?" The anger's there, bubbling beneath the surface—I can see that, but his tone is neutral.

"I care." And it's true. Possibly the most honest thing I've said in a long time.

"Do you?"

"Of course I care, Lucas." He shakes his head and stares out the window. Except it's dark outside and light inside, so he's actually staring at a reflection of us sitting at this table in this depressing place. "She's not…going to die, is she?"

"They don't think so. But it's serious—really serious. Her face…" He shakes his head again. I'm pretty sure we're both thinking about how beautiful she is. Was.

"But they can do amazing things these days, can't they? The doctors, I mean? I saw this program…" I sound like a child.

"It's bad, Jem. OK?" Is there a note of pity in his voice or am I imagining it? I must be imagining it.

"This is all my fault." The very act of voicing what everyone must be thinking makes me feel a little better somehow.

He says nothing. Clenches his fist.

"I'm sorry, Lucas." I make a move to reach across the table to touch his hand, but then I realize what I'm doing. The space between us couldn't be any wider.

"What for? The accident? The graffiti? The magazines? Being a complete bitch to Sasha?"

"All of the above?" He doesn't crack a smile at my lame attempt to lighten the mood. "And I'm sorry for how I treated *you*."

"Are you going to tell me why? Because I can't even begin to guess…it makes *no* sense. Bugs, Sasha, even Stu in his own way, I guess…they've been nothing but nice to you. *Especially* Sasha. And I…well, you know exactly how I feel about you."

My heart does a little leap at the word "feel," even though deep down I know he means "felt." Because there's no way. There's just no way.

There's no reason to lie anymore. I've been keeping this secret so long, so deeply wrapped up inside me, that it takes a moment or two for me to find the words, and when I do, they're not even the right ones—not exactly. "I did it for Kai."

"*What?*" Too loud. The guy with the mop turns to see what's going on. Lucas doesn't notice because he's too busy looking at me like I'm deranged.

I wait until the mop guy has turned his attention back to page three of *The Sun*, then I lean toward Lucas and lower my voice. "The video?"

Lucas shakes his head again. He's doing a lot of that. "What video? You mean, the one where he…"

"What other video *is* there?!" My anger seems to have returned from nowhere.

"I don't understand. What's that got to do with us? With me?"

Now it's my turn to shake my head. "Lucas, come on." I'm not going to forgive him if he admits it now, but I'll feel a whole lot more charitable if he doesn't make me drag it out of him.

"What are you getting at? Wait…you don't think we…?" My facial expression makes it abundantly clear that this is *exactly* what I think. "Why the hell would you think that? Jesus, Jem. I would never do something like that. You know that. You know *me*." He's doing a really good job of looking wounded.

I whisper fiercely, "I know it was you, so can you just cut the crap? So maybe it was Stu's idea and he did all the dirty work, but you were involved, which makes you just as guilty as far as I'm concerned."

He holds his hands up as if I'm pointing a gun at him. "Jem, I swear to you. It wasn't us. Look at me, OK?" I meet his eyes and I really look, and I know I'm crap at this sort of thing, but suddenly I'm not sure anymore and…"What made you think it was us? Because it was at Max's party?"

"No…I…someone told me. And as soon as they did, it all made sense. Stu was pissed off that I wouldn't have sex with him— wounded pride or whatever—and everyone knew me and Kai were best friends, so he went after Kai to get back at me. Fucking cowardly bastard. And I *saw* you and Bugs messing around, pretending to be gay or whatever." I don't mention the fact that I saw Stu on his phone too, because suddenly that little bit of evidence doesn't seem as convincing as it did before. Suddenly *none* of it seems quite as convincing as it did before.

He's looking at me like I'm crazy. "What are you even *talking* about? I can't believe you thought I'd be involved with something like that. Why didn't you just *ask* me if you were so sure it was true?"

"Yeah, 'cause that would have really worked. None of you even knew I *existed* a year ago. And like you'd have admitted it *anyway*!"

"Of course I wouldn't have admitted it! It's not bloody true! So all this was just…what, exactly?"

"I wanted to pay you back. All of you." And it all seems so stupid now—so pointless and pathetic.

Lucas leans his elbows on the table and puts his head in his hands. The only sound in the cafeteria is the doctor giggling flirtatiously. Eventually Lucas looks up at me, and I know exactly what's just occurred to him. "You never really liked me, did you? So why did you…?"

There's no point in lying anymore. "It was part of the Plan."

"You're kidding, right?" The look on my face makes it painfully clear that this isn't the case. "Jesus fucking Christ." He sniffs and continues. "I've got to hand it to you, Jem. You did a pretty stellar job. Bugs, Stu, me…you really knew how to hit us where it hurts, didn't you? Shame you hurt the wrong people though, isn't it? Shame Sasha's going to be scarred for life because you couldn't be bothered to find out the truth before you went off on some mad revenge kick. I mean, who *does* that?"

And I think there's a real chance he might be telling the truth. Maybe it *wasn't* them. Maybe Jon was wrong after all. Maybe Bugs and Lucas were just messing around that night. Maybe Stu was so intent on his phone because he'd been nutted by a girl.

My brain can't compute, can't wrap itself around the idea that I've been wrong—so fucking wrong—all this time. It can't possibly be true…can it? But I look at Lucas's face and I *know* that he would never do something like that. I know it with absolute certainty and it's hard to believe that I didn't see it before. I fell in love with him, for fuck's sake. That would never have happened if I'd really truly totally believed he'd done that to Kai. Would it?

I struggle to find some words to say. "I…I'm sorry, Lucas. I was so sure. I needed someone to pay for it. You have to understand, I miss him *so* much." I had no intention of crying, but the tears come easily. My hand is so close to his on the table. I want to reach out to him so badly but I'm afraid of what he'll do.

"Of course you miss him. It's OK to miss him. But what you did…" He exhales slowly, painfully almost.

"Who told you it was us?"

"It doesn't matter."

"Like fuck it doesn't matter!"

"It was a note. An anonymous note."

"And you *believed* it? Just like that? Without even bothering to…Jesus."

I'm confused and upset and tired beyond belief, but I can't let this go. "Who do you think did it then? You must have known most of the people at the party, right? I only knew a couple of people…You probably didn't even realize I was there until tonight, did you?" There's a bitter note to my voice that I don't even bother to disguise.

What he says next comes as a complete surprise. "I knew you were there. I saw Stu follow you to the end of the yard."

"You…you *knew* about that?"

He shrugs, maybe a little embarrassed. "I had a pretty good idea what you two were up to."

"And you never said anything?!" Lucas just shoots me this look that shuts me right up.

"I knew a lot of people at the party, I guess. But no one who would do something like *that*. I mean, we all talked about it afterward. Max wasn't exactly happy that it had all…um…gone down in his room."

"And nobody saw anything?" I shouldn't be obsessing about this now. I know Sasha is what I should be thinking about. But I'm running out of time.

I ask Lucas if there's anything he can think of—anything at all—that might help me work out who did it. And for some reason he doesn't tell me to fuck off. I push him to try to remember if he saw anyone looking shifty.

"I was pretty wasted, to be honest. I remember me and Sasha looking for somewhere to…go. Max didn't want anyone upstairs, but I figured he'd make an exception. The only person we saw was Louise. She was sitting in the hallway looking about as wrecked as I felt. She pointed us in the direction of Max's folks' room. And we…er…yeah."

The only person they saw was Louise.

Louise.

chapter fifty-four

I go back to the bridge. I have a couple hours to kill and I can't stand the thought of going home. Mom would put her arms around me and make me drink tea from my favorite mug. I can't face her. Not yet.

Bugs interrupted us in the cafeteria, right after the Louise revelation. It was obvious that Lucas had no idea what he'd said. He didn't think for a minute that it could have been her, and I wanted to keep it that way. For now at least.

Bugs didn't look at all pleased to find Lucas sitting with me. He completely blanked me, asked Lucas if he wanted a lift home with him and his dad. Lucas asked if I could come too, and Bugs looked at him as if he was crazy. Before he had a chance to reply I said Mom was coming to pick me up, so there was really no need.

Bugs said he'd wait for Lucas in the car and was just about to leave when I asked him if he'd managed to get in touch with Max and Louise. For a second there I thought he wouldn't answer, but he said they were at Max's house. He'd been keeping them up to date on Sasha's condition. He addressed Lucas rather than me. I couldn't exactly blame him. I wanted to say something; I wanted to apologize. But I couldn't.

I hadn't noticed that Lucas and I were now the only ones left in the cafeteria. Maybe Flirty Doctor was off shagging her conquest somewhere. Or more likely he'd taken off when he came to his senses and realized she was old enough to be his mother.

Lucas pushed back his chair and it made an ugly screeching sound on the green linoleum. "I…I'll see you around, I guess." He gripped the back of the chair and I wondered if it was to stop himself reaching out to me. Probably not. More likely he was so tired he could barely stand up straight.

I looked up at him. His face had a yellowish tinge, almost like a faded bruise. I wondered if this would be the last time I'd ever see him. There was so much I should say to try to fix things, but it was too late. No words I could say would ever be enough to undo the things I'd done. The words I did manage to stutter out were so pathetically inadequate I almost laughed. "I'm sorry." It's what you say when you step on someone's toes or accidentally cut in line. Not when you have used someone in the worst possible way, accused them of doing something they would never ever do, and nearly killed their ex-girlfriend. His eyes were on mine for the longest time before he turned to walk away. It was not the most comfortable of silences. He was a few paces away when he stopped. He didn't turn to look at me though. He kept his back to me as he said the words that seared themselves onto my brain.

"I did notice you, you know. Before. I remember the day you came to school wearing those purple Docs and Miss Maynard marched you out of the cafeteria. I remember you and Kai laughing. You always seemed to be laughing at something. And I used to wonder what was so funny."

"Lucas? Look at me. Please look at me."

His hands clenched into fists and his shoulders tensed up. "I can't."

Then he walked away. His progress toward the door was painfully slow, almost as if he wanted me to stop him. I watched to see if he looked back before the doors swung closed behind him. He didn't. The boy I loved—the boy who'd loved me like I wanted to be loved—didn't look back.

⌒

It's still not light by the time I get to the bridge. A fine mist cloaks the water below. The rain starts to fall almost as soon as I get there. Then it starts to bucket down and my teeth are chattering within minutes. This must have been what it was like for him.

I don't even know what I'm doing here. It's not like I'm going to jump or anything. And it's not as if being here makes me feel particularly close to him. But it's as good a way as any to pass the time.

I call Mom and tell her I'm heading to Lucas's house for a couple of hours. She's not happy, but she doesn't fight me on it. She just tells me she's worried about me and that I should call her if I want a lift home. Before she has a chance to change her mind, I say that Mrs. Mahoney has just pulled up outside the hospital so I'd really better go. I don't even have to think about lying these days—it's no effort at all.

I stand there for God knows how long, hands gripping the railing even though it's wet and icy cold. My hands look red and raw.

I feel a hand on my shoulder. It startles me so much I stumble into the railing, and for a microsecond I imagine it breaking and me falling. Would it really be so bad? But the railing holds fast and I turn to face the owner of the mystery hand.

It's a red-haired woman, about thirty years old, dressed for the gym. Black cropped leggings and a neon pink cropped tank top. I look over her shoulder and see a car with the driver's door wide open.

She stands in front of me, the rain gradually turning her hair a darker red. I'm determined not to be the first one to speak.

"Hi. Is everything…OK?" She starts to shiver and I bet she wished she'd worn a hoodie. Or just stayed in her stupid car.

"Yes."

353

"Can I give you a lift or something?"

"No." My tone's a little harsh and I can't help adding a quiet "thank you," even though I really don't want to. Old habits die hard, I guess.

"Are you sure? Is there someone I can call then?" I shake my head.

"Look, I'm not going to leave you here, OK? I wouldn't want you to…" She nods her head, indicating the river below and half laughs in a self-conscious sort of way.

"What makes you think I would?"

"Oh, I don't know…maybe something to do with the fact that you're standing here in the pissing rain at an ungodly hour on a Saturday morning?"

A snort of laughter escapes me even though there's really nothing to laugh about. "Good point. No need to worry, I'm not going to off myself…" I don't add the *yet* that I'm screaming inside. I look at my watch and it's just about a respectable time to turn up at someone's front door, and I *am* freezing. "Actually, I could do with a lift back into town, if it's not too much trouble."

The woman's face lights up, and you can tell she thinks she's just saved a life. She'll probably go home and tell her husband or boyfriend or cat all about it. She probably reckons there's some seriously good karma coming her way. Who knows? Maybe there is, for making sure I don't die of hypothermia before I'm ready.

As we're getting into the car, she tells me her name is Melissa. "And you are…?"

"Kai." I say it without thinking.

"That's an unusual name. Kai—it suits you." Melissa turns the heating up and talks pretty much nonstop the rest of the way. It's only a five-minute journey, but I find out a lot about her in those five minutes. It's amazing how much a complete stranger is willing to share with you when they think they've saved your life.

When she pulls up outside the house, she puts her hand on my arm. "Are you going to be OK, Kai?" She really seems to care. It's sort of sweet actually.

"I'll be fine. Thank you. I'm glad you stopped."

She reaches into the glove compartment and hands me a card. I hold the edges of the card between my thumb and forefinger and stare at it. It's a business card—all fancy and embossed. Melissa Hill. She's an estate agent. I thought estate agents were supposed to be the spawn of the devil? That's what Dad's always saying.

Melissa looks embarrassed all of a sudden. "Look, I know this is a bit weird, but call me, won't you, if you ever—I don't know—need someone to talk to? OK…now you think I'm crazy, don't you? I don't blame you. Just…remember there's always another option. And things *do* get better, you know. Trust me." Her face is flushed red and she's staring at the raindrops trickling down the windscreen instead of looking at me. She's talking about herself now—that's as clear as anything. It makes me itch with embarrassment for her. That she would expose herself like this.

"Thanks, Melissa." I clamber out of the car and shut the door before she has a chance to say anything else. I watch as she drives away—all the way along the street until the car turns the corner. There are no other cars for me to watch. No joggers. No dog walkers. Not even a plastic bag blowing down the street that I could pretend to be interested in.

The sensation in the pit of my stomach is similar to the feeling I had the last time I walked up this particular driveway. It's fear, plain and simple. But I have no reason to be afraid anymore. The worst has already happened. Kai. Sasha. This is just about finding out *why.*

Why would a sister do something like that to a brother she adored?

Why would *anyone* do something like that?

chapter fifty-five

Sebastian opens the front door wearing a pair of tight white boxers slung low over his bony hips. He scratches his armpit and looks confused. "Gemma, right?"

I hate people calling me Gemma. HATE IT.

"Yeah. Are Max and Louise up yet?"

Sebastian yawns and his face transforms into something gargoyle-like. "Fuck knows. I think I heard the shower going earlier, so you might be in luck." He clearly has no idea what happened last night. Either that or he doesn't care. I wonder if Amber's here, sprawled on Sebastian's bed, completely unaware that one of her best friends very nearly died last night.

Sebastian ushers me into the house and hitches up his pants. "Go on up. Better knock first in case they're getting it on. On second thoughts, don't bother."

I'm not sure how to take this, so I say nothing and head up the stairs. I turn and catch Sebastian checking out my butt, and he doesn't even bother to pretend otherwise. "Third door on the left," he says with a smirk on his face. Tool.

I stand in front of the door. There's no telltale sign saying: "Max's room—KEEP OUT," but that's probably because Max isn't ten years old. I knock before I can change my mind.

Max calls out, "Come in." And then I'm there. I'm in the room

I've only seen in that hideous video. I'm staring at the bed that Kai knelt in front of. The duvet cover's the same.

Louise is sitting cross-legged on the bed, nibbling on a slice of toast with peanut butter. Peanut butter was Kai's favorite too. Max is sitting on the floor, tapping away on an impossibly slimline Apple laptop. They're both fully dressed, thank God. Max seems surprised to see me; Louise does not.

"Drowned rat is a really good look for you, Jem. Also, nice work last night. Really."

"Louise!" Max slams the lid of his laptop. "How are you doing, Jem? It must have been awful."

I close the door behind me and lean against it. I don't want to be any closer to Louise than is absolutely necessary.

Louise speaks through a mouthful of toast. "What are you doing here? Just popped by for a cup of tea on your way to church? Off to confess your sins, are you?"

This is the Louise I've always known. The only downside to being friends with Kai. This is the Louise she's been hiding so carefully for the past couple months. I wonder why she's decided to unleash the beast now, before I've even said anything. It makes me wonder if she knows what's coming. Or maybe she's just tired of putting on an act; I know I am.

Max is looking uncomfortable and I can hardly blame him. No boy wants to get caught in the crossfire between two girls who hate each other. "Max, would you mind leaving us alone for a couple of minutes?"

He's halfway to his feet before Louise tells him to sit down. And he does—without a word. He's a well-trained dog, knowing full well that if he disobeys his master he'll get a good kicking later. Louise turns to me. "You're not coming here and kicking him out of his own room. You can say what you have to say in front of Max or you can just fuck off home. Maybe think about something to buy Sasha…though Clinton's didn't make a 'Sorry I melted your face' card last time I checked. What the fuck were you thinking?"

Max isn't looking at either of us. He's fiddling with the upturned corner of a stripy rug. Kai knelt on that rug.

I turn to Louise. "Well, if you're sure you don't mind Max hearing this, I don't mind either. And don't play games with me, Louise. You know full well what I was thinking. Mostly because you're the one who made me think it." I'd only realized this a few seconds before I said it. Jon hadn't written the note—*of course* he hadn't.

She licks some peanut butter from her thumb and smiles. "I don't know what you're talking about."

"How could you do it? Just answer me that and I'll go. And I'm not going to tell anyone if that's what you're wondering. Kai wouldn't want everyone knowing that his own *sister* would betray him like that. So—tell me how you could do something like that to your own brother, and I'll leave you in peace."

Silence stretches right out to the corners of the room. I'm looking at Louise, and I'm pretty sure Max is too. Louise is looking at me, cool as you like, utterly unfazed by this turn of events. "How could I do what?" She's not smiling anymore.

"You really want me to say it? Fine. How could you film Kai and *email* it to people?" Another thought occurs to me. "Did he know it was you?"

I glance at Max, expecting him to say something.

He's fiddling with the corner of the rug again.

"What makes you think it was me?" Louise licks her lips. They look cracked and dry. She glances toward the door, then the window, like she's looking for an escape route. Then she shakes her head and I can see the facade crumbling before my eyes. "I didn't mean to do it." She sounds like a child.

I take a couple steps toward her because I want to hurt her. I really, really want to make her feel pain. She doesn't move, doesn't even look bothered, maybe because she thinks she deserves it. Or maybe she knows that I'm not actually going to touch her. I stand there and wait her out.

"Look…I made a mistake, OK? A really terrible, really fucking big mistake. And nothing you can say or do will make me feel any worse about it than I already do, so don't even bother. And no, he didn't know who did it." She crosses her arms defensively; she looks small, weak almost. It's some consolation, I suppose. That he didn't know his sister had ruined his life.

"I don't understand how you could have…You must have known it would destroy him."

A flicker of fire returns to her eyes. "Did *you* think he was going to jump off a bridge?" The words make me flinch, but I say nothing. "No. Of course you didn't. Because you wouldn't have left his side for a second if you thought there was even the slightest chance."

She's right about that. It never crossed my mind—not a glimmer of a hint of a possibility. It's hardly the point though, is it? She knew he would be devastated. She knew it would make his life a misery.

Louise takes my silence for agreement. "Thought so. Now, if you don't mind, we've got things to do…" She stands up to usher me out of the room.

The "we" reminds me that Max is still here, no matter how hard he tries to blend into the background. I look at him. "Aren't you going to say something?"

He looks up at me and shakes his head. There's something there though—a look in his eyes that's hard to place. "Doesn't this bother you?" And then I realize that I might not know what the look means, but I know what it *doesn't* mean. It doesn't mean surprise. "What the…? Fuck. You *knew*, didn't you? You knew it was her and you didn't say anything. Wow. That's a whole new level of spineless I never knew existed. You're as bad as your sleazy brother—worse in fact." Max clenches his jaw but still says nothing. "You do realize that she made me think it was Stu and the others? She's the reason I wrote the graffiti. She's the reason I went out with Lucas. It's *all* her fault." Not true. Not even close.

Louise gets right in my face now. "I think you should leave. Now." We're exactly the same height because she's barefoot. She looks even worse up close—tired and haggard and old. But her eyes look so much like Kai's that for a second it's hard to breathe.

"Actually, Louise, while we're on the subject, why *did* you blame them? I thought they were supposed to be your friends? Or is that what passes for loyalty with you guys?"

I think she's going to lie or fob me off, so it's surprising when she says, "They deserved it. They've never been my *friends*. Lucas barely even noticed I existed before I started going out with Max, and Bugs was the same—fawning over Sasha like she's something special. And Stu…he's a fucking animal and you know it. Thought he could have me on tap whenever he wanted me, then chuck me aside as soon as someone new caught his eye. I showed him." She's almost smirking.

Another light bulb flashes in my brain. *She* was the one who kept writing the graffiti. I shake my head in disbelief. I know I haven't liked her in years, but I had no idea she'd turned into someone so bitter. So hard and cold. And without even realizing, I've been following in Louise's footsteps, faking my way into Team Popular, pretending to like people I despise.

I back up a little because she's still right in my face, but she takes another step toward me. Like we're locked together in some hideous dance. Max is finally getting to his feet, hopefully to make sure Louise doesn't do anything crazy. But he just picks up his laptop and puts it carefully in its case. I want to grab the fucking thing and throw it out the window.

Louise reaches out suddenly and I flinch before I realize she's just opening the door. It's not like I thought she was going to hit me or anything.

"I don't know how you can live with yourself. Kai was ten times the person you'll ever be, you know that, don't you?" Even knowing everything she's done, I feel a twinge of guilt as my words hang in the air.

"I've always known that," she snaps. "Even if it hadn't been made clear to me every single day of my life, I'd still know that. But he shouldn't have—" She shakes her head quickly, eyes closed.

"Shouldn't have what?"

"Nothing." And it's the type of nothing that makes you absolutely certain it's something.

"Louise, if there's something you're not telling me…" I sound like I'm in control now. I sound like someone who should be listened to. Someone dangerous almost. It's an act, but she's not to know that.

She shakes her head again and looks away. Looks at Max.

And that's when I know. That's when I realize I've been stupid. We've all been so very stupid.

chapter fifty-six

"You. It was you." Not a question. A statement of fact.

Max slumps down onto the bed. Louise closes the door. And then the most bizarre thing happens: Max starts to cry. Louise says, "Oh for fuck's sake," and stomps over to the window, turning her back on us both.

As Max sits there sniffling, I can't help but notice he's sitting in the same position he was sitting in that night. It would be funny if it wasn't so awful. "So you're…gay?"

"No! Fuck no!" He swipes at the tears with the sleeve of his shirt. "I liked *him*. That's all." A derisory snort from Louise.

My brain's working hard to put together the pieces. It's all so simple now. Like one of those four-piece jigsaws for toddlers. So. Fucking. Obvious. "That wasn't the first time, was it? At the party?" My voice is gentle; for some reason the fight has gone out of me. I actually find myself feeling sorry for this boy. It's not his fault. Not really.

Louise answers, "Oh no. They'd been at it for a good few weeks by then. My brother fucking my boyfriend. Can you even *begin* to imagine how that feels?" For the very first time, I try to put myself in her shoes; they're not very comfortable shoes to be in.

"I found a text from Kai on his phone, talking about hooking up at the party." She shudders with revulsion and I can't tell if it's the thought of two boys hooking up, or these two boys in particular.

"So you...filmed them?" This is the thing that's hardest to understand. It's cruel, calculated. But I have never, ever been able to understand this girl.

She leans on the windowsill and crosses her arms defensively. "I wasn't planning it or anything. I was upset. And wasted."

"You weren't wasted when you emailed it though, were you?" It's a petty point to make, but I can't help myself. I already know that she's going to get away with it. That no one will ever know the truth. I could tell people if I really wanted to. I could tell Lucas and the others, tell the police. But it wouldn't make anything better. Lucas and Sasha would never forgive me. Kai would still be dead, but it would be even worse because the newspapers would be raking over his personal life. And two more lives would be ruined—the lives of people that Kai really cared about. I won't tell.

Max has his head in his hands and I want to put my arms around him. I want to tell him that it's OK—that I don't blame him. That it really doesn't matter if he's gay or bi or whatever. That he doesn't need to stay with Louise if he doesn't want to. He doesn't need to have a girlfriend, and especially not one as fucked up as her. I want to ask him how he could have stayed with her all this time, knowing what she'd done. Had she been holding it over him, threatening to out him if he did anything wrong? Did she *remind* him of Kai in some way? Or did he actually care about her and want to make a go of things? Had he loved Kai? Had Kai loved him? There are so many things I want to say and questions I want to ask. But I won't. I don't know this boy at all, even though he's the key to everything.

I feel stretched and flattened by the truth. It's time for me to go.

I turn my back on them.

I'm opening the door when Max says, "You're not going to say anything to anyone are you, Jem?" He doesn't sound too hopeful.

I take one last look at him. One last look at her.

They're broken too. I shouldn't forget that. But I can't quite bring myself to reassure them. I'm not sure they deserve it.

They'll know the answer to Max's question soon enough.

⌒

I walk home so slowly that sometimes I'm hardly moving forward at all. I keep trying to picture it all going differently.

Max and Louise would never have gotten together. No. That's not the start. Kai and I would be living in a world where nobody cared about your sexual orientation. Being gay wouldn't be gossiped about or frowned upon—it wouldn't even be worth mentioning. It would just be a fact. A mundane sort of fact. Max would arrive at school and Kai would fancy him and he would fancy Kai, and one of them would ask the other one out (Max would do the asking, most probably). And I wouldn't be jealous because I would see how happy Kai was.

A year later and they would still be together. And they would be *that* couple. The one that just seems right. You can imagine them staying together forever because they're just so damn perfect for each other. You don't resent them though, because they give you hope. Maybe one day you could be as happy as they are.

But you're happy to wait, because for now you have your best friend (and favorite person in the world) by your side and that's enough.

I don't let myself think about the dreamworld I used to harbor deep inside my heart. It was too painful to think about then and it's even worse now. Plus I was never able to properly picture Kai loving me the way I wanted him to. My brain would never let me go there, probably because it knew there was zero chance of that dream becoming reality.

Wishful thinking doesn't change anything. What happened to

Sasha doesn't change anything. Knowing the truth about Max and Louise doesn't change anything.

I live in a world in which Kai doesn't exist anymore. I'm not willing to do that for much longer.

chapter fifty-seven

The rest of Saturday was not particularly pleasant. Mom wouldn't leave me alone, asking questions and fretting about Sasha. Dad stayed out of the way after hugging me and saying, "Thank God you're OK." I couldn't help wondering if that would be the last time I would get to hug him.

After a couple hours of tea and sympathy that went exactly as I'd expected, I finally escaped to my room on the pretext of needing sleep. A nasty shock was awaiting me—a shock that wouldn't have been a shock if I'd been thinking clearly.

Sasha's things were everywhere. One of her boots was peeking out from under the bed. The top she'd been wearing when she came over was slung over the back of my chair, on top of my favorite hoodie. Her makeup bag was lying on its side, the contents spilling onto a purple folder on my desk.

I gathered everything up, trying not to think or feel. Put everything in her bag, put the bag by the door. Then lay curled up on my bed and closed my eyes. It was no good; I could smell the fire. My clothes, my body, were coated in the stench of smoke.

Even after a shower, I could still smell it. That's when I realized it was in my head.

I tried to sleep, but all I could think about was burning and blistering and screaming. I stopped trying after an hour or so, because what was the point? I could manage without sleep for another twenty-four hours and then it wouldn't matter.

I needed to know if there was any news about Sasha. Mom was bound to ask, and it would be weird for me not to know. Lucas was the best bet, in spite of everything. The others were sure to ignore me. I rewrote the message seven times before I was happy with it: I know I'm the last person you want to talk to, but pls let me know how S is doing. Please. I won't bother you again after this. I'm sorry. I didn't add any Xs. It didn't seem appropriate somehow.

I stared at my phone for God knows how long before I realized he wasn't going to reply. When Mom asked at dinner I said Sasha was stable and that the doctors were pleased with her progress so far. I had no idea if this was anywhere close to convincing, but Mom nodded and patted my hand. She said, "There but for the grace of God..." which was an odd thing for someone who doesn't believe in God to say.

It was the last supper. I noticed every detail. Dad's foot tapping out an annoying rhythm on the linoleum. Mom cutting up all her food before she started eating; Noah and I used to laugh at her for that. I'd say, "OCD much?" and he would sing, "OCD! OCD!" over and over again even though he had no idea what it meant.

Noah ate his lasagna and barely said a word. I desperately wanted him to be his usual motormouth self, as if I could store up the memories of the nonsense he spouted and take them with me to the grave. Mom and Dad both tried their best to engage him, but he was having none of it. The three of us exchanged glances before I spoke up. "So what do you say I kick your skinny butt on the X-box after dinner? Game of your choice, best of three. Loser has to..." I was going to say "do the winner's chores for a whole week" but the words dried up in my mouth. Noah would be doing all the chores from now on. Or maybe none of the chores, because Mom and Dad would go easy on him on account of his dead sister. I didn't need to finish the sentence because Noah said he didn't feel like it. Mom chipped in to ask him if he was sure. She even said she'd make him an ice cream float, which was his absolute favorite. Noah just shrugged and said it was too cold for ice cream floats.

As soon as he finished eating, Noah went up to his room. Mom followed him a couple of minutes later. Dad and I watched a David Attenborough documentary that he'd recorded during the week, and it was nearly finished by the time Mom trudged down the stairs. Noah had been crying. He was upset about Sasha. He was worried about something happening to me. He wanted to know why bad things kept happening to people he knows.

If hell exists, I will be going there.

~

On Sunday morning it's the same routine as always. I seem to be the only one who remembers what day it is. Dad goes out to get the papers (stopping off for an espresso on the way home). Mom's rushing around trying to find Noah's swimming goggles, while he sits at the table rolling up his towel around his trunks. I choke down some Cheerios while Noah watches me closely.

"What are you looking at, shrimp?" He sticks his tongue out at me and I laugh. It's one of our little rituals.

The only change in the routine is that I hug Noah before he leaves. Mom doesn't notice; she's halfway to the car already. Normally Noah would wriggle out of my grasp, but today he hugs me back. I tell him I love him and he tells me he loves me. It's the perfect good-bye—so perfect it makes me wonder if on some level he knows. That's not possible, but I can't shake the thought as I get on the bus.

I obsessively check my phone for the duration of the journey. No messages from Lucas, or anyone else for that matter. Just before my stop I switch off the phone and tuck it down between the seat and the window.

I hang out in the woods to kill time. I sit on a rock so cold it numbs my butt in a matter of minutes. The last envelope is in my hands but I'm scared to open it.

He died one year ago today. I have lived on this planet for 365 days without him.

366 days would be one too many.

chapter fifty-eight

I make my way onto the bridge at 10:13. I don't know the exact time Kai jumped, but this has to be close enough. To deter any Melissa-like do-gooders I have Dad's old camera slung round my neck. It's bloody massive—looks like it'd be at home among the paparazzi or something. You can't miss it; the idea being that anyone driving past will clock it and decide that I'm not about to dive headfirst off the railings.

I can't put my finger on the moment I decided to do it here, do it this way, rather than with pills. I never thought I'd have the guts, but I feel surprisingly calm about it. It feels right. If Kai can do it, I can too. The local newspaper will love it.

I put my bag on the pavement and lean over the railing. The rocks aren't visible at least, but I know they're lurking beneath the surface ready to smash my skull.

It's time to open Kai's last letter. I want his words to be the only words in my head right now. I want to forget about the world and hear his voice for the last time.

The envelope looks the same as all the others. The word "October" is printed in Kai's freakishly neat handwriting. I bring it to my lips and kiss it.

Something stops me every time I go to open it. Because as soon as I open it, I'll have to read it, and once I've read it, there will be nothing else for me to do. I'm not chickening out—there's no *way* I'm chickening out. I just need to make sure I'm ready.

Fuck it. This is getting ridiculous. I shake my head at my ridiculousness and tear into the envelope with my thumb. A single, precious sheet of paper inside.

A truck speeds past me and a blast of air blows the paper out of my hands and up into the air. I lunge forward to grab it and I can feel my center of gravity shift. My whole upper body lurches over the railing and I'm reaching for the sheet of paper, my arm stretched painfully, hand clawing at the air. Only one foot on the pavement now, but if I can just reach that little bit farther I'll be able to…

I start to fall and there's a moment—and I'm not even sure this is possible—when I *know* I can reach the letter. I can reach it and keep it safe in my hand as I fall. If I can't read his words, I can at least hold them in my hand as I die. I can just close my eyes and let myself fall into oblivion. Maybe I'll hit the exact same rocks and my blood will mingle with his and maybe there's some kind of life after death and he's waiting for me there with his hand outstretched just like mine.

But…

I don't want to die.

I try to twist my body backward and pain shoots up my neck.

It's too late.

I chose life too late.

chapter fifty-nine

Received:

09:53

October 23

Hey. S doing OK. I spoke to her mom this morning. She's talking—she wants to see you. You can come down with me tomorrow. If you want to. I've been thinking…We should talk. L.

My dearest Jem,

So here we are at the end of the journey together. It's hard to imagine you a year older (wiser?), holding this letter in your hands and reading these words. It gives me hope. It comforts me to think of you living your life and learning to be happy and doing all the things I can't because I'm too scared. You always were the brave one, you know.

I trust you'll forgive me if I'm brief in this final missive? Better brief than maudlin, I think.

In no particular order, here are my top five hopes and dreams for you, my dear best friend Jemima Halliday:

1. I hope you finally get to beat someone other than me at table tennis.

2. I hope you go backpacking in India. Yes, I know full well you've never expressed the slightest interest in backpacking in the Lake District let alone India, but it's something I can picture you doing—and loving. Call it a hunch.

3. I want you to dance and sing and laugh whenever you get the chance and never be self-conscious about it.

4. (THIS IS THE REALLY, REALLY
IMPORTANT ONE… JUST IN CASE YOU'RE
SKIM READING BY NOW). I want you to be
happy. When happiness comes knocking on
your door (and knock on your door it most
certainly will), you fling that door open and
welcome it with open arms, I'm half tempted
to ORDER you to be happy, but I've done
quite enough of the telling-you-what-to-do
shtick, don't you think?

a. If it helps with number 4, I want you
to forget all about me. Or if that's not
possible, just wrap up the memory of me in
a silk cloth and store it somewhere deep
inside your heart for safekeeping. You can
bring it out every once in a while, as and
when you need to. I'll always be there.

b. Yes, I'm aware this is cheating. But I
hope that one day you and Louise will be
friends, or at the very least two people
who don't hate each other. She's not a
bad person, you know. She made a mistake,
but so did I. Maybe we're even. Maybe it's
a strange quirk of human nature that we
can't help hurting the ones we love the
most. But when you love someone that

much, you can usually find it in your heart to forgive. It's surprisingly easy to do.

I could go on and on and on forever and it would never be enough. Words are never enough, when it comes down to it.

I love you, pickle. You are going to do great things in this life—enough great things for both of us.

Your best friend always,

Kai
xxx

Acknowledgments

First of all, I'd like to thank YOU, the lovely reader for picking up this book. I'm ever so grateful.

Mahoosive thanks to:

Victoria Birkett, Nancy Miles, and Caroline Hill-Trevor.

Sarah Lilly, Alice Hill, Niamh Mulvey, Talya Baker, and all at Quercus.

Leah Hultenschmidt, Cat Clyne, Steve Geck, Jillian Bergsma, and everyone at Sourcebooks.

The UKYA blogging community—a knowledgeable, passionate, lovely bunch if ever there was one. A special *muppet flail* must go to Laura Heath for being ace.

Sarah Stewart, Lara Williamson, Conrad Mason, Nova Ren Suma, Karen Mahoney, Louie Stowell, Keris Stainton, Luisa Plaja, Susie Day, Kay Woodward, Tamsyn Murray, Sophia Bennett, James Dawson, and Zoë Marriott. Fabulous writerly folk, each and every one.

Nina Douglas, for letting me steal her name even though the character description didn't much extend beyond the word "vapid."

My cat, Jem, for letting me steal *her* name for my main character. (Not to mention my other cat Scout, for not getting jealous.)

Cate James, for handwriting Kai's words so perfectly. And for being the best Cava buddy in the all the land.

Lauren James, bestest critique buddy and general Yoda-like figure (albeit significantly less green and wrinkly).

Robert Clarke, for too many things to mention.

Finally, there have been a couple of new additions to the Clarke household since I started writing *Undone*. I'd like to extend some extra special big fat thank-you hugs to Caro and Griffpup for:

1. Providing EPIC levels of distraction against which I had to battle to get the book finished. I always did enjoy a challenge. *coughs*
2. Providing EPIC levels of awesome, making me beam on a regular basis and just being too adorable for words.